Praise for previous volumes of
Nebula Awards Showcase

"Reading all of *Nebula Awards Showcase 2002* is a way of reading a bunch of good stories. It is also a very good way to explore the writing of tomorrow."
—John Clute, scifi.com

"Conveys a sense of the vitality and excitement that have characterized the field's internal dialogues and debate over the last few years. One of the most entertaining *Nebula* volumes in years."
—*Locus*

"An essential index of one year in SF and fantasy."
—*Booklist*

"A stellar collection. . . . This is not only a must read for anyone with an interest in the field, but a pleasure to read. . . . That's more reassuring than surprising, of course, given that this collection has little if any agenda besides quality writing, but it is reassuring to see that so many fresh voices are so much fun. . . . Worth picking up."
—SF Revu

"While the essays offer one answer to the question of where does SF go now, the stories show that science fiction writers continue to re-examine their vision of the future. It's a continuing dialogue, and by including critical essays along with the stories, the *Nebula Awards Showcase 2002* does more to present the SF field as an ongoing conversation and discussion of ideas than any of the other best of the year anthologies. It's a worthy contribution and a good volume to have on your shelf."
—SF Site

"Very impressive."
—Off the Shelf

"Presents the usual quality mix of literary SF and fantasy with critical essays."
—*Publishers Weekly*

"Provocative essays. . . . [Jack] Dann's introductions and story notes are knowledgeable, graceful, and to the point. Here's another for the fan's bookshelf."
—*Kirkus Reviews*

Gardner Dozois was the longtime editor of ⬚⬚⬚⬚⬚⬚⬚⬚ *zine*, having won the Hugo Award for Best Edi⬚⬚⬚⬚⬚⬚⬚⬚⬚⬚⬚⬚ his tenure, and currently holds the position o⬚⬚⬚⬚⬚⬚⬚⬚⬚us with the magazine. He lives in Philadelphia with his wife.

NEBULA AWARDS© SHOWCASE

2006

THE YEAR'S BEST SF AND FANTASY

Selected by the Science Fiction and
Fantasy Writers of America®

EDITED BY
Gardner Dozois

A ROC BOOK

ROC
Published by New American Library, a division of
Penguin Group (USA) Inc., 375 Hudson Street,
New York, New York 10014, USA
Penguin Group (Canada), 90 Eglinton Avenue East, Suite 700, Toronto,
Ontario M4P 2Y3, Canada (a division of Pearson Penguin Canada Inc.)
Penguin Books Ltd., 80 Strand, London WC2R 0RL, England
Penguin Ireland, 25 St. Stephen's Green, Dublin 2,
Ireland (a division of Penguin Books Ltd.)
Penguin Group (Australia), 250 Camberwell Road, Camberwell, Victoria 3124,
Australia (a division of Pearson Australia Group Pty. Ltd.)
Penguin Books India Pvt. Ltd., 11 Community Centre, Panchsheel Park,
New Delhi–110 017, India
Penguin Group (NZ), cnr Airborne and Rosedale Roads, Albany,
Auckland 1310, New Zealand (a division of Pearson New Zealand Ltd.)
Penguin Books (South Africa) (Pty.) Ltd., 24 Sturdee Avenue,
Rosebank, Johannesburg 2196, South Africa
Penguin Books Ltd., Registered Offices:
80 Strand, London WC2R 0RL, England

First published by Roc, an imprint of New American Library,
a division of Penguin Group (USA) Inc.

First Printing, March 2006
10 9 8 7 6 5 4 3 2

 REGISTERED TRADEMARK—MARCA REGISTRADA

Set in Bembo
Designed by Ginger Legato

Printed in the United States of America

ACKNOWLEDGMENTS

The editor would like to thank the following people for their help and support: Jack Dann, Walter Jon Williams, Eleanor Wood, Susan Casper, Ellen Datlow, Gordon Van Gelder, Mark Kreighbaum, Brian Bienowski, Pamela Sargent, Vaughne Hanson, G. O. Clark, Mike Allen, Jack Williamson, Robert Silverberg, Frederik Pohl, Betty Anne Hull, Ursula K. Le Guin, Brian W. Aldiss, Anne McCaffrey, Todd McCaffrey, Kathi Maio, Jody Lynn Nye, Harry Harrison, Eileen Gunn, Ellen Klages, Mike Resnick, Roger Dutcher, Theodora Goss, Diane Taylor, Susan Smith, Jennifer Brehl, Peter London, and special thanks to my editor, Ginjer Buchanan.

CONTENTS

INTRODUCTION

GARDNER DOZOIS

I t's been said so many times now that it's become a sarcastic cliché on the lips of disappointed Nebula finalists who didn't actually *win* the award, or who think that they have no chance of winning it, often said with a bitter, cynical, mocking smile: "It's an honor just to be nominated!"

But you know, it really *is*.

Hundreds (if not thousands) of stories are published every year in the science fiction and fantasy genres, in the professional magazines, in anthologies, as novella chapbooks, in semiprozines, and as previously unpublished stories in single-author collections, in addition to those "published" (we really need a new word for this!) electronically on-line in any of dozens of e-zines and Web sites, some of them very far off the beaten track indeed (2004, for instance, saw first-rate stories published on the Web site of an association of electrical engineers, and as an *advertisement* for an upcoming novel on Amazon.com!) . . . and the brutal truth is that most of those hundreds of stories are going to vanish without a trace and never be heard from again. Most stories published (or "published") during the year are *not* going to make it on to the Nebula Award ballot; most are not going to arouse a lot of word-of-mouth buzz; most are not going to generate any fan letters or trigger flamewars on Internet bulletin boards, are not going to be reprinted later on (or perhaps ever be seen in any form again, from now until the end of the universe)—most are not even going to get reviewed. At all. Ever. (There are very few places that review genre short fiction, other than the newsmagazines *Locus* and *Chronicle,* and a couple of online venues such as *Tangent Online* and the *Internet Review of Science Fiction*.) For most writers, with most stories, publishing short fiction is like tying the story to an anvil and throwing it off the end of the dock into the sea. It sinks without even a splash, swallowed by black water, and, without a ripple, it is gone. You may grow old and die, and still never hear anything about that story ever again.

(Nor, with 642 SF and fantasy novels published in 2004, according to *Locus,* is the situation necessarily any better with novels. How many of those novels even get reviewed? Let *alone* make it on to the Final Nebula Ballot? A considerably lesser number than 642, believe me.)

On the other hand, for a story or a novel to make it on to the Final Nebula Ballot, it has to have impressed a number of the author's peers enough for them to expend the time and effort required to nominate it in the first place, then seem worthy enough to an even larger number of the author's peers that they're willing to actually vote for it when the preliminary ballot comes out, over all the other choices available to them there. Unlike the vast majority of stories that came out that year, the hundreds of stories that were consigned to blank oblivion, it has been *noticed.* It's been approved of, and judged worthy to be in competition to win an award by the harshest jury of all, a fellowship of other working writers who know all the tricks and who are not easy to fool.

So it really *is* "an honor just to be nominated." It really is. If you're a finalist and you're tempted to put on the mask of sophisticated blasé cynicism and sneer at that, embracing the idea that it's only *winning* that counts, just ask all the authors who *didn't* get nominated if they would change places with you if they could. Boy, *would* they! In a hot second.

All the stories we're bringing you in *Nebula Award Showcase 2006* have been through this rugged peer-vetting system; the winners are here, of course (including an excerpt from the winning novel), and as many finalists as we could fit into the book. In an ideal world, we would be able to bring you *all* the finalists; back here in the real world, though, constraints on the length of the anthology make that, sadly, impossible, and I've been forced to choose among them—a tough choice, since they all deserve to be included.

The stories that *are* here are a varied group, though, ranging from the hardest of hard science fiction to political/economic/sociological thrillers to speculations on the nature of the Posthuman Condition to gentle fantasy to creepy and exotic horror, with a few hard-to-classify stories thrown in along the way. Add insightful commentary on where the field's come from and where it's going by SFFWA Grand

Masters Jack Williamson, Robert Silverberg, Ursula K. Le Guin, Frederik Pohl, and Brian W. Aldiss, the year's Rhysling Award–winning poetry, a classic story by new SFFWA Grand Master Anne McCaffrey and an appreciation of her by Jody Lynn Nye, lists of past winners and of this year's finalists, and a review of the films on this year's final ballot by the film reviewer for *The Magazine of Fantasy & Science Fiction,* Kathi Maio, and you have as good a snapshot of what the year in science fiction was like, in all its variety and richness of expression, in all its different forms, as you are likely to get anywhere. I hope you enjoy it!

THE 2005 NEBULA AWARDS
FINAL BALLOT

NOVEL

Paladin of Souls, by **Lois McMaster Bujold** (Eos, October 2003)

Down and Out in the Magic Kingdom, by Cory Doctorow (Tor, February 2003)

Omega, by Jack McDevitt (Ace, November 2003)

Cloud Atlas: A Novel, by David Mitchell (Sceptre, January 2004)

Perfect Circle, by Sean Stewart (Small Beer Press, June 2004)

The Knight, by Gene Wolfe (Tor, January 2004)

NOVELLA

"Walk in Silence," by Catherine Asaro (*Analog Science Fiction and Fact,* April 2003)

"The Tangled Strings of the Marionettes," by Adam-Troy Castro (*The Magazine of Fantasy & Science Fiction,* July 2003)

"The Cookie Monster," by Vernor Vinge (*Analog Science Fiction and Fact,* October 2003)

"The Green Leopard Plague," by **Walter Jon Williams** (*Asimov's Science Fiction,* October/November 2003)

"Just Like the Ones We Used to Know," by Connie Willis (*Asimov's Science Fiction,* December 2003)

NOVELETTE

"Zora and the Zombie," by Andy Duncan (*SCI FICTION,* Feb. 4, 2004)

"Basement Magic," by **Ellen Klages** (*The Magazine of Fantasy & Science Fiction,* May 2003)

"The Voluntary State," by Christopher Rowe (*SCI FICTION,* May 2004)

"Dry Bones," by William Sanders (*Asimov's Science Fiction,* May 2003)

"The Gladiator's War: A Dialogue," by Lois Tilton (*Asimov's Science Fiction,* June 2004)

SHORT STORY

"Coming to Terms," by **Eileen Gunn** (*Stable Strategies and Others,* September 2004)

"The Strange Redemption of Sister Mary Anne," by Mike Moscoe (*Analog Science Fiction and Fact,* November 2004)

"Travels with My Cats," by Mike Resnick (*Asimov's Science Fiction,* February 2004)

"Embracing-The-New," by Benjamin Rosenbaum (*Asimov's Science Fiction,* January 2004)

"In the Late December," by Greg van Eekhout (*Strange Horizons,* Dec. 22, 2003)

"Aloha," by Ken Wharton (*Analog Science Fiction and Fact,* June 2003)

SCRIPTS

The Incredibles, by Brad Bird (Pixar, November 2004)

The Butterfly Effect, by J. Mackye Gruber and Eric Bress (New Line Cinema, January 2004)

Eternal Sunshine of the Spotless Mind, by Charlie Kaufman and Michel Gondry (Anonymous Content/Focus Features, March 2004)

The Lord of the Rings: The Return of the King, by Fran Walsh, Philippa Boyens, and Peter Jackson, based on the novel by J.R.R. Tolkien (New Line Cinema, December 2003)

The fortieth annual Nebula Awards banquet was held at the Allegro Hotel in Chicago, Illinois, on April 30, 2005, where Nebula Awards were given in the categories of novel, novella, novelette, short story, script, and lifetime achievement (Grand Master). Four of the six winners, including new Grand Master Anne McCaffrey, were present to accept their awards in person. A "Service to SFFWA Award" was also given to Kevin O'Donnell, Jr. Neil Gaiman was the elegant and eloquent Toastmaster.

Walter Jon Williams was born in Minnesota and now lives in Albuquerque, New Mexico. His short fiction has appeared frequently in *Asimov's Science Fiction,* as well as in *The Magazine of Fantasy & Science Fiction, Wheel of Fortune, Global Dispatches, Alternate Outlaws,* and in other markets, and has been gathered in the collections *Facets* and *Frankensteins and Other Foreign Devils.* His novels include *Ambassador of Progress, Knight Moves, Hardwired, The Crown Jewels, Voice of the Whirlwind, House of Shards, Days of Atonement, Aristoi, Metropolitan, City on Fire,* a huge disaster thriller called *The Rift,* and a *Star Trek* novel, *Destiny's Way.* His most recent books are the first two novels in his acclaimed modern space opera epic, "Dread Empire's Fall," *Dread Empire's Fall: The Praxis* and *Dread Empire's Fall: The Sundering.* Coming up are two new novels, *Orthodox War* and *Conventions of War.* He won a long-overdue Nebula Award in 2001 for his story "Daddy's World," and now has taken the award again with "The Green Leopard Plague."

About "The Green Leopard Plague," the Nebula winner in the novella category, he says:

" 'The Green Leopard Plague' was the result of a collision of many ideas. I began with the notion of a postscarcity economy, and the dangers that this might pose to human liberty. To this was added another question relating to economics: How valuable is a human life that can be easily duplicated and reconstituted, and would the crime of murder then be any more serious than vandalism?

"My two protagonists, in addition to whatever lives they may enjoy within the structure of the story, are examples of two conflicting philosophical points of view: Baudrillard's 'the self does not exist,' versus Richard Rorty's 'I don't care.' To this I added scenery viewed in recent journeys to Palau and to Europe, the political situation in Transnistria, and the background of an earlier story, 'Lethe,' which I always thought deserved a sequel.

"I would like to thank Ted Chiang for the 'back-of-the-envelope' calculations that showed my initial scientific solution to the problem in the story was bogus, and Dr. Stephen C. Lee, professor of biomedical nanotech, for fixing my problem once Ted had detected it."

THE GREEN LEOPARD PLAGUE

WALTER JON WILLIAMS

Kicking her legs out over the ocean, the lonely mermaid gazed at the horizon from her perch in the overhanging banyan tree.

The air was absolutely still and filled with the scent of night flowers. Large fruit bats flew purposefully over the sea, heading for their daytime rest. Somewhere a white cockatoo gave a penetrating squawk. A starling made a brief flutter out to sea, then came back again. The rising sun threw up red-gold sparkles from the wavetops and brought a brilliance to the tropical growth that crowned the many islands spread out on the horizon.

The mermaid decided it was time for breakfast. She slipped from her hanging canvas chair and walked out along one of the banyan's great limbs. The branch swayed lightly under her weight, and her bare feet found sure traction on the rough bark. She looked down to see the deep blue of the channel, distinct from the turquoise of the shallows atop the reefs. ·

She raised her arms, poised briefly on the limb, the ruddy light of the sun glowing bronze on her bare skin, and then pushed off and dove headfirst into the Philippine Sea. She landed with a cool impact and a rush of bubbles.

Her wings unfolded, and she flew away.

After her hunt, the mermaid—her name was Michelle—cached her fishing gear in a pile of dead coral above the reef, and then ghosted easily over the sea grass with the rippled sunlight casting patterns on her wings. When she could look up to see the colossal, twisted tangle that was the roots of her banyan tree, she lifted her head from the water and gulped her first breath of air.

The Rock Islands were made of soft limestone coral, and tide and chemical action had eaten away the limestone at sea level, undercutting the stone above. Some of the smaller islands looked like mushrooms, pointed green pinnacles balanced atop thin stems. Michelle's island was larger and irregularly shaped, but it still had steep limestone walls undercut six meters by the tide, with no obvious way for a person to clamber from the sea to the land. Her banyan perched on the saucer-edge of the island, itself undercut by the sea.

Michelle had arranged a rope elevator from her nest in the tree, just a loop on the end of a long nylon line. She tucked her wings away—they were harder to retract than to deploy, and the gills on the undersides were delicate—and then slipped her feet through the loop. At her verbal command, a hoist mechanism lifted her in silence from the sea to her resting place in the bright green-dappled forest canopy.

She had been an ape once, a siamang, and she felt perfectly at home in the treetops.

During her excursion, she had speared a yellowlip emperor, and this she carried with her in a mesh bag. She filleted the emperor with a blade she kept in her nest, and tossed the rest into the sea, where it became a subject of interest to a school of bait fish. She ate a slice of one fillet raw, enjoying the brilliant flavor, sea and trembling pale flesh together, then cooked the fillets on her small stove, eating one with some rice she'd cooked the previous evening and saving the other for later.

By the time Michelle finished breakfast, the island was alive. Geckoes scurried over the banyan's bark, and coconut crabs sidled beneath the leaves like touts offering illicit downloads to passing tourists. Out in the deep water, a flock of circling, diving black noddies marked where a school of skipjack tuna was feeding on swarms of bait fish.

It was time for Michelle to begin her day as well. With sure, steady feet, she moved along a rope walkway to the ironwood tree that held her satellite uplink in its crown, straddled a limb, took her deck from the mesh bag she'd roped to the tree, and downloaded her messages.

There were several journalists requesting interviews—the legend of the lonely mermaid was spreading. This pleased her more often than not, but she didn't answer any of the queries. There was a message from Darton, which she decided to savor for a while before opening. And then she saw a note from Dr. Davout, and opened it at once.

Davout was, roughly, twelve times her age. He'd actually been carried for nine months in his mother's womb, not created from scratch in a nanobed like almost everyone else she knew. He had a sib who was a famous astronaut, a McEldowny Prize for his *Lavoisier and His Age,* and a red-haired wife who was nearly as well-known as he was. A couple of years ago, Michelle had attended a series of his lectures at the College of Mystery, and been interested despite her specialty being, strictly speaking, biology.

He had shaved off the little goatee he'd worn when she'd last seen him, which Michelle considered a good thing. "I have a research project for you, if you're free," the recording said. "It shouldn't take too much effort."

Michelle contacted him at once. He was a rich old bastard with a thousand years of tenure and no notion of what it was to be young in these times, and he'd pay her whatever outrageous fee she asked.

Her material needs at the moment were few, but she wouldn't stay on this island forever.

Davout answered right away. Behind him, working at her own console, Michelle could see his red-haired wife Katrin.

"Michelle!" Davout said, loudly enough for Katrin to know who'd called without turning around. "Good!" He hesitated, and then his fingers formed the mudra for <concern>. "I understand you've suffered a loss," he said.

"Yes," she said, her answer delayed by a second's satellite lag.

"And the young man—?"

"Doesn't remember."

Which was not exactly a lie, the point being *what* was remembered.

Davout's fingers were still fixed in <concern>. "Are you all right?" he asked.

Her own fingers formed an equivocal answer. "I'm getting better." Which was probably true.

"I see you're not an ape any more."

"I decided to go the mermaid route. New perspectives, all that." And welcome isolation.

"Is there any way we can make things easier for you?"

She put on a hopeful expression. "You said something about a job?"

"Yes." He seemed relieved not to have to probe further—he'd had a realdeath in his own family, Michelle remembered, a chance-in-a-billion thing, and perhaps he didn't want to relive any part of that.

"I'm working on a biography of Terzian," Davout said.

". . . And his Age?" Michelle finished.

"And his *Legacy*." Davout smiled. "There's a three-week period in his life where he—well, he drops right off the map. I'd like to find out where he went—and who he was with, if anyone."

Michelle was impressed. Even in comparatively unsophisticated times such as that inhabited by Jonathan Terzian, it was difficult for people to disappear.

"It's a critical time for him," Davout went on. "He'd lost his job at Tulane, his wife had just died—realdeath, remember—and if he decided he simply wanted to get lost, he would have all my sympathies." He raised a hand as if to tug at the chin-whiskers that were no longer there, made a vague pawing gesture, then dropped the hand. "But my problem is that when he resurfaces, everything's changed for him. In June, he delivered an undistinguished paper at the Athenai conference in Paris, then vanished. When he surfaced in Venice in mid-July, he didn't deliver the paper he was scheduled to read, instead he delivered the first version of his Cornucopia Theory."

Michelle's fingers formed the mudra <highly impressed>. "How have you tried to locate him?"

"Credit card records—they end on June 17, when he buys a lot of euros at American Express in Paris. After that, he must have paid for everything with cash."

"He really *did* try to get lost, didn't he?" Michelle pulled up one bare leg and rested her chin on it. "Did you try passport records?"

<No luck.> "But if he stayed in the European Community he wouldn't have had to present a passport when crossing a border."

"Cash machines?"

"Not till after he arrived in Venice, just a couple of days prior to the conference."

The mermaid thought about it for a moment, then smiled. "I guess you need me, all right."

<I concur> Davout flashed solemnly. "How much would it cost me?"

Michelle pretended to consider the question for a moment, then named an outrageous sum.

Davout frowned. "Sounds all right," he said.

Inwardly, Michelle rejoiced. Outwardly, she leaned toward the camera lens and looked businesslike. "I'll get busy, then."

Davout looked grateful. "You'll be able to get on it right away?"

"Certainly. What I need you to do is send me pictures of Terzian, from as many different angles as possible, especially from around that period of time."

"I have them ready."

"Send away."

An eyeblink later, the pictures were in Michelle's deck. <Thanks> she flashed. "I'll let you know as soon as I find anything."

At university, Michelle had discovered that she was very good at research, and it had become a profitable sideline for her. People—usually people connected with academe in one way or another—hired her to do the duller bits of their own jobs, finding documents or references, or, in this case, three missing weeks out of a person's life. It was almost always work they could do themselves, but Michelle was simply better at research than most people, and she was considered worth the extra expense. Michelle herself usually enjoyed the work—it gave her interesting sidelights on fields about which she knew little, and provided a welcome break from routine.

Plus, this particular job required not so much a researcher as an artist, and Michelle was very good at this particular art.

Michelle looked through the pictures, most scanned from old photographs. Davout had selected well: Terzian's face or profile was clear in every picture. Most of the pictures showed him young, in his twenties, and the ones that showed him older were of high quality, or showed parts of the body that would be crucial to the biometric scan, like his hands or his ears.

The mermaid paused for a moment to look at one of the old photos: Terzian smiling with his arm around a tall, long-legged woman with a wide mouth and dark, bobbed hair, presumably the wife who had died. Behind them was a Louis Quinze table with a blaze of gladiolas in a cloisonné vase, and, above the table, a large portrait of a stately-looking horse in a heavy gilded frame. Beneath the table were stowed—temporarily, Michelle assumed—a dozen or so trophies, which to judge from the little golden figures balanced atop them were awarded either for gymnastics or martial arts. The opulent setting seemed a little at odds with the young, informally dressed couple: she wore a flowery tropical shirt tucked into khakis, and Terzian was dressed in a tank top and shorts. There was a sense that the photographer had caught them almost in motion, as if they'd paused for the picture en route from one place to another.

Nice shoulders, Michelle thought. Big hands, well-shaped muscular legs. She hadn't ever thought of Terzian as young, or large, or strong, but he had a genuine, powerful physical presence that came across even in the old, casual photographs. He looked more like a football player than a famous thinker.

Michelle called up her character-recognition software and fed in all the pictures, then checked the software's work, something she was reasonably certain her employer would never have done if he'd been doing this job himself. Most people using this kind of canned software didn't realize how the program could be fooled, particularly when used with old media, scanned film prints heavy with grain and primitive digital images scanned by machines that simply weren't very intelligent. In the end, Michelle and the software between them managed an excellent job of mapping Terzian's body and calibrating its precise ratios: the distance between the eyes, the length of nose and curve of lip, the distinct shape of the ears, the length of limb and trunk. Other men might share some of these biometric ratios, but none would share them all.

The mermaid downloaded the data into her specialized research spiders, and sent them forth into the electronic world.

A staggering amount of the trivial past existed there, and nowhere else. People had uploaded pictures, diaries, commentary, and video; they'd digitized old home movies, complete with the garish, deteriorating colors of the old film stock; they'd scanned in family trees, postcards, wedding lists, drawings, political screeds, and images of handwritten letters. Long, dull hours of security video. Whatever had meant something to someone, at some time, had been turned into electrons and made available to the universe at large.

A surprising amount of this stuff had survived the Lightspeed War—none of it had seemed worth targeting, or, if trashed, had been reloaded from backups.

What all this meant was that Terzian was somewhere in there. Wherever Terzian had gone in his weeks of absence—Paris, Dalmatia, or Thule—there would have been someone with a camera. In stills of children eating ice cream in front of Notre Dame, or moving through the video of buskers playing saxophone on the Pont des Artistes, there would be a figure in the background, and that figure would be Terzian. Terzian might be found lying on a beach in Corfu, reflected in a bar mirror in Gdynia, or negotiating with a prostitute in Hamburg's St. Pauli district—Michelle had found targets in exactly those places during the course of her other searches.

Michelle sent her software forth to find Terzian, then lifted her arms above her head and stretched—stretched fiercely, thrusting out her bare feet and curling the toes, the muscles trembling with tension, her mouth yawned in a silent shriek.

Then she leaned over her deck again, and called up the message from Darton, the message she'd saved till last.

"I don't understand," he said. "Why won't you talk to me? I love you!"

His brown eyes were a little wild.

"Don't you understand?" he cried. "I'm not dead! *I'm not really dead!*"

Michelle hovered three or four meters below the surface of Zigzag Lake, gazing upward at the inverted bowl of the heavens, the brilliant blue of the Pacific sky surrounded by the dark, shadowy towers of mangrove. Something caught her eye, something black and falling, like a bullet: and then there was a splash and a boil of bubbles, and the daggerlike bill of a collared kingfisher speared a blue-eyed apogonid that had been hovering over a bright red coral head. The kingfisher flashed its pale underside as it stroked to the surface, its wings doing efficient double duty as fins, and then there was a flurry of wings and feet and bubbles and the kingfisher was airborne again.

Michelle floated up and over the barrel-shaped coral head, then over a pair of giant clams, each over a meter long. The clams drew shut as Michelle slid across them, withdrawing the huge siphons as thick as her wrist. The fleshy lips that overhung the scalloped edges of the shells were a riot of colors: purples, blues, greens, and reds interwoven in an eye-boggling pattern.

Carefully drawing in her gills so their surfaces wouldn't be inflamed by coral stings, she kicked up her feet and dove beneath the mangrove roots into the narrow tunnel that connected Zigzag Lake with the sea.

Of the three hundred or so Rock Islands, seventy or thereabouts had marine lakes. The islands were made of coral limestone and porous to one degree or another: some lakes were connected to the ocean through tunnels and caves, and others through seepage. Many of the lakes contained forms of life unique in all the world, evolved distinctly from their remote ancestors: even now, after all this time, new species were being described.

During the months Michelle had spent in the islands, she thought she'd discovered two undescribed species: a variation on the *Entacmaea medusivora* white anemone that was patterned strangely with scarlet and a cobalt-blue; and a nudibranch, deep violet with yellow polka dots, that had undulated past her one night on the reef, flapping like a tea towel in a strong wind as a seven-knot tidal current tore it along. The nudi and samples of the anemone had been sent to the appropriate authorities, and perhaps in time Michelle would be immortalized by having a Latinate version of her name appended to the scientific description of the two marine animals.

The tunnel was about fifteen meters long, and had a few narrow twists where Michelle had to pull her wings in close to her sides and maneuver by the merest fluttering of their edges. The tunnel turned up, and brightened with the sun; the mermaid extended her wings and flew over brilliant pink soft corals toward the light.

Two hours' work, she thought, *plus a hazardous environment. Twenty-two hundred calories, easy.*

The sea was brilliantly lit, unlike the gloomy marine lake surrounded by tall cliffs, mangroves, and shadow, and for a moment Michelle's sun-dazzled eyes failed to see the boat bobbing on the tide. She stopped short, her wings cupping to brake her motion, and then she recognized the boat's distinctive paint job, a bright red meant to imitate the natural oil of the *cheritem* fruit.

Michelle prudently rose to the surface a safe distance away—Torbiong might be fishing, and sometimes he did it with a spear. The old man saw her, and stood to give a wave before Michelle could unblock her trachea and draw air into her lungs to give a hail.

"I brought you supplies," he said.

"Thanks," Michelle said as she wiped a rain of sea water from her face.

Torbiong was over two hundred years old, and Paramount Chief of Koror, the capital forty minutes away by boat. He was small and wiry and black-haired, and had a broad-nosed, strong-chinned, unlined face. He had traveled over the world and off it while young, but returned to Belau as he aged. His duties as chief were mostly ceremonial, but counted for tax purposes; he had money from hotels and restaurants that his ancestors had built and that others managed for him, and he spent most of his time visiting his neighbors, gossiping, and fishing. He had befriended Darton and Michelle when they'd first come to Belau, and helped them in securing the permissions for their researches on the Rock Islands. A few months back, after Darton died, Torbiong had agreed to bring supplies to Michelle in exchange for the occasional fish.

His boat was ten meters long and featured a waterproof canopy amidships made from interwoven pandanas leaves. Over the scarlet faux-*cheritem* paint were zigzags, crosses, and stripes in the brilliant yellow of the ginger plant. The ends of the thwarts were decorated with grotesque carved faces, and dozens of white cowrie shells were glued to the gunwales. Wooden statues of the kingfisher bird sat on the prow and stern.

Thrusting above the pandanas canopy were antennae, flagpoles, deep-sea fishing rods, fish spears, radar, and a satellite uplink. Below the canopy, where Torbiong could command the boat from an elaborately carved throne of breadfruit-tree wood, were the engine and rudder controls, radio, audio, and video sets, a collection of large audio speakers, a depth finder, a satellite navigation relay, and radar. Attached to the uprights that supported the canopy were whistles tuned to make an eerie, discordant wailing noise when the boat was at speed.

Torbiong was fond of discordant wailing noises. As Michelle swam closer, she heard the driving, screeching electronic music that Torbiong loved trickling from the earpieces of his headset—he normally howled it out of speakers, but when sitting still he didn't want to scare the fish. At night, she could hear Torbiong for miles, as he raced over the darkened sea blasted out of his skull on betel-nut juice with his music thundering and the whistles shrieking.

He removed the headset, releasing a brief audio onslaught before switching off his sound system.

"You're going to make yourself deaf," Michelle said.

Torbiong grinned. "Love that music. Gets the blood moving."

Michelle floated to the boat and put a hand on the gunwale between a pair of cowries.

"I saw that boy of yours on the news," Torbiong said. "He's making you famous."

"I don't want to be famous."

"He doesn't understand why you don't talk to him."

"He's dead," Michelle said.

Torbiong made a spreading gesture with his hands. "That's a matter of opinion."

"Watch your head," said Michelle.

Torbiong ducked as a gust threatened to bring him into contact with a pitcher plant that drooped over the edge of the island's overhang. Torbiong evaded the plant and then stepped to the bow to haul in his mooring line before the boat's canopy got caught beneath the overhang.

Michelle submerged and swam till she reached her banyan tree, then surfaced and called down her rope elevator. By the time Torbiong's boat hissed up to her, she'd folded away her gills and wings and was sitting in the sling, kicking her legs over the water.

Torbiong handed her a bag of supplies: some rice, tea, salt, vegetables, and fruit. For the last several weeks Michelle had experienced a craving for blueberries, which didn't grow here, and Torbiong had included a large package fresh off the shuttle, and a small bottle of cream to go with them. Michelle thanked him.

"Most tourists want corn chips or something," Torbiong said pointedly.

"I'm not a tourist," Michelle said. "I'm sorry I don't have any fish to swap—I've been hunting smaller game." She held out the specimen bag, still dripping sea water.

Torbiong gestured toward the cooler built into the back of his boat. "I got some *chai* and a *chersuuch* today," he said, using the local names for barracuda and mahi mahi.

"Good fishing."

"Trolling." With a shrug. He looked up at her, a quizzical look on his face. "I've got some calls from reporters," he said, and then his betel-stained smile broke out. "I always make sure to send them tourist literature."

"I'm sure they enjoy reading it."

Torbiong's grin widened. "You get lonely, now," he said, "you come visit the family. We'll give you a home-cooked meal."

She smiled. "Thanks."

They said their farewells and Torbiong's boat hissed away on its jets, the whistles building to an eerie, spine-shivering chord. Michelle rose into the trees and stashed her specimens and groceries. With a bowl of blueberries and cream, Michelle crossed the rope walkway to her deck, and checked the progress of her search spiders.

There were pointers to a swarm of articles about the death of Terzian's wife, and Michelle wished she'd given her spiders clearer instructions about dates.

The spiders had come up with three pictures. One was a not-very-well-focused tourist video from July 10, showing a man standing in front of the Basilica di Santa Croce in Florence. A statue of Dante, also not in focus gloomed down at him from beneath thick-bellied rain clouds. As the camera panned across him, he stood with his back to the camera, but turned to the right, one leg turned out as he scowled down at the ground—the profile was a little smeared, but the big, broad-shouldered body seemed right. The software reckoned that there was a 78 percent chance that the man was Terzian.

Michelle got busy refining the image, and after a few passes of the software, decided the chances of the figure being Terzian were more on the order of 95 percent.

So maybe Terzian had gone on a Grand Tour of European cultural sites. He didn't look happy in the video, but then the day was rainy and Terzian didn't have an umbrella.

And his wife had died, of course.

Now that Michelle had a date and a place she refined the instructions from her search spiders to seek out images from Florence a week either way from July 3, and then expand the search from there, first all Tuscany, then all Italy.

If Terzian was doing tourist sites, then she surely had him nailed.

The next two hits, from her earlier research spiders, were duds. The software gave a less than 50 percent chance of Terzian's being in Lisbon or Cape Sounion, and refinements of the image reduced the chance to something near zero.

Then the next video popped up, with a time stamp right there in the image—Paris, June 26, 13:41:44 hours, just a day before Terzian bought a bankroll of euros and vanished.

<*Bingo!*> Michelle's fingers formed.

The first thing Michelle saw was Terzian walking out of the frame—no doubt this time that it was him. He was looking over his shoulder at a small crowd of people. There was a dark-haired woman huddled on his arm, her face turned away from the camera. Michelle's heart warmed at the thought of the lonely widower Terzian having an affair in the City of Love.

Then she followed Terzian's gaze to see what had so drawn his attention. A dead man stretched out on the pavement, surrounded by hapless bystanders.

And then, as the scene slowly settled into her astonished mind, the video sang at her in the piping voice of Pan.

Terzian looked at his audience as anger raged in his backbrain. A wooden chair creaked, and the sound spurred Terzian to wonder how long the silence had gone on. Even the Slovenian woman who had been drowsing realized that something had changed, and blinked herself to alertness.

"I'm sorry," he said in French. "But my wife just died, and I don't feel like playing this game any more."

His silent audience watched as he gathered his papers, put them in his case, and left the lecture room, his feet making sharp, murderous sounds on the wooden floor.

Yet up to that point his paper had been going all right. He'd been uncertain about commenting on Baudrillard in Baudrillard's own country, and in Baudrillard's own language, a cheery compare-and-contrast exercise between Baudrillard's "the self does not exist" and Rorty's "I don't care," the stereotypical French and American answers to modern life. There had been seven in his audience, perched on creaking wooden chairs, and none of them had gone to sleep, or walked out, or condemned him for his audacity.

Yet, as he looked at his audience and read on, Terzian had felt the anger growing, spawned by the sensation of his own uselessness. Here he was, in the City of Light, its every cobblestone a monument to European civilization, and he was in a dreary lecture hall on the Left Bank, reading to his audience of seven from a paper that was nothing more than a footnote, and a footnote to a footnote at that. To come to the land of *cogito ergo sum* and to answer, *I don't care?*

I came to Paris for this? he thought. *To read this* drivel? *I paid for the privilege of doing* this?

I do care, he thought as his feet turned toward the Seine. *Desiderio, ergo sum,* if he had his Latin right. I am in pain, and therefore I *do* exist.

He ended in a Norman restaurant on the Ile de la Cité, with lunch as his excuse and the thought of getting hopelessly drunk not far from his thoughts. He had absolutely nothing to do until August, after which he would return to the States and collect his belongings from the servants' quarters of the house on Esplanade, and then he would go about looking for a job.

He wasn't certain whether he would be more depressed by finding a job or by not finding one.

You are alive, he told himself. *You are alive and in Paris with the whole summer ahead of you, and you're eating the cuisine of Normandy in the Place Dauphine. And if that isn't a command to be joyful, what is?*

It was then that the Peruvian band began to play. Terzian looked up from his plate in weary surprise.

When Terzian had been a child his parents—both university professors—had first taken him to Europe, and he'd seen then that every European city had its own Peruvian or Bolivian street band, Indians in black bowler hats and colorful blankets crouched in some public place, gazing with impassive brown eyes from over their guitars and reed flutes.

Now, a couple of decades later, the musicians were still here, though they'd exchanged the blankets and bowler hats for European styles, and their presentation had grown more slick. Now they had amps, and cassettes and CDs for sale. Now they had congregated in the triangular Place Dauphine, overshadowed by the neo-classical mass of the Palais de Justice, and commenced a Latin-flavored medley of old Abba songs.

Maybe, after Terzian finished his veal in calvados sauce, he'd go up to the band and kick in their guitars.

The breeze flapped the canvas overhead. Terzian looked at his empty plate. The food had been excellent, but he could barely remember tasting it.

Anger still roiled beneath his thoughts. And—for God's *sake*—was that band now playing *Oasis?* Those chords were beginning to sound suspiciously like "Wonderwall." "Wonderwall" on Spanish guitars, reed flutes, and a mandolin!

Terzian had nearly decided to call for a bottle of cognac and stay here all afternoon, but not with that noise in the park. He put some euros on the table, anchoring the bills with a saucer against the fresh spring breeze that rattled the green canvas canopy over his head. He was stepping through the restaurant's little wrought-iron gate to the sidewalk when the scuffle caught his attention.

The man falling into the street, his face pinched with pain. The hands of the three men on either side who were, seemingly, unable to keep their friend erect.

Idiots, Terzian thought, fury blazing in him.

There was a sudden shrill of tires, of an auto horn.

Papers streamed in the wind as they spilled from a briefcase.

And over it all came the amped sound of pan pipes from the Peruvian band. *"Wonderwall."*

Terzian watched in exasperated surprise as the three men sprang after the papers. He took a step toward the fallen man—*someone* had to take charge here. The fallen man's hair had spilled in a shock over his forehead and he'd curled on his side, his face still screwed up in pain.

The pan pipes played on, one distinct hollow shriek after another.

Terzian stopped with one foot still on the sidewalk and looked around at faces that all registered the same sense of shock. Was there a doctor here? he wondered. A *French* doctor? All his French seemed to have just drained from his head. Even such simple questions as *Are you all right?* and *How are you feeling?* seemed beyond him now. The first-aid course he'd taken in his Kenpo school was *ages* ago.

Unnaturally pale, the fallen man's face relaxed. The wind floated his shock of thinning dark hair over his face. In the park, Terzian saw a man in a baseball cap panning a video camera, and his anger suddenly blazed up again at the fatuous uselessness of the tourist, the uselessness that mirrored his own.

Suddenly there was a crowd around the casualty, people coming out of stopped cars, off the sidewalk. Down the street, Terzian saw the distinctive flat-topped kepis of a pair of policemen bobbing toward him from the direction of the Palais de Justice, and felt a surge of relief. Someone more capable than this lot would deal with this now.

He began, hesitantly, to step away. And then his arm was seized by a pair of hands and he looked in surprise at the woman who had just huddled her face into his shoulder, cinnamon-dark skin and eyes invisible beneath wraparound shades.

"Please," she said in English a bit too musical to be American. "Take me out of here."

The sound of the reed pipes followed them as they made their escape.

He walked her past the statue of the Vert Galant himself, good old lecherous Henri IV, and onto the Pont Neuf. To the left, across the Seine, the Louvre glowed in mellow colors beyond a screen of plane trees.

Traffic roared by, a stampede of steel unleashed by a green light. Unfocused anger blazed in his mind. He didn't want this woman attached to him, and he suspected she was running some kind of scam. The gym bag she wore on a strap over one shoulder kept banging him on the ass. Surreptitiously, he slid his hand into his right front trouser pocket to make sure his money was still there.

"Wonderwall," he thought. *Christ.*

He supposed he should offer some kind of civilized comment, just in case the woman was genuinely distressed.

"I suppose he'll be all right," he said, half-barking the words in his annoyance and anger.

The woman's face was still half-buried in his shoulder. "He's dead," she murmured into his jacket. "Couldn't you tell?"

For Terzian, death had never occurred under the sky, but shut away, in hospice rooms with crisp sheets and warm colors and the scent of disinfectant. In an explosion of tumors and wasting limbs and endless pain masked only in part by morphia.

He thought of the man's pale face, the sudden relaxation.

Yes, he thought, death came with a sigh.

Reflex kept him talking. "The police were coming," he said. "They'll—they'll call an ambulance or something."

"I only hope they catch the bastards who did it," she said.

Terzian's heart gave a jolt as he recalled the three men who let the victim fall, and then dashed through the square for his papers. For some reason, all he could remember about them were their black-laced boots, with thick soles.

"Who were they?" he asked blankly.

The woman's shades slid down her nose, and Terzian saw startling green eyes narrowed to murderous slits. "I suppose they think of themselves as cops," she said.

Terzian parked his companion in a café near Les Halles, within sight of the dome of the Bourse. She insisted on sitting indoors, not on the sidewalk, and on facing the front door so that she could scan whoever came in. She put her gym bag, with its white Nike swoosh, on the floor between the table legs and the wall, but Terzian noticed she kept its shoulder strap in her lap, as if she might have to bolt at any moment.

Terzian kept his wedding ring within her sight. He wanted her to see it; it might make things simpler.

Her hands were trembling. Terzian ordered coffee for them both. "No," she said suddenly. "I want ice cream."

Terzian studied her as she turned to the waiter and ordered in French. She was around his own age, twenty-nine. There was no question that she was a mixture of races, but *which* races? The flat nose could be African or Asian or Polynesian, and Polynesia was again confirmed by the black, thick brows. Her smooth brown complexion could be from anywhere but Europe, but her pale green eyes were nothing but European. Her broad, sensitive mouth suggested Nubia. The black ringlets yanked into a knot behind her head could be African or East Indian, or, for that matter, French. The result was too striking to be beautiful—and also too striking, Terzian thought, to belong to a successful criminal. Those looks could be too easily identified.

The waiter left. She turned her wide eyes toward Terzian, and seemed faintly surprised that he was still there.

"My name's Jonathan," he said.

"I'm," hesitating, "Stephanie."

"Really?" Terzian let his skepticism show.

"Yes." She nodded, reaching in a pocket for cigarettes. "Why would I lie? It doesn't matter if you know my real name or not."

"Then you'd better give me the whole thing."

She held her cigarette upward, at an angle, and enunciated clearly. "Stephanie América Pais e Silva."

"America?"

Striking a match. "It's a perfectly ordinary Portuguese name."

He looked at her. "But you're not Portuguese."

"I carry a Portuguese passport."

Terzian bit back the comment, *I'm sure you do.*

Instead he said, "Did you know the man who was killed?"

Stephanie nodded. The drags she took off her cigarette did not ease the tremor in her hands.

"Did you know him well?"

"Not very." She dragged in smoke again, then let the smoke out as she spoke.

"He was a colleague. A biochemist."

Surprise silenced Terzian. Stephanie tipped ash into the Cinzano ashtray, but her nervousness made her miss, and the little tube of ash fell on the tablecloth.

"Shit," she said, and swept the ash to the floor with a nervous movement of her fingers.

"Are you a biochemist, too?" Terzian asked.

"I'm a nurse." She looked at him with her pale eyes. "I work for Santa Croce—it's a—"

"A relief agency." A Catholic one, he remembered. The name meant *Holy Cross*.

She nodded.

"Shouldn't you go to the police?" he asked. And then his skepticism returned. "Oh, that's right—it was the police who did the killing."

"Not the *French* police." She leaned across the table toward him. "This was a different sort of police, the kind who think that killing someone and making an arrest are the same thing. You look at the television news tonight. They'll report the death, but there won't be any arrests. Or any suspects." Her face darkened, and she leaned back in her chair to consider a new thought. "Unless they somehow manage to blame it on me."

Terzian remembered papers flying in the spring wind, men in heavy boots sprinting after. The pinched, pale face of the victim.

"Who, then?"

She gave him a bleak look through a curl of cigarette smoke. "Have you ever heard of Transnistria?"

Terzian hesitated, then decided "No" was the most sensible answer.

"The murderers are Transnistrian." A ragged smile drew itself across Stephanie's face. "Their intellectual property police. They killed Adrian over a copyright."

At that point, the waiter brought Terzian's coffee, along with Stephanie's order. Hers was colossal, a huge glass goblet filled with pastel-colored ice creams and fruit syrups in bright primary colors, topped by a mountain of cream and a toy pinwheel on a candy-striped stick. Stephanie looked at the creation in shock, her eyes wide.

"I love ice cream," she choked, and then her eyes brimmed with tears and she began to cry.

Stephanie wept for a while, across the table, and, between sobs, choked down heaping spoonfuls of ice cream, eating in great gulps and swiping at her lips and tear-stained cheeks with a paper napkin.

The waiter stood quietly in the corner, but from his glare and the set of his jaw it was clear that he blamed Terzian for making the lovely woman cry.

Terzian felt his body surge with the impulse to aid her, but he didn't know what to do. Move around the table and put an arm around her? Take her hand? Call someone to take her off his hands?

The latter, for preference.

He settled for handing her a clean napkin when her own grew sodden.

His skepticism had not survived the mention of the Transnistrian copyright police. This was far too bizarre to be a con—a scam was based on basic human desire, greed, or lust, not something as abstract as intellectual property. Unless there was a gang who made a point of targeting academics from the States, luring them with a tantalizing hook about a copyright worth murdering for. . . .

Eventually, the storm subsided. Stephanie pushed the half-consumed ice cream away, and reached for another cigarette.

He tapped his wedding ring on the table top, something he did when thinking. "Shouldn't you contact the local police?" he asked. "You know something about this . . . death." For some reason he was reluctant to use the word *murder*. It was as if using the word would make something true, not the killing itself but his relationship to the killing . . . to call it murder would grant it some kind of power over him.

She shook her head. "I've got to get out of France before those guys find me. Out of Europe, if I can, but that would be hard. My passport's in my hotel room, and they're probably watching it."

"Because of this copyright."

Her mouth twitched in a half-smile. "That's right."

"It's not a literary copyright, I take it."

She shook her head, the half-smile still on her face.

"Your friend was a biologist." He felt a hum in his nerves, a certainty that he already knew the answer to the next question.

"Is it a weapon?" he asked.

She wasn't surprised by the question. "No," she said. "No, just the opposite." She took a drag on her cigarette and sighed the smoke out. "It's an antidote. An antidote to human folly."

"Listen," Stephanie said. "Just because the Soviet Union fell doesn't mean that *Sovietism* fell with it. Sovietism is still there—the only difference is that its moral justification is gone, and what's left is vio-lence and extortion disguised as law enforcement and taxation. The old empire breaks up, and in the West you think it's great, but more countries just meant more palms to be greased—all throughout the former Soviet empire you've got more 'inspectors' and 'tax collec-tors,' more 'customs agents' and 'security directorates' than there ever were under the Russians. All these people do is prey off their own populations, because no one else will do business with them unless they've got oil or some other resource that people want."

"Trashcanistans," Terzian said. It was a word he'd heard used of his own ancestral homeland, the former Soviet Republic of Armenia, whose looted economy and paranoid, murderous, despotic Russian puppet regime was supported only by millions of dollars sent to the country by Americans of Armenian descent, who thought that prop-ping up the gang of thugs in power somehow translated into freedom for the fatherland.

Stephanie nodded. "And the worst Trashcanistan of all is Transnistria."

She and Terzian had left the café and taken a taxi back to the Left Bank and Terzian's hotel. He had turned the television to a local sta-tion, but muted the sound until the news came on. Until then the sta-tion showed a rerun of an American cop show, stolid, businesslike detectives underplaying their latest sordid confrontation with tragedy.

The hotel room hadn't been built for the queen-sized bed it now held, and there was an eighteen-inch clearance around the bed and no room for chairs. Terzian, not wanting Stephanie to think he wanted to get her in the sack, perched uncertainly on a corner of the bed, while Stephanie disposed herself more comfortably, sitting cross-legged in its center.

"Moldova was a Soviet republic put together by Stalin," she said. "It was made up of Bessarabia, which was a part of Romania that Stalin chewed off at the beginning of the Second World War, plus a strip of industrial land on the far side of the Dniester. When the So-viet Union went down, Moldova became 'independent'—" Terzian could hear the quotes in her voice. "But independence had nothing to do with the Moldovan *people*, it was just Romanian-speaking So-viet elites going off on their own account once their own superiors were no longer there to restrain them. And Moldova soon split—first the Turkish Christians . . ."

"Wait a second," Terzian said. "There are *Christian Turks?*"

The idea of Christian Turks was not a part of his Armenian-American worldview.

Stephanie nodded. "Orthodox Christian Turks, yes. They're called Gagauz, and they now have their own autonomous republic of Gagauzia within Moldova."

Stephanie reached into her pocket for a cigarette and her lighter.

"Uh," Terzian said. "Would you mind smoking out the window?"

Stephanie made a face. "Americans," she said, but she moved to the window and opened it, letting in a blast of cool spring air. She perched on the windowsill, sheltered her cigarette from the wind, and lit up.

"Where was I?" she asked.

"Turkish Christians."

"Right." Blowing smoke into the teeth of the gale. "Gagauzia was only the start—after that, a Russian general allied with a bunch of crooks and KGB types created a rebellion in the bit of Moldova that was on the far side of the Dniester—another collection of Soviet elites, representing no one but themselves. Once the Russian-speaking rebels rose against their Romanian-speaking oppressors, the Soviet Fourteenth Army stepped in as 'peacekeepers,' complete with blue helmets, and created a twenty-mile-wide state recognized by no other government. And that meant more military, more border guards, more administrators, more taxes to charge, and customs duties, and uniformed ex-Soviets whose palms needed greasing. And over a hundred thousand refugees who could be put in camps while the administration stole their supplies and rations. . . .

"But—" She jabbed the cigarette like a pointer. "Transnistria had a problem. No other nation recognized their existence, and they were tiny and had no natural resources, barring the underage girls they enslaved by the thousands to export for prostitution. The rest of the population was leaving as fast as they could, restrained only slightly by the fact that they carried passports no other state recognized, and that meant there were fewer people whose productivity the elite could steal to support their predatory post-Soviet lifestyles. All they had was a lot of obsolete Soviet heavy industry geared to produce stuff no one wanted.

"But they still had the *infrastructure*. They had power plants—running off Russian oil they couldn't afford to buy—and they had a transportation system. So the outlaw regime set up to attract other outlaws who needed industrial capacity—the idea was that they'd

attract entrepreneurs who were excused paying most of the local
'taxes' in exchange for making one big payoff to the higher echelon."

"Weapons?" Terzian asked.

"Weapons, sure." Stephanie nodded. "Mostly they're producing
cheap knockoffs of other people's guns, but the guns are up to the size
of howitzers. They tried banking and data havens, but the authorities
couldn't restrain themselves from ripping those off—banks and data
run on trust and control of information, and when the regulators are
greedy, shortsighted crooks, you don't get either one. So what they
settled on was, well, *biotech*. They've got companies creating cheap
generic pharmaceuticals that evade Western patents. . . ." Her look
darkened. "Not that I've got a problem with *that,* not when I've seen
thousands dying of diseases they couldn't afford to cure. And they've
also got other companies who are ripping off Western genetic research to develop their own products. And as long as they make their
payoffs to the elite, these companies remain *completely unregulated.* Nobody, not even the government, knows what they're doing in those
factories, and the government gives them security free of charge."

Terzian imagined gene-splicing going on in a rusting Soviet fac-
tory, rows and rows of mutant plants with untested, unregulated genetics, all set to be released on an unsuspecting world. Transgenic
elements drifting down the Dniester to the Black Sea, growing quietly in its saline environment . . .

"The news," Stephanie reminded, and pointed at the television.

Terzian reached for the control and hit the mute button, just as
the throbbing, anxious music that announced the news began to fade.

The murder on the Ile de la Cité was the second item on the
broadcast. The victim was described as a "foreign national" who had
been fatally stabbed, and no arrests had been made. The motive for
the killing was unknown.

Terzian changed the channel in time to catch the same item on
another channel. The story was unchanged.

"I told you," Stephanie said. "No suspects. No motive."

"You could tell them."

She made a negative motion with her cigarette. "I couldn't tell
them who did it, or how to find them. All I could do is put myself
under suspicion."

Terzian turned off the TV. "So what happened exactly? Your
friend stole from these people?"

Stephanie swiped her forehead with the back of her wrist. "He stole something that was of no value to them. It's only valuable to poor people, who can't afford to pay. And——" She turned to the window and spun her cigarette into the street below. "I'll take it out of here as soon as I can," she said. "I've got to try to contact some people." She closed the window, shutting out the spring breeze. "I wish I had my passport. That would change everything."

I saw a murder this afternoon, Terzian thought. He closed his eyes and saw the man falling, the white face so completely absorbed in the reality of its own agony.

He was so fucking sick of death.

He opened his eyes. "I can get your passport back," he said.

Anger kept him moving until he saw the killers, across the street from Stephanie's hotel, sitting at an outdoor table in a café-bar. Terzian recognized them immediately—he didn't need to look at the heavy shoes, or the broad faces with their disciplined military mustaches— one glance at the crowd at the café showed the only two in the place who weren't French. That was probably how Stephanie knew to speak to him in English, he just didn't dress or carry himself like a Frenchman, for all that he'd worn an anonymous coat and tie. He tore his gaze away before they saw him gaping at them.

Anger turned very suddenly to fear, and as he continued his stride toward the hotel he told himself that they wouldn't recognize him from the Norman restaurant, that he'd changed into blue jeans and sneakers and a windbreaker, and carried a soft-sided suitcase. Still he felt a gunsight on the back of his neck, and he was so nervous that he nearly ran headfirst into the glass lobby door.

Terzian paid for a room with his credit card, took the key from the Vietnamese clerk, and walked up the narrow stair to what the French called the second floor, but what he would have called the third. No one lurked in the stairwell, and he wondered where the third assassin had gone. Looking for Stephanie somewhere else, probably, an airport or train station.

In his room Terzian put his suitcase on the bed—it held only a few token items, plus his shaving kit—and then he took Stephanie's key from his pocket and held it in his hand. The key was simple, attached to a weighted doorknob-shaped ceramic plug.

The jolt of fear and surprise that had so staggered him on first sighting the two men began to shift again into rage.

They were drinking *beer,* there had been half-empty mugs on the table in front of them, and a pair of empties as well.

Drinking on duty. Doing surveillance while drunk.

Bastards. Trashcanians. They could kill someone simply through drunkenness.

Perhaps they already had.

He was angry when he left his room and took the stairs to the floor below. No foes kept watch in the hall. He opened Stephanie's room and then closed the door behind him.

He didn't turn on the light. The sun was surprisingly high in the sky for the hour: he had noticed that the sun seemed to set later here than it did at home. Maybe France was very far to the west for its time zone.

Stephanie didn't have a suitcase, just a kind of nylon duffel, a larger version of the athletic bag she already carried. He took it from the little closet, and enough of Terzian's suspicion remained so that he checked the luggage tag to make certain the name was *Steph. Pais,* and not another.

He opened the duffel, then got her passport and travel documents from the bedside table and tossed them in. He added a jacket and a sweater from the closet, then packed her toothbrush and shaver into her plastic travel bag and put it in the duffel.

The plan was for him to return to his room on the upper floor and stay the night and avoid raising suspicion by leaving a hotel he'd just checked into. In the morning, carrying two bags, he'd check out and rejoin Stephanie in his own hotel, where she had spent the night in his room, and where the air would by now almost certainly reek with her cigarette smoke.

Terzian opened a dresser drawer and scooped out a double handful of Stephanie's T-shirts, underwear, and stockings, and then he remembered that the last time he'd done this was when he cleaned Claire's belongings out of the Esplanade house.

Shit. Fuck. He gazed down at the clothing between his hands and let the fury rage like a tempest in his skull.

And then, in the angry silence, he heard a creak in the corridor, and then a stumbling thud.

Thick rubber military soles, he thought. With drunk baboons in them.

Instinct shrieked at him not to be trapped in this room, this dead-end where he could be trapped and killed. He dropped Stephanie's clothes back into the drawer and stepped to the bed and picked up the duffel in one hand. Another step took him to the door, which he opened with one hand while using the other to fling the duffel into the surprised face of the drunken murderer on the other side.

Terzian hadn't been at his Kenpo school in six years, not since he'd left Kansas City, but certain reflexes don't go away after they've been drilled into a person thousands of times—certainly not the front kick that hooked upward under the intruder's breastbone and drove him breathless into the corridor wall opposite.

A primitive element of his mind rejoiced in the fact that he was bigger than these guys. He could really knock them around.

The second Trashcanian tried to draw a pistol, but Terzian passed outside the pistol hand and drove the point of an elbow into the man's face. Terzian then grabbed the automatic with both hands, took a further step down the corridor, and spun around, which swung the man around Terzian's hip a full two hundred and seventy degrees and drove him head first into the corridor wall. When he'd finished falling and opened his eyes he was staring into the barrel of his own gun.

Red rage gave a fangs-bared roar of animal triumph inside Terzian's skull. Perhaps his tongue echoed it. It was all he could do to stop himself from pulling the trigger.

Get Death working for *him* for a change. Why not?

Except that the first man hadn't realized that his side had just lost. He had drawn a knife—a glittering chromed single-edged thing that may have already killed once today—and now he took a dangerous step toward Terzian.

Terzian pointed the pistol straight at the knife man and pulled the trigger. Nothing happened.

The intruder stared at the gun as if he'd just realized at just this moment it wasn't his partner who held it.

Terzian pulled the trigger again, and when nothing happened his rage melted into terror and he ran. Behind him he heard the drunken knife man trip over his partner and crash to the floor.

Terzian was at the bottom of the stair before he heard the thick-soled military boots clatter on the risers above him. He dashed through the small lobby—he sensed the Vietnamese night clerk, who was facing away, begin to turn toward him just as he pushed open the glass door and ran into the street.

He kept running. At some point he discovered the gun still in his fist, and he put it in the pocket of his windbreaker.

Some moments later, he realized that he wasn't being pursued. And he remembered that Stephanie's passport was still in her duffel, which he'd thrown at the knife man and hadn't retrieved.

For a moment, rage ran through him, and he thought about taking out the gun and fixing whatever was wrong with it and going back to Stephanie's room and getting the documents one way or another.

But then the anger faded enough for him to see what a foolish course that would be, and he returned to his own hotel.

Terzian had given Stephanie his key, so he knocked on his own door before realizing she was very unlikely to open to a random knock. "It's Jonathan," he said. "It didn't work out."

She snatched the door open from the inside. Her face was taut with anxiety. She held pages in her hand, the text of the paper he'd delivered that morning.

"Sorry," he said. "They were there, outside the hotel. I got into your room, but—"

She took his arm and almost yanked him into the room, then shut the door behind him. "Did they follow you?" she demanded.

"No. They didn't chase me. Maybe they thought I'd figure out how to work the gun." He took the pistol out of his pocket and showed it to her. "I can't believe how stupid I was—"

"Where did you get that? Where did you get that?" Her voice was nearly a scream, and she shrank away from him, her eyes wide. Her fist crumpled papers over her heart. To his astonishment, he realized that she was afraid of him, that she thought he was *connected* somehow, with the killers.

He threw the pistol onto the bed and raised his hands in a gesture of surrender. "No really!" he shouted over her cries. "It's not mine! I took it from one of them!"

Stephanie took a deep gasp of air. Her eyes were still wild. "Who the hell are you, then?" she said. "James Bond?"

He gave a disgusted laugh. "James Bond would have known how to shoot."

"I was reading your—your article." She held out the pages toward him. "I was thinking, my God, I was thinking, what have I got this poor guy into. Some professor I was sending to his death." She passed a hand over her forehead. "They probably bugged my room. They would have known right away that someone was in it."

"They were drunk," Terzian said. "Maybe they've been drinking all day. Those assholes really pissed me off."

He sat on the bed and picked up the pistol. It was small and blue steel and surprisingly heavy. In the years since he'd last shot a gun, he had forgotten that purposefulness, the way a firearm was designed for a single, clear function. He found the safety where it had been all along, near his right thumb, and flicked it off and then on again.

"There," he said. "That's what I should have done."

Waves of anger shivered through his limbs at the touch of the adrenaline still pouring into his system. A bitter impulse to laugh again rose in him, and he tried to suppress it.

"I guess I was lucky after all," he said. "It wouldn't have done you any good to have to explain a pair of corpses outside your room." He looked up at Stephanie, who was pacing back and forth in the narrow lane between the bed and the wall, and looking as if she badly needed a cigarette. "I'm sorry about your passport. Where were you going to go, anyway?"

"It doesn't so much matter if *I* go," she said. She gave Terzian a quick, nervous glance. "You can fly it out, right?"

"It?" He stared at her. "What do you mean, it?"

"The biotech." Stephanie stopped her pacing and stared at him with those startling green eyes. "Adrian gave it to me. Just before they killed him." Terzian's gaze followed hers to the black bag with the Nike swoosh, the bag that sat at the foot of Terzian's bed.

Terzian's impulse to laugh faded. Unregulated, illegal, stolen biotech, he thought. Right in his own hotel room. Along with a stolen gun and a woman who was probably out of her mind.

Fuck.

The dead man was identified by news files as Adrian Cristea, a citizen of Ukraine and a researcher. He had been stabbed once in the right kidney and bled to death without identifying his assailants. Witnesses reported two or maybe three men leaving the scene immediately after Cristea's death. Michelle set more search spiders to work.

For a moment, she considered calling Davout and letting him know that Terzian had probably been a witness to a murder, but decided to wait until she had some more evidence one way or another.

For the next few hours, she did her real work, analyzing the samples she'd taken from Zigzag Lake's sulphide-tainted deeps. It wasn't very physical, and Michelle figured it was only worth a few hundred calories.

A wind floated through the treetops, bringing the scent of night flowers and swaying Michelle's perch beneath her as she peered into her biochemical reader, and she remembered the gentle pressure of Darton against her back, rocking with her as he looked over her shoulder at her results. Suddenly she could remember, with a near-perfect clarity, the taste of his skin on her tongue.

She rose from her woven seat and paced along the bough. *Damn it,* she thought, *I watched you die.*

Michelle returned to her deck and discovered that her spiders had located the police file on Cristea's death. A translation program handled the antique French without trouble, even producing modern equivalents of forensic jargon. Cristea was of Romanian descent, had been born in the old USSR, and had acquired Ukranian citizenship on the breakup of the Soviet Union. The French files themselves had translations of Cristea's Ukranian travel documents, which included receipts showing that he had paid personal insurance, environmental insurance, and departure taxes from Transnistria, a place of which she'd never heard, as well as similar documents from Moldova, which at least was a province, or country, that sounded familiar.

What kind of places were these, where you had to buy *insurance* at the *border?* And what was environmental insurance anyway?

There were copies of emails between French and Ukranian authorities, in which the Ukranians politely declined any knowledge of their citizen beyond the fact that he *was* a citizen. They had no addresses for him.

Cristea apparently lived in Transnistria, but the authorities there echoed the Ukranians in saying they knew nothing of him.

Cristea's tickets and vouchers showed that he had apparently taken a train to Bucharest, and there he'd got on an airline that took him to Prague, and thence to Paris. He had been in the city less than a day before he was killed. Found in Cristea's hotel room was a curious document certifying that Cristea was carrying medical supplies, specifically a vaccine against hepatitis A. Michelle wondered why he would be carrying a hepatitis vaccine from Transnistria to France. France presumably had all the hepatitis vaccine it needed.

No vaccine had turned up. Apparently Cristea had got into the European Community without having his bags searched, as there was no evidence that the documents relating to the alleged vaccine had ever been examined.

The missing "vaccine"—at some point in the police file the skeptical quotation marks had appeared—had convinced the Paris police that Cristea was a murdered drug courier, and at that point they'd lost interest in the case. It was rarely possible to solve a professional killing in the drug underworld.

Michelle's brief investigation seemed to have come to a dead end. That Terzian might have witnessed a murder would rate maybe half a sentence in Professor Davout's biography.

Then she checked what her spiders had brought her in regard to Terzian, and found something that cheered her.

There he was inside the Basilica di Santa Croce, a tourist still photograph taken before the tomb of Machiavelli. He was only slightly turned away from the camera and the face was unmistakable. Though there was no date on the photograph, only the year, he wore the same clothes he wore in the video taken outside the church, and the photo caught him in the act of speaking to a companion. She was a tall woman with deep brown skin, but she was turned away from the camera, and a wide-brimmed sun hat made her features indistinguishable.

Humming happily, Michelle deployed her software to determine whether this was the same woman who had been on Terzian's arm on the Place Dauphine. Without facial features or other critical measurements to compare, the software was uncertain, but the proportion of limb and thorax was right, and the software gave an estimate of 41 percent, which Michelle took to be encouraging.

Another still image of Terzian appeared in an undated photograph taken at a festival in southern France. He wore dark glasses, and he'd grown heavily tanned; he carried a glass of wine in either hand, but the person to whom he was bringing the second glass was out of the frame. Michelle set her software to locating the identity of the church seen in the background, a task the two distinctive bell towers would make easy. She was lucky and got a hit right away: the church was the Eglise St-Michel in Salon-de-Provence, which meant Terzian had attended the Fête des Aires de la Dine in June. Michelle set more search spiders to seeking out photo and video from the festivals. She had no doubt that she'd find Terzian there, and perhaps again his companion.

Michelle retired happily to her hammock. The search was going well. Terzian had met a woman in Paris and traveled with her for weeks. The evidence wasn't quite there yet, but Michelle would drag it out of history somehow.

Romance. The lonely mermaid was in favor of romance, the kind where you ran away to faraway places to be more intently one with the person you adored.

It was what she herself had done, before everything had gone so wrong, and Michelle had had to take steps to re-establish the moral balance of her universe.

Terzian paid for a room for Stephanie for the night, not so much because he was gallant as because he needed to be alone to think. "There's a breakfast buffet downstairs in the morning," he said. "They have hard-boiled eggs and croissants and Nutella. It's a very un-French thing to do. I recommend it."

He wondered if he would ever see her again. She might just vanish, particularly if she read his thoughts, because another reason for wanting privacy was so that he could call the police and bring an end to this insane situation.

He never quite assembled the motivation to make the call. Perhaps Rorty's *I don't care* had rubbed off on him. And he never got a chance to taste the buffet, either. Stephanie banged on his door very early, and he dragged on his jeans and opened the door. She entered, furiously smoking from her new cigarette pack, the athletic bag over her shoulder.

"How did you pay for the room at my hotel?" she asked.

"Credit card," he said, and in the stunned, accusing silence that followed he saw his James Bond fantasies sink slowly beneath the slack, oily surface of a dismal lake.

Because credit cards leave trails. The Transnistrians would have checked the hotel registry, and the credit card impression taken by the hotel, and now they knew who *he* was. And it wouldn't be long before they'd trace him at this hotel.

"Shit, I should have warned you to pay cash." Stephanie stalked to the window and peered out cautiously. "They could be out there right now."

Terzian felt a sudden compulsion to have the gun in his hand. He took it from the bedside table and stood there, feeling stupid and cold and shirtless.

"How much money do you have?" Terzian asked.

"Couple of hundred."

"I have less."

"You should max out your credit card and just carry euros. Use your card now before they cancel it."

"Cancel it? How could they cancel it?"

She gave him a tight-lipped, impatient look. "Jonathan. They may be assholes, but they're still a *government*."

They took a cab to the American Express near the Opéra and Terzian got ten thousand Euros in cash from some people who were extremely skeptical about the validity of his documents, but who had, in the end, to admit that all was technically correct. Then Stephanie got a cell phone under the name A. Silva, with a bunch of prepaid hours on it, and within a couple of hours they were on the TGV, speeding south to Nice at nearly two hundred seventy kilometers per hour, all with a strange absence of sound and vibration that made the French countryside speeding past seem like a strangely unconvincing special effect.

Terzian had put them in first class and he and Stephanie were alone in a group of four seats. Stephanie was twitchy because he hadn't bought seats in a smoking section. He sat uncertain, unhappy about all the cash he was carrying and not knowing what to do with it—he'd made two big rolls and zipped them into the pockets of his windbreaker. He carried the pistol in the front pocket of his jeans and its weight and discomfort was a perpetual reminder of this situation that he'd been dragged into, pursued by killers from Trashcanistan and escorting illegal biotechnology.

He kept mentally rehearsing drawing the pistol and shooting it. Over and over, remembering to thumb off the safety this time. Just in case Trashcanian commandos stormed the train.

"Hurled into life," he muttered. "An object lesson right out of Heidegger."

"Beg pardon?"

He looked at her. "Heidegger said we're hurled into life. Just like

I've been hurled into—" He flapped his hands uselessly. "Into what-ever this is. The situation exists before you even got here, but here you are anyway, and the whole business is something you inherit and have to live with." He felt his lips draw back in a snarl. "He also said that a fundamental feature of existence is anxiety in the face of death, which would also seem to apply to our situation. And his answer to all of this was to make existence, *dasein* if you want to get technical, an authentic project." He looked at her. "So what's your authentic proj-ect, then? And how authentic is it?"

Her brow furrowed. "What?"

Terzian couldn't stop, not that he wanted to. It was just Stephanie's hard luck that he couldn't shoot anybody right now, or break some-thing up with his fists, and was compelled to lecture instead. "Or," he went on, "to put this in a more accessible context, just pretend we're in a Hitchcock film, okay? This is the scene where Grace Kelly tells Cary Grant exactly who she is and what the maguffin is."

Stephanie's face was frozen into a hostile mask. Whether she un-derstood what he was saying or not, the hostility was clear.

"I don't get it," she said.

"What's in the fucking bag?" he demanded.

She glared at him for a long moment, then spoke, her own anger plain in her voice. "It's the answer to world hunger," she said. "Is that authentic enough for you?"

Stephanie's father was from Angola and her mother from East Timor, both former Portuguese colonies swamped in the decades since inde-pendence by war and massacre. Both parents had, with great foresight and intelligence, retained Portuguese passports, and had met in Rome, where they worked for UNESCO, and where Stephanie had grown up with a blend of their genetics and their service ethic.

Stephanie herself had received a degree in administration from the University of Virginia, which accounted for the American lights in her English, then she'd gotten another degree in nursing and went to work for the Catholic relief agency Santa Croce, which sent her to its every war-wrecked, locust-blighted, warlord-ridden, sandstorm-blasted camp in Africa. And a few that *weren't* in Africa.

"Trashcanistan," Terzian said.

"Moldova," Stephanie said. "For three months, on what was sup-posed to be my vacation." She shuddered. "I don't mind telling you that it was a frightening thing. I was used to that kind of thing in Africa, but to see it all happening in the developed world . . . warlords, ethnic hatreds, populations being moved at the point of a gun, whole forested districts being turned to deserts because people suddenly need firewood. . . ." Her emerald eyes flashed. "It's all politics, okay? Just like in Africa. Famine and camps are all politics now, and have been since before I was born. A whole population starves, and it's because someone, somewhere, sees a profit in it. It's difficult to just kill an ethnic group you don't like, war is expensive and there are questions at the UN and you may end up at the Hague being tried for war crimes. But if you just wait for a bad harvest and then arrange for the whole population to *starve,* it's different—suddenly your enemies are giving you all their money in return for food, you get aid from the UN instead of grief, and you can award yourself a piece of the relief action and collect bribes from all the relief agencies, and your enemies are rounded up into camps and you can get your armed forces into the country without resistance, make sure your enemies disappear, control everything while some deliveries disappear into government warehouses where the food can be sold to the starving or just sold abroad for a profit. . . ." She shrugged. "That's the way of the world, okay? *But no more!*" She grabbed a fistful of the Nike bag and brandished it at him.

What her time in Moldova had done was to leave Stephanie contacts in the area, some in relief agencies, some in industry and government. So that when news of a useful project came up in Transnistria, she was among the first to know.

"So what is it?" Terzian asked. "Some kind of genetically modified food crop?"

"No." She smiled thinly. "What we have here is a genetically modified *consumer.*"

Those Transnistrian companies had mostly been interested in duplicating pharmaceuticals and transgenic food crops created by other companies, producing them on the cheap and underselling the patent-owners. There were bits and pieces of everything in those labs, DNA human and animal and vegetable. A lot of it had other people's trademarks and patents on it, even the human codes, which U.S. law permitted companies to patent provided they came up with something useful to do with it. And what these semi-outlaw companies were doing was making two things they figured people couldn't do without: drugs and food.

And not just people, since animals need drugs and food, too. Starving, tubercular sheep or pigs aren't worth much at market, so there's as much money in keeping livestock alive as in doing the same for people. So at some point one of the administrators—after a few too many shots of vodka flavored with bison grass—said, "Why should we worry about feeding the animals at all? Why not have them grow their own food, like plants?"

So then began the Green Swine Project, an attempt to make pigs fat and happy by just herding them out into the sun.

"Green swine," Terzian repeated, wondering. "People are getting killed over green swine."

"Well, no." Stephanie waved the idea away with a twitchy swipe of her hand. "The idea never quite got beyond the vaporware stage, because at that point another question was asked—why swine? Adrian said, Why stop at having animals do photosynthesis—why not *people?*"

"No!" Terzian cried, appalled. "You're going to turn people green?"

Stephanie glared at him. "Something wrong with fat, happy green people?" Her hands banged out a furious rhythm on the armrests of her seat. "I'd have skin to match my eyes. Wouldn't that be attractive?"

"I'd have to see it first," Terzian said, the shock still rolling through his bones.

"Adrian was pretty smart," Stephanie said. "The Transnistrians killed themselves a real genius." She shook her head. "He had it all worked out. He wanted to limit the effect to the skin—no green muscle tissue or skeletons—so he started with a virus that has a tropism for the epidermis—papilloma, that's warts, okay?"

So now we've got green warts, Terzian thought, but he kept his mouth shut.

"So if you're Adrian, what you do is gut out the virus and re-encode to create chlorophyll. Once a person's infected, exposure to sunlight will cause the virus to replicate and chlorophyll to reproduce in the skin."

Terzian gave Stephanie a skeptical look. "That's not going to be very efficient," he said. "Plants get sugars and oxygen from chlorophyll, okay, but they don't need much food, they stand in one place and don't walk around. Add chlorophyll to a person's skin, how many calories do you get each day? Tens? Dozens?"

Stephanie's lips parted in a fierce little smile. "You don't stop with just the chlorophyll. You have to get really efficient electron transport. In a plant that's handled in the chloroplasts, but the human body already has mitochondria to do the same job. You don't have to create these huge support mechanisms for the chlorophyll, you just make use of what's already there. So if you're Adrian, what you do is add trafficking tags to the reaction center proteins so that they'll target the mitochondria, which *already* are loaded with proteins to handle electron transport. The result is that the mitochondria handle transport from the chlorophyll, which is the sort of job they do anyway, and once the virus starts replicating, you can get maybe a thousand calories or more just from standing in the sun. It won't provide full nutrition, but it can keep starvation at bay, and it's not as if starving people have much to do besides stand in the sun anyway."

"It's not going to do much good for Icelanders," Terzian said.

She turned severe. "Icelanders aren't starving. It so happens that most of the people in the world who are starving happen to be in hot places."

Terzian flapped his hands. "Fine. I must be a racist. Sue me."

Stephanie's grin broadened, and she leaned toward Terzian. "I didn't tell you about Adrian's most interesting bit of cleverness. When people start getting normal nutrition, there'll be a competition within the mitochondria between normal metabolism and solar-induced electron transport. So the green virus is just a redundant backup system in case normal nutrition isn't available."

A triumphant smile crossed Stephanie's face. "Starvation will no longer be a weapon," she said. "Green skin can keep people active and on their feet long enough to get help. It will keep them healthy enough to fend off the epidemics associated with malnutrition. The point is—" She made fists and shook them at the sky. *"The bad guys don't get to use starvation as a weapon anymore!* Famine *ends!* One of the Four Horsemen of the Apocalypse *dies,* right here, right now, as a result of *what I've got in this bag!"* She picked up the bag and threw it into Terzian's lap, and he jerked on the seat in defensive reflex, knees rising to meet elbows. Her lips skinned back in a snarl, and her tone was mocking.

"I think even that Nazi fuck Heidegger would think my *project* is pretty damn *authentic.* Wouldn't you agree, Herr Doktor Terzian?"

Got you, Michelle thought. Here was a still photo of Terzian at the Fête des Aires de la Dine, with the dark-skinned woman. She had the same wide-brimmed straw hat she'd worn in the Florence church, and had the same black bag over her shoulder, but now Michelle had a clear view of a three-quarter profile, and one hand, with its critical alignments, was clearly visible, holding an ice cream cone.

Night insects whirled around the computer display. Michelle batted them away and got busy mapping. The photo was digital and Michelle could enlarge it.

To her surprise, she discovered that the woman had green eyes. Black women with green irises—or irises of orange or chartreuse or chrome steel—were not unusual in her own time, but she knew that in Terzian's time they were rare. That would make the search much easier.

"Michelle . . ." The voice came just as Michelle sent her new search spiders into the ether. A shiver ran up her spine.

"Michelle . . ." The voice came again.

It was Darton.

Michelle's heart gave a sickening lurch. She closed her console and put it back in the mesh bag, then crossed the rope bridge between the ironwood tree and the banyan. Her knees were weak, and the swaying bridge seemed to take a couple of unexpected pitches. She stepped out onto the banyan's sturdy overhanging limb and gazed out at the water.

"Michelle . . ." To the southwest, in the channel between the mermaid's island and another, she could see a pale light bobbing, the light of a small boat.

"Michelle, where are you?"

The voice died away in the silence and surf. Michelle remembered the spike in her hand, the long, agonized trek up the slope above Jellyfish Lake. Darton pale, panting for breath, dying in her arms.

The lake was one of the wonders of the world, but the steep path over the ridge that fenced the lake from the ocean was challenging even for those who were not dying. When Michelle and Darton—at that time, apes—came up from their boat that afternoon, they didn't climb the steep path, but swung hand-over-hand through the trees overhead, through the hardwood and guava trees, and avoided the poison trees with their bleeding, allergenic black sap. Even though their trip was less exhausting than if they'd gone over the land route, the two were ready for the cool water by the time they arrived at the lake.

Tens of thousands of years in the past, the water level was higher, and when it receded, the lake was cut off from the Pacific, and with it the *Mastigias* sp. jellyfish, which soon exhausted the supply of small fish that were its food. As the human race did later, the jellies gave up hunting and gathering in exchange for agriculture, and permitted themselves to be farmed by colonies of algae that provided the sugars they needed for life. At night, they'd descend to the bottom of the lake, where they fertilized their algae crops in the anoxic, sulfurous waters; at dawn, the jellies rose to the surface, and during the day, they crossed the lake, following the course of the sun, and allowed the sun's rays to supply the energy necessary for making their daily ration of food.

When Darton and Michelle arrived, there were ten million jellyfish in the lake, from fingertip-sized to jellies the size of a dinner plate, all in one warm throbbing golden-brown mass in the center of the water. The two swam easily on the surface with their long siamang arms, laughing and calling to one another as the jellyfish in their millions caressed them with the most featherlike of touches. The lake was the temperature of their own blood, and it was like a soupy bath, the jellyfish so thick that Michelle felt she could almost walk on the surface. The warm touch wasn't erotic, exactly, but it was sensual in the way that an erotic touch was sensual, a light brush over the skin by the pad of a teasing finger.

Trapped in a lake for thousands of years without suitable prey, the jellyfish had lost most of their ability to sting. Only a small percentage of people were sensitive enough to the toxin to receive a rash or feel a modest burning.

A very few people, though, were more sensitive than that.

Darton and Michelle left at dusk, and, by that time Darton was already gasping for breath. He said he'd overexerted himself, that all he needed was to get back to their base for a snack, but as he swung through the trees on the way up the ridge, he lost his hold on a Palauan apple tree and crashed through a thicket of limbs to sprawl, amid a hail of fruit, on the sharp algae-covered limestone of the ridge.

Michelle swung down from the trees, her heart pounding. Darton was nearly colorless and struggling to breathe. They had no way of calling for help unless Michelle took their boat to Koror or to their base camp on another island. She tried to help Darton walk, taking one of his long arms over her shoulder, supporting him up the steep island trail. He collapsed, finally, at the foot of a poison tree, and Michelle bent over him to shield him from the drops of venomous sap until he died.

Her back aflame with the poison sap, she'd whispered her parting words into Darton's ear. She never knew if he heard.

The coroner said it was a million-to-one chance that Darton had been so deathly allergic, and tried to comfort her with the thought that there was nothing she could have done. Torbiong, who had made the arrangements for Darton and Michelle to come in the first place, had been consoling, had offered to let Michelle stay with his family. Michelle had surprised him by asking permission to move her base camp to another island, and to continue her work alone.

She also had herself transformed into a mermaid, and subsequently, a romantic local legend.

And now Darton was back, bobbing in a boat in the nearby channel and calling her name, shouting into a bullhorn.

"Michelle, I love you." The words floated clear into the night air. Michelle's mouth was dry. Her fingers formed the sign <go away>.

There was a silence, and then Michelle heard the engine start on Darton's boat. He motored past her position, within five hundred meters or so, and continued on to the northern point of the island.

<go away> . . .

"Michelle . . ." Again his voice floated out onto the breeze. It was clear that he didn't know where she was. She was going to have to be careful about showing lights.

<go away> . . .

Michelle waited while Darton called out a half-dozen more times, and then he started his engine and moved on. She wondered if he would search all three hundred islands in the Rock Island group.

No, she knew he was more organized than that.

She'd have to decide what to do when he finally found her.

While a thousand questions chased each other's tails through his mind, Terzian opened the Nike bag and withdrew the small hard plastic case inside, something like a box for fishing tackle. He popped the locks on the case and opened the lid, and he saw glass vials resting in slots cut into dark grey foam. In them was a liquid with a faint golden cast.

"The papilloma," Stephanie said.

Terzian dropped the lid on the case as he cast a guilty look over his shoulder, not wanting anyone to see him with this stuff. If he were arrested under suspicion of being a drug dealer, the wads of cash and the pistol certainly wouldn't help.

"What do you do with the stuff once you get to where you're going?"

"Brush it on the skin. With exposure to solar energy, it replicates as needed."

"Has it been tested?"

"On people? No. Works fine on rhesus monkeys, though."

He tapped his wedding ring on the arm of his seat. "Can it be . . . caught? I mean, it's a virus, can it go from one person to another?"

"Through skin-to-skin contact."

"I'd say that's a yes. Can mothers pass it on to their children?"

"Adrian didn't think it would cross the placental barrier, but he didn't get a chance to test it. If mothers want to infect their children, they'll probably have to do it deliberately." She shrugged. "Whatever the case, my guess is that mothers won't mind green babies, as long as they're green *healthy* babies." She looked down at the little vials in their secure coffins of foam. "We can infect tens of thousands of people with this amount," she said. "And we can make more very easily."

If mothers want to infect their children . . . Terzian closed the lid of the plastic case and snapped the locks. "You're out of your mind," he said.

Stephanie cocked her head and peered at him, looking as if she'd anticipated his objections and was humoring him. "How so?"

"Where do I start?" Terzian zipped up the bag, then tossed it in Stephanie's lap, pleased to see her defensive reflexes leap in response. "You're planning on unleashing an untested transgenic virus on Africa—on *Africa* of all places, a continent that doesn't exactly have a happy history with pandemics. And it's a virus that's cooked up by a bunch of illegal pharmacists in a non-country with a murderous secret police, facts that don't give me much confidence that this is going to be anything but a disaster."

Stephanie tapped two fingers on her chin as if she were wishing there were a cigarette between them. "I can put your mind to rest on the last issue. The animal study worked. Adrian had a family of bright green rhesus in his lab, till the project was canceled and the rhesus were, ah, liquidated."

"So if the project's so terrific, why'd the company pull the plug?"

"Money." Her lips twisted in anger. "Starving people can't afford to pay for the treatments, so they'd have to practically give the stuff away. Plus they'd get reams of endless bad publicity, which is exactly what outlaw biotech companies in outlaw countries don't want. There are millions of people who go ballistic at the very thought of a genetically engineered *vegetable*—you can imagine how people who can't abide the idea of a transgenic bell pepper would freak at the thought of infecting people with an engineered virus. The company decided it wasn't worth the risk. They closed the project down."

Stephanie looked at the bag in her hands. "But Adrian had been in the camps himself, you see. A displaced person, a refugee from the civil war in Moldova. And he couldn't stand the thought that there was a way to end hunger sitting in his refrigerator in the lab, and that nothing was being done with it. And so . . ." Her hands outlined the case inside the Nike bag. "He called me. He took some vacation time and booked himself into the Henri IV on the Place Dauphine. And I guess he must have been careless, because . . ."

Tears starred in her eyes, and she fell silent. Terzian, strong in the knowledge that he'd shared quite enough of her troubles by now, stared out the window, at the green landscape that was beginning to take on the brilliant colors of Provence. The Hautes-Alpes floated blue and whitecapped in the distant east, and nearby were orchards of almonds and olives with shimmering leaves, and hillsides covered with rows of orderly vines. The Rhone ran silver under the westering sun.

"I'm not going to be your bagman," he said. "I'm not going to contaminate the world with your freaky biotech."

"Then they'll catch you and you'll die," Stephanie said. "And it will be for nothing."

"My experience of death," said Terzian, "is that it's *always* for nothing."

She snorted then, angry. "My experience of death," she mocked, "is that it's too often for *profit*. I want to make mass murder an un-profitable venture. I want to crash the market in starvation by *giving away life*." She gave another snort, amused this time. "It's the ultimate anti-capitalist gesture."

Terzian didn't rise to that. Gestures, he thought, were just that.

Gestures didn't change the fundamentals. If some jefe couldn't starve his people to death, he'd just use bullets, or deadly genetic technology he bought from outlaw Transnistrian corporations.

The landscape, all blazing green, raced past at over two hundred kilometers per hour. An attendant came by and sold them each a cup of coffee and a sandwich.

"You should use my phone to call your wife," Stephanie said as she peeled the cellophane from her sandwich. "Let her know that your travel plans have changed."

Apparently she'd noticed Terzian's wedding ring.

"My wife is dead," Terzian said.

She looked at him in surprise. "I'm sorry," she said.

"Brain cancer," he said.

Though it was more complicated than that. Claire had first complained of back pain, and there had been an operation, and the tumor removed from her spine. There had been a couple of weeks of mad joy and relief, and then it had been revealed that the cancer had spread to the brain and that it was inoperable. Chemotherapy had failed. She died six weeks after her first visit to the doctor.

"Do you have any other family?" Stephanie said.

"My parents are dead, too." Auto accident, aneurysm. He didn't mention Claire's uncle Geoff and his partner Luis, who had died of HIV within eight months of each other and left Claire the Victorian house on Esplanade in New Orleans. The house that, a few weeks ago, he had sold for six hundred and fifty thousand dollars, and the furnishings for a further ninety-five thousand, and Uncle Geoff's collection of equestrian art for a further forty-one thousand.

He was disinclined to mention that he had quite a lot of money, enough to float around Europe for years.

Telling Stephanie that might only encourage her.

There was a long silence. Terzian broke it. "I've read spy novels," he said. "And I know that we shouldn't go to the place we've bought tickets for. We shouldn't go anywhere *near* Nice."

She considered this, then said, "We'll get off at Avignon."

They stayed in Provence for nearly two weeks, staying always in unrated hotels, those that didn't even rise to a single star from the Ministry of Tourism, or in *gîtes ruraux,* farmhouses with rooms for rent. Stephanie spent much of her energy trying to call colleagues in

Africa on her cell phone and achieved only sporadic success, a frustration that left her in a near-permanent fury. It was never clear just who she was trying to call, or how she thought they were going to get the papilloma off her hands. Terzian wondered how many people were involved in this conspiracy of hers.

They attended some local fêtes, though it was always a struggle to convince Stephanie it was safe to appear in a crowd. She made a point of disguising herself in big hats and shades and ended up looking like a cartoon spy. Terzian tramped rural lanes or fields or village streets, lost some pounds despite the splendid fresh local cuisine, and gained a suntan. He made a stab at writing several papers on his laptop, and spent time researching them in Internet cafés.

He kept thinking he would have enjoyed this trip, if only Claire had been with him.

"What is it you *do,* exactly?" Stephanie asked him once, as he wrote. "I know you teach at university, but . . ."

"I don't teach anymore," Terzian said. "I didn't get my post-doc renewed. The department and I didn't exactly get along."

"Why not?"

Terzian turned away from the stale, stalled ideas on his display. "I'm too interdisciplinary. There's a place on the academic spectrum where history and politics and philosophy come together—it's called 'political theory' usually—but I throw in economics and a layman's understanding of science as well, and it confuses everybody but me. That's why my MA is in American Studies—nobody in my philosophy or political science department had the nerve to deal with me, and nobody knows what American Studies actually *are,* so I was able to hide out there. And my doctorate is in philosophy, but only because I found one rogue professor emeritus who was willing to chair my committee.

"The problem is that if you're hired by a philosophy department, you're supposed to teach Plato or Hume or whoever, and they don't want you confusing everybody by adding Maynard Keynes and Leo Szilard. And if you teach history, you're supposed to confine yourself to acceptable stories about the past and not toss in ideas about perceptual mechanics and Kant's ideas of the noumenon, and of course you court crucifixion from the laity if you mention Foucault or Nietzsche."

Amusement touched Stephanie's lips. "So where do you find a job?"

"France?" he ventured, and they laughed. "In France, 'thinker' is a job description. It's not necessary to have a degree, it's just something you do." He shrugged. "And if that fails, there's always Burger King."

She seemed amused. "Sounds like burgers are in your future."

"Oh, it's not as bad as all that. If I can generate enough interesting, sexy, highly original papers, I might attract attention and a job, in that order."

"And have you done that?"

Terzian looked at his display and sighed. "So far, no."

Stephanie narrowed her eyes and she considered him. "You're not a conventional person. You don't think inside the box, as they say."

"As they say," Terzian repeated.

"Then you should have no objections to radical solutions to world hunger. Particularly ones that don't cost a penny to white liberals throughout the world."

"Hah," Terzian said. "Who says I'm a liberal? I'm an *economist*."

So Stephanie told him terrible things about Africa. Another famine was brewing across the southern part of the continent. Mozambique was plagued with flood *and* drought, a startling combination. The Horn of Africa was worse. According to her friends, Santa Croce had a food shipment stuck in Mogadishu and before letting it pass, the local warlord wanted to renegotiate his bribe. In the meantime, people were starving, dying of malnutrition, infection, and dysentery in camps in the dry highlands of Bale and Sidamo. Their own government in Addis Ababa was worse than the Somali warlord, at this stage permitting no aid at all, bribes or no bribes.

And as for the southern Sudan, it didn't bear thinking about.

"What's *your* solution to this?" she demanded of Terzian. "Or do you have one?"

"Test this stuff, this papilloma," he said, "show me that it works, and I'm with you. But there are too many plagues in Africa as it is."

"Confine the papilloma to labs while thousands die? Hand it to governments who can suppress it because of pressure from religious loons and hysterical NGOs? You call *that* an answer?" And Stephanie went back to working her phone while Terzian walked off in anger for another stalk down country lanes.

Terzian walked toward an old ruined castle that shambled down the slope of a nearby hill. And if Stephanie's plant-people proved viable? he wondered. All bets were off. A world in which humans could become plants was a world in which none of the old rules applied.

Stephanie had said she wanted to crash the market in starvation. But, Terzian thought, that also meant crashing the market in *food*. If people with no money had all the food they needed, that meant *food itself had no value in the marketplace*. Food would be so cheap that there would be no profit in growing or selling it.

And this was all just *one application* of the technology. Terzian tried to keep up with science: he knew about nanoassemblers. Green people was just the first magic bullet in a long volley of scientific musketry that would change every fundamental rule by which humanity had operated since they'd first stood upright. What happened when *every* basic commodity—food, clothing, shelter, maybe even health—was so cheap that it was free? What then had value?

Even *money* wouldn't have value then. Money only had value if it could be exchanged for something of equivalent worth.

He paused in his walk and looked ahead at the ruined castle, the castle that had once provided justice and security and government for the district, and he wondered if he was looking at the future of *all* government. Providing an orderly framework in which commodities could be exchanged was the basic function of the state, that and providing a secure currency. If people didn't need government to furnish that kind of security and if the currency was worthless, the whole future of government itself was in question. Taxes weren't worth the expense of collecting if the money wasn't any good, anyway, and without taxes, government couldn't be paid for.

Terzian paused at the foot of the ruined castle and wondered if he saw the future of the civilized world. Either the castle would be rebuilt by tyrants, or it would fall.

❀

Michelle heard Darton's bullhorn again the next evening, and she wondered why he was keeping fruit-bat hours. Was it because his calls would travel farther at night?

If he were sleeping in the morning, she thought, that would make it easier. She'd finished analyzing some of her samples, but a principle of science was not to do these things alone: she'd have to travel to Koror to mail her samples to other people, and now she knew to do it in the morning, when Darton would be asleep.

The problem for Michelle was that she was a legend. When the lonely mermaid emerged from the sea and walked to the post office in the little foam booties she wore when walking on pavement, she was noticed. People pointed; children followed her on their boards, people in cars waved. She wondered if she could trust them not to contact Darton as soon as they saw her.

She hoped that Darton wasn't starting to get the islanders on his side.

Michelle and Darton had met on a field trip in Borneo, their obligatory government service after graduation. The other field workers were older, paying their taxes or working on their second or third or fourth or fifth careers, and Michelle knew on sight that Darton was no older than she, that he, too, was a child among all these elders. They were pulled to each other as if drawn by some violent natural force, cataloguing snails and terrapins by day and spending their nights wrapped in each other in their own shell, their turtleback tent. The ancients with whom they shared their days treated them with amused condescension, but then, that was how they treated everything. Darton and Michelle didn't care. In their youth they stood against all creation.

When the trip came to an end, they decided to continue their work together, just a hop across the equator in Belau. Paying their taxes ahead of time. They celebrated by getting new bodies, an exciting experience for Michelle, who had been built by strict parents who wouldn't allow her to have a new body until adulthood, no matter how many of her friends had been transforming from an early age into one newly fashionable shape or another.

Michelle and Darton thought that anthropoid bodies would be suitable for the work, and so they went to the clinic in Delhi and settled themselves on nanobeds and let the little machines turn their bodies, their minds, their memories, their desires and their knowledge and their souls, into long strings of numbers. All of which were fed into their new bodies when they were ready, and reserved as backups to be downloaded as necessary.

Being a siamang was a glorious discovery. They soared through the treetops of their little island, swinging overhand from limb to limb in a frenzy of glory. Michelle took a particular delight in her body hair—she didn't have as much as a real ape, but there was enough on her chest and back to be interesting. They built nests of foliage in trees and lay tangled together, analyzing data or making love or shaving their hair into interesting tribal patterns. Love was far from placid—it was a flame, a fury. An obsession that, against all odds, had been fulfilled, only to build the flame higher.

The fury still burned in Michelle. But now, after Darton's death, it had a different quality, a quality that had nothing to do with life or youth.

Michelle, spooning up blueberries and cream, riffled through the names and faces her spiders had spat out. There were, now she added them up, a preposterous number of pictures of green-eyed women with dark skin whose pictures were somewhere in the net. Nearly all of them had striking good looks. Many of them were unidentified in the old scans, or identified only by a first name. The highest probability the software offered was 43 percent.

That 43 percent belonged to a Brazilian named Laura Flor, who research swiftly showed was home in Aracaju during the critical period, among other things having a baby. A video of the delivery was available, but Michelle didn't watch it. The way women delivered babies back then was disgusting.

The next most likely female was another Brazilian seen in some tourist photographs taken in Rio. Not even a name given. A further search based on this woman's physiognomy turned up nothing, not until Michelle broadened the search to a different gender, and discovered that the Brazilian was a transvestite. That didn't seem to be Terzian's scene, so she left it alone.

The third was identified only as Stephanie, and posted on a site created by a woman who had done relief work in Africa. Stephanie was shown with a group of other relief workers, posing in front of a tin-roofed, cinderblock building identified as a hospital.

The quality of the photograph wasn't very good, but Michelle mapped the physiognomy anyway, and sent it forth along with the name "Stephanie" to see what might happen.

There was a hit right away, a credit card charge to a Stephanie América Pais e Silva. She had stayed in a hotel in Paris for the three nights before Terzian disappeared.

Michelle's blood surged as the data flashed on her screens. She sent out more spiders and the good news began rolling in.

Stephanie Pais was a dual citizen of Portugal and Angola, and had been educated partly in the States—a quick check showed that her time at university didn't overlap Terzian's. From her graduation, she had worked for a relief agency called Santa Croce.

Then a news item turned up, a sensational one. Stephanie Pais had been spectacularly murdered in Venice on the night of July 19, six days before Terzian had delivered the first version of his Cornucopia Theory.

Two murders . . .

One in Paris, one in Venice. And one of them of the woman who seemed to be Terzian's lover.

Michelle's body shivered to a sudden gasping spasm, and she realized that in her suspense she'd been holding her breath. Her head swam. When it cleared, she worked out what time it was in Maryland, where Dr. Davout lived, and then told her deck to page him at once.

Davout was unavailable at first, and by the time he returned her call, she had more information about Stephanie Pais. She blurted the story out to him while her fingers jabbed at the keyboard of her deck, sending him copies of her corroborating data.

Davout's startled eyes leaped from the data to Michelle and back. "How much of this . . ." he began, then gave up. "How did she die?" he managed.

"The news article says stabbed. I'm looking for the police report."

"Is Terzian mentioned?"

<No> she signed. "The police report will have more details."

"Any idea what this is about? There's no history of Terzian *ever* being connected with violence."

"By tomorrow," Michelle said, "I should be able to tell you. But I thought I should send this to you because you might be able to tie this in with other elements of Terzian's life that I don't know anything about."

Davout's fingers formed a mudra that Michelle didn't recognize—an old one, probably. He shook his head. "I have no idea what's happening here. The only thing I have to suggest is that this is some kind of wild coincidence."

"I don't believe in that kind of coincidence," Michelle said.

Davout smiled. "A good attitude for a researcher," he said. "But experience—well," he waved a hand.

But he loved her, Michelle insisted inwardly. She knew that in her heart. She was the woman he loved after Claire died, and then she was killed and Terzian went on to create the intellectual framework on

which the world was now built. He had spent his modest fortune building pilot programs in Africa that demonstrated his vision was a practical
one. The whole modern world was a monument to Stephanie.

Everyone was young then, Michelle thought. Even the seventy-
year-olds were young compared to the people now. The world must
have been *ablaze* with love and passion. But Davout didn't understand
that because he was old and had forgotten all about love.

"*Michelle* . . ." Darton's voice came wafting over the waters.

Bastard. Michelle wasn't about to let him spoil this.

Her fingers formed <gotta go>. "I'll send you everything once it
comes in," she said. "I think we've got something amazing here."

She picked up her deck and swung it around so that she could be
sure that the light from the display couldn't be seen from the ocean.
Her bare back against the rough bark of the ironwood, she began
flashing through the data as it arrived.

She couldn't find the police report. Michelle went in search of it
and discovered that all police records from that period in Venetian
history had been wiped out in the Lightspeed War, leaving her only
with what had been reported in the media.

"*Where are you? I love you!*" Darton's voice came from farther
away. He'd narrowed his search, that was clear, but he still wasn't sure
exactly where Michelle had built her nest.

Smiling, Michelle closed her deck and slipped it into its pouch.
Her spiders would work for her tirelessly till dawn while she dreamed
on in her hammock and let Darton's distant calls lull her to sleep.

They shifted their lodgings every few days. Terzian always arranged
for separate bedrooms. Once, as they sat in the evening shade of a
farm terrace and watched the setting sun shimmer on the silver leaves
of the olives, Terzian found himself looking at her as she sat in an old
cane chair, at the profile cutting sharp against the old limestone of the
Vaucluse. The blustering wind brought gusts of lavender from the
neighboring farm, a scent that made Terzian want to inhale until his
lungs creaked against his ribs.

From a quirk of Stephanie's lips, Terzian was suddenly aware that
she knew he was looking at her. He glanced away.

"You haven't tried to sleep with me," she said.

"No," he agreed.

"But you *look*" she said. "And it's clear you're not a eunuch."

"We fight all the time," Terzian pointed out. "Sometimes we can't stand to be in the same room."

Stephanie smiled. "That wouldn't stop most of the men I've known. Or the women, either."

Terzian looked out over the olives, saw them shimmer in the breeze. "I'm still in love with my wife," he said.

There was a moment of silence. "That's well," she said.

And I'm angry at her, too, Terzian thought. Angry at Claire for deserting him. And he was furious at the universe for killing her and for leaving him alive, and he was angry at God even though he didn't believe in God. The Trashcanians had been good for him, because he could let his rage and his hatred settle there, on people who deserved it.

Those poor drunken bastards, he thought. Whatever they'd expected in that hotel corridor, it hadn't been a berserk grieving American who would just as soon have ripped out their throats with his bare hands.

The question was, could he do that again? It had all occurred without his thinking about it, old reflexes taking over, but he couldn't count on that happening a second time. He'd been trying to remember the Kenpo he'd once learned, particularly all the tricks against weapons. He found himself miming combats on his long country hikes, and he wondered if he'd retained any of his ability to take a punch.

He kept the gun with him, so the Trashcanians wouldn't get it if they searched his room when he was away. When he was alone, walking through the almond orchards or on a hillside fragrant with wild thyme, he practiced drawing it, snicking off the safety, and putting pressure on the trigger . . . the first time the trigger pull would be hard, but the first shot would cock the pistol automatically and after that the trigger pull would be light.

He wondered if he should buy more ammunition. But he didn't know how to buy ammunition in France and didn't know if a foreigner could get into trouble that way.

"We're both angry," Stephanie said. He looked at her again, her hand raised to her head to keep the gusts from blowing her long ringlets in her face. "We're angry at death. But love must make it more complicated for you."

Her green eyes searched him. "It's not death you're in love with, is it? Because—"

Terzian blew up. She had no right to suggest that he was in a secret alliance with death just because he didn't want to turn a bunch of Africans green. It was their worst argument, and this one ended with both of them stalking away through the fields and orchards while the scent of lavender pursued them on the wind.

When Terzian returned to his room, he checked his caches of money, half-hoping that Stephanie had stolen his euros and run. She hadn't.

He thought of going into her room while she was away, stealing the papilloma, and taking a train north, handing it over to the Pasteur Institute or someplace. But he didn't.

In the morning, during breakfast, Stephanie's cell phone rang, and she answered. He watched while her face turned from curiosity to apprehension to utter terror. Adrenaline sang in his blood as he watched, and he leaned forward, feeling the familiar rage rise in him, just where he wanted it. In haste, she turned off the phone, then looked at him. "That was one of them. He says he knows where we are, and wants to make a deal."

"If they know where we are," Terzian found himself saying coolly, "why aren't they here?"

"We've got to *go,*" she insisted.

So they went. Clean out of France and into the Tuscan hills, with Stephanie's cell phone left behind in a trash can at the train station and a new phone purchased in Siena. The Tuscan countryside was not unlike Provence, with vine-covered hillsides, orchards a-shimmer with the silver-green of olive trees, and walled medieval towns perched on crags; but the slim, tall cypress standing like sentries gave the hills a different profile, and there were different types of wine grapes, and many of the vineyards rented rooms where people could stay and sample the local hospitality. Terzian didn't speak the language, and because Spanish was his first foreign language, consistently pronounced words like "villa" and "panzanella" as if they were Spanish. But Stephanie had grown up in Italy and spoke the language not only like a native, but like a native Roman.

Florence was only a few hours away, and Terzian couldn't resist visiting one of the great living monuments to civilization. His parents had taken him to Europe several times as a child, but somehow never made it here.

Terzian and Stephanie spent a day wandering the center of town, on occasion taking shelter from one of the pelting rainstorms that shattered the day. At one point, with thunder booming overhead, they found themselves in the Basilica di Santa Croce.

"Holy Cross," Terzian said, translating. "That's your outfit."

"We have nothing to do with this church," Stephanie said. "We don't even have a collection box here."

"A pity," Terzian said as he looked at the soaked swarms of tourists packed in the aisles. "You'd clean up."

Thunder accompanied the camera strobes that flashed against the huge tomb of Galileo like a vast lightning storm. "Nice of them to forget about that Inquisition thing and bury him in a church," Terzian said.

"I expect they just wanted to keep an eye on him."

It was the power of capital, Terzian knew, that had built this church, that had paid for the stained glass and the Giotto frescoes and the tombs and cenotaphs to the great names of Florence: Dante, Michelangelo, Bruni, Alberti, Marconi, Fermi, Rossini, and of course Machiavelli. This structure, with its vaults and chapels and sarcophagi and chanting Franciscans, had been raised by successful bankers, people to whom money was a real, tangible thing, and who had paid for the centuries of labor to build the basilica with caskets of solid, weighty coined silver.

"So what do you think he would make of this?" Terzian asked, nodding at the resting place of Machiavelli, now buried in the city from which he'd been exiled in his lifetime.

Stephanie scowled at the unusually plain sarcophagus with its Latin inscription. "No praise can be high enough," she translated, then turned to him as tourist cameras flashed. "Sounds overrated."

"He was a republican, you know," Terzian said. "You don't get that from just *The Prince*. He wanted Florence to be a republic, defended by citizen soldiers. But when it fell into the hands of a despot, he needed work, and he wrote the manual for despotism. But he looked at despotism a little too clearly, and he didn't get the job." Terzian turned to Stephanie. "He was the founder of modern political theory, and that's what I do. And he based his ideas on the belief that all human beings, at all times, have the same passions." He turned his eyes deliberately to Stephanie's shoulder bag. "That may be about to end, right? You're going to turn people into plants. That should change the passions if anything would."

"Not *plants*," Stephanie hissed, and glanced left and right at the crowds. "And not *here*." She began to move down the aisle, in the direction of Michelangelo's ornate tomb, with its draped figures who appeared not in mourning, but as if they were trying to puzzle out a difficult engineering problem.

"What happens in your scheme," Terzian said, following, "is that the market in food crashes. But that's not the *real* problem. The real problem is, what happens to the market in *labor?*"

Tourist cameras flashed. Stephanie turned her head away from the array of Kodaks. She passed out of the basilica and to the portico. The cloudburst had come to an end, but rainwater still drizzled off the structure. They stepped out of the droplets and down the stairs into the piazza.

The piazza was walled on all sides by old palaces, most of which now held restaurants or shops on the ground floor. To the left, one long palazzo was covered with canvas and scaffolding. The sound of pneumatic hammers banged out over the piazza. Terzian waved a hand in the direction of the clatter.

"Just imagine that food is nearly free," he said. "Suppose you and your children can get most of your food from standing in the sunshine. My next question is, *Why in hell would you take a filthy job like standing on a scaffolding and sandblasting some old building?*"

He stuck his hands in his pockets and began walking at Stephanie's side along the piazza. "Down at the bottom of the labor market, there are a lot of people whose labor goes almost entirely for the necessities. Millions of them cross borders illegally in order to send enough money back home to support their children."

"You think I don't know that?"

"The only reason that there's a market in illegal immigrants is that *there are jobs that well-off people won't do*. Dig ditches. Lay roads. Clean sewers. Restore old buildings. Build *new* buildings. The well-off might serve in the military or police, because there's a certain status involved and an attractive uniform, but we won't guard prisons, no matter how pretty the uniform is. That's strictly a job for the laboring classes, and if the laboring classes are too well-off to labor, who guards the prisons?"

She rounded on him, her lips set in an angry line. "So I'm supposed to be afraid of people having more choice in where they work?"

"No," Terzian said, "you should be afraid of people having *no choice at all*. What happens when markets collapse is *intervention*—and that's state intervention, if the market's critical enough, and you can bet the labor market's critical. And because the state depends on ditch-diggers and prison guards and janitors and road-builders for its very being, then if these classes of people are no longer available, and the very survival of civil society depends on their existence, in the end, the state will just *take* them.

"You think our friends in Transnistria will have any qualms about rounding up people up at gunpoint and forcing them to do labor? The powerful are going to want their palaces kept nice and shiny. The liberal democracies will try volunteerism or lotteries or whatever, but you can bet that we're going to want our sewers to work, and somebody to carry our grandparents' bedpans, and the trucks to the supermarkets to run on time. And what *I'm* afraid of is that when things get desperate, we're not going to be any nicer about getting our way than those Sovietists of yours. We're going to make sure that the lower orders do their jobs, even if we have to kill half of them to convince the other half that we mean business. And the technical term for that is *slavery*. And if someone of African descent isn't sensitive to *that* potential problem, then I am very surprised!"

The fury in Stephanie's eyes was visible even through her shades, and he could see the pulse pounding in her throat. Then she said, "I'll save the *people,* that's what I'm good at. You save the rest of the world, *if* you can." She began to turn away, then swung back to him. "And by the way," she added, "fuck you!" turned, and marched away.

"Slavery or anarchy, Stephanie!" Terzian called, taking a step after. "That's the choice you're forcing on people!"

He really felt he had the rhetorical momentum now, and he wanted to enlarge the point by saying that he knew some people thought anarchy was a good thing, but no anarchist he'd ever met had ever even *seen* a real anarchy, or been in one, whereas Stephanie had— drop your anarchist out of a helicopter into the eastern Congo, say, with all his theories and with whatever he could carry on his back, and see how well he prospered. . . .

But Terzian never got to say any of these things, because Stephanie was gone, receding into the vanishing point of a busy street, the shoulder bag swinging back and forth across her butt like a pendulum powered by the force of her convictions.

Terzian thought that perhaps he'd never see her again, that he'd finally provoked her into abandoning him and continuing on her quest alone, but when he stepped off the bus in Montespèrtoli that night, he saw her across the street, shouting into her cell phone.

A day later, as with frozen civility they drank their morning coffee, she said that she was going to Rome the next day. "They might be looking for me there," she said, "because my parents live there. But I won't go near the family, I'll meet Odile at the airport and give her the papilloma."

Odile? Terzian thought. "I should go along," he said.

"What are you going to do?" she said. "Carry that gun into an *airport?*"

"I don't have to take the gun. I'll leave it in the hotel room in Rome."

She considered. "Very well."

Again, that night, Terzian found the tumbled castle in Provence haunting his thoughts, that ruined relic of a bygone order, and once more considered stealing the papilloma and running. And again, he didn't.

They didn't get any farther than Florence, because Stephanie's cell phone rang as they waited in the train station. Odile was in Venice. *"Venezia?"* Stephanie shrieked in anger. She clenched her fists. There had been a cache of weapons found at the Fiumicino airport in Rome, and all planes had been diverted, Odile's to Marco Polo outside Venice. Frenzied booking agents had somehow found rooms for her despite the height of the tourist season.

Fiumicino hadn't been re-opened, and Odile didn't know how she was going to get to Rome. "Don't try!" Stephanie shouted. "I'll come to *you.*"

This meant changing their tickets to Rome for tickets to Venice. Despite Stephanie's excellent Italian, the ticket seller clearly wished the crazy tourists would make up their mind which monuments of civilization they really wanted to see.

Strange—Terzian had actually *planned* to go to Venice in five days or so. He was scheduled to deliver a paper at the Conference of Classical and Modern Thought.

Maybe, if this whole thing was over by then, he'd read the paper after all. It wasn't a prospect he coveted: he would just be developing another footnote to a footnote.

The hills of Tuscany soon began to pour across the landscape like a green flood. The train slowed at one point—there was work going on on the tracks, men with bronze arms and hard hats—and Terzian wondered how, in the Plant People Future, in the land of Cockaigne, the tracks would ever get fixed, particularly in this heat. He supposed there were people who were meant by nature to fix tracks, who would repair tracks as an *avocation* or out of boredom regardless of whether they got paid for their time or not, but he suspected that there wouldn't be many of them.

You could build machines, he supposed, robots or something. But they had their own problems, they'd cause pollution and absorb resources and, on top of everything, they'd break down and have to be repaired. And who would do *that?*

If you can't employ the carrot, Terzian thought, if you can't reward people for doing necessary labor, then you have to use the stick. You march people out of the cities at gunpoint, like Pol Pot, because there's work that needs to be done.

He tapped his wedding ring on the arm of his chair and wondered what jobs would still have value. Education, he supposed; he'd made a good choice there. Some sorts of administration were necessary. There were people who were natural artists or bureaucrats or salesmen and who would do that job whether they were paid or not.

A woman came by with a cart and sold Terzian some coffee and a nutty snack product that he wasn't quite able to identify. And then he thought, *labor.*

"Labor," he said. In a world in which all basic commodities were provided, the thing that had most value was actual labor. Not the stuff that labor bought, but the work *itself*.

"Okay," he said, "it's labor that's rare and valuable, because people don't *have* to do it anymore. The currency has to be based on some kind of labor exchange—you purchase *x* hours with *y* dollars. Labor is the thing you use to pay taxes."

Stephanie gave Terzian a suspicious look. "What's the difference between that and slavery?"

"Have you been reading Nozick?" Terzian scolded. "The difference is the same as the difference between *paying taxes* and *being a slave*. All the time you don't spend paying your taxes is your own." He barked a laugh. "I'm resurrecting Labor Value Theory!" he said. "Adam Smith and Karl Marx are dancing a jig on their tombstones! In Plant People Land, the value is the *labor itself!* The *calories!*" He laughed again, and almost spilled coffee down his chest.

"You budget the whole thing in calories! The government promises to pay you a dollar's worth of calories in exchange for their currency! In order to keep the roads and the sewer lines going, a citizen owes the government a certain number of calories per year—he can either pay in person or hire someone else to do the job. And jobs can be budgeted in calories-per-hour, so that if you do hard physical labor, you owe fewer hours than someone with . . . a desk job—that should keep the young, fit, impatient people doing the nasty jobs, so that they have more free time for their other pursuits." He chortled. "Oh, the intellectuals are going to just hate this! They're used to valuing their brain power over manual labor—I'm going to reverse their whole scale of values!"

Stephanie made a pffing sound. "The people I care about have no money to pay taxes at all."

"They have bodies. They can still be enslaved." Terzian got out his laptop. "Let me put my ideas together."

Terzian's frenetic two-fingered typing went on for the rest of the journey, all the way across the causeway that led into Venice. Stephanie gazed out the window at the lagoon soaring by, the soaring water birds, and the dirt and stink of industry. She kept the Nike bag in her lap until the train pulled into the Stazione Ferrovia della Stato Santa Lucia at the end of its long journey.

Odile's hotel was in Cannaregio, which, according to the map purchased in the station gift shop, was the district of the city nearest the station and away from most of the tourist sites. A brisk wind almost tore the map from their fingers as they left the station, and their vaporetto bucked a steep chop on the grey-green Grand Canal as it took them to the Ca' d'Oro, the fanciful white High Gothic palazzo that loomed like a frantic wedding cake above a swarm of bobbing gondolas and motorboats.

Stephanie puffed cigarettes, at first with ferocity, then with satisfaction. Once they got away from the Grand Canal and into Cannaregio itself, they quickly became lost. The twisted medieval streets were broken on occasion by still, silent canals, but the canals didn't seem to lead anywhere in particular. Cooking smells demonstrated that it was dinnertime and there were few people about, and no tourists. Terzian's stomach rumbled. Sometimes the streets deteriorated into mere passages. Stephanie and Terzian were in such a passage, holding their map open against the wind and shouting directions at each other, when someone slugged Terzian from behind.

He went down on one knee with his head ringing and the taste of blood in his mouth, and then two people rather unexpectedly picked him up again, only to slam him against the passage wall. Through some miracle, he managed not to hit his head on the brickwork and knock himself out. He could smell garlic on the breath of one of the attackers. Air went out of him as he felt an elbow to his ribs.

It was the scream from Stephanie that concentrated his attention. There was violent motion in front of him, and he saw the Nike swoosh, and remembered that he was dealing with killers, and that he had a gun.

In an instant, Terzian had his rage back. He felt his lungs fill with the fury that spread through his body like a river of scalding blood. He planted his feet and twisted abruptly to his left, letting the strength come up his legs from the earth itself, and the man attached to his right arm gave a grunt of surprise and swung counterclockwise. Terzian twisted the other way, which budged the other man only a little, but which freed his right arm to claw into his right pants pocket.

And from this point on it was just the movement that he had rehearsed. Draw, thumb the safety, pull the trigger hard. He shot the man on his right and hit him in the groin. For a brief second, Terzian saw his pinched face, the face that reflected such pain that it folded in on itself, and he remembered Adrian falling in the Place Dauphine with just that look. Then he stuck the pistol in the ribs of the man on his left and fired twice. The arms that grappled him relaxed and fell away.

There were two more men grappling with Stephanie. That made four altogether, and Terzian reasoned dully that after the first three fucked up in Paris, the home office had sent a supervisor. One was trying to tug the Nike bag away, and Terzian lunged toward him and fired at a range of two meters, too close to miss, and the man dropped to the ground with a whuff of pain.

The last man had hold of Stephanie and swung her around, keeping her between himself and the pistol. Terzian could see the knife in his hand and recognized it as one he'd seen before. Her dark glasses were cockeyed on her face and Terzian caught a flash of her angry green eyes. He pointed the pistol at the knife man's face. He didn't dare shoot.

"*Police!*" he shrieked into the wind. "*Policia!*" He used the Spanish word. Bloody spittle spattered the cobblestones as he screamed.

In the Trashcanian's eyes, he saw fear, bafflement, rage.

"*Polizia!*" He got the pronunciation right this time. He saw the rage in Stephanie's eyes, the fury that mirrored his own, and he saw her struggle against the man who held her.

"*No!*" he called. Too late. The knife man had too many decisions to make all at once, and Terzian figured he wasn't very bright to begin with. *Kill the hostages* was probably something he'd been taught on his first day at Goon School.

As Stephanie fell, Terzian fired, and kept firing as the man ran away. The killer broke out of the passageway into a little square, and then just fell down.

The slide of the automatic locked back as Terzian ran out of ammunition, and then he staggered forward to where Stephanie was bleeding to death on the cobbles.

Her throat had been cut and she couldn't speak. She gripped his arm as if she could drive her urgent message through the skin, with her nails. In her eyes, he saw frustrated rage, the rage he knew well, until at length he saw there nothing at all, a nothing he knew better than any other thing in the world.

He shouldered the Nike bag and staggered out of the passageway into the tiny Venetian square with its covered well. He took a street at random, and there was Odile's hotel. Of course: the Trashcanians had been staking it out.

It wasn't much of a hotel, and the scent of spice and garlic in the lobby suggested that the desk clerk was eating his dinner. Terzian went up the stair to Odile's room and knocked on the door. When she opened—she was a plump girl with big hips and a suntan—he tossed the Nike bag on the bed.

"You need to get back to Mogadishu right away," he said. "Stephanie just died for that."

Her eyes widened. Terzian stepped to the wash basin to clean the blood off as best he could. It was all he could do not to shriek with grief and anger.

"You take care of the starving," he said finally, "and I'll save the rest of the world."

Michelle rose from the sea near Torbiong's boat, having done thirty-six hundred calories' worth of research and caught a honeycomb grouper into the bargain. She traded the fish for the supplies he brought. "Any more blueberries?" she asked.

"Not this time." He peered down at her, narrowing his eyes against the bright shimmer of sun on the water. "That young man of yours is being quite a nuisance. He's keeping the turtles awake and scaring the fish."

The mermaid tucked away her wings and arranged herself in her rope sling. "Why don't you throw him off the island?"

"My authority doesn't run that far." He scratched his jaw. "He's interviewing people. Adding up all the places you've been seen. He'll find you pretty soon, I think."

"Not if I don't want to be found. He can yell all he likes, but I don't have to answer."

"Well, maybe." Torbiong shook his head. "Thanks for the fish."

Michelle did some preliminary work with her new samples, and then abandoned them for anything new that her search spiders had discovered. She had a feeling she was on the verge of something colossal.

She carried her deck to her overhanging limb and let her legs dangle over the water while she looked through the new data. While paging through the new information, she ate something called a Raspberry Dynamo Bar that Torbiong had thrown in with her supplies. The old man must have included it as a joke: it was over-sweet and sticky with marshmallow and strangely flavored. She chucked it in the water and hoped it wouldn't poison any fish.

Stephanie Pais had been killed in what the news reports called a "street fight" among a group of foreign visitors. Since the authorities couldn't connect the foreigners to Pais, they had to assume she was an innocent bystander caught up in the violence. The papers didn't mention Terzian at all.

Michelle looked through pages of followup. The gun that had shot the four men had never been found, though nearby canals were dragged. Two of the foreigners had survived the fight, though one died eight weeks later from complications of an operation. The survivor maintained his innocence and claimed that a complete stranger had opened fire on him and his friends, but the judges hadn't believed him and sent him to prison. He lived a great many years and died in the Lightspeed War, along with most people caught in prisons during that deadly time.

One of the four men was Belorussian. Another Ukrainian. Another two Moldovan. All had served in the Soviet military in the past, in the Fourteenth Army in Transnistria. It frustrated Stephanie that she couldn't shout back in time to tell the Italians to connect these four to the murder of another ex-Soviet, seven weeks earlier, in Paris.

What the hell had Pais and Terzian been up to? Why were all

these people with Transnistrian connections killing each other, and Pais?

Maybe it was Pais they'd been after all along. Her records at Santa Croce were missing, which was odd, because other personnel records from the time had survived. Perhaps someone was arranging that certain things not be known.

She tried a search on Santa Croce itself, and slogged through descriptions and mentions of a whole lot of Italian churches, including the famous one in Florence where Terzian and Pais had been seen at Machiavelli's tomb. She refined the search to the Santa Croce relief organization, and found immediately the fact that let it all fall into place.

Santa Croce had maintained a refugee camp in Moldova during the civil war following the establishment of Transnistria. Michelle was willing to bet that Stephanie Pais had served in that camp. She wondered if any of the other players had been residents there.

She looked at the list of other camps that Santa Croce had maintained in that period, which seemed to have been a busy one for them. One name struck her as familiar, and she had to think for a moment before she remembered why she knew it. It was at a Santa Croce camp in the Sidamo province of Ethiopia where the Green Leopard Plague had first broken out, the first transgenic epidemic.

It had been the first real attempt to modify the human body at the cellular level, to help marginal populations synthesize their own food, and it had been primitive compared to the more successful mods that came later. The ideal design for the efficient use of chlorophyll was a leaf, not the homo sapien—the designer would have been better advised to create a plague that made its victims leafy, and later designers, aiming for the same effect, did exactly that. And Green Leopard's designer had forgotten that the epidermis already contains a solar-activated enzyme: melanin. The result on the African subjects was green skin mottled with dark splotches, like the black spots on an implausibly verdant leopard.

The Green Leopard Plague broke out in the Sidamo camp, then at other camps in the Horn of Africa. Then it leaped clean across the continent to Mozambique, where it first appeared at a Oxfam camp in the flood zone, spread rapidly across the continent, then leaped across oceans. It had been a generation before anyone found a way to disable it, and by then other transgenic modifiers had been released into the population, and there was no going back.

The world had entered Terzian's future, the one he had proclaimed at the Conference of Classical and Modern Thought.

What, Michelle thought excitedly, if Terzian had known about Green Leopard ahead of time? His Cornucopia Theory had seemed prescient precisely because Green Leopard appeared just a few weeks after he'd delivered his paper. But if those Eastern bloc thugs had been involved somehow in the plague's transmission, or were attempting to prevent Pais and Terzian from sneaking the modified virus to the camps . . .

Yes! Michelle thought exultantly. That had to be it. No one had ever worked out where Green Leopard originated, but there had always been suspicion directed toward several semi-covert labs in the former Soviet empire. This was *it*. The only question was how Terzian, that American in Paris, had got involved. . . .

It had to be Stephanie, she thought. Stephanie, who Terzian had loved and who had loved him, and who had involved him in the desperate attempt to aid refugee populations.

For a moment, Michelle bathed in the beauty of the idea. Stephanie dedicated and in love, had been murdered for her beliefs— realdeath!—and Terzian, broken-hearted, had carried on and brought the future—Michelle's present—into being. A *wonderful* story! And no one had known it till *now,* no one had understood Stephanie's sacrifice, or Terzian's grief . . . not until the lonely mermaid, working in isolation on her rock, had puzzled it out.

"Hello, Michelle," Darton said.

Michelle gave a cry of frustration and glared in fury down at her lover. He was in a yellow plastic kayak—kayaking was popular here, particularly in the Rock Islands—and had slipped his electric-powered boat along the margin of the island, moving in near-silence. He looked grimly up at her from below the pitcher plant that dangled below the overhang.

They had rebuilt him, of course, after his death. All the data was available in backup, in Delhi where he'd been taken apart, recorded, and rebuilt as an ape. He was back in a conventional male body, with the broad shoulders and white smile and short hairy bandy legs she remembered.

Michelle knew that he hadn't made any backups during their time in Belau. He had his memories up to the point where he'd lain down on the nanobed in Delhi. That had been the moment when his love of Michelle had been burning its hottest, when he had just made the commitment to live with Michelle as an ape in the Rock Islands.

That burning love had been consuming him in the weeks since his resurrection, and Michelle was glad of it, had been rejoicing in every desperate, unanswered message that Darton sent sizzling through the ether.

"Damn it," Michelle said, "I'm working."

<Talk to me> Darton's fingers formed. Michelle's fingers made a ruder reply.

"I don't understand," Darton said. "We were in love. We were going to be together."

"I'm not talking to you," Michelle said. She tried to concentrate on her video display.

"We were still together when the accident happened," Darton said. "I don't understand why we can't be together now."

"I'm not listening, either," said Michelle.

"I'm not leaving, Michelle!" Darton screamed. *"I'm not leaving till you talk to me!"*

White cockatoos shrieked in answer. Michelle quietly picked up her deck, rose to her feet, and headed inland. The voice that followed her was amplified, and she realized that Darton had brought his bull-horn.

"You can't get away, Michelle! You've got to tell me what happened!"

I'll tell you about Lisa Lee, she thought, *so you can send her desperate messages, too.*

Michelle had been deliriously happy for her first month in Belau, living in arboreal nests with Darton and spending the warm days de-scribing their island's unique biology. It was their first vacation, in Prague, that had torn Michelle's happiness apart. It was there that they'd met Lisa Lee Baxter, the American tourist who thought apes were cute, and who wondered what these shaggy kids were doing so far from an arboreal habitat.

It wasn't long before Michelle realized that Lisa Lee was at least two hundred years old, and that behind her diamond-blue eyes was the withered, mummified soul that had drifted into Prague from some waterless desert of the spirit, a soul that required for its contin-ued existence the blood and vitality of the young. Despite her age and presumed experience, Lisa Lee's ploys seemed to Michelle to be so *ob-vious,* so *blatant.* Darton fell for them all.

It was only because Lisa Lee had finally tired of him that Darton returned to Belau, chastened and solemn and desperate to be in love with Michelle again. But by then it was Michelle who was tired. And who had access to Darton's medical records from the downloads in Delhi.

"You can't get away, Michelle!"

Well, maybe not. Michelle paused with one hand on the banyan's trunk. She closed her deck's display and stashed it in a mesh bag with some of her other stuff, then walked out again on the overhanging limb.

"I'm not going to talk to you like this," she said. "And you can't get onto the island from that side, the overhang's too acute."

"Fine," Darton said. The shouting had made him hoarse. "Come down here, then."

She rocked forward and dived off the limb. The salt water world exploded in her senses. She extended her wings and fluttered close to Darton's kayak, rose, and shook sea water from her eyes.

"There's a tunnel," she said. "It starts at about two meters and exits into the lake. You can swim it easily if you hold your breath."

"All right," he said. "Where is it?"

"Give me your anchor."

She took his anchor, floated to the bottom, and set it where it wouldn't damage the live coral.

She remembered the needle she'd taken to Jellyfish Lake, the needle she'd loaded with the mango extract to which Darton was violently allergic. Once in the midst of the jellyfish swarm, it had been easy to jab the needle into Darton's calf, then let it drop to the anoxic depths of the lake.

He probably thought she'd given him a playful pinch.

Michelle had exulted in Darton's death, the pallor, the labored breathing, the desperate pleading in the eyes.

It wasn't murder, after all, just a fourth-degree felony. They'd build a new Darton in a matter of days. What was the value of a human life, when it could be infinitely duplicated, and cheaply? As far as Michelle was concerned, Darton had amusement value only.

The rebuilt Darton still loved her, and Michelle enjoyed that as well, enjoyed the fact that she caused him anguish, that he would pay for ages for his betrayal of her love.

Lisa Lee Baxter could take a few lessons from the mermaid, Michelle thought.

Michelle surfaced near the tunnel and raised a hand with the

fingers set at <follow me>. Darton rolled off the kayak, still in his
clothes, and splashed clumsily toward her.

"Are you sure about this?" he asked.

"Oh yes," Michelle replied. "You go first, I'll follow and pull you
out if you get in trouble."

He loved her, of course. That was why he panted a few times for
breath, filled his lungs, and dove.

Michelle had not, of course, bothered to mention that the tunnel
was fifteen meters long, quite far to go on a single breath. She followed him, very interested in how this would turn out, and when
Darton got into trouble in one of the narrow places and tried to back
out, she grabbed his shoes and held him right where he was.

He fought hard but none of his kicks struck her. She would remember the look in his wide eyes for a long time, the thunderstruck
disbelief in the instant before his breath exploded from his lungs and
he died.

She wished that she could speak again the parting words she'd
whispered into Darton's ear when he lay dying on the ridge above
Jellyfish Lake. *"I've just killed you. And I'm going to do it again."*

But even if she could have spoken the words underwater, they
would have been untrue. Michelle supposed this was the last time she
could kill him. Twice was dangerous, but a third time would be too
clear a pattern. She could end up in jail, though, of course, you only
did severe prison time for realdeath.

She supposed that she would have to discover his body at some
point, but if she cast the kayak adrift, it wouldn't have to be for a
while. And then she'd be thunderstruck and grief-stricken that he'd
thrown away his life on this desperate attempt to pursue her after
she'd turned her back on him and gone inland, away from the sound
of his voice.

Michelle looked forward to playing that part.

She pulled up the kayak's anchor and let it coast away on the six-
knot tide, then folded away her wings and returned to her nest in the
banyan tree. She let the breeze dry her skin and got her deck from its
bag and contemplated the data about Terzian and Stephanie Pais and
the outbreak of the Green Leopard Plague.

Stephanie had died for what she believed in, killed by the agents
of an obscure, murderous regime. It had been Terzian who had shot
those four men in her defense, that was clear to her now. And Terzian,
who lived a long time and then died in the Lightspeed War along

with a few billion other people, had loved Stephanie and kept her secret till his death, a secret shared with the others who loved Stephanie
and who had spread the plague among the refugee populations of the
world.

It was realdeath that people suffered then, the death that couldn't
be corrected. Michelle knew that she understood that kind of death
only as an intellectual abstract, not as something she would ever have
to face or live with. To lose someone *permanently* . . . that was something she couldn't grasp. Even the ancients, who faced realdeath every
day, hadn't been able to accept it, that's why they'd invented the myth
of Heaven.

Michelle thought about Stephanie's death, the death that must
have broken Terzian's heart, and she contemplated the secret Terzian
had kept all those years, and she decided that she was not inclined to
reveal it.

Oh, she'd give Davout the facts, that was what he paid her for.
She'd tell him what she could find out about Stephanie and the
Transnistrians. But she wouldn't mention the camps that Santa Croce
had built across the starvation-scarred world, she wouldn't point him
at Sidamo and Green Leopard. If he drew those conclusions himself,
then obviously the secret was destined to be revealed. But she suspected he wouldn't—he was too old to connect those dots, not when
obscure ex-Soviet entities and relief camps in the Horn of Africa
were so far out of his reference.

Michelle would respect Terzian's love, and Stephanie's secret. She
had some secrets of her own, after all.

The lonely mermaid finished her work for the day and sat on her
overhanging limb to gaze down at the sea, and she wondered how
long it would be before Darton called her again, and how she would
torture him when he did.

—*With thanks to Dr. Stephen C. Lee.*

Ellen Klages divides her time between Cleveland, Ohio, and anywhere else. Her short fiction has been on the final ballot for the Nebula and Hugo awards, and has been reprinted in Harwell and Cramer's *Year's Best Fantasy* volumes. She was also a finalist for the John W. Campbell Award, and is a graduate of the Clarion South writing workshop.

She has recently sold her first novel, *Green Glass Sea,* about two eleven-year-old girls living in Los Alamos during the war, while Mom and Dad are building the bomb.

In addition to her writing, she also serves on the Motherboard of the James Tiptree, Jr., Award, and is somewhat notorious as the auctioneer/entertainment for the Tiptree auctions. When she's not writing fiction, she sells old toys on eBay, and collects lead civilians.

About "Basement Magic," the Nebula winner in the novelette category, she says:

"This story grew out of a conversation with Nalo Hopkinson, about an anthology she was editing, *Mojo: Conjure Stories*. She was looking for stories about personal, subversive magic arising from traditions of the African diaspora. Not exactly my ethnic background. But I wrote 'Basement Magic' for her anyway. It was supposed to be a short story, and ended up a novelette, too long for the anthology. Nalo liked it, but didn't buy it. Fortunately, Gordon Van Gelder gave it a home in *F&SF,* my first major magazine sale.

" 'Basement Magic' is about power and how it is used and abused. It is a fairy tale, set against the beginning of the Space Age, because that was my childhood. For me, magic and fairy tales were a mix of Disney and Grimm, and so my sense of what it means to be a princess—or a witch—and what constitutes a happy ending are all a little skewed."

BASEMENT MAGIC

ELLEN KLAGES

Mary Louise Whittaker believes in magic. She knows that somewhere, somewhere else, there must be dragons and princes, wands and wishes. Especially wishes. And happily ever after. Ever after is not now.

Her mother died in a car accident when Mary Louise was still a toddler. She misses her mother fiercely but abstractly. Her memories are less a coherent portrait than a mosaic of disconnected details: soft skin that smelled of lavender; a bright voice singing "Sweet and Low" in the night darkness; bubbles at bath time; dark curls; zwieback.

Her childhood has been kneaded, but not shaped, by the series of well-meaning middle-aged women her father has hired to tend her. He is busy climbing the corporate ladder, and is absent even when he is at home. She does not miss him. He remarried when she was five, and they moved into a two-story Tudor in one of the better suburbs of Detroit. Kitty, the new Mrs. Ted Whittaker, is a former Miss Bloomfield Hills, a vain divorcée with a towering mass of blond curls in a shade not her own. In the wild, her kind is inclined to eat their young.

Kitty might have tolerated her new stepdaughter had she been sweet and cuddly, a slick-magazine cherub. But at six, Mary Louise is an odd, solitary child. She has unruly red hair the color of Fiestaware, the dishes that might have been radioactive, and small round pink glasses that make her blue eyes seem large and slightly distant. She did not walk until she was almost two, and propels herself with a quick shuffle-duckling gait that is both urgent and awkward.

One spring morning, Mary Louise is camped in one of her favorite spots, the window seat in the guest bedroom. It is a stage set of a room, one that no one else ever visits. She leans against the wall, a thick book with lush illustrations propped up on her bare knees. Bright sunlight, filtered through the leaves of the oak outside, is broken into geometric patterns by the mullioned windows, dappling the floral cushion in front of her.

The book is almost bigger than her lap, and she holds it open with one elbow, the other anchoring her Bankie, a square of pale blue flannel with pale blue satin edging that once swaddled her infant self, carried home from the hospital. It is raveled and graying, both tattered and beloved. The thumb of her blanket arm rests in her mouth in a comforting manner.

Mary Louise is studying a picture of a witch with purple robes and hair as black as midnight when she hears voices in the hall. The door to the guest room is open a crack, so she can hear clearly, but cannot see or be seen. One of the voices is Kitty's. She is explaining something about the linen closet, so it is probably a new cleaning lady. They have had six since they moved in.

Mary Louise sits very still and doesn't turn the page, because it is stiff paper and might make a noise. But the door opens anyway, and she hears Kitty say, "This is the guest room. Now unless we've got company—and I'll let you know—it just needs to be dusted and the linens aired once a week. It has an—oh, there you are," she says, coming in the doorway, as if she has been looking all over for Mary Louise, which she has not.

Kitty turns and says to the air behind her, "This is my husband's daughter, Mary Louise. She's not in school yet. She's small for her age, and her birthday is in December, so we decided to hold her back a year. She never does much, just sits and reads. I'm sure she won't be a bother. Will you?" She turns and looks at Mary Louise but does not wait for an answer. "And this is Ruby. She's going to take care of the house for us."

The woman who stands behind Kitty nods, but makes no move to enter the room. She is tall, taller than Kitty, with skin the color of gingerbread. Ruby wears a white uniform and a pair of white Keds. She is older, there are lines around her eyes and her mouth, but her hair is sleek and black, black as midnight.

Kitty looks at her small gold watch. "Oh, dear. I've got to get going or I'll be late for my hair appointment." She looks back at Mary Louise. "Your father and I are going out tonight, but Ruby will make you some dinner, and Mrs. Banks will be here about six." Mrs. Banks is one of the babysitters, an older woman in a dark dress who smells like dusty licorice and coos too much. "So be a good girl. And for god's sake get that thumb out of your mouth. Do you want your teeth to grow in crooked, too?"

Mary Louise says nothing, but withdraws her damp puckered thumb and folds both hands in her lap. She looks up at Kitty, her eyes expressionless, until her stepmother looks away. "Well, an-y-wa-y," Kitty says, drawing the word out to four syllables, "I've really got to be going." She turns and leaves the room, brushing by Ruby, who stands silently just outside the doorway.

Ruby watches Kitty go, and when the high heels have clattered onto the tiles at the bottom of the stairs, she turns and looks at Mary Louise. "You a quiet little mouse, ain't you?" she asks in a soft, low voice.

Mary Louise shrugs. She sits very still in the window seat and waits for Ruby to leave. She does not look down at her book, because it is rude to look away when a grownup might still be talking to you. But none of the cleaning ladies talk to her, except to ask her to move out of the way, as if she were furniture.

"Yes siree, a quiet little mouse," Ruby says again. "Well, Miss Mouse, I'm fixin to go downstairs and make me a grilled cheese sandwich for lunch. If you like, I can cook you up one too. I make a mighty fine grilled cheese sandwich."

Mary Louise is startled by the offer. Grilled cheese is one of her very favorite foods. She thinks for a minute, then closes her book and tucks Bankie securely under one arm. She slowly follows Ruby down the wide front stairs, her small green-socked feet making no sound at all on the thick beige carpet.

It is the best grilled cheese sandwich Mary Louise has ever eaten. The outside is golden brown and so crisp it crackles under her teeth. The cheese is melted so that it soaks into the bread on the inside, just a little. There are no burnt spots at all. Mary Louise thanks Ruby and returns to her book.

The house is large, and Mary Louise knows all the best hiding places. She does not like being where Kitty can find her, where their paths might cross. Before Ruby came, Mary Louise didn't go down to the basement very much. Not by herself. It is an old house, and the basement is damp and musty, with heavy stone walls and banished, battered furniture. It is not a comfortable place, nor a safe one. There is the furnace, roaring fire, and the cans of paint and bleach and other frightful potions. Poisons. Years of soap flakes, lint, and furnace soot coat the walls like household lichen.

The basement is a place between the worlds, within Kitty's domain, but beneath her notice. Now, in the daytime, it is Ruby's, and Mary Louise is happy there. Ruby is not like other grownups. Ruby talks to her in a regular voice, not a scold, nor the singsong Mrs. Banks uses, as if Mary Louise is a tiny baby. Ruby lets her sit and watch while she irons, or sorts the laundry, or runs the sheets through the mangle. She doesn't sigh when Mary Louise asks her questions.

On the rare occasions when Kitty and Ted are home in the evening, they have dinner in the dining room. Ruby cooks. She comes in late on those days, and then is very busy, and Mary Louise does not get to see her until dinnertime. But the two of them eat in the kitchen, in the breakfast nook. Ruby tells stories, but has to get up every few minutes when Kitty buzzes for her, to bring more water or another fork, or to clear away the salad plates. Ruby smiles when she is talking to Mary Louise, but when the buzzer sounds, her face changes. Not to a frown, but to a kind of blank Ruby mask.

One Tuesday night in early May, Kitty decrees that Mary Louise will eat dinner with them in the dining room, too. They sit at the wide mahogany table on stiff brocade chairs that pick at the backs of her legs. There are too many forks and even though she is very careful, it is hard to cut her meat, and once the heavy silverware skitters across the china with a sound that sets her teeth on edge. Kitty frowns at her.

The grownups talk to each other and Mary Louise just sits. The worst part is that when Ruby comes in and sets a plate down in front of her, there is no smile, just the Ruby mask.

"I don't know how you do it, Ruby," says her father when Ruby comes in to give him a second glass of water. "These pork chops are the best I've ever eaten. You've certainly got the magic touch."

"She does, doesn't she?" says Kitty. "You must tell me your secret."

"Just shake 'em up in flour, salt and pepper, then fry 'em in Crisco," Ruby says.

"That's all?"

"Yes, ma'am."

"Well, isn't that marvelous. I must try that. Thank you, Ruby. You may go now."

"Yes, ma'am." Ruby turns and lets the swinging door between the kitchen and the dining room close behind her. A minute later Mary Louise hears the sound of running water, and the soft clunk of plates being slotted into the racks of the dishwasher.

"Mary Louise, don't put your peas into your mashed potatoes that way. It's not polite to play with your food," Kitty says.

Mary Louise sighs. There are too many rules in the dining room.

"Mary Louise, answer me when I speak to you."

"Muhff-mum," Mary Louise says through a mouthful of mashed potatoes.

"Oh, for god's sake. Don't talk with your mouth full. Don't you have any manners at all?"

Caught between two conflicting rules, Mary Louise merely shrugs.

"Is there any more gravy?" her father asks.

Kitty leans forward a little and Mary Louise hears the slightly muffled sound of the buzzer in the kitchen. There is a little bump, about the size of an Oreo, under the carpet just beneath Kitty's chair that Kitty presses with her foot. Ruby appears a few seconds later and stands inside the doorway, holding a striped dishcloth in one hand.

"Mr. Whittaker would like some more gravy," says Kitty.

Ruby shakes her head. "Sorry, Miz Whittaker. I put all of it in the gravy boat. There's no more left."

"Oh." Kitty sounds disapproving. "We had plenty of gravy last time."

"Yes, ma'am. But that was a beef roast. Pork chops just don't make as much gravy," Ruby says.

"Oh. Of course. Well, thank you, Ruby."

"Yes, ma'am." Ruby pulls the door shut behind her.

"I guess that's all the gravy, Ted," Kitty says, even though he is sitting at the other end of the table, and has heard Ruby himself.

"Tell her to make more next time," he says, frowning. "So what did you do today?" He turns his attention to Mary Louise for the first time since they sat down.

"Mostly I read my book," she says. "The fairy tales you gave me for Christmas."

"Well, that's fine," he says. "I need you to call the Taylors and cancel." Mary Louise realizes he is no longer talking to her, and eats the last of her mashed potatoes.

"Why?" Kitty raises an eyebrow. "I thought we were meeting them out at the club on Friday for cocktails."

"Can't. Got to fly down to Florida tomorrow. The space thing. We designed the guidance system for Shepard's capsule, and George wants me to go down with the engineers, talk to the press if the launch is a success."

"Are they really going to shoot a man into space?" Mary Louise asks.

"That's the plan, honey."

"Well, you don't give me much notice," Kitty says, smiling. "But I suppose I can pack a few summer dresses, and get anything else I need down there."

"Sorry, Kit. This trip is just business. No wives."

"No, only to Grand Rapids. Never to Florida," Kitty says, frowning. She takes a long sip of her drink. "So how long will you be gone?"

"Five days, maybe a week. If things go well, Jim and I are going to drive down to Palm Beach and get some golf in."

"I see. Just business." Kitty drums her lacquered fingernails on the tablecloth. "I guess that means I have to call Barb and Mitchell, too. Or had you forgotten my sister's birthday dinner next Tuesday?" Kitty scowls down the table at her husband, who shrugs and takes a bite of his chop.

Kitty drains her drink. The table is silent for a minute, and then she says, "Mary Louise! Don't put your dirty fork on the tablecloth. Put it on the edge of your plate if you're done. Would you like to be excused?"

"Yes, ma'am," says Mary Louise.

As soon as she is excused, Mary Louise goes down to the basement to wait. When Ruby is working it smells like a cave full of soap and warm laundry.

A little after seven, Ruby comes down the stairs carrying a brown paper lunch sack. She puts it down on the ironing board. "Well, Miss Mouse. I thought I'd see you down here when I got done with the dishes."

"I don't like eating in the dining room," Mary Louise says. "I want to eat in the kitchen with you."

"I like that, too. But your stepmomma says she got to teach you some table manners, so when you grow up you can eat with nice folks."

Mary Louise makes a face, and Ruby laughs.

"They ain't such a bad thing, manners. Come in real handy some-day, when you're eatin with folks you *want* to have like you."

"I guess so," says Mary Louise. "Will you tell me a story?"

"Not tonight, Miss Mouse. It's late, and I gotta get home and give my husband his supper. He got off work half an hour ago, and I told him I'd bring him a pork chop or two if there was any left over." She gestures to the paper bag. "He likes my pork chops even more than your daddy does."

"Not even a little story?" Mary Louise feels like she might cry. Her stomach hurts from having dinner with all the forks.

"Not tonight, sugar. Tomorrow, though, I'll tell you a long one, just to make up." Ruby takes off her white Keds and lines them up next to each other under the big galvanized sink. Then she takes off her apron, looks at a brown gravy stain on the front of it, and crumples it up and tosses it into the pink plastic basket of dirty laundry. She pulls a hanger from the line that stretches across the ceiling over the washer and begins to undo the white buttons on the front of her uniform.

"What's that?" Mary Louise asks. Ruby has rucked the top of her uniform down to her waist and is pulling it over her hips. There is a green string pinned to one bra strap. The end of it disappears into her left armpit.

"What's what? You seen my underwear before."

"Not that. That string."

Ruby looks down at her chest. "Oh. That. I had my auntie make me up a conjure hand."

"Can I see it?" Mary Louise climbs down out of the chair and walks over to where Ruby is standing.

Ruby looks hard at Mary Louise for a minute. "For it to work, it gotta stay a secret. But you good with secrets, so I guess you can take a look. Don't you touch it, though. Anybody but me touch it, all the conjure magic leak right out and it won't work no more." She reaches under her armpit and draws out a small green flannel bag, about the size of a walnut, and holds it in one hand.

Mary Louise stands with her hands clasped tight behind her back so she won't touch it even by accident and stares intently at the bag. It doesn't look like anything magic. Magic is gold rings and gowns spun of moonlight and silver, not a white cotton uniform and a little stained cloth bag. "Is it really magic? Really? What does it do?"

"Well, there's diff'rent kinds of magic. Some conjure bags bring luck. Some protects you. This one, this one gonna bring me money. That's why it's green. Green's the money color. Inside there's a silver dime, so the money knows it belong here, a magnet—that attracts the money right to me—and some roots, wrapped up in a two-dollar bill. Every mornin I gives it a little drink, and after nine days, it gonna bring me my fortune." Ruby looks down at the little bag fondly, then tucks it back under her armpit.

Mary Louise looks up at Ruby and sees something she has never seen on a grownup's face before: Ruby believes. She believes in magic, even if it is armpit magic.

"Wow. How does—"

"Miss Mouse, I *got* to get home, give my husband his supper." Ruby steps out of her uniform, hangs it on a hanger, then puts on her blue skirt and a cotton blouse.

Mary Louise looks down at the floor. "Okay," she says.

"It's not the end of the world, sugar." Ruby pats Mary Louise on the back of the head, then sits down and puts on her flat black shoes. "I'll be back tomorrow. I got a big pile of laundry to do. You think you might come down here, keep me company? I think I can tell a story and sort the laundry at the same time." She puts on her outdoor coat, a nubby, burnt-orange wool with chipped gold buttons and big square pockets, and ties a scarf around her chin.

"Will you tell me a story about the magic bag?" Mary Louise asks. This time she looks at Ruby and smiles.

"I think I can do that. Gives us both somethin to look forward to. Now scoot on out of here. I gotta turn off the light." She picks up her brown paper sack and pulls the string that hangs down over the ironing board. The light bulb goes out, and the basement is dark except for the twilight filtering in through the high single window. Ruby opens the outside door to the concrete stairs that lead up to the driveway. The air is warmer than the basement.

"Nitey-nite, Miss Mouse," she says, and goes outside.

"G'night Ruby," says Mary Louise, and goes upstairs.

When Ruby goes to vacuum the rug in the guest bedroom on Thursday morning, she finds Mary Louise sitting in the window seat, staring out the window.

"Mornin, Miss Mouse. You didn't come down and say hello."

Mary Louise does not answer. She does not even turn around.

Ruby pushes the lever on the vacuum and stands it upright, dropping the gray fabric cord she has wrapped around her hand. She walks over to the silent child. "Miss Mouse? Somethin wrong?"

Mary Louise looks up. Her eyes are cold. "Last night I was in bed, reading. Kitty came home. She was in a really bad mood. She told me I read too much and I'll just ruin my eyes—more—reading in bed. She took my book and told me she was going to throw it in the 'cinerator and burn it up." She delivers the words in staccato anger, through clenched teeth.

"She just bein mean to you, sugar." Ruby shakes her head. "She tryin to scare you, but she won't really do that."

"But she *did!*" Mary Louise reaches behind her and holds up her fairy tale book. The picture on the cover is soot-stained, the shiny coating blistered. The gilded edges of the pages are charred and the corners are gone.

"Lord, child, where'd you find that?"

"In the 'cinerator, out back. Where she said. I can still read most of the stories, but it makes my hands all dirty." She holds up her hands, showing her sooty palms.

Ruby shakes her head again. She says, more to herself than to Mary Louise, "I burnt the trash after lunch yesterday. Must of just been coals, come last night."

Mary Louise looks at the ruined book in her lap, then up at Ruby. "It was my favorite book. Why'd she do that?" A tear runs down her cheek.

Ruby sits down on the window seat. "I don't know, Miss Mouse," she says. "I truly don't. Maybe she mad that your daddy gone down to Florida, leave her behind. Some folks, when they're mad, they just gotta whup on somebody, even if it's a little bitty six-year-old child. They whup on somebody else, they forget their own hurts for a while."

"You're bigger than her," says Mary Louise, snuffling. "You could—*whup*—*her* back. You could tell her that it was bad and wrong what she did."

Ruby shakes her head. "I'm real sorry, Miss Mouse," she says quietly, "but I can't do that."

"Why not?"

"'Cause she the boss in this house, and if I say anythin crosswise to Miz Kitty, her own queen self, she gonna fire me same as she fire all them other colored ladies used to work for her. And I needs this job. My husband's just workin part-time down to the Sunoco. He tryin to get work in the Ford plant, but they ain't hirin right now. So my paycheck here, that's what's puttin groceries on our table."

"But, but—" Mary Louise begins to cry without a sound. Ruby is the only grownup person she trusts, and Ruby cannot help her.

Ruby looks down at her lap for a long time, then sighs. "I can't say nothin to Miz Kitty. But her bein so mean to you, that ain't right, neither." She puts her arm around the shaking child.

"What about your little bag?" Mary Louise wipes her nose with the back of her hand, leaving a small streak of soot on her cheek.

"What 'bout it?"

"You said some magic is for protecting, didn't you?"

"Some is," Ruby says slowly. "Some is. Now, my momma used to say, 'an egg can't fight with a stone.' And that's the truth. Miz Kitty got the power in this house. More'n you, more'n me. Ain't nothin to do 'bout that. But conjurin—" She thinks for a minute, then lets out a deep breath.

"I think we might could put some protection 'round you, so Miz Kitty can't do you no more misery," Ruby says, frowning a little. "But I ain't sure quite how. See, if it was your house, I'd put a goopher right under the front door. But it ain't. It's your daddy's house, and she married to him legal, so ain't no way to keep her from comin in her own house, even if she is nasty."

"What about my room?" asks Mary Louise.

"Your room? Hmm. Now, that's a different story. I think we can goopher it so she can't do you no harm in there."

Mary Louise wrinkles her nose. "What's *a goopher?*"

Ruby smiles. "Down South Carolina, where my family's from, that's just what they calls a spell, or a hex, a little bit of rootwork."

"Root—?"

Ruby shakes her head. "It don't make no never mind what you calls it, long as you does it right. Now if you done cryin, we got work to do. Can you go out to the garage, to your Daddy's toolbox, and get me nine nails? Big ones, all the same size, and bright and shiny as you can find. Can you count that many?"

Mary Louise snorts. "I can count up to *fifty,*" she says.

"Good. Then you go get nine shiny nails, fast as you can, and meet me down the hall, by your room."

When Mary Louise gets back upstairs, nine shiny nails clutched

tightly in one hand, Ruby is kneeling in front of the door of her bedroom, with a paper of pins from the sewing box, and a can of Drano.
Mary Louise hands her the nails.

"These is just perfect," Ruby says. She pours a puddle of Drano
into its upturned cap, and dips the tip of one of the nails into it, then
pokes the nail under the edge of the hall carpet at the left side of
Mary Louise's bedroom door, pushing it deep until not even its head
shows.

"Why did you dip the nail in Drano?" Mary Louise asks. She
didn't know any of the poison things under the kitchen sink could be
magic.

"Don't you touch that, hear? It'll burn you bad, 'cause it's got lye
in it. But lye the best thing for cleanin away any evil that's already
been here. Ain't got no Red Devil like back home, but you got to use
what you got. The nails and the pins, they made of iron, and iron keep
any new evil away from your door." Ruby dips a pin in the Drano as
she talks and repeats the poking, alternating nails and pins until she
pushes the last pin in at the other edge of the door.

"That oughta do it," she says. She pours the few remaining drops
of Drano back into the can and screws the lid on tight, then stands up.
"Now all we needs to do is set the protectin charm. You know your
prayers?" she asks Mary Louise.

"I know 'Now I lay me down to sleep.'"

"Good enough. You get into your room and you kneel down,
facin the hall, and say that prayer to the doorway. Say it loud and as
best you can. I'm goin to go down and get the sheets out of the dryer.
Meet me in Miz Kitty's room when you done."

Mary Louise says her prayers in a loud, clear voice. She doesn't
know how this kind of magic spell works, and she isn't sure if she is
supposed to say the God Blesses, but she does. She leaves Kitty out
and adds Ruby. "And help me to be a good girl, amen," she finishes,
and hurries down to her father's room to see what other kinds of
magic Ruby knows.

The king-size mattress is bare. Mary Louise lies down on it and
rolls over and over three times before falling off the edge onto the
carpet. She is just getting up, dusting off the knees of her blue cotton
pants, when Ruby appears with an armful of clean sheets, which she
dumps onto the bed. Mary Louise lays her face in the middle of the
pile. It is still warm and smells like baked cotton. She takes a deep
breath.

"You gonna lay there in the laundry all day or help me make this bed?" Ruby asks, laughing.

Mary Louise takes one side of the big flowered sheet and helps Ruby stretch it across the bed and pull the elastic parts over all four corners so it is smooth everywhere.

"Are we going to do a lot more magic?" Mary Louise asks. "I'm getting kind of hungry."

"One more bit, then we can have us some lunch. You want tomato soup?"

"Yes!" says Mary Louise.

"I thought so. Now fetch me a hair from Miz Kitty's hairbrush. See if you can find a nice long one with some dark at the end of it."

Mary Louise goes over to Kitty's dresser and peers at the heavy silver brush. She finds a darker line in the tangle of blond and carefully pulls it out. It is almost a foot long, and the last inch is definitely brown. She carries it over to Ruby, letting it trail through her fingers like the tail of a tiny invisible kite.

"That's good," Ruby says. She reaches into the pocket of her uniform and pulls out a scrap of red felt with three needles stuck into it lengthwise. She pulls the needles out one by one, makes a bundle of them, and wraps it round and round, first with the long strand of Kitty's hair, then with a piece of black thread.

"Hold out your hand," she says.

Mary Louise holds out her hand flat, and Ruby puts the little black-wrapped bundle into it.

"Now, you hold this until you get a picture in your head of Miz Kitty burnin up your pretty picture book. And when it nice and strong, you spit. Okay?"

Mary Louise nods. She scrunches up her eyes, remembering, then spits on the needles.

"You got the knack for this," Ruby says, smiling. "It's a gift."

Mary Louise beams. She does not get many compliments, and stores this one away in the most private part of her thoughts. She will visit it regularly over the next few days until its edges are indistinct and there is nothing left but a warm glow labeled RUBY.

"Now put it under this mattress, far as you can reach." Ruby lifts up the edge of the mattress and Mary Louise drops the bundle on the box spring.

"Do you want me to say my prayers again?"

"Not this time, Miss Mouse. Prayers is for protectin. This here is a sufferin hand, bring some of Miz Kitty's meanness back on her own self, and it need another kind of charm. I'll set this one myself." Ruby lowers her voice and begins to chant:

> Before the night is over,
> Before the day is through.
> What you have done to someone else
> Will come right back on you.

"There. That ought to do her just fine. Now we gotta make up this bed. Top sheet, blanket, bedspread all smooth and nice, pillows plumped up just so."

"Does that help the magic?" Mary Louise asks. She wants to do it right, and there are almost as many rules as eating in the dining room. But different.

"Not 'zactly. But it makes it look like it 'bout the most beautiful place to sleep Miz Kitty ever seen, make her want to crawl under them sheets and get her beauty rest. Now help me with that top sheet, okay?"

Mary Louise does, and when they have smoothed the last wrinkle out of the bedspread, Ruby looks at the clock.

"Shoot. How'd it get to be after one o'clock? Only fifteen minutes before my story comes on. Let's go down and have ourselves some lunch."

In the kitchen, Ruby heats up a can of Campbell's tomato soup, with milk, not water, the way Mary Louise likes it best, then ladles it out into two yellow bowls. She puts them on a metal tray, adds some saltine crackers and a bottle of ginger ale for her, and a lunchbox bag of Fritos and a glass of milk for Mary Louise, and carries the whole tray into the den. Ruby turns on the TV and they sip and crunch their way through half an hour of *As the World Turns*.

During the commercials, Ruby tells Mary Louise who all the people are, and what they've done, which is mostly bad. When they are done with their soup, another story comes on, but they aren't people Ruby knows, so she turns off the TV and carries the dishes back to the kitchen.

"I gotta do the dustin and finish vacuumin, and ain't no way to talk over that kind of noise," Ruby says, handing Mary Louise a handful of Oreos. "So you go off and play by yourself now, and I'll get my chores done before Miz Kitty comes home."

Mary Louise goes up to her room. At 4:30 she hears Kitty come home, but she only changes into out-to-dinner clothes and leaves and doesn't get into bed. Ruby says good-bye when Mrs. Banks comes at 6:00, and Mary Louise eats dinner in the kitchen and goes upstairs at 8:00, when Mrs. Banks starts to watch *Dr. Kildare*.

On her dresser there is a picture of her mother. She is beautiful, with long curls and a silvery white dress. She looks like a queen, so Mary Louise thinks she might be a princess. She lives in a castle, imprisoned by her evil stepmother, the false queen. But now that there is magic, there will be a happy ending. She crawls under the covers and watches her doorway, wondering what will happen when Kitty tries to come into her room, if there will be flames.

Kitty begins to scream just before nine Friday morning. Clumps of her hair lie on her pillow like spilled wheat. What is left sprouts from her scalp in irregular clumps, like a crabgrass-infested lawn. Clusters of angry red blisters dot her exposed skin.

By the time Mary Louise runs up from the kitchen, where she is eating a bowl of Kix, Kitty is on the phone. She is talking to her beauty salon. She is shouting, "This is an emergency! An emergency!"

Kitty does not speak to Mary Louise. She leaves the house with a scarf wrapped around her head like a turban, in such a hurry that she does not even bother with lipstick. Mary Louise hears the tires of her T-bird squeal out of the driveway. A shower of gravel hits the side of the house, and then everything is quiet.

Ruby comes upstairs at ten, buttoning the last button on her uniform. Mary Louise is in the breakfast nook, eating a second bowl of Kix. The first one got soggy. She jumps up excitedly when she sees Ruby.

"Miz Kitty already gone?" Ruby asks, her hand on the coffeepot.

"It worked! It worked! Something *bad* happened to her hair. A lot of it fell out, and there are chicken pox where it was. She's at the beauty shop. I think she's going to be there a long time."

Ruby pours herself a cup of coffee. "That so?"

"Uh-huh." Mary Louise grins. "She looks like a *goopher*."

"Well, well, well. That come back on her fast, didn't it? Maybe now she think twice 'bout messin with somebody smaller'n her. But you, Miss Mouse"—Ruby wiggles a semi-stern finger at Mary Louise. "Don't you go jumpin up and down shoutin 'bout goophers, hear? Magic ain't nothin to be foolin around with. It can bring sickness, bad luck, a whole heap of misery if it ain't done proper. You hear me?"

Mary Louise nods and runs her thumb and finger across her lips, as if she is locking them. But she is still grinning from ear to ear.

Kitty comes home from the beauty shop late that afternoon. She is in a very, very bad mood, and still has a scarf around her head. Mary Louise is behind the couch in the den, playing seven dwarfs. She is Snow White and is lying very still, waiting for the prince.

Kitty comes into the den and goes to the bar. She puts two ice cubes in a heavy squat crystal glass, then reaches up on her tiptoes and feels around on the bookshelf until she finds a small brass key. She unlocks the liquor cabinet and fills her glass with brown liquid. She goes to the phone and makes three phone calls, canceling cocktails, dinner, tennis on Saturday. "Sorry," Kitty says. "Under the weather. Raincheck?" When she is finished she refills her glass, replaces the key, and goes upstairs. Mary Louise does not see her again until Sunday.

Mary Louise stays in her room most of the weekend. It seems like a good idea, now that it is safe there. Saturday afternoon she tiptoes down to the kitchen and makes three peanut butter and honey sandwiches. She is not allowed to use the stove. She takes her sandwiches and some Fritos upstairs and touches one of the nails under the carpet, to make sure it is still there. She knows the magic is working, because Kitty doesn't even try to come in, not once.

At 7:30 on Sunday night, she ventures downstairs again. Kitty's door is shut. The house is quiet. It is time for Disney. *Walt Disney's Wonderful World of Color.* It is her favorite program, the only one that is not black and white, except for *Bonanza,* which comes on after her bedtime.

Mary Louise turns on the big TV that is almost as tall as she is, and sits in the middle of the maroon leather couch in the den. Her feet stick out in front of her, and do not quite reach the edge. There is a commercial for Mr. Clean. He has no hair, like Kitty, and Mary Louise giggles, just a little. Then there are red and blue fireworks over the castle where Sleeping Beauty lives. Mary Louise's thumb wanders up to her mouth, and she rests her cheek on the soft nap of her Bankie.

The show is Cinderella, and when the wicked stepmother comes on, Mary Louise thinks of Kitty, but does not giggle. The story unfolds and Mary Louise is bewitched by the colors, by the magic of television. She does not hear the creaking of the stairs. She does not hear the door of the den open, or hear the rattle of ice cubes in an empty crystal glass. She does not see the shadow loom over her until it is too late.

It is a sunny Monday morning. Ruby comes in the basement door and changes into her uniform. She switches on the old brown table radio, waits for its tubes to warm up and begin to glow, then turns the yellowed plastic dial until she finds a station that is more music than static. The Marcels are singing "Blue Moon" as she sorts the laundry, and she dances a little on the concrete floor, swinging and swaying as she tosses white cotton panties into one basket and black nylon socks into another.

She fills the washer with a load of whites, adds a measuring cup of Dreft, and turns the dial to Delicate. The song on the radio changes to "Runaway" as she goes over to the wooden cage built into the wall, where the laundry that has been dumped down the upstairs chute gathers.

"As I walk along . . . ," Ruby sings as she opens the hinged door with its criss-cross of green painted slats. The plywood box inside is a cube about three feet on a side, filled with a mound of flowered sheets and white terry cloth towels. She pulls a handful of towels off the top of the mound and lets them tumble into the pink plastic basket waiting on the floor below. "An' I wonder. I wa-wa-wa-wa-wuh-under," she sings, and then stops when the pile moves on its own, and whimpers.

Ruby parts the sea of sheets to reveal a small head of carrot-red hair.

"Miss Mouse? What on God's green earth you doin in there? I like to bury you in all them sheets!"

A bit more of Mary Louise appears, her hair in tangles, her eyes red-rimmed from crying.

"Is Kitty gone?" she asks.

Ruby nods. "She at the beauty parlor again. What you *doin* in there? You hidin from Miz Kitty?"

"Uh-huh." Mary Louise sits up and a cascade of hand towels and washcloths tumbles out onto the floor.

"What she done this time?"

"She—she—" Mary Louise bursts into ragged sobs.

Ruby reaches in and puts her hands under Mary Louise's arms, lifting the weeping child out of the pile of laundry. She carries her over to the basement stairs and sits down, cradling her. The tiny child shakes and holds on tight to Ruby's neck, her tears soaking into the white cotton collar. When her tears subside into trembling, Ruby reaches into a pocket and proffers a pale yellow hankie.

"Blow hard," she says gently. Mary Louise does.

"Now scooch around front a little so you can sit in my lap." Mary Louise scooches without a word. Ruby strokes her curls for a minute. "Sugar? What she do this time?"

Mary Louise tries to speak, but her voice is still a rusty squeak. After a few seconds she just holds her tightly clenched fist out in front of her and slowly opens it. In her palm is a wrinkled scrap of pale blue flannel, about the size of a playing card, its edges jagged and irregular.

"Miz Kitty do that?"

"Uh-huh," Mary Louise finds her voice. "I was watching Disney and *she* came in to get another drink. She said Bankie was just a dirty old rag with germs and sucking thumbs was for babies—" Mary Louise pauses to take a breath. "She had scissors and she cut up all of Bankie on the floor. She said next time she'd get bigger scissors and cut off my thumbs! She threw my Bankie pieces in the toilet and flushed, three times. This one fell under the couch," Mary Louise says, looking at the small scrap, her voice breaking.

Ruby puts an arm around her shaking shoulders and kisses her forehead. "Hush now. Don't you fret. You just sit down here with me. Everything gonna be okay. You gotta—" A buzzing noise from the washer interrupts her. She looks into the laundry area, then down at Mary Louise and sighs. "You take a couple deep breaths. I gotta move the clothes in the washer so they're not all on one side. When I come back, I'm gonna tell you a story. Make you feel better, okay?"

"Okay," says Mary Louise in a small voice. She looks at her lap, not at Ruby, because nothing is really very okay at all.

Ruby comes back a few minutes later and sits down on the step next to Mary Louise. She pulls two small yellow rectangles out of her pocket and hands one to Mary Louise. "I like to set back and hear a story with a stick of Juicy Fruit in my mouth. Helps my ears open up or somethin. How about you?"

"I like Juicy Fruit," Mary Louise admits.

"I thought so. Save the foil. Fold it up and put it in your pocket."

"So I have someplace to put the gum when the flavor's all used up?"

"Maybe. Or maybe we got somethin else to do and that foil might could come in handy. You save it up neat and we'll see."

Mary Louise puts the gum in her mouth and puts the foil in the pocket of her corduroy pants, then folds her hands in her lap and waits.

"Well, now," says Ruby. "Seems that once, a long, long time ago, down South Carolina, there was a little mouse of a girl with red, red hair and big blue eyes."

"Like me?" asks Mary Louise.

"You know, I think she was just about 'zactly like you. Her momma died when she was just a little bit of a girl, and her daddy married hisself a new wife, who was very pretty, but she was mean and lazy. Now, this stepmomma, she didn't much like stayin home to take care of no child weren't really her own and she was awful cruel to that poor little girl. She never gave her enough to eat, and even when it was snowin outside, she just dress her up in thin cotton rags. That child was awful hungry and cold, come winter.

"But her real momma had made her a blanket, a soft blue blanket, and that was the girl's favorite thing in the whole wide world. If she wrapped it around herself and sat real quiet in a corner, she was warm enough, then.

"Now, her stepmomma, she didn't like seein that little girl happy. That little girl had power inside her, and it scared her stepmomma. Scared her so bad that one day she took that child's most favorite special blanket and cut it up into tiny pieces, so it wouldn't be no good for warmin her up at all."

"That was really mean of her," Mary Louise says quietly.

"Yes it was. Awful mean. But you know what that little girl did next? She went into the kitchen, and sat down right next to the cookstove, where it was a little bit warm. She sat there, holdin one of the little scraps from her blanket, and she cried, 'cause she missed havin her real momma. And when her tears hit the stove, they turned into steam, and she stayed warm as toast the rest of that day. Ain't nothin warmer than steam heat, no siree.

"But when her stepmomma saw her all smilin and warm again, what did that woman do but lock up the woodpile, out of pure spite. See, she ate out in fancy rest'rants all the time, and she never did cook, so it didn't matter to her if there was fire in the stove or not.

"So finally that child dragged her cold self down to the basement. It was mighty chilly down there, but she knew it was someplace her stepmomma wouldn't look for her, 'cause the basement's where work gets done, and her stepmomma never did do one lick of work.

"That child hid herself back of the old wringer washer, in a dark, dark corner. She was cold, and that little piece of blanket was only big enough to wrap a mouse in. She wished she was warm. She wished and wished and between her own power and that magic blanket, she found her mouse self. Turned right into a little gray mouse, she did. Then she wrapped that piece of soft blue blanket around her and hid herself away just as warm as if she was in a feather bed.

"But soon she heard somebody comin down the wood stairs into the basement, clomp, clomp, clomp. And she thought it was her mean old stepmomma comin to make her life a misery again, so she scampered quick like mice do, back into a little crack in the wall. 'Cept it weren't her stepmomma. It was the cleanin lady, comin down the stairs with a big basket of mendin."

"Is that you?" Mary Louise asks.

"I reckon it was someone pretty much like me," Ruby says, smiling. "And she saw that little mouse over in the corner with that scrap of blue blanket tight around her, and she said, ''Scuse me, Miss Mouse, but I needs to patch me up this old raggy sweater, and that little piece of blanket is just the right size. Can I have it?' "

"Why would she talk to a mouse?" Mary Louise asks, puzzled.

"Well, now, the lady knew that it wasn't no regular mouse, 'cause she weren't no ordinary cleanin lady, she was a conjure woman too. She could see that magic girl spirit inside the mouse shape clear as day."

"Oh. Okay."

Ruby smiles. "Now, the little mouse-child had to think for a minute, because that piece of blue blanket was 'bout the only thing she loved left in the world. But the lady asked so nice, she gave over her last little scrap of blanket for the mendin and turned back into a little girl.

"Well sir, the spirit inside that blue blanket was powerful strong, even though the pieces got all cut up. So when the lady sewed that blue scrap onto that raggy old sweater, what do you know? It turned into a big warm magic coat, just the size of that little girl. And when she put on that magic coat, it kept her warm and safe, and her step-momma never could hurt her no more."

"I wish there really was magic," says Mary Louise sadly. "Because she *did* hurt me again."

Ruby sighs. "Magic's there, sugar. It truly is. It just don't always work the way you think it will. That sufferin hand we put in Miz Kitty's bed, it work just fine. It scared her plenty. Trouble is, when she scared, she get mad, and then she get mean, and there ain't no end to it. No tellin what she might take it into her head to cut up next."

"My thumbs," says Mary Louise solemnly. She looks at them as if she is saying good-bye.

"That's what I'm afraid of. Somethin terrible bad. I been thinkin on this over the weekend, and yesterday night I call my Aunt Nancy down in Beaufort, where I'm from. She's the most powerful conjure woman I know, taught me when I was little. I ask her what she'd do, and she says, 'Sounds like you all need a Peaceful Home hand, stop all the angry, make things right.'"

"Do we have to make the bed again?" asks Mary Louise.

"No, sugar. This is a wearin hand, like my money hand. 'Cept it's for you to wear. Got lots of special things in it."

"Like what?"

"Well, first we got to weave together a hair charm. A piece of yours, a piece of Miz Kitty's. Hers before the goopher, I think. And we need some dust from the house. And some rosemary from the kitchen. I can get all them when I clean today. The rest is stuff I bet you already got."

"I have magic things?"

"I b'lieve so. That piece of tinfoil from your Juicy Fruit? We need that. And somethin lucky. You got somethin real lucky?"

"I have a penny what got run over by a train," Mary Louise offers.

"Just so. Now the last thing. You know how my little bag's green flannel, 'cause it's a money hand?"

Mary Louise nods.

"Well, for a Peaceful Home hand, we need a square of light blue flannel. You know where I can find one of those?"

Mary Louise's eyes grow wide behind her glasses. "But it's the only piece I've got left."

"I know," Ruby says softly.

"It's like in the story, isn't it?"

"Just like."

"And like in the story, if I give it to you, Kitty can't hurt me ever again?"

"Just like."

Mary Louise opens her fist again and looks at the scrap of blue flannel for a long time. "Okay," she says finally, and gives it to Ruby.

"It'll be all right, Miss Mouse. I b'lieve everything will turn out just fine. Now I gotta finish this laundry and do me some housework. I'll meet you in the kitchen round one-thirty. We'll eat and I'll fix up your hand right after my story."

At two o'clock the last credits of *As the World Turns* disappear from the TV. Ruby and Mary Louise go down to the basement. They lay out all the ingredients on the padded gray surface of the ironing board. Ruby assembles the hand, muttering under her breath from time to time. Mary Louise can't hear the words. Ruby wraps everything in the blue flannel and snares the neck of the walnut-sized bundle with three twists of white string.

"Now all we gotta do is give it a little drink, then you can put it on," she tells Mary Louise.

"Drink of what?"

Ruby frowns. "I been thinkin on that. My Aunt Nancy said best thing is to get me some Peaceful oil. But I don't know no root doctors up here. Ain't been round Detroit long enough."

"We could look in the phone book."

"Ain't the kind of doctor you finds in the Yellow Pages. Got to know someone who knows someone. And I don't. I told Aunt Nancy that, and she says in that case, reg'lar whiskey'll do just fine. That's what I been givin my money hand. Little bit of my husband's whiskey every mornin for six days now. I don't drink, myself, 'cept maybe a cold beer on a hot summer night. But whiskey's strong magic, comes to conjurin. Problem is, I can't take your hand home with me to give it a drink, 'long with mine."

"Why not?"

" 'Cause once it goes round your neck, nobody else can touch it, not even me, else the conjure magic leak right out."

Ruby looks at Mary Louise thoughtfully. "What's the most powerful drink you ever had, Miss Mouse?"

Mary Louise hesitates for a second, then says, "Vernor's ginger ale.

The bubbles are *very* strong. They go up my nose and make me sneeze."

Ruby laughs. "I think that just might do. Ain't as powerful as whiskey, but it fits, you bein just a child and all. And there's one last bottle up in the Frigidaire. You go on up now and fetch it."

Mary Louise brings down the yellow and green bottle. Ruby holds her thumb over the opening and sprinkles a little bit on the flannel bag, mumbling some more words that end with "father son and holy ghost amen." Then she ties the white yarn around Mary Louise's neck so that the bag lies under her left armpit, and the string doesn't show.

"This bag's gotta be a secret," she says. "Don't talk about it, and don't let nobody else see it. Can you do that?"

Mary Louise nods. "I dress myself in the morning, and I change into my jammies in the bathroom."

"That's good. Now the next three mornings, before you get dressed, you give your bag a little drink of this Vernor's, and say, 'Lord, bring an end to the evil in this house, amen.' Can you remember that?"

Mary Louise says she can. She hides the bottle of Vernor's behind the leg of her bed. Tuesday morning she sprinkles the bag with Vernor's before putting on her T-shirt. The bag is a little sticky.

But Mary Louise thinks the magic might be working. Kitty has bought a blond wig, a golden honey color. Mary Louise thinks it looks like a helmet, but doesn't say so. Kitty smiles in the mirror at herself and is in a better mood. She leaves Mary Louise alone.

Wednesday morning the bag is even stickier. It pulls at Mary Louise's armpit when she reaches for the box of Kix in the cupboard. Ruby says this is okay.

By Thursday, the Vernor's has been open for too long. It has gone flat and there are no bubbles at all. Mary Louise sprinkles her bag, but worries that it will lose its power. She is afraid the charm will not work, and that Kitty will come and get her. Her thumbs ache in anticipation.

When she goes downstairs Kitty is in her new wig and a green dress. She is going out to a luncheon. She tells Mary Louise that Ruby will not be there until noon, but she will stay to cook dinner. Mary Louise will eat in the dining room tonight, and until then she should be good and not to make a mess. After she is gone, Mary Louise eats some Kix and worries about her thumbs.

When her bowl is empty, she goes into the den, and stands on the desk chair so she can reach the tall books on the bookshelf. They are still over her head, and she cannot see, but her fingers reach. The dust on the tops makes her sneeze; she finds the key on a large black book called *Who's Who in Manufacturing 1960*. The key is brass and old-looking.

Mary Louise unlocks the liquor cabinet and looks at the bottles. Some are brown, some are green. One of the green ones has Toto dogs on it, a black one and a white one, and says SCOTCH WHISKEY. The bottle is half-full and heavy. She spills some on the floor, and her little bag is soaked more than sprinkled, but she thinks this will probably make up for the flat ginger ale.

She puts the green bottle back and carefully turns it so the Toto dogs face out, the way she found it. She climbs back up on the chair and puts the key back up on top of *Manufacturing,* then climbs down.

The little ball is cold and damp under her arm, and smells like medicine. She changes her shirt and feels safer. But she does not want to eat dinner alone with Kitty. That is not safe at all. She thinks for a minute, then smiles. Ruby has shown her how to make a *room* safe.

There are only five nails left in the jar in the garage. But she doesn't want to keep Kitty *out* of the dining room, just make it safe to eat dinner there. Five is probably fine. She takes the nails into the kitchen and opens the cupboard under the sink. She looks at the Drano. She is not allowed to touch it, not by Kitty's rules, not by babysitter rules, not by Ruby's rules. She looks at the pirate flag man on the side of the can. The poison man. He is bad, bad, bad, and she is scared. But she is more scared of Kitty.

She carries the can over to the doorway between the kitchen and the dining room and kneels down. When she looks close she sees dirt and salt and seeds and bits of things in the thin space between the linoleum and the carpet.

The can is very heavy, and she doesn't think she can pour any Drano into the cap. Not without spilling it. So she tips the can upside down three times, then opens it. There is milky Drano on the inside of the cap. She carefully dips in each nail and pushes them, one by one, under the edge of the dining room carpet. It is hard to push them all the way in, and the two in the middle go crooked and cross over each other a little.

"This is a protectin' hand," she says out loud to the nails. Now she needs a prayer, but not a bedtime prayer. A dining room prayer.

She thinks hard for a minute, then says, "For what we are about to receive may we be truly thankful amen." Then she puts the Drano back under the sink and washes her hands three times with soap, just to make sure.

Ruby gets there at noon. She gives Mary Louise a quick hug and a smile, and then tells her to scoot until dinnertime, because she has to vacuum and do the kitchen floor and polish the silver. Mary Louise wants to ask Ruby about magic things, but she scoots.

Ruby is mashing potatoes in the kitchen when Kitty comes home. Mary Louise sits in the corner of the breakfast nook, looking at the comics in the paper, still waiting for Ruby to be less busy and come and talk to her. Kitty puts her purse down and goes into the den. Mary Louise hears the rattle of ice cubes. A minute later, Kitty comes into the kitchen. Her glass has an inch of brown liquid in it. Her eyes have an angry look.

"Mary Louise, go to your room. I need to speak to Ruby in private."

Mary Louise gets up without a word and goes into the hall. But she does not go upstairs. She opens the basement door silently and pulls it almost shut behind her. She stands on the top step and listens.

"Ruby, I'm afraid I'm going to have to let you go," says Kitty. Mary Louise feels her armpits grow icy cold and her eyes begin to sting.

"Ma'am?"

"You've been drinking."

"No, ma'am. I ain't—"

"Don't try to deny it. I know you coloreds have a weakness for it. That's why Mr. Whittaker and I keep the cabinet in the den locked. For your own good. But when I went in there, just now, I found the cabinet door open. I cannot have servants in my house that I do not trust. Is that clear?"

"Yes, ma'am."

Mary Louise waits for Ruby to say something else, but there is silence.

"I will pay you through the end of the week, but I think it's best if you leave after dinner tonight." There is a rustling and the snap of Kitty's handbag opening. "There," she says. "I think I've been more than generous, but of course I cannot give you references."

"No, ma'am," says Ruby.

"Very well. Dinner at six. Set two places. Mary Louise will eat with me." Mary Louise hears the sound of Kitty's heels marching off, then the creak of the stairs going up. There is a moment of silence, and the basement door opens.

Ruby looks at Mary Louise and takes her hand. At the bottom of the stairs she sits, and gently pulls Mary Louise down beside her.

"Miss Mouse? You got somethin you want to tell me?"

Mary Louise hangs her head.

"You been in your Daddy's liquor?"

A tiny nod. "I didn't *drink* any. I just gave my bag a little. The Vernor's was flat and I was afraid the magic wouldn't work. I put the key back. I guess I forgot to lock the door."

"I guess you did."

"I'll tell Kitty it was me," Mary Louise says, her voice on the edge of panic. "You don't have to be fired. I'll tell her."

"Tell her what, Miss Mouse? Tell her you was puttin your Daddy's whiskey on a conjure hand?" Ruby shakes her head. "Sugar, you listen to me. Miz Kitty thinks I been drinkin, she just fire me. But she find out I been teachin you black juju magic, she gonna call the police. Better you keep quiet, hear?"

"But it's not fair!"

"Maybe it is, maybe it ain't." Ruby strokes Mary Louise's hair and smiles a sad smile, her eyes as gentle as her hands. "But, see, after she talk to me that way, ain't no way I'm gonna keep workin for Miz Kitty nohow. It be okay, though. My money hand gonna come through. I can feel it. Already startin to, maybe. The Ford plant's hirin again, and my husband's down there today, signin up. Maybe when I gets home, he's gonna tell me good news. May just be."

"You can't *leave* me!" Mary Louise cries.

"I got to. I got my own life."

"Take me with you."

"I can't, sugar." Ruby puts her arms around Mary Louise. "Poor Miss Mouse. You livin in this big old house with nice things all 'round you, 'cept nobody nice to you. But angels watchin out for you. I b'lieve that. Keep you safe till you big enough to make your own way, find your real kin."

"What's kin?"

"Fam'ly. Folks you belong to."

"Are you my kin?"

"Not by blood, sugar. Not hardly. But we're heart kin, maybe.
'Cause I love you in my heart, and I ain't never gonna forget you.
That's a promise." Ruby kisses Mary Louise on the forehead and pulls
her into a long hug. "Now since Miz Kitty already give me my pay, I
'spect I oughta go up, give her her dinner. I reckon you don't want to
eat with her?"

"No."

"I didn't think so. I'll tell her you ain't feelin well, went on up to
bed. But I'll come downstairs, say good-bye, 'fore I leave." Ruby
stands up and looks fondly down at Mary Louise. "It'll be okay, Miss
Mouse. There's miracles every day. Why, last Friday, they put a fella up
in space. Imagine that? A man up in space? So ain't nothin impossible,
not if you wish just hard as you can. Not if you believe." She rests her
hand on Mary Louise's head for a moment, then walks slowly up the
stairs and back into the kitchen.

Mary Louise sits on the steps and feels like the world is crumbling
around her. This is not how the story is supposed to end. This is not
happily ever after.

She cups her tiny hand around the damp, sticky bag under her arm
and closes her eyes and thinks about everything that Ruby has told
her. She wishes for the magic to be real.

And it is. There are no sparkles, no gold. This is basement magic,
deep and cool. Power that has seeped and puddled, gathered slowly,
beneath the notice of queens, like the dreams of small awkward girls.
Mary Louise believes with all her heart, and finds the way to her
mouse self.

Mouse sits on the bottom step for a minute, a tiny creature with a
round pink tail and fur the color of new rust. She blinks her blue
eyes, then scampers off the step and across the basement floor. She is
quick and clever, scurrying along the baseboards, seeking familiar
smells, a small ball of blue flannel trailing behind her.

When she comes to the burnt-orange coat hanging inches from
the floor, she leaps. Her tiny claws find purchase in the nubby fabric,
and she climbs up to the pocket, wriggles over and in. Mouse burrows
into a pale cotton hankie that smells of girl tears and wraps herself
tight around the flannel ball that holds her future. She puts her pink
nose down on her small pink paws and waits for her true love to
come.

Kitty sits alone at the wide mahogany table. The ice in her drink has melted. The kitchen is only a few feet away, but she does not get up. She presses the buzzer beneath her feet, to summon Ruby. The buzzer sounds in the kitchen. Kitty waits. Nothing happens. Impatient, she presses on the buzzer with all her weight. It shifts, just a fraction of an inch, and its wire presses against the two lye-tipped nails that have crossed it. The buzzer shorts out with a hiss. The current, diverted from its path to the kitchen, returns to Kitty. She begins to twitch, as if she were covered in stinging ants, and her eyes roll back in her head. In a gesture that is both urgent and awkward, she clutches at the tablecloth, pulling it and the dishes down around her. Kitty Whittaker, a former Miss Bloomfield Hills, falls to her knees and begins to howl wordlessly at the Moon.

Downstairs, Ruby hears the buzzer, then a crash of dishes. She starts to go upstairs, then shrugs. She takes off her white uniform for the last time. She puts on her green skirt and her cotton blouse, leaves the white Keds under the sink, puts on her flat black shoes. She looks in the clothes chute, behind the furnace, calls Mary Louise's name, but there is no answer. She calls again, then, with a sigh, puts on her nubby orange outdoor coat and pulls the light string. The basement is dark behind her as she opens the door and walks out into the soft spring evening.

William Sanders makes his home in Tahlequah, Oklahoma, but his formative years were spent in the hill country of western Arkansas, where this story is set. He appeared on the SF scene in the early eighties with a couple of alternate-history comedies, *Journey to Fusang* (a finalist for the John W. Campbell Award) and *The Wild Blue and the Gray.* Sanders then turned to mystery and suspense, producing a number of critically acclaimed titles. He credits his old friend Roger Zelazny with persuading him to return to SF, this time via the short-story form; his stories have appeared in *Asimov's Science Fiction, The Magazine of Fantasy & Science Fiction,* and numerous anthologies, earning himself a well-deserved reputation as one of the best short-fiction writers of the last decade, and winning him two Sidewise Awards for Best Alternate History story. He has also returned to novel writing, with books such as *The Ballad of Billy Badass and the Rose of Turkestan* and *The Bernadette Operations,* a new SF novel, *J.,* and a mystery novel, *Smoke.* Some of his acclaimed short stories have been collected in *Are We Having Fun Yet? American Indian Fantasy Stories.* His most recent book is a historical study, *Conquest: Hernando de Soto and the Indians: 1539–1543.* Coming up is a new collection, *Is It Now Yet?* (Most of his books, including reissues of his earlier novels, are available from Wildside Press, or on Amazon.com.)

About "Dry Bones," he says:

"I can't think of anything that needs to be said about this story. Either it works on its own or it doesn't.

"About the only thing I would point out is that this is an example of a long-established but seldom-seen subcategory of science fiction: the Great Lost Scientific Discovery. Kipling did it with 'The Eye of Allah'; Waldrop did it with 'The Ugly Chickens.' In between, examples have been pretty rare; I can't think why.

"I would like to thank those people who voted for the story, and assure them that the videotapes will be destroyed as promised."

DRY BONES

WILLIAM SANDERS

It was a hot summer day and I was sitting under the big tree down by the road, where we caught the bus when school was in, when Wendell Haney came up the road on his bike and told me somebody had found a skeleton in a cave down in Moonshine Hollow.

"No lie," he said. "My cousin Wilma Jean lives in town and she came by the house just now and told Mama about it."

I put down the Plastic Man comic book I had been reading. "You mean a human skeleton?" I said, not really believing it.

Wendell made this kind of impatient face. "Well, of *course* a human one," he said. "What did you *think?*"

He was a skinny kid with a big head and pop eyes like a frog and when he was excited about something, like now, he was pretty funny-looking. He was only a year younger than me, but I'd just turned thirteen last month and a twelve-year-old looked like a little kid now.

He said, "Gee, Ray, don't you want to go see? Everybody's down there, the sheriff and all."

Sure enough, when I looked off up the blacktop I saw there was a lot of dust hanging over the far end of Tobe Nelson's pasture, where the dirt road ran down toward Moonshine Hollow. Somebody in a pickup truck was just turning in off the road.

I stood up. "I'll go get my bike," I told him. "Go on, I'll catch up with you."

I went back to the house, hoping Mama hadn't seen me talking to Wendell. She didn't like for me to have anything to do with him because she said his family was trashy. They lived down a dirt road a little way up the valley from us, in an old house that looked about ready to fall down, with a couple of old cars up on blocks in the front yard. Everybody knew his daddy was a drunk.

Mama was back in the kitchen, though—I could hear her through the window, singing along with Johnny Ray on the radio—and I got my bicycle from behind the house and rode off before she could ask me where I was going and probably tell me not to.

I caught up with Wendell about a quarter of the way across Tobe Nelson's pasture. That wasn't hard to do, with that rusty old thing he had to ride. When I came even with him, I slowed down and we rode the rest of the way together.

It was a long way across the field, with no shade anywhere along the road. Really it wasn't much more than a cow path, all bumpy and rutty and dusty, and I worked up a good sweat pedaling along in the sun. On the far side of the pasture, the ground turned downhill, sloping toward the creek, and we could ease off and coast the rest of the way. Now I could see a lot of cars and trucks parked all along the creek bank where the road ended.

At the bottom of the hill I stopped and got off and put the kickstand down and stood for a minute looking around, while Wendell leaned his bike against a tree. A good many people, men and women both, were standing around in the shade of the willows and the big sycamores, talking and looking off across the creek in the direction of Moonshine Hollow.

Moonshine Hollow was a strange place. It was a little like what they call a box canyon out west, only not as big. I guess you could call it a ravine. Anyway it ran back into the side of the ridge for maybe half a mile or so and then ended in this big round hole of a place with high rock cliffs all around, and a couple of waterfalls when it was wet season.

I'd been up in the hollow a few times, like all the kids around there. It was kind of creepy and I didn't much like it. The trees on top of the bluffs blocked out the sun so the light was dim and gloomy even on a sunny day. The ground was steep and rocky and it was hard to walk.

It wasn't easy even getting there, most of the year. First you had to get across the creek, which ran strong and fast through this stretch, especially in the spring. It was only about thirty or forty feet across but you'd have had to be crazy to try to swim it when the water was high.

And that was just about the only way in there, unless you wanted to take the road up over the ridge and work your way down the bluffs. A few people had done that, or said they had.

In a dry summer, like now, it was no big deal because you could just walk across without even getting your feet wet. Except that right now Deputy Pritchard was standing in the middle of the dry creek bed and not letting anyone cross.

"Sheriff's orders," he was saying as I moved up to where I could see. "Nobody goes in there till he comes back."

There was a little stir as somebody came pushing through the crowd. Beside me, Wendell said softly, "Uh oh," and a second later I saw why.

Wendell's daddy was tall and lean, with black hair and dark skin— he beat a man up pretty bad once, I heard, for asking him if he was part Indian—and mean-looking eyes. He stopped on the edge of the creek bank and stared at Deputy Pritchard. "Sheriff's orders, huh?" he said. "Who's he think he is?"

Deputy Pritchard looked back at him. "Thinks he's the sheriff, I expect," he said. "Like he did the last couple of times he locked you up."

Everything got quiet for a minute. Then, farther down the bank, Tobe Nelson spoke up. "What's he doing," he said, "asking the skeleton to vote for him?"

He was a fat bald-headed man with a high voice like a woman, always grinning and laughing and making jokes. Everybody laughed now, even Wendell's daddy, and things felt easier. I heard Wendell let his breath out.

Somebody said, "There they are now."

Sheriff Cowan was coming through the trees on the far side of the creek, pushing limbs and brush out of his way. There was somebody behind him and at first I couldn't see who it was, but then I said, "Hey, it's Mr. Donovan!"

"Well, *sure*." Wendell said, like I'd said something dumb. "He was the one who *found* it."

Mr. Donovan taught science at the junior high school in town. Everybody liked him even though his tests were pretty hard. He was big and husky like a football player and the girls all talked about how handsome he was. The boys looked up to him because he'd been in the Marines and won the Silver Star on Okinawa. I guess half the men around there had been in the service during the war—that was what we still called it, "the war," even though the fighting in Korea had been going on for almost a year now—but he was the only one I knew who had a medal.

I always enjoyed his class because he made it interesting, showing us things like rocks and plants and even live animals. Sometimes he let me help when he did experiments. When he saw I liked science, he helped me pick out some books in the school library. He offered to loan me some science fiction magazines he had, but I had to tell him no because there would have been big trouble if Daddy had caught me reading them.

Sheriff Cowan climbed down the far bank of the creek and walked over to stand next to Deputy Pritchard. His face was red and sweaty and his khaki uniform was all wrinkled and dusty. He looked up and down the line of people standing on the creek bank. "I don't know what you all heard," he said, "and I don't know what you thought you were going to see, but you're not going to see anything here today."

A couple of people started to speak and he raised his hand. "No, just listen. I've examined the site, and it's obvious the remains are too old to come under my jurisdiction." He tilted his head at Mr. Donovan, who had come up beside him. "Mr. Donovan, here, thinks the bones might be thousands of years old. Even I don't go back that far."

After the laughter stopped he said, "He says this could be an important discovery. So he's going to get in touch with some people he knows at the university, and have them come take a look. Meanwhile, since the site is on county land—"

"Is not," Wendell's daddy said in a loud voice. "That's our land, on that side of the creek. My family's. Always has been."

"No, it isn't," Sheriff Cowan said. "It *used* to be your family's land, but the taxes weren't paid and finally the county took over the property. And nobody ever wanted to buy it."

"I guess not," Tobe Nelson said. "Just a lot of rocks and brush, not even any decent timber."

"I don't care," Wendell's daddy said. "It was ours and they taken it. It ain't right."

"That's so," Sheriff Cowan said. "It's not right that you managed to throw away everything your daddy worked so hard for, while your brother was off getting killed for his country. Just like it's not right that your own family have to do without because you'd rather stay higher than a Georgia pine than do an honest day's work. And now, Floyd Haney, you just shut up while I talk."

Wendell's daddy looked madder than ever but he shut up. "All right, then," Sheriff Cowan said, "as I was saying, since it's county property, I'm closing it to the public till further notice. Tobe, I want you to lock that gate up at the main road, and don't let anybody cross your land to come down here without checking with me first. Or with Mr. Donovan."

A man said, "You mean we can't even go look?"

"Yep," the sheriff said. "You hard of hearing?"

Mr. Donovan spoke up. "Actually there's not much to see. Just a hand and a little bit of the wrist, sticking out from under a pile of rocks and dirt, and even that's partly buried. We're just assuming that there's a whole skeleton under there somewhere."

"Not that any of you could find that cave," Sheriff Cowan said, "even if I let you try. I'd have walked right past it if he hadn't been there to show me."

He started waving his hands, then, at the crowd, like somebody shooing a flock of chickens. "Go on, now. Everybody go home or back to the pool hall or something. Nothing to see down here."

People started moving, heading toward their cars, talking among themselves and glancing back in the direction of Moonshine Hollow. Wendell's daddy was walking our way and Wendell sort of scooched down behind me, but he went right past us and climbed into his old pickup truck and drove away, throwing gravel and dirt as he went up the hill. When he was gone, we went over and got our bikes, without speaking or looking at each other. There was a lot I wanted to talk about but I could tell Wendell wasn't in the mood.

"Lot of foolishness," Daddy said that evening over supper when I told him the story. "Going to have a bunch of damn fool scientists, now, poking around and spouting off a bunch of crap."

Daddy didn't like scientists because they believed in evolution. He used to ask me if Mr. Donovan was teaching evolution at the school. He said he could get him fired if he was.

He said, "I'm not surprised, though. There's a good many caves and holes up in that hollow. That's why they call it Moonshine Hollow, you know, the bootleggers used to hide their whiskey there during Prohibition. Could be some bootlegger's bones," he said, "that hid in there running from the law. Or maybe a runaway nigger back in slave times. Probably not even an Indian at all."

"Mr. Donovan says the bones are a lot older than that," I said, and Mama gave me a warning look. She didn't like for me to argue with Daddy about anything. She said it wasn't my place.

Daddy said, "Oh, that's a crock. Damn scientists know everything, to hear them tell it. I heard one on the radio telling how far it is to the moon." He snorted. "Guess he'd been there and measured it off."

Mama said, "Who wants pie?"

Later on Mr. Donovan told me how he happened to find the skeleton.

He was hiking up in the hollow, looking for things he might be able to use in class next year. He was working his way along the foot of a bluff, where there were a lot of great big boulders that had fallen down from above, when he saw a snake of a kind he didn't recognize. Before he could get a good look, it slipped in behind a boulder that rested against the rock of the bluff.

So Mr. Donovan went up to the boulder, and after walking around it and pushing aside some brush, he found a gap between it and the bluff. He got out his flashlight from his pack and shone it into the hole, still looking for the snake, and saw what looked like a dark opening in the face of the rock. Without stopping to think about it, he squeezed himself through the gap to have a closer look.

"One of the dumbest things I've ever done," he told me. "You never, *never* go into a place like that alone. Don't tell the school board, Raymond, but I'm a real idiot sometimes."

Behind the boulder, sure enough, a hole led back into the rock. The opening was so low he had to bend over double and then get down on his hands and knees and craw—"getting stupider by the minute," he said—but then it opened up and he found himself in a small cave.

The floor was covered with loose rock that he guessed had fallen from the ceiling. He squatted down and picked up a few pieces and looked at them by the light of his flashlight, hoping for fossils, but they were just plain old rock.

Then he turned over a big flat slab and saw the hand bones.

"It took a few seconds to register," he said. "The light was bad and the bones were still half buried, just barely exposed. I started to poke at them, and then I realized what I was looking at and yanked my fingers back. Then I just sat there for a little while, as the implications sank in."

I said, "How'd you know they were so old?"

"I didn't," he admitted. "Archaeology isn't my field, after all. But they sure as hell *looked* old, and if there was any chance they were then they needed to be protected. So maybe I bluffed the sheriff a little. But that's our secret, right?"

Mr. Donovan didn't waste any time and neither did his friends from the university. They showed up next Saturday afternoon.

"I'm just an ignorant old country boy," Tobe Nelson said, talking to a bunch of people in front of the church after service let out the next morning. "When that schoolteacher said some scientists were coming, I was expecting old men in beards and white coats, you know?"

He shook his head, grinning. "Then here come this nice-looking young couple driving up in front of my house in a brand-new bright red Mercury, with a little house trailer hitched on behind. I took them for tourists that had lost their way, till they got out and came up and introduced theirselves and wanted to know if they could set up camp down by the creek."

Daddy said, "You let those fools onto your land?"

"Hey," Tobe Nelson said, "they asked me real nice, and they paid me some good money. The nice part would have been enough, but I sure didn't turn down the money either."

He laughed his high-pitched laugh. "But I tell you what, if I was young and I had me a car like that and a woman like that, you wouldn't see me spending my time digging up a bunch of old bones. I could think of a *lot* better things to do."

It stayed hot and dry. Wednesday afternoon I rode my bike down toward the little crossroads store to get myself a soda pop. On the way, though, I stopped by Tobe Nelson's pasture gate and got off and stood for a while leaning on the fence and looking off down the trail toward Moonshine Hollow. The gate wasn't locked now and I could have gone on in but I was pretty sure I wasn't supposed to.

Then I heard somebody pull up behind me, and when I turned around there was Mr. Donovan, sitting behind the wheel of the war surplus jeep he drove. "Hey, Raymond!" he called. "Be a buddy and open the gate for me, will you?"

I went over and undid the latch and swung the big gate open and held it back while he drove through, and then closed it and pushed until the latch snapped shut. "Thanks," Mr. Donovan said, stopping the jeep. "So what have you been doing with your summer, Raymond? Anything interesting?"

"Not really," I said. "Too hot to do very much."

"I heard that. Say," he said, "how would you like to meet a couple of real scientists?"

Would I? I said, "Sure," and he got out and picked up my bike and tossed it in the back of the jeep while I got in, and off we went. That was when he told me about how he found the cave, while we were bumping across Tobe Nelson's pasture.

Pretty soon we were rolling down the hill toward the creek. Even before we got to the bottom I saw the red car parked near the creek bank, and, just beyond, a shiny bare-metal trailer.

Mr. Donovan stopped the jeep in the shade of a big tree and we got out and walked toward the trailer, which I saw now had a big canvas awning coming off one side, with a table and some chairs underneath. A man got up from the table and came toward us. "David," Mr. Donovan called. "Working hard, I see."

"To the verge of exhaustion," the man said, and turned his head and yelled back over his shoulder, "Maddy! Bob's here!"

The trailer door opened and a woman came out. "Oh, hi," she said, and then, looking at me, "And who's this?"

"This is Raymond," Mr. Donovan said, "one of my best students. Raymond, meet David and Madeleine Sloane."

The man stuck out his hand and I took it. The woman came trotting over from the trailer and put out her hand too. "So," she said, "you like science, Raymond?"

"Yes, ma'am," I said, and she threw her head back and laughed.

"'Ma'am,'" she said, "my God, you make me sound like your grandmother. Call me Maddy. Everybody does."

"Come sit down in the shade," the man said. "We're just taking a little break."

He was a medium-sized young man with blond crewcut hair and glasses. That was about all I noticed. He wasn't the one I was looking at.

The woman said, "Well, Raymond, would you like a Coke?"

She was the prettiest lady I'd ever seen outside of the movies. She was taller than me and I'd hit five feet five right before my birthday. She had light brown hair, cut off short at the nape of her neck, and dark blue eyes and nice white teeth.

She was wearing a red top thing with no sleeves, tied up so her stomach was showing, and shorts that I saw were blue jeans with the legs cut off. Whoever cut them off hadn't left much. Her legs were tanned and they just went on and on.

I said, "Yes, ma'am. Uh, Maddy."

"Bob? Anything for you? He shook his head and she went back to the trailer.

We went over and sat down at the table under the awning. I noticed there was a noise coming from somewhere nearby, like a power lawnmower, but I couldn't see where it was coming from. "Generator," David Sloane said, seeing me looking around. "You know, for electricity."

"Quite a fancy setup you've got here," Mr. Donovan said.

"Oh, yes," David said. "All the civilized comforts money can buy." His face got a little funny when he said that last part. "What a good thing some of us have it," he added, so low I could barely hear him, and he looked off toward the trailer just as Maddy came back out carrying a bottle of Coke.

"Did you want a glass and ice?" she asked me. I shook my head. "Good," she said. "I had you figured for a bottle man." She dragged up a chair and sat down. "Bob Donovan, I'm going to strangle you, bringing company around when I'm looking like this." I saw now there were some dusty smudges on her arms and legs. "Just look at me," she said. "Like a field hand."

"Been grubbing away?" Mr. Donovan said, grinning. "How's it going?"

"Slowly," David said, "As it's supposed to."

"It's quite a process," Mr. Donovan said to me. "The earth's got to be removed very gradually, just a little bit at a time, so as not to damage whatever's underneath. And everything's got to be measured and recorded. Takes a lot of patience and steady hands."

"Actually," Maddy said, "we're still working through that pile of loose rock from the ceiling fall. And having to examine every bit of it too, in case—" She stopped and looked at David. "Show them the point, why don't you?"

David started to say something, but then he grunted and got up and headed for the trailer. "Wait till you see this," Maddy said. I sipped my Coke and tried not to stare at her. Around our part of the state you didn't see very many grown women in shorts, because most of the churches said it was a sin. My Uncle Miles, who was the pastor of the Baptist church where we belonged, even said they weren't sup- posed to wear their hair bobbed short.

Just about the only women you saw dressed the way Maddy Sloane was right now were the trashy ones who hung around the pool hall in town, or the honky-tonks out at the county line. But it was easy to see that this one wasn't trashy at all.

David came back carrying a little flat wooden box and set it down on the table in front of me. He opened it and pulled back some cot- ton and said, "There. Look what we found this morning."

I tried not to look disappointed. I'd seen Indian arrowheads be- fore, who hadn't? People were always finding them along the creek banks, or turning them up plowing. A couple of the boys at school had regular collections.

Now I looked closer, though, this one didn't look like any arrow- head I'd seen. It was sure a beauty, made of some kind of shiny yellowish-brown stone with dark bands running through it, and really well made. It was pretty big, maybe three inches long, and it didn't have the usual notches on the sides, just one big notch at the bottom. There was a kind of groove going up the middle.

Mr. Donovan said, "I'll be damned. Clovis?"

"I'd bet on it," David said. "And I saw enough of them last year, on that dig in New Mexico."

I said, "Do you know what kind of Indians made this kind of ar- rowhead?"

"Not Indians. At least not the kind you're thinking about. More like their prehistoric ancestors."

"And it's a spearhead," Maddy said. "Bows and arrows hadn't been invented yet."

"Wow." I ran my finger over the smooth stone. "Old huh?"

David nodded. "Just how old, well, there's still some pretty hot ar- guing going on. Well over ten thousand years, though."

"To give you an idea," Mr. Donovan said to me, "that thing was very likely made to hunt mammoths with."

"Wow," I said again. "But you don't really know if it goes with the skeleton, do you?"

They all looked at each other. "Damn," Maddy said. "You're right, Bob, this one's sharp."

"That's right," David told me. "No guarantee the skeleton's from the same time period. Not even safe to guess yet."

"Still nothing on that?" Mr. Donovan asked.

David shrugged. "It's damned old, all right. Just from a superficial examination of the exposed bones, I'm nearly sure there's some degree of fossilization. But so far there's nothing to date it." He sighed. "Best would be the new radiocarbon test, that Dr. Libby's been working on up at the University of Chicago. But half the archaeologists in the country are waiting in line for that. Could be a long time before we have an answer."

"But," Maddy said, "now you see why we're excited about this site. It could be really important."

David stood up and stretched. "And so we need to get back to work. Sorry."

He picked up the box and closed it carefully. I saw that there were some numbers marked on the lid. As he carried it back to the trailer Maddy said, "Raymond, it was great meeting you." She reached over and put her hand on my shoulder. "Come back and see us again some time, won't you?"

"Sure." My voice didn't come out quite right. "I will."

But as it turned out I didn't see the Sloanes again for quite a while. I rode down there several times over the next few days, but there was never any sign of them, just the trailer sitting there and the generator running. I guessed they were up at the cave, working, and I thought about going up the hollow and trying to find them, but I didn't know the way.

By now everybody was talking about them. Especially about Maddy. "Parades around practically naked," my Aunt Ethel, who worked at the Ben Franklin five-and-dime store in town, said to Mama. "She was in the store yesterday. Looked like a you-know-what."

Uncle Miles even worked them into his sermon the next Sunday. "I'm reminded," he said, "of the old colored spiritual, 'Them bones, them bones, them dry bones, now hear the word of the Lord.' Some people need to quit worrying about a lot of dry bones and start hearing the word of the Lord."

Next morning I woke up with a head cold. It wasn't all that bad, but it was enough for Mama to keep me in bed for a couple of days and indoors for the rest of the week. I spent the time reading and listening to the radio and mostly being bored and wishing I could go see David and Maddy again.

Daddy came in from town one evening with a big grin on his face. "That schoolteacher of yours," he said to me, "I got to say one thing for him, he's no sissy."

"What happened?" I asked, and Daddy laughed.

"Damnedest thing," he said. "Floyd Haney came up to him in front of the diner, drunk as a skunk as usual, and started cussing him out—still going on about that land across the creek—and when the schoolteacher tried to walk past him, Floyd took a swing at him. Next thing you know Floyd was flat on his ass. I saw the whole thing from across the street."

"Mr. Donovan hit him?"

"Fastest left I ever saw. Deputy Pritchard drove up while Floyd was still laying there, but the schoolteacher said he didn't want to press charges. Probably right," Daddy said. "It never does no good, locking Floyd's kind up. Some folks are just the way they are."

Finally I got to feeling better and Mama let me out of the house again. Naturally I took off right away for the creek.

Mr. Donovan's jeep was sitting there when I came down the hill, and as I stopped the bike I saw they were all three up by the trailer sitting under the awning. As I walked toward them I could hear Maddy talking, sounding angry.

"I don't believe this," she was saying. "The most important discovery of the century, and you're acting as if it's a bomb that's going to explode in your face."

"It is," David said. "Oh, sure, maybe not for you. Your tight little rich-bitch ass isn't the one on the line, is it? Nobody pays any attention to graduate students." His voice was getting louder. "I'm the poor son of a bitch with the ink still fresh on his doctorate. If I blow this I'll be lucky to get a job at City College of Rooster Poot, Arkansas."

They looked up and saw me, then, and they got all quiet and embarrassed-looking, the way grown people do when kids catch them quarreling. After a second Maddy said, "Why, hello, Raymond."

I said, "Maybe I ought to go?"

"No, no." Maddy waved her hands. "I bet you'd like a Coke, wouldn't you? Why don't you just go help yourself? The box is just inside the door, you can't miss it."

I went over to the trailer and climbed up the little steps and opened the door. Sure enough, there was a refrigerator, the littlest one I'd ever seen, just inside. I could see up into the front part of the trailer, which was mostly taken up by a bed that needed making. I got myself a Coke and went back out just as Mr. Donovan was saying, "Anyway, I hope these are all right."

I saw now that there was a big yellow envelope on the table and a couple of stacks of big glossy photographs. David was holding a picture up and looking at it from different angles. "Oh, yes," he said, "this is really first-class work. Thanks, Bob."

"Been a while since I've done any darkroom work," Mr. Donovan said "Took a couple of hours just to dig out my old equipment and get it dusted off. Glad the prints turned out okay."

I walked over and looked at the photos while they talked. One of the ones on top was a close-up shot of a skull, half buried in the ground. Another one looked like a full-length view of the whole skeleton. I picked that one up for a closer look and then I saw something that didn't make any sense at all.

"Hey," I said. "He's wearing clothes!"

They all turned and stared at me. I said, "If the skeleton's as old as you said, wouldn't they have rotted away by now?"

"Oh, shit," David said, and reached over and snatched the picture out of my hand. "Bob, why'd you have to bring—"

"Shut up, David," Maddy said. "Raymond, come here."

I walked around the table and stood in front of her. She took both my hands in hers and looked right into my face. "Raymond," she said, "you wouldn't do anything to hurt us, would you?"

"No, ma'am," I said. My throat had tightened up till I could barely talk. "No, Maddy."

"And if you knew something that could cause trouble for us, you wouldn't tell? I don't mean anything bad or illegal," she said quickly. "Just something that could make a lot of trouble."

"No." I didn't know what she was talking about but I would have agreed with anything she said.

"Then come on," she said, standing up and picking up a big battery lantern that was sitting on the table. "There's something I want to show you."

David stood up too, fast. "You will like hell!"

"Don't be stupid, David," Maddy said without looking at him. "And for once in your life try trusting someone."

"Raymond's a smart boy," Mr. Donovan said. "He'll cooperate, once he understands."

"Oh, all right," David said, throwing up his hands, "why not? Hell, let's hold a press conference. Call the White House, invite Truman for a look. Bring in the damn United *Nations.*"

"Watch your step," Maddy said as we started across the dry creek bed.

It was a long hard walk up the hollow to the cave, and hot even in the deep shade under the trees. By the time we got there, I was wishing I'd brought the rest of that Coke along.

About halfway up the hollow Maddy turned left and started up a steep slope, covered with big loose rocks, to the foot of the bluff. "Here," she said, and I saw what Sheriff Cowan had meant. If I hadn't known there was a cave there I'd never have guessed.

"It's a little rough getting through the brush," she said, "but we didn't want to advertise the location by clearing it away."

She walked around to the side of a gray boulder, big as a good-sized car, that rested against the face of the bluff. She switched on the battery lantern and pushed aside some bushes and disappeared behind the boulder.

"You know," Mr. Donovan said as we started after her, "I believe this must have been sealed off until recently. Look at all that loose rock and earth down below. There's been a slide, not too long ago. Maybe that last big rainstorm in May set it off."

"You could be right," David said. "There's hardly any animal sign in the cave."

I pushed through the brush and found myself in a narrow little space, dark except for the light that was coming from off to my right. "You'll have to get down and crawl a little way," Maddy called back. "It's not too bad."

It was as far as I was concerned. The light from up ahead helped, but it was still a scary place, and going through the tightest part I could feel the whole world pressing in on me. The air was cold, too, with a creepy dead smell. I wanted to yell but I choked it down because I didn't want Maddy to think I was a coward. Then the hole got bigger and the light got brighter and there I was in the cave.

"Sorry about the light," Maddy said as I straightened up. "We usually use carbide lamps, which are brighter. But they're a pain to get started and I don't feel like fooling with it."

It wasn't a fancy cave like the ones in the books, with stalactites and all. It was just a kind of room, about the size of a one-car garage. It looked even smaller because of all the stuff stacked and piled over by the walls—shovels and trowels, big round screen-wire dirt sifters, boxes and bags and a lot of things I didn't recognize.

In the middle of the floor, a space had been marked off with wooden pegs and lengths of twine. Inside that, the ground had been dug or scraped down for a foot or so, and in the dug-out space lay the skeleton.

It didn't look much like the ones in the Halloween decorations. It looked more like a bundle of loose sticks, till you got a good look. It lay on its left side with its knees drawn up part way, and its left arm flung out straight. The right hand was out of sight up near its chest.

And sure enough, it was wearing clothes, and they didn't look like Indian clothes to me. It was hard to be sure, but it looked more like some kind of one-piece outfit, like the coveralls my cousin Larry wore when he worked at the Texaco station in town. Maddy held the light up higher and now I saw it had on shoes, too. Or rather boots, with big heavy-looking soles. Actually, I could only see one, because the left foot was still buried.

After a minute I said, "I don't get it."

David said, "Welcome to the club, kid."

"Don't feel bad," Maddy said. "Neither does anyone else."

David went around and squatted down by the hole and reached down and touched the right sleeve. "You asked a good question, back there," he said. "Fabric should have rotted away a long time ago, but just look at this stuff. Oh, it's deteriorated badly, it's brittle and flimsy, but it's still in a hell of a lot better condition than it should be. Than it *can* be."

"But then," I said, thinking I got it now, "it must not be as old as you thought. Must be, uh, modern."

David nodded. "That would be the logical conclusion. The condition of the bones, the partial fossilization, well, there might be some other explanation, chemicals in the soil or something. The Clovis point you saw could have been here long before this guy arrived. But there's just one other thing."

He moved a little to one side and motioned to me. "Come look at this."

I went over and hunkered down beside him, though I didn't really want to get any closer to that skeleton. He said, "Hold that light closer, Maddy. Look here, Raymond."

He was pointing at a big long rip in the material covering the right shoulder. He pushed the cloth aside with his fingertips. "See that?"

I saw it. I'd seen one like it a couple of weeks ago, lying on a bed of cotton in a little box on the table by the creek.

"And so," David said, "what we have here is a man in modern clothes with a ten-thousand-year-old Clovis point embedded in his shoulder. Which, of course, is flatly impossible."

"Modern is right," Maddy said. "I cut a tiny little piece from the cuff and studied it under the microscope, and it's not any natural fiber. In fact it's not exactly woven fiber at all, it's more—I don't know what the hell it is, that's the truth, I've never seen anything like it and textiles are a specialty of mine."

"The boots are synthetic too," David said. "And the fasteners are some kind of hard plastic."

I thought it over for a minute. "But that's—" I remembered, then, a story in a science fiction magazine I'd had, before Daddy took it away from me and told me he'd whip me if he ever caught me reading that crap again.

I said, "You think he was a time traveler."

"Did I say that?" David made a big show of looking around. "I didn't hear anybody say that, did you?"

"Now you see," Maddy said, "why we're having to keep this secret for now. David's got to be careful how he handles this, because a lot of people are sure to call it a fake. It could destroy his career."

There was something sticking out of the ground just behind the skeleton's lower back, a dark object about the size of a kid's book satchel. Or that was my guess, though you really couldn't see much of it. I said, "What's this?"

"Once again," David said, "I'm damned if I know. Looks like some kind of pack he was carrying, but what's in it I couldn't tell you. Maybe his lunch, maybe his spare socks, maybe something we wouldn't even recognize."

"Like," Maddy said, "whatever got him here. From wherever—whenever—he came from."

"I didn't hear that either," David said. "Anyway, I haven't looked inside and I'm not going to. Not even going to dig it out so it *can* be opened. If and when it gets opened, it's going to be by somebody of absolutely impeccable professional standing, with a bunch of other respected paragons on hand for witnesses."

"Have you got anyone yet?" Mr. Donovan asked.

David shook his head. "Everybody's out on digs right now. Most of all I want Dr. Hoban of the University of Pennsylvania, but he's in Iraq for the rest of the summer."

"That old bastard," Maddy said. "You know damn well he'll steal all the credit for himself."

"I wish I had your optimism," David said. "More likely he'll denounce the whole thing as a fraud and me as a lunatic or worse."

"Of course," Mr. Donovan said, "if the government gets wind of this, and somebody thinks there might be something in that pack with possible military applications—"

"Oh, my God," David said. He put his hands up to his face. "I hadn't even thought of that. Marvelous."

I was looking at the skull. It wasn't "grinning," as they say. The jaws were open and it looked like it was screaming in pain. I shivered. It really was cold in there.

I said, "It was the spear that killed him, wasn't it?"

"Looks that way," Maddy said. "Looks as if he dragged himself in here—maybe for shelter, maybe trying to hide—and simply bled to death. That's got to have been a terrible wound."

"Wonder what happened," Mr. Donovan said. "To cause them to kill him, I mean."

"Maybe he broke some local taboo," Maddy said. "We found a few small objects, that apparently fell out of his pockets—another point like that one you saw, a bone scraping tool, a kind of awl made from deer horn. Evidently he was doing some collecting. Maybe he picked up something he shouldn't."

"Or maybe they just killed him because he was a stranger." David looked down at the skeleton. "Poor bastard, you sure wound up a long way from home, didn't you?"

"How'd he get buried?" I asked.

"Flooding," Maddy said. "Silt and sand washing in. This cave's been flooded several times in the distant past."

"The floor of the hollow would have been a lot higher back then," Mr. Donovan added. "Say, that's another possible dating clue, isn't it?"

"Maybe." David shrugged. "When you get right down to it, the date doesn't really matter now. If this burial is even a hundred years old, we're looking at the impossible. Christ, *fifty.*"

He stood up. "Come on. Raymond's seen enough. Probably wondering by now if we're crazy or he is."

By the time I got home it was nearly supper time. Daddy came in a little bit later, while I was sitting on the couch in the living room trying to think, and right away he said, "Raymond, you been hanging around with them college people, down at the creek? Don't lie to me," he added before I could answer. "Two different people said they saw you on your bicycle headed that way."

I said, "Tobe Nelson said it was all right, Daddy. I asked him and he said it was all right, long as I close the gate."

"That's *Mister* Nelson to you," Mama said from the doorway.

Daddy said, "I don't care if General MacArthur told you it was all right for you to go down there. I'm the one says what you can and can't do, and I'm telling you to stay away from them people. I don't want you having nothing to do with them and I don't want you going down there as long as they're there."

I said, "Why?"

"Because I say so," he said, starting to get red in the face, "and you're not so big I can't still whip your ass if you don't mind me." I started to speak and he said, "Or I can do it right now if you keep talking back."

So I didn't say any more. I wasn't really afraid of him—he hadn't laid a hand on me since I was six, he just liked to talk tough—but I knew he'd get all mad and stomp and holler around, and Mama would start crying, and I didn't feel like going through all that right now. I had enough on my mind.

I did stay away, though, for the next couple of days. I figured David and Maddy didn't need me coming around, with all they had to do and think about.

Wednesday, I decided to go into town to the library and see if they had some books about archaeology. I told Mama where I was going and she said, "You're not going down to the creek, are you, to see those people? You know what your daddy said."

"Just to the library," I said. "Promise."

"You be careful, then," she said. "I don't really like you riding that thing down the road."

It was only a couple of miles into town, but the weather was still hot, so by the time I got there I was pretty sweaty. Going by the Texaco station I slowed down, thinking about getting me a cold drink, and then I saw the red Mercury parked out front.

David Sloane came out of the side door as I pulled up. "Raymond," he said, raising a hand. He looked at my bike and said, "Hm. You get around pretty well on that bike, don't you? Wonder if you'd consider doing me a big favor."

He got out his wallet. "Five bucks," he said, "if you'll go tell Maddy that I'm stuck in town with car trouble, and I'll probably be coming in pretty late."

I hesitated for a second. Daddy would be really mad if I went down there again. I was taking a big enough chance just standing here talking to David.

But I was too embarrassed to tell David about Daddy, and I really did want to see Maddy again. And if it came down to it, I could say I was doing a Christian duty by helping someone. There wouldn't be much Daddy could say to that.

Besides, there was a lot I could do with five dollars. I said, "Sure," and took the five and stuck it in my pocket and off I went, back up the road, standing on the pedals to get up speed.

When I got down to the creek things looked funny, somehow, and then I realized it was because I was used to seeing the red car sitting there by the trailer. Mr. Donovan's jeep was there, though. Good, I thought, maybe he'd give me a ride back to town.

But I didn't see him or Maddy anywhere, so I figured they must be up at the cave. I leaned the bike on its stand and started toward the creek, but then I stopped and looked back at the trailer. I really was dry from riding in the hot sun, and I knew Maddy wouldn't mind if I got myself a nice cold Coke first.

The generator motor was rattling away as I walked toward the trailer. I went up the little metal steps and saw that the door wasn't quite shut. I pushed it open and started to go in, but then I caught something moving out of the corner of my eye and I turned my head and saw them on the bed.

Mr. Donovan was lying on top of Maddy. Her legs were sticking up in the air and they were both sort of thrashing around. Neither of them had any clothes on.

I stood there for a minute or so, standing on the top step with my head and shoulders inside the door, just staring with my mouth open. They didn't look around. I don't think they were noticing much just then.

Finally I got myself unstuck and jumped down off the steps and ran, up the creek bank, not really looking where I was going, just getting away from that trailer. I felt sick and angry and ashamed and yet kind of excited too. My skin felt hot and not just from the sun.

I mean, I knew about what they were doing. I was thirteen, after all. But it just didn't look at *all* like I'd imagined.

I got my bike and wobbled off up the road, nearly falling a couple of times. At the top of the hill I remembered David's message, and the five dollars. So now he was going to think I'd cheated him, but I couldn't help that. I wouldn't have gone back down there for all the money in the United States.

Saturday night I woke up in the middle of a dream about Maddy and the skeleton—I don't want to tell about it, it was pretty awful—and sat up in bed, listening, the way you do when you don't know what woke you. It seemed like I could hear the echo of a big loud boom, and then a rumbling sound dying away. In the next room, Mama's voice said, "What was that?"

"Thunder," Daddy said. "Go back to sleep."

Next morning as we left for church I saw a lot of dust hanging over the road across Tobe Nelson's pasture, and what looked like a police car heading toward the creek. The dust was still there when we came home, but I didn't see any more cars.

Late in the afternoon while we were sitting on the porch Sheriff Cowan came by. "Afternoon," he said to Daddy. "Wonder if I could ask your boy a couple of questions. Don't worry, he's not in any trouble," he added, smiling at Mama.

Daddy said, "Raymond, answer the sheriff's questions."

Sheriff Cowan sat down on the edge of the porch and looked up at me. "I understand you've been spending a lot of time down by the creek lately. Been friendly with those friends of Mr. Donovan's?"

"He was," Daddy said, not giving me a chance to answer. "That's over."

"That right?" Sheriff Cowan raised one eyebrow. "Well, then I'm probably wasting my time. You haven't been down there in the last couple of days?"

"No, sir," I said.

"Oh, well." He let out a big loud sigh. "So much for that. Sorry to bother you folks."

Daddy said, "Mind if I ask what this is about?"

Sheriff Cowan turned his head and looked off across the valley. "Night before last, somebody broke into Huckaby's Feed and Supply and stole half a case of dynamite. Last night they used it to blow up that cave."

I said, "*What?*" and Mama made little astonished noises. Daddy said, "Well, I'll be damned."

Sheriff Cowan nodded. "Yep, did a pretty thorough job, too. The whole bluff's all busted up and caved in, great big chunks of rock every which way."

He took off his hat and scratched his head. "Tell you the truth, I can't hardly believe somebody did that much damage with half a case of DuPont stump-blower. It's strange," he said. "Tobe Nelson claimed there were two explosions, too, a little one and then a big one, but nobody else heard it that way." He shrugged. "Maybe some kind of gas in the ground there? Who knows?"

Mama said, "My Lord. Who would do such a thing?"

"Oh," Sheriff Cowan said, "there's no doubt in my mind who did it. But I don't expect I'll ever prove it."

Daddy said, "Floyd Haney."

"Yep. Nobody else around here that crazy and mean," Sheriff Cowan said. "And he was sure nursing a grudge about that land."

He stood up and put his hat back on. "But like I say, I'll never prove it. I thought maybe Raymond might have seen or heard something, but I should have known that was too much to hope for."

He chuckled down deep in his throat. "You know the funny part? He had all that work and risk for nothing. Those two scientists already pulled out."

"They're gone?" I said, louder than I meant to.

"Yep," Sheriff Cowan said. "Drove right through town, late

yesterday afternoon, pulling that trailer. So they must have found out there wasn't anything important there after all. Probably just some old animal bones or something."

"Probably," Daddy said. "Bunch of foolishness."

And that's about all there is to tell. David and Maddy never came back, and nobody else ever tried to find that cave again. Not that it would have done them any good. I went up into Moonshine Hollow once, a long time later, and the whole place was smashed up so bad you couldn't even tell where you were.

Mr. Donovan left too, that summer. He went back into the Marines and I heard he got killed in Korea, but I don't really know.

Wendell's daddy got caught with a stolen truck, later on that year, and got sent off to the penitentiary, where everybody said he belonged. Sheriff Cowan never did charge him with blowing up the cave, but he didn't make any secret of believing he did it.

And maybe he was right, but I wasn't so sure. My cousin Larry was working the evening shift at the Texaco station when David and Maddy stopped for gas on their way out of town, and he said Maddy was crying and it looked like she'd been roughed up some. And Aunt Ethel mentioned to Mama that David had been in the store on Saturday buying an alarm clock. But I never said anything to anybody.

People talked, for a while there, about that strange business in Moonshine Hollow. But it didn't last long. Everybody's mind was on the news from Korea, which was mostly bad, and then by next year all anybody wanted to talk about was the election. I guess by now I'm the only one who even remembers.

And sometimes I sure wish I didn't.

THE MASTERS SPEAK

INTRODUCTION

GARDNER DOZOIS

For the last several years, it's been customary for the editors of the Nebula Award anthologies to assemble a bunch of hot young Turks to have a symposium about the state of SF at the moment and its future, and that was my first thought as well when I was tapped to edit this year's volume. But then I remembered all the Nebula banquets I'd been to where I'd suffered through speeches by numbingly inappropriate or irrelevant guest speakers, and I remembered that on each of those occasions, I'd looked around the room and seen writers like Jack Williamson and Frederik Pohl sitting there looking politely bored as well, and that each time I'd thought: Why aren't we listening to *them,* instead of to this guy? With writers in the room who had been present at the very beginnings of science fiction as an individual genre, writers who knew what it was like to sell stories to Gernsback or Campbell or H. L. Gold, writers who had survived in a turbulent and changing market for almost the entire length of the twentieth century, why would an organization of professional writers want to listen to Hugh Downs instead?

So this year, I've decided to do something different with the symposium feature. Instead of tapping a group of hot young Turks, I decided to get some historical perspective by going to the Grand Masters instead, to see what they had to say about where the field has been, what it was like, what it's like now, what ground has been gained or lost in the process—and yes, where the genre may be going tomorrow.

So, then, following are a series of essays by a selection of the living Grand Masters: Jack Williamson, Robert Silverberg, Ursula K. Le Guin, Brian W. Aldiss, and Frederik Pohl. Between them, they have

289 years of experience in writing and selling science fiction! Which ought to be enough to earn them a few moments of our attention, eh?

Jack Williamson's career has stretched over an incredible seventy-seven years, from his first sale in 1928 to the present day. No science fiction writer has ever had a career arc that spanned a greater percentage of science fiction history (when Williamson was making his first sales, John W. Campbell's famous "Golden Age" at *Astounding*, now more than sixty years in the past, was still more than a decade in the future!), from the very start of the field's beginnings as a separate genre all the way through the twentieth century and into the twenty-first. During that career, Williamson has produced a steady stream of dozens of novels and hundreds of stories, and has been always in the forefront of the field as one of the genre's most acclaimed authors. His sequence of novels about the Legion of Space were among the highlights of the "superscience" era of the twenties and thirties just as his story "With Folded Hands" was one of the most famous stories of the Campbellian "Golden Age" mentioned above. His novels include *The Humanoids* (an expansion of "With Folded Hands"), *The Humanoid Touch, Darker Than You Think* (almost as important to the evolution of fantasy as *The Humanoids* was to SF), *The Legion of Space, The Legion of Time, The Queen of the Legion, The Black Sun, Demon Moon, The Trial of Terra, Firechild, Seetee Ship, Manseed, Beachhead,* and many others, including a long series of collaborative novels written with Frederik Pohl. His short fiction has been collected in *The Best of Jack Williamson, People Machines, The Early Williamson, The Pandora Effect, Dreadful Sleep, The Metal Man and Others: The Collected Stories of Jack Williamson, Volume One, Wolves of Darkness: The Collected Stories of Jack Williamson, Volume Two, Wizard's Isle: The Collected Stories of Jack Williamson, Volume Three,* and *Wizard's Isle: The Collected Stories of Jack Williamson, Volume Four.* He won the Hugo Award in 1985 for his autobiography, *Wonder's Child: My Life in Science Fiction,* and both Hugo and Nebula awards for his novella *The Ultimate Earth* in 2001. His most recent book is a massive retrospective collection *Seventy-Five: The Diamond Anniversary of a Science Fiction Pioneer,* and coming up is a new novel, *The Stonehenge Gate.* He was named SFFWA Grand Master in 1976.

Robert Silverberg is one of the most famous SF writers of modern times, with dozens of novels, anthologies, and collections to his credit. As both writer and editor, Silverberg continues to be at the forefront of the field to this very day, having won a total of five Nebula Awards and four Hugo Awards. His novels include the acclaimed *Dying Inside, Lord Valentine's Castle, The Book of Skulls, Downward to the Earth, Tower of Glass, Son of Man, Nightwings, The World Inside, Born with the Dead, Shadrack in the Furnace, Thorns, Up the Line, The Man in the Maze, Tom O' Bedlam, Star of Gypsies, At Winter's End, The Face of the Waters, Kingdoms of the Wall, Hot Sky at Morning, The Alien Years, Lord Prestimion,* and *Mountains of Majipoor.* His collections include *Unfamiliar Territory, Capricorn Games, Majipoor Chronicles, The Best of Robert Silverberg, At the Conglomeroid Cocktail Party, Beyond the Safe Zone,* and *The Secret Sharers.* His most recent books are the novel *The Long Way Home,* the mosaic novel *Roma Eterna,* and a massive retrospective collection, *Phases of the Moon: Stories from Six Decades.* He lives with his wife, writer Karen Haber, in Oakland, California. He was named SFFWA Grand Master in 2004.

Ursula K. Le Guin is probably one of the best-known and most universally respected SF writers in the world today. Her famous novel *The Left Hand of Darkness* may have been the most influential SF novel of its decade, and shows every sign of becoming one of the enduring classics of the genre. (Her 1968 fantasy novel, *A Wizard of Earthsea,* would be almost as influential on future generations of high fantasy and young adult writers.) *The Left Hand of Darkness* won both the Hugo and Nebula awards, as did Le Guin's monumental novel *The Dispossessed* a few years later. Her novel *Tehanu* won her another Nebula in 1990, and she has also won three other Hugo Awards and a Nebula Award for her short fiction, as well as the National Book Award for Children's Literature for her novel *The Farthest Shore,* part of her Earthsea trilogy. Her other novels include *Planet of Exile, The Lathe of Heaven, City of Illusions, Rocannon's World, The Beginning Place, A Wizard of Earthsea, The Tombs of Atuan, Tehanu, Searoad, Always Coming Home,* and *The Telling.* She has had eight collections: *The Wind's Twelve Quarters, Orsinian Tales, The Compass Rose, Buffalo Gals and Other Animal Presences, A Fisherman of the Inland Sea, Four Ways to Forgiveness, Tales of Earthsea,* and *The Birthday of the World.* Her most recent books are a collection of her critical essays, *The Wave in the Mind: Tales and Essays on the Reader, and the Imagination,* and a YA novel, *Gifts.* She lives with her husband in Portland, Oregon. She was named SFFWA Grand Master in 2003.

Brian W. Aldiss is one of the true giants of the field, someone who has been publishing science fiction for more than a quarter of a century, and has more than two dozen books to his credit. *The Long Afternoon of Earth* won a Hugo Award in 1962. "The Saliva Tree" won a Nebula Award in 1965, and Aldiss's novel *Starship* won the Prix Jules Verne in 1977. He took another Hugo Award in 1987 for his critical study of science fiction, *Trillion Year Spree*, written with David Wingrove. His other books include *An Island Called Moreau*, *Graybeard*, *Enemies of the System*, *A Rude Awakening*, *Life in the West*, *Forgotten Life*, *Dracula Unbound*, and *Remembrance Day*, and a memoir, *Bury My Heart at W. H. Smith's*, and an autobiography, *The Twinkling of an Eye, or, My Life as an Englishman*. His short fiction has been collected in *Space, Time, and Nathaniel*, *Who Can Replace a Man?*, *New Arrivals, Old Encounters*, *Galaxies Like Grains of Sand*, *Seasons in Flight*, and *Common Clay*, and he's published a collection of poems, *Home Life with Cats*. His many anthologies include *The Penguin Science Fiction Omnibus*, and, with Harry Harrison, *Decade: the 1940s*, *Decade: the 1950s*, and *Decade: the 1960s*. His latest books are two new novels, *Affairs at Hampden Ferrers* and *Jocasta*. Coming up are a new collection, *Cultural Breaks*, and a new novel, *Sanity and the Lady*. He lives in Oxford. He was named SFFWA Grand Master in 2000.

Frederik Pohl is a seminal figure whose career spans almost the entire development of modern SF, having been one of the genre's major shaping forces—as writer, editor, agent, and anthologist—for more than fifty years. He was the founder of the Star series, SF's first continuing anthology series, and was the editor of the *Galaxy* group of magazines from 1960 to 1969, during which time *Galaxy*'s sister magazine, *Worlds of If*, won three consecutive Best Professional Magazine Hugos. As a writer, he won both Hugo and Nebula awards for his novel *Gateway*, has also won the Hugo for his stories "The Meeting" (a collaboration with C. M. Kornbluth) and "Fermi and Frost," and won an additional Nebula for his novel *Man Plus*; he has also won the American Book Award and the French Prix Apollo. His many books include several written in collaboration with the late C. M. Kornbluth—including *The Space Merchants*, *Wolfbane*, and *Gladiator-at-Law*—and many solo novels, including the award-winning *Gateway* and *Man Plus*, *Beyond the Blue Event Horizon*, *The Coming of the Quantum Cats*, *Mining the Oort*, *O Pioneer!*, *The Siege of Eternity*, and *The Far Shore of Time*. Among his many collections are *The Gold at the Star-*

bow's End, In the Problem Pit, and The Best of Frederik Pohl. His most recent books are the novel The Boy Who Would Live Forever, and a massive retrospective collection, Platinum Pohl. He lives in Palatine, Illinois, with his wife, writer Elizabeth Ann Hull. He was named SFFWA Grand Master in 1993.

SCIENCE FICTION CENTURY

JACK WILLIAMSON

The editor asked me to contribute a thumbnail sketch of the field as I've seen it change since 1926, when I discovered the classics of Jules Verne, H. G. Wells, and Edgar Allan Poe, along with the best of A. Merritt and Edgar Rice Burroughs, reprinted by Hugo Gernsback in the early issues of Amazing Stories. The genre had yet to find a name. In 1928 Gernsback printed my own first story as "scientifiction." He coined the term "science fiction" in 1929 for the contents of his new Science Wonder Stories.

The genre itself, of course, was hardly new. Its beginnings go back beyond Wells and Verne to Mary Shelley and Jonathan Swift, even to The Odyssey. Through the first half of the century, American science fiction was shaped by a few influential magazine editors. There were yet no regular book markets; novels were generally published as magazine serials.

One long-forgotten but once legendary editor was Bob Davis, at Argosy and other Monsey pulps, which ran the work of Burroughs, Merritt, and Ray Cummings as "unusual" or "different" stories. Cummings had been the lab assistant of Thomas Alva Edison. Davis launched him on a long pulp career when he got him to rewrite Wells's Time Machine into a lost-race romance, The Girl in the Golden Atom, his most notable work.

Gernsback himself was no such editor, though the Hugos were named to honor him as "the father of science fiction." He did name the field. Reprinting the classics in Amazing, he found a modern readership for it. Contemporary critics are apt to call him a pernicious influence, but actually I think he had almost no editorial influence at all.

Never creative, he rejected the first stories I sent him without comment, and printed later stories still with no comment except blurbs for the reader. Even as publisher he was finally a failure. He never paid a prevailing rate for new work, sometimes nothing at all. When he owed me for a hundred thousand words, at a promised half a cent, I had to get a lawyer to collect. Yet, like a few other beginners, I felt happy to get into print for anything at all.

Such pulp editors as Harry Bates and Desmond Hall were far more influential. Bates was the founding editor of *Astounding Stories of Super Science* for the Clayton pulp chain in 1930, Hall the first editor at Street and Smith, which took it over after Clayton failed. They paid real money. In those depression times, two cents a word for my first stories for *Astounding* and five hundred for a novelette in the Clayton *Strange Tales* made me rich for a day.

Street and Smith cut the rate to one cent, good money then, roughly equal to ten cents today. Gernsback preached the value of the genre as sugarcoating for science, though nothing stopped him from republishing Merritt's "Moon Pool," a dreamlike fantasy with no science at all. Bates and his fellow pulp editors cared nothing for science and little for literary excellence, but their influence was far more positive.

Their money went for stories that would sell their magazines. Stories with beginning, middle, and end. Stories generally about likable people overcoming difficult odds. The *Harper's* editor Bernard DeVoto called it "sub-literate trash." Much of it was, but Sturgeon's law applies. Isaac Asimov made a collection of stories worth reprinting in *Before the Golden Age*.

"The Golden Age" was a sudden flowering of the genre beginning when John W. Campbell became an editor at *Astounding* in 1937. He knew science and cared about it. A skeptical critic of conservative orthodoxy, he looked at possible worlds to come with an active imagination. Though apt to fall for crackpot ideas, he cherished a magnificent vision of the human future.

He breathed a fresh life into science fiction, finding and inspiring a whole generation of able writers, among them Asimov, Robert Heinlein, and A. E. van Vogt. His dream of the conquest of space is perhaps expressed most vividly in the dozen young adult novels Heinlein wrote for *Scribner's,* beginning with two kids building a rocket in their backyard and ending in *Have Space Suit, Will Travel,* with the hero negotiating with the Lords of the Three Galaxies for the admission of the human race into civilization.

In translation, the same dream inspired German fans as well as American, leading to V2 rockets, ballistic missiles, men on the moon, and the world as we know it. World War II marks a watershed in the history of science fiction. Gernsback had opened it to a new generation of readers. The pulp editors trained a new generation of writers. Campbell inspired them with his vision of future human greatness. The war wiped it out.

Back in the last decade of the 1800s, Wells had painted a darker future when he dramatized the limits to progress in his great early work. The world ignored his warning. The worship of technology went on, inspiring rocket engineers and many others. I attended the Century of Progress exposition in Chicago in the 1930s, and saw my first television at the world fair in New York. The future could look golden.

Pearl Harbor changed everything. Technology unsheathed its sharper edge. In the shadow of the mushroom cloud, the old dream of endless progress toward some peaceful utopia faded into Cold War hysteria. Grisly mutants came to haunt the short story, and post-holocaust novels were published by the score.

Campbell's influence faded when L. Ron Hubbard converted him to Dianetics. Other able editors appeared: Horace Gold, with his own pessimistic vision in *Galaxy*, Tony Boucher with *Fantasy and Science Fiction* and an eye for traditional literary values that steered the genre toward the mainstream.

Yet no new editor has dominated the field as Campbell did. The sands are always shifting. The magazines themselves are now in danger. Book markets opened after the war, when fans began setting up their own small presses to reprint the serials they had loved. Major publishers followed, with their editors making new demands and helping new writers to find new voices. Film and TV created new audiences for hybrid "sci-fi." No longer American, science fiction became international.

Back in the 1930s we could know everybody and read everything. The field has now diversified too widely for any single perspective. Scores of writers have found circles of fans who may read little else. On one side science fiction is merging into fantasy and horror, on the other into sci-fi and the mainstream, with a robust corps of the old school still standing in the middle. It has grown too far for any simple description. Its future seems impossible to predict.

Literary forms are shaped by technologies of communication, and change as they change. Homer's epics were composed in verse to be memorized for oral transmission. The invention of writing gave permanence to prose. The novel was invented for the printing press. The short story was born in mass magazines and orphaned when TV claimed the audience for sitcoms. Yet no genre is gone forever, and literature is left richer for the growing variety.

The effects of the information revolution are not yet clear. Worldwide communication is cheaper and faster. Literacy should become universal. The e-book may be perfected. Electronic "paper" could save forests and alter every aspect of our culture. Copyright law may change. The economics of distribution certainly will. The roles of editor and publisher as well, though they can hardly be replaced.

Science fiction itself was a child of changing technology. New technologies have always reshaped culture and society, but beginning at a glacial rate, hardly noticed until the time of Jonathan Swift, a stout defender of the past. Gulliver's flying island of Laputa was his horrified response to the dawn of modern science and the creation of the Royal Society. Mary Shelley's idea for the animation of Frankenstein's monster must have come from Volta's experiments with frog legs. New technologies seem now about to bury the globe beneath an avalanche of change. We are left to wait and wonder at what is to come. Speculative fiction will surely live on.

THE WAY IT WAS

ROBERT SILVERBERG

It was all very different once upon a time, of course. In the old days, fifty-some years ago, the magazines were the center of the whole thing—the soul of science fiction, as Barry Malzberg has said. The magazines were where nearly all science fiction was published, and the magazine editors were the suns around which we orbited. The Hugos hadn't been invented yet, in that far-off antique era, nor the Nebulas, nor, for that matter, the Science Fiction Writers of America itself; and what I dreamed of then was not anything like getting a book on the *New York Times* best-seller list, or winning an award, or being named a Grand Master—that last one would have been a fantasy too absurd to waste a moment's mental energy on, even if such an honor had existed then—but simply selling a short story, just one story, to any of the magazines. That was the big career-launching breakthrough that any would-be writer of the era yearned for—selling a story to one of the magazines.

By which I meant, back there around 1952, magazines named *Startling Stories* or *Thrilling Wonder Stories* or *Planet Stories;* or, more probably, the lowest-paying market in the field, *Future Science Fiction.* As the gaudy names of most of them indicate, they were pulp magazines, crudely printed on cheap, shaggy paper that left bits of itself all over your lap as you read them, and their bright, flashy, posterlike covers, showing wide-eyed brass-brassiered maidens being menaced by monsters or robots, were no more than half a notch up from comic-book covers in artistic quality. Those few disreputable-looking pulp magazines were the bastions that novices like me dreamed of storming: what we would think of today the entry-level markets.

There were, it's true, a couple of magazines even pulpier than those—the Ziff-Davis pair, *Amazing Stories* and *Fantastic Adventures,* two bulky monthlies devoted to the publication of simple adventure fiction. But I had already discovered, by dint of sending stories to them over a period of two or three years and getting them all back with the speed of light, that they were entirely staff-written, and paid no attention whatever to submissions from the outside. Also there was what we called the Big Three—a trio of elite non-pulp magazines, neat little jobs, dignified in look and manner, published in what was called the "digest" format because it was the size that *The Reader's Digest,* the dominant general-circulation magazine of the day, employed. I had slightly more hope of selling to one of them than I did to *Amazing* or *Fantastic,* because the editors of all three did, at least, read unsolicited submissions with some degree of sympathy. But I knew I wasn't likely, at the age of sixteen or thereabouts, to be pushing Theodore Sturgeon or Hal Clement or A. E. van Vogt aside on the contents page of John Campbell's austerely intellectual *Astounding Science Fiction,* nor did I have the polished narrative technique that Horace Gold demanded for his shiny new *Galaxy Science Fiction,* or the sophistication and literary breadth required by Anthony Boucher and J. F. McComas for *Fantasy and Science Fiction.* If I was ever going to make that first sale, I was going to have to make it to one of the pulps.

You'll note that I say nothing about book publishers. It was entirely a short-story market then. A little hardback science fiction was being published by the children's-book houses, where I would, in fact, make my first big sale in 1954. But when it came to adult science fiction there were, essentially, just two book publishers, each doing, at most, a book or two a month. Doubleday was the established leader, but its list was strictly top-echelon: Ray Bradbury, Robert A. Heinlein, John Wyndham, Isaac Asimov. Not for another few years would writers of merely middling fame like Edgar Pangborn, Poul Anderson, and Jack Vance be getting published there, and they certainly had no interest in beginners like me. The other major house, just getting started in 1952, was Ballantine Books, but at the outset it, too, was publishing the likes of Bradbury and Wyndham, along with such other big-name writers as Arthur C. Clarke, Frederik Pohl, Theodore Sturgeon, and one gifted newcomer who was making a spectacular splash that year, Robert Sheckley. We also had a handful of semi-pro houses—Fantasy Press, Shasta Press, etc.—but those concentrated mostly on reprinting classic magazine material of earlier years. For most science fiction writers of those early postwar days, selling a novel to a major publisher was a little like winning the lottery. It did happen to people now and then, yes, but counting on it wasn't a smart career plan. Nearly everyone who hoped to earn some substantial fraction of his livelihood from writing science fiction, or was already doing so, looked to the magazines for his income, and (to minimize the risks inherent in putting in many months writing a novel and finding no taker for it) concentrated on short stories and novelets.

It's all so different today. *Astounding Science Fiction* is still with us, transmogrified into *Analog,* and so is *Fantasy and Science Fiction,* and alongside them is a newcomer of 1970s vintage, *Asimov's Science Fiction.* Those are today's Big Three. Then there's a fantasy magazine—*Realms of Fantasy*—and some titles like *Absolute Magnitude* that have been fighting their way up from semi-pro status, and a host of electronic "magazines," of which the best-known is Ellen Datlow's *SCI FICTION.* A list like that makes it appear that magazine science fiction is still a thriving operation, but what it actually is is a ghostly relic of its former self. The surviving magazines are all minor players in the vast, hectic marketplace that is modern SF. Even the top ones have only modest circulations, and the others are largely the work of publishers and writers who must be considered devoted hobbyists, amateurs in the best sense of that word. The real action is in the book field. And from the point of view of the reader seriously concerned with science fiction as an art form, or even the writer with the same concerns, it's mostly the wrong kind of action.

One big difference between today's book-centered SF world and the magazine-centered world of fifty years ago is that book publishing is almost entirely sales-driven, magazine publishing much less so. Oh, of course, magazines had to maintain a certain sales level or they would go under, as did *Space Science Fiction* and *Marvel Science Fiction* and *Dynamic Science Fiction* and many another ephemeral title of the early fifties. But once a magazine succeeded in establishing a modestly profitable basic level of circulation, the main task of its editor was just to keep the core readership happy by providing, month after month, the sort of fiction it seemed to prefer. The habit of regular purchase was easily instilled—everybody knew the right time of month to find the new *Astounding* or *Galaxy* on the newsstands—and that devoted cadre of faithful month-by-month buyers, along with a considerable nucleus of annual subscribers for, at least, the top three, allowed the most shrewdly edited magazines to survive for years.

But each book that is published today is an individual entity that must stand or fall on its own pulling power. Perhaps the name of the author provides that power—a *lot* of people will buy any new book by X or Y—or, if the author isn't a brand name, perhaps a provocative blurb will do the job, or a powerful cover painting, such as the celebrated one Michael Whelan did for Heinlein's *Friday*. (Not that Heinlein needed anybody's painting to pull in the readers, but the sexy Whelan painting certainly was a plus.) Nobody, though, except a fanatic collector decides to buy a book simply because its publisher is Tor or Del Rey or Roc. There is almost no way for a publisher to create the sort of brand continuity that the old magazines could, when readers looked for a familiar magazine name, even a familiar logotype or cover format, without caring particularly about what stories were likely to be in any one issue. They knew they could be confident of getting *something* they'd want to read. The only way a paperback publisher can achieve something similar is to make each new book resemble all the previous titles of its line in format and content—the Harlequin Books approach—and while this tactic has been marginally successful on occasion, it is no recipe for producing great science fiction. And it is essentially impossible for a hardcover house to do anything of that sort.

So each new book usually stands alone, unsheltered by the other titles its publisher may have issued, and if it sells badly, its author will very quickly find himself in commercial trouble, because everybody knows everybody else's sales figures. One conspicuous failure from a big house can doom a writer in the eyes of the book-chain buyers for years to come. And if a publishing house puts out a long string of books that sell badly, not just the writers will be in trouble. Editors and higher-level executives will lose their jobs.

Caution, therefore, is the watchword in the book field. Publish wisely; publish warily; take no chances, because your job may be at stake. Editors rightly abjure risk. Artistic risk means commercial risk; commercial risk means trouble.

Once in a while an innovative novelist like William Gibson will come along, yes, and turn everything upside down with a single book. But books of that sort are rare, and it takes a courageous editor to take a chance on publishing them. Gibson emerged because one brave editor managed to create a whole line of innovative SF novels—Terry Carr's Ace Science Fiction Specials—that also gave us outstanding pathbreaking work by Joanna Russ, R. A. Lafferty, Ursula K. Le Guin, D. G. Compton, and others of that ilk. But the specials were a kind of loss leader for Ace, which made its real money doing action SF of the old pulp kind. The fact is that such books as *Neuromancer* and *Left Hand of Darkness* also happened to turn out to be tremendous commercial properties, but would any of today's paperback editors have taken a chance on publishing them if they turned up in manuscript form now? They will, of course, all loudly insist that they would, but that's with the advantage of twenty-twenty hindsight, which provides an awareness of the immense fame and influence that the books of Le Guin and Gibson have gathered over the years, and their huge sales figures. I'm not so sure, remembering as I do that Le Guin was a little-known writer of paperback originals and one still-obscure Earthsea novel in 1969 when *Left Hand* came along, and that *Neuromancer,* in 1984, was the almost unknown Gibson's first novel. Both are challenging books. I can think of a couple of modern-day editors who might be willing to gamble on books like that as unheralded new properties—but only a couple.

The science fiction magazines of the 1950s were not greatly sympathetic to trailblazing material either, but it's important to remember that in the 1950s most of the SF magazines still were pitched to the primarily young and unsophisticated pulp-magazine readership, and that the Eisenhower era was not, in general, a time of brave literary experimentation. Still, the editors of some well-established magazines could afford to take risks from time to time, knowing that a single unusual story wasn't likely to drive their entire readership away. Thus

Fantasy and Science Fiction was willing to devote a couple of pages to Richard Matheson's strange, haunting first story, "Born of Man and Woman," in 1950, though no one would have touched a book written in that tone of voice. Campbell and Gold both rejected Philip José Farmer's taboo-breaking "The Lovers," but Sam Mines of *Starting Stories* used it as the lead novella in a 1952 issue and turned Farmer into a famous SF writer then and there. Robert W. Lowndes made room for such unusual James Blish stories as "Testament of Andros" and "Common Time" in his low-paying pulp.

I could provide many other examples. The stories that Ray Bradbury was doing throughout the 1940s and 1950s were very different from standard pulp-magazine fare, but pulp editors recognized their power and slipped them into their magazines anyway. So too with the work of Theodore Sturgeon, Fritz Leiber, C. M. Kornbluth, and, a decade later, Harlan Ellison and Barry Malzberg: they all ignored the pulp formulas and got published anyway. The reader who didn't care for their radical work would find something else more to his taste elsewhere in the same issue. (I don't mean to imply, of course, that *any* unconventional or experimental story would find a market easily back then. As I've already noted, Farmer's "Lovers" had a hard time getting into print. Cordwainer Smith's "Scanners Live in Vain" was rejected everywhere until a semi-pro magazine called *Fantasy Book* finally picked it up. My own bleak, pessimistic "Road to Nightfall" bounced around for four years before one of the minor magazines agreed to print it. But at least all three stories did get printed eventually.)

By fits and starts, then, the evolution of science fiction away from its pulp antecedents continued throughout the 1950s and 1960s, first in the shorter forms, then in the explosion of brilliant novels of what we now call the New Wave period, 1967 or so through the early 1970s. Most of those New Wave novels didn't sell very well, alas. Before long some editors were getting their pink slips: those who had not been able to see that although one or two experimental stories tucked into an issue of a monthly magazine could do no real harm, a whole line of books, each sent out to make its way on its own and failing, could be a major financial disaster for their company. A few paperback houses and most hardcover ones withdrew from SF entirely. Which led, quite rationally and appropriately, to the play-it-safe attitude that typifies science fiction publishing today.

What we have now in SF is a largely derivative enterprise. Serving up familiar stuff, not breaking new paths, is the primary goal. The trilogy is the standard publishing unit. What is now termed a "standalone" book is considered risky. The hope of the publishers is to get a series going—the Dune books, the Foundation books, the Pern books, the Ender books—and make a "franchise" out of it, extending it indefinitely, often even beyond the lifetime of the original writer. A big media-related series—*Star Trek* novels, *Star Wars* novels—is, of course, the ultimate jackpot. The books themselves observe rigid conventions of format—the huge lettering, the space-battle illustrations—that hearken back to the old pulp days. And, perhaps most troublesome of all, even those books that are not part of some established series are given spurious links to previous best-selling titles by other writers with that appalling and preposterous cover line, "In the tradition of . . ."

Some of the traditions thus proclaimed are strangely desperate ones. The one closest to my heart was emblazoned on a fantasy novel of a decade or so ago: "In the tradition of Stephen Donaldson, David Eddings, and Robert Silverberg." Perhaps more unlikely yokings could be conceived—"In the tradition of J.R.R. Tolkien, Clifford D. Simak, and Philip K. Dick," say, or "In the tradition of Lois McMaster Bujold, Neil Gaiman, and Avram Davidson," a nice party game for late at night, but still—Donaldson, Eddings, Silverberg?

In any case this whole business of "traditions," proudly advertising the derivative nature of the product being marketed, is pernicious. Imagine a magazine of the 1950s splashing this on its cover: "A new novella by James Blish . . . closely imitating Robert A. Heinlein and Isaac Asimov." Not likely. We each wanted to be writing in our own traditions, not someone else's. Since we all read the magazines, and discussed their contents among ourselves, there was, of course, that ongoing dialog among writers, that colloquium of ideas—Heinlein would toss in waldos, Sturgeon would give us synergy, Blish genetic modification, or Campbell would send *Astounding* off on some new thematic tangent and ask us to dream up our own variations on it—but when we picked up those themes and worked with them ourselves, as we inevitably had to do for the sake of employing up-to-date furniture in our stories, we tried to deal with them in our own ways, not produce imitation Heinlein or Sturgeon or Blish. Anything too blatantly written in someone else's tradition would get a quick rejection from editors who knew that their readers weren't interested in secondhand merchandise. But today, when marketing is all, derivative is good.

What we had back then, and don't have now, was a small—*very* small—publishing universe in which science fiction was dominated by a handful of magazine editors, powerful creative figures who gathered a nucleus of regular contributors around them, nurtured and encouraged them, guided them, and sponsored a continuous conceptual dialog that led to the steady growth of the ideational foundations of the field. Most of us lived in or around New York City, then— something else that has changed—and not only did the writers know one another, they dropped in frequently at the editorial offices (all but the office of the Boucher-McComas team, which was in Berkeley, California) and maintained close personal relationships with the men who actually bought their stories. So we all talked about that lead novelette in last month's *Astounding,* or the flabbergasting novel by Alfred Bester that Horace Gold had just serialized in *Galaxy,* or the utterly original stuff that Phil Farmer was selling to *Startling* and *Thrilling Wonder.* And I was able to learn at first hand of John Campbell's latest intellectual hobbyhorses, I got vitriolic but valuable tongue-lashings from the voluble and impassioned Horace Gold, and I helped out such editors as Bob Lowndes and Larry T. Shaw when they came up a story or two short as deadlines approached, all this before I was twenty-five. Whenever I began getting too cocky for my own good, as early success will cause one to do, there was some older colleague like Fred Pohl or Lester del Rey on hand to set me straight in a kindly dutch-uncle way.

It's not like that any more. The field has no coherent center. There are too many publishers, too many writers, too many books hitting the stores every month. There are no editorial titans like Campbell and Gold and Boucher. Modern-day editors, by and large, are young and harried, frantically trying to find enough publishable material to fill their huge lists and making their editorial decisions, mostly, on the basis of potential sales figures and "traditions." The closest thing we have to a coherent center is the *Locus* best-seller list. That tells us what to imitate; it doesn't tell us how to forge our own way. Meanwhile the books pour out by the hundreds. No one could possibly keep track of them all: the *Locus* list of upcoming books is pages and pages and pages of small type every three months. I miss the old organic coherence of the field I grew up in, when the appearance of a new magazine (*If, Fantastic, Infinity*) brought excitement and promise, and when the emergence of a dazzling new writer (Philip K. Dick, Wyman Guin, Philip José Farmer) was the subject of immediate ubiquitous discussion.

And yet . . . and yet . . .

I'm not really advocating a return to the time when that handful of dominant and very forceful editors, a couple of whom verged on being tyrants, ran the SF world, and the only way a science fiction writer could earn a living was to turn out dozens of short stories a year, for fees of fifty to four hundred dollars apiece, while keeping a watchful eye on each editor's special "slant." That was a tough, practically impossible thing to do, and only a dozen or so were able to manage it. Most writers were part-timers with outside jobs, like Blish or Asimov or Clement. Even the few full-time pros in the field usually lived the most marginal of lives: you would be amazed to learn what the annual incomes of such great writers as Theodore Sturgeon, Philip K. Dick, and Fritz Leiber were back then. (Heinlein and Clarke did well, on sales to the slick magazines and royalties from big book publishers; but those were fields closed to all but a few. Ellison, Anderson, and I had decent incomes also, but that was only by dint of inordinate prolificity, a jillion words a year at two cents a word. Dick was very prolific too, of course, but his output could never keep up with the high price of divorce.)

Things are a lot better today, economically speaking. It's a huge market, and those writers who manage to establish themselves as novelists with faithful audiences can depend on selling a book or two a year forever, with none of the uncertainties involved in submitting short stories on spec to Campbell or Gold or Boucher, hoping that somebody like Lowndes would catch them (for one-third as much) if they bounced. As noted above, hardly anyone made a living wage in science fiction fifty years ago. Today there are vast platoons of full-time writers earning decent, if unspectacular, livings, and some writers make a lot of money indeed. There are also hundreds and hundreds of part-timers now whose stories and novels get published with fair regularity and who can legitimately regard themselves as professionals. I can only regard that as a positive development. Plenty of worthwhile books and stories are published every year, too, and a few great ones, though it's harder to find them in today's world of megapublishing than it was when the total monthly ouput of published science fiction was less than half a million words. Of course, there's a lot of conformity to established norms, an enormous amount of derivative work being produced, but that's only to be expected in such a vast field that needs huge quantities of material each month to sustain its own momentum. And if you don't like writing in other people's traditions nowadays, or want to try literary experiments that are clearly not going to reap immense sales, there's a vigorous small-press cosmos available, both in conventional print format and, now, online as well. All in all, it's not a ghastly time to be a science-fiction writer. It is just not a time conducive to the production of stunning work like *The Stars My Destination* or *West of the Sun* or *More Than Human* or *Fahrenheit 451,* to mention just four novels of the glorious early fifties.

I know that the kind of SF world we had fifty years ago isn't going to come back. That just isn't possible, in today's bigger and noisier time, and I wouldn't even want it to. A return to the diminished publishing conditions of the old days would mean disaster for 98 percent of today's science fiction writers, for one thing. And it probably would come about only as a result of some general economic cataclysm that I have no desire to see.

Even so, I look back fondly at that little village that SF once was, where all of us, readers and writers both, knew what was going on all the time. We could see the boundaries of the field and we knew how we wanted to expand them, and thought we could do it. As the evolution of science fiction occurred, month by month, we perceived it happening, and to the best of our abilities we each helped that evolution along. Today, when so much is being published that nothing attains much visibility for long, and the great mass of mediocre work churned out every month crowds out excellence, it's quite possible that a writer of the originality of Farmer or Sturgeon could arise and work in utter obscurity for a decade or more before most of us had heard about him. Even when some brilliant new book or story comes along that might cause the rest of us to reevaluate our whole approach to the concepts and techniques of science fiction, it is buried by the inexorable tonnage of material that the following month brings, and within a year or two it is forgotten.

We were heading somewhere exciting fifty years ago, as American science fiction began to emerge from its pulp-magazine origins. I don't think we managed to get there. In the United States today, SF is just a branch of commercial fiction that tends to be regarded by discerning mainstream readers as nothing more than silly stuff for kids.

There's a good reason for that, too: All too many of the hundreds of books a year that bear the SF label offer a commodity that's only slightly evolved beyond the old *Captain Future* sort of thing, evil empires and mad robots and swaggering space-pirates. I can't help but regard that as a sad situation. We had hopes, once, of making it into something more than that.

TEACHING THE ART

URSULA K. LE GUIN

All old writers of SF are self-taught. We didn't take courses in writing SF, because there weren't any. Most of us didn't take courses in writing anything, because they were lectures by asses with egos. We learned how to write SF by reading it—still the basic requirement—and then imitating, as all artists do, till we got the hang of it. (Anybody who really suffers from the anxiety of influence has no business being a writer. He should go invent the wheel.)

This primitive anarchy was changed by a revolutionary discovery—the first valid method of teaching writing as an art. It's now the method used, on all levels, everywhere, and has almost totally replaced the asses with egos. I don't know whether it actually first appeared in Robin Wilson's peer-group SF workshops in Clarion, Pennsylvania, but I met it as the Clarion Method, and saw it used only much later in "mainstream" workshops and writing programs. Its basic ploy is to have everyone write, read one another's work, and critique, under strict and simple rules, with a professional writer as facilitator. The group dynamic is central, and very powerful. The pro's experience is accessible, but the system eliminates the asinine lecture and helps minimize ego trips. It builds both critical and self-critical capacity and toughens the young writer's delicate hide. It is a most extraordinary teaching device. If it came out of SF, as it seems to have, we should be boasting about it.

I was introduced to it, as the pro facilitator, in the first Clarion workshop, which was in Seattle in 1971. I had no experience teaching anything but French. Vonda N. McIntyre (who had been at the 1970 workshop in Clarion, Pennsylvania, and was running the show, while trying to grow teratoma cells in vitro in her other life) explained how it worked to me. And even with a terrified amateur in charge who didn't know an epiphany from the *passé composé,* it worked. The twenty of them were better writers at the end of my week. They were better writers yet at the end of six weeks.

They were mostly male, that first group. In those first Clarions, women were few, and they often had a hard time of it. One of them had been savaged by the pro the week before me (no method can prevent an ass from kicking) and couldn't write at all. (When the famous Iowa Writing School was taught entirely by Great Men, a common effect it had on the few women allowed to attend it was to keep them from writing, for years after, or forever. Some of the Great Men boasted about it.) Another young woman had wandered in from the UW English Department's Creative Writing program and didn't have a clue what the hell FTL was, but she was game. You had to be game, if you were a woman, because guys ruled SF, okay? This is a man's world, ma'am. You go back and teach kindergarten now. Some of the tough guys couldn't handle critiques from woman workshoppers at all. What they really wanted was to take orders from a man.

They were also mostly pretty young.

That's all changed strikingly in the decades since. Clarion students now are at least half and sometimes predominantly women, and they're mostly over thirty.

Another thing that's changed is that SF is taught not only at the two Clarion workshops but also in writing classes and programs in respectable, even distinguished colleges and universities. Not all of them—only the intelligent ones. There are many creative writing programs in which SF is still on an Index of Loathly and Prohibited Genres. When I taught fiction writing at an undergraduate college in the upper Midwest some years ago, my students told me they were forbidden to write anything but realism, unless they could convince the professors that it was magic realism. I immediately demanded that they write me a romance, a fantasy or SF or horror story, a mystery, or a Western. The poor kids were so intimidated they had a hard time with the assignment, though there was one good ghost, and a girl wrote an excellent nursy romance. Mostly they couldn't handle love at all, only sex. That had to do with being undergraduates. The department had another rule, which sounded arbitrary but made sense: You couldn't end a story with a murder. They had to have the rule or all the boys would end all their stories with murders, because they didn't know how else to stop. (*Stop me, stop meee . . .*)

I came out of this and other experiences with the belief that people under twenty are probably too young for any serious fiction-writing class, unless it focuses on deliberate imitation and on basic technique (sentence structure, syntax, and other stuff kids no longer learn in school).

I also feel that going to a high-powered workshop like Clarion before about age twenty-five is risky. The competition can be over-whelming; and the emphasis on publication, on a narrowly defined commercial professionalism, may be really destructive to a tentative, insecure originality.

There of course arises the big question about the Clarion work-shops in SF, as about the huge proliferation of writing programs in the mainstream. The method has been proven: It can increase a writer's confidence and skill. The contact with professionals is challenging and often exciting, and working with fellow writers can be a discov-ery of real fellowship. The experience, for many students (and teach-ers), both socially and artistically, is rewarding. And the publication rate of ex-Clarion students is amazingly high. But what kind of writ-ing is coming out of these programs? If commercial publication is the standard, what's published is likely to be ever more standardized. If what will sell easily is the highest goal to aim at, the target is going to sag pretty low. Do we need a rebirth of anarchy?

CHANGE AND OKAY IN ALL AROUND I SEE

BRIAN W. ALDISS

At an early age, I was reading H. G. Wells and Weird Tales, and almost anything that represented this world as differing from the one I perforce inhabited. I became really engaged with magazine science fiction when, or shortly after, John W. Campbell took over the editorship of *Astounding*. SF fandom was then still en-gaged in Gernsback worship, enthralled by H. P. Lovecraft, and de-lighted by tales with titles like, "The Gnurrs Come from the Woodwork Out." I speak here of U.S. fandom, since British fandom was belly-up proletarian, ruled by a writer called E. C. Tubb, who brewed his own alcoholic drinks.

Four men have markedly changed the course of science fiction (if indeed "course" has meaning in this context): Hugo Gernsback, John

W. Campbell, Michael Moorcock, and Philip K. Dick. Oh, and I suppose one must add J.R.R. Tolkien, but he lies beyond my brief. Gernsback formed SF fandom, which remains a powerful and a unique institution. Such was the Gernsback effect that many readers of his magazine—whom I conceive of as largely unlettered blue-collar workers—believed him to have invented SF single-handedly. That was certainly never the case; indeed, it would be miserable to think that SF had crawled out of those cheap magazines, those horror-oriented yearns. "Moon of Mad Atavism" indeed!

It was Campbell who gathered real able writers to his magazine, Campbell who instructed and inspired them, who was indefatigable. True, yes, that all arteries harden in the end, but Campbell was a real-life force for many years and umpteen stories. He reigned supreme until other magazines came along, notably *Galaxy* and *The Magazine of Fantasy & Science Fiction,* both edited by intelligent men who knew one end of a sentence from the other.

Michael Moorcock was a fantasy writer who woke one morning to find himself editing *New Worlds*. His was a divine discontent. Out went the old shags; in bustled the new mob. Americans found the (I utter the words with caution) New Wave alarming. Here were stories about men going no longer to Mars but shortly to bed, speaking not in corny lingo but of cunnilingus! Here was a new vision of the future as arriving today, of all as now, now as all, and of style as well as substance.

Those thrilling days! You felt the difference. Charles Platt, standing barefoot in Notting Hill, sold copies of *New Worlds* to the bemused populace. (This was the sixties, when the people themselves were changing and the miniskirt was the newly hoisted female flag.) The old drunken orgies, the old ragged lads that secretly hated the new, those staples hitherto of British cons, were swept away. A new, bright, engaged generation swept in. And gradually America too changed, in the same computer-savvy direction.

So to the fourth bringer of changes, Philip K. Dick. Dick was no Robert Heinlein. I had fallen under the spell of Heinlein, like many another reader. My first SF novel, *Non-Stop* (wretchedly marketed by Criterion as *Starship*) had as its inspiration Heinlein's "Universe," the story of generations imprisoned in a starship. I was enthralled by "Universe"; it echoed my life, when I felt myself imprisoned in circumstances not of my own creation. This was SF as metaphor. I wanted to paint it with emotion, with heart, showing the humor and

tragedy—not merely the rough stuff—of people involved in this cos-
mic trap.

Is it not true of Heinlein that he was . . . well, *unfeeling,* caught up
in his own narcissism, which became more pronounced as time went
by? While his big, brash heroes swaggered to the heights of Heinlein's
popularity, Philip K. Dick was writing of the fallen, the unheroic. A
parallel prompts us here. During the Italian Renaissance, when the
grandeur and heroism of the adult male was being extolled in statuary
and canvas and fresco, a Flemish painter, Pieter Brueghel, went to
Rome and Florence to see what was going on, only to return to
Antwerp to create the most striking and meaningful depictions of
peasant life ever achieved. So, Dick in California gave us unforget-
table pictures of the humble, the artificers, the people with success
and even reality leaking from their lives.

Gradually, this vision—wistful, weird, wired, wacky, wondrous to
behold—superceded the Heinleinian world-shatterers. More truth-
ful? Your judgment depends on your temperament—and your drug
bill.

Perhaps a word about Tolkien, or his followers. SF used to have a
little sister, pearls in her hair, called Fantasy. Fantasy grew up to be a
big tough lass and to rule the roost. She cleared herself a space among
the hardware for magic and dragons and the hairy-footed. Well, we
have learned to live with her; it's still storytelling, after all.

So we find ourselves today, standing here in our T-shirts, donkey
jackets, and chinos, without the bold scenarios we enjoyed when the
moon was young and untrodden. Those bold scenarios have effec-
tively migrated to the wide-open spaces of the cinema screen, the circular spaces of the DVD. *Alien,* with its scrubby spaceship full of
ill-dressed crew, bears a Dick hallmark. The *Terminator* franchise, based
on an old SF idea. *Star Wars,* owing much to Doc Smith's *Lensman* series. *Matrix,* a dark Dickian idea. Other one-offs, debasing Dick's
concepts—remember *Total Recall?* We'll say nothing of *AI,* debasing
my ideas. . . .

Of course, I simplify. Every writer worth his salt slightly changes
the timbre of our uniform voice. While fans naturally always want
more of the same, a real writer needs his individuality to be acknowl-
eged (and to be loved, or else to hell with them!). I wrote *Billion Year
Spree,* my history of science fiction, not only for my love, my obses-
sive love, of the field, but to distance myself from what I regarded as
the rubbish of *Ralph 124C41+,* to clear a space in which I could live

and breathe and create. And what goes for me goes for Cordwainer Smith, Kurt Vonnegut, Michael Bishop, James Morrow, China Miéville, any number of other writers. And despite all the changes, the dwindling of space-travel narratives, SF continues on its surreal way much as it ever did—as indeed the great world does, give or take a few suicide bombers.

So now we work on in black and white, we and our computers, to appear modestly on the printed page. Is it better or worse than it was? Will it be better in the future? I can answer that one with assurance: *Plus ça change, plus c'est la meme chose . . .*

THEN AND NOW

FREDERIK POHL

Back in the days when I made my first professional sale to a science fiction magazine, which was in . . .

Well, let's think about that date for a moment. What I sold was a poem. I wrote it in 1935. It was accepted by T. O'Conor Sloane, Ph.D., the editor of *Amazing Stories,* in 1936. It was published in 1937 (in their October issue) . . . and paid for—in the amount of two dollars—in early 1938. So at some time over that period, however minimally, I made my first professional sale and thus became eligible to join in the wonderful world of the science fiction pro.

That world, of course, was most wonderful only in the eyes of the yearning unpublished. There was certainly nothing wondrous about its financial aspects, because those in fact were pretty sad. In the mid-thirties there were three science fiction magazines. One was the monthly *Astounding,* the class of the field, which paid a lordly penny a word on acceptance for all it bought. The other two, *Amazing Stories* and *Wonder Stories,* were bimonthlies that paid only half as much a word, and didn't pay at all until the work was actually published. Occasionally not even then.

I once did the arithmetic on these financial matters, and it came out pretty discouraging. The three magazines together generated something around ten thousand dollars a year to pour into the collective coffers of the period's SF writers. If you add in the income from such subsidiary rights as book publication, foreign-language translations, and motion-picture sales, you come up with a yearly total of . . . well, still ten thousand dollars, because the American SF writers of the 1930s never saw any of that kind of money. With negligible exceptions, the only science fiction published in book form in America in the 1930s was by English authors, and the other kinds of subsidiary-rights income didn't exist at all.

Even so (you may think) ten thousand dollars, especially ten thousand of the dollars of the 1930s, worth so much more apiece than our own inflated twenty-first-century play money, was not a contemptible sum. Indeed it was not. If any single writer had gotten it all he could have lived a kingly existence, perhaps with a staff of servants to take care of all the nonpleasurable parts of his daily life, conceivably with a pied-à-terre in Paris as well and maybe a winter place in the Florida keys. (Well, maybe not *all* of that, but pretty kingly all the same.)

Unfortunately that ten grand didn't go to a single writer; it was divided among sixty or seventy impecunious individuals. The average income for a 1930s science fiction writer was somewhere between three and four dollars a week. A few of the most prolific of the pulpsters—Arthur J. Burks, L. Ron Hubbard, and hardly anybody else—did better, but not out of science fiction alone. Most of what they wrote went to the magazines of the more popular pulp categories (detective, Western, sports, even love stories) as well as to the SF ones . . . and were the result of long daily hours pounding those old typewriter keys. In the lap of luxury no American science fiction writer resided in the 1930s.

That's the bad part. There was a good part, though, and that was that science fiction was catching on.

Not in book publishing, of course—that didn't happen until after World War II—and certainly not in any other of the subrights. But there was a sudden and wholly unexpected florescence of more of the same. New pulp SF magazines began popping up all over the place, until by the end of the decade there were some twenty of the things.

This did not mean great enrichment for the writers. The new magazines were almost all bimonthlies, if that; few of them lasted more than a handful of issues; their payment rates were uniformly at the low end of the already low publishing scale (Don Wollheim's two magazines, in fact, budgeted no payment at all for writers) . . . and the number of new writers entering the field was increasing as rapidly as the number of magazines, so that, instead of enriching the existing pros, the new outlets were pretty much just spreading the poverty around.

The spirit of change was not limited to the new magazine pop-ups, either. By the end of the decade all three of the canonical magazines—*Amazing, Astounding, Wonder*—were still around, but all three of them were under new, and significantly different, management.

T. O'Conor Sloane had been an editor, then *the* editor, of *Amazing* almost since its inception. He was eighty-six years old when he bought that pivotal bit of poetry from me—beard long and white, fingers trembling, and mind pretty firmly locked into the late nineteenth century. (He was convinced that spaceflight was a physical impossibility.) Mailing me that tiny check may have been one of the last things he did as *Amazing*'s editor, because early in 1938 the magazine was sold to the Ziff-Davis Publishing Company of Chicago, and Sloane was out of a job.

His replacement was Raymond A. Palmer, who may or may not have believed in space travel but definitely did believe (or came to believe) that the stories by Richard S. Shaver that he published, dealing with great swarms of deranged robots that lived under the surface of the Earth and had malevolent plans for the human race, weren't fiction at all. Although Palmer also published straight SF stories by old-timers like Eando Binder and newcomers like the teenage Isaac Asimov, it is the "Shaver mysteries" that define his tenure.

Wonder Stories throughout most of the period was owned by Hugo Gernsback and, under his watchful eye, edited by the fairly undistinguished Charles D. Hornig. Like *Amazing,* it had seen better days, but then, when it was sold to the Thrilling Group in mid-decade, its fortunes changed. Its new editor was Leo Margulies, and its title was, of course, changed to *Thrilling Wonder Stories. Thrilling Wonder* wasn't the only magazine Margulies edited; the company owned forty-five others, and Margulies was listed as the editor of all forty-six of them. (With, it is true, a large stable of assistants—including at one time or another H. L. Gold, Mort Weisinger, Samuel Mines, and half a dozen others.) But Margulies's was the guiding intelligence. He had no particular interest in science fiction, but he knew what he wanted from its writers. It was the same thing he demanded from his Western and mystery and air-war authors, and it could be summed up in one word:

Action.

Margulies had no objection to stories with a social message (as, for instance, Heinlein's "Jerry Is a Man") or to interesting new kinds of planets and alien creatures (like John Campbell's tour of the solar system in his "Penton and Blake" series or Stanley Weinbaum's superintelligent Venusian plants). All he insisted on was that, if the writer was determined to have his characters debate alien customs, they should do so while having a ray-gun battle with the aliens. It was his conviction that his pulp readership, whatever the genre, was composed principally of eleven-year-olds, thus such childishness as his "Sergeant Saturn" letter columns.

But there was one editor who considered his readers to be capable of adult thought (even though not of being exposed to matters of adult sexuality). That was John Campbell. *Astounding* was lucky in having had the great good fortune of being picked up by the high-end pulp chain of Street & Smith when Clayton, its original publisher, went belly-up, luckier still when, in 1938, it was given over to John W. Campbell, Jr., to edit. Campbell is generally considered the greatest editor science fiction has ever seen, and perhaps his willingness to consider his readers grown-ups is why. Campbell's editoral policy, he himself said, was to publish stories that could be read as contemporary fiction, but in a magazine of the twenty-fifth century. And he came pretty close.

That was then. Now it's the twenty-first century and much has changed almost unrecognizably. Money, for instance. Even when inflation is discounted, now there is much, much more of it to spread around, and it comes not only from the handful of surviving specialist magazines but from book publishers, television and movie producers, and even such grace notes as lecture fees and corporate consultancies. Respectability: Even the most elevated of literatures will now sometimes admire certain science fiction stories, provided only that they are permitted to deny that those stories are SF at all. Accessibility: In the 1930s a beginning writer who had not yet persuaded any of the paying magazines to take on any of his stories—the young Ray Bradbury, say—had only one recourse, which was to publish them, free, in a (typically mimeographed) fan magazine, where they would be read by perhaps a couple of dozen human beings. Now the World Wide Web has provided countless e-publishers. Often the payment is the same—that's to say, somewhere around zero—but the readership may now be in the thousands.

So in that way and in most others it is now a considerably better world for the average SF writer. Easy, no . . . but then if it were really easy everybody would be doing it, and what would be the fun of that?

New writer Christopher Rowe was born in Kentucky and lives there still. With Gwenda Bond, he operates a small press and edits the critically acclaimed magazine *Say*. His stories have appeared in *SCI FICTION*, *Realms of Fantasy*, *Electric Velocipede*, *Idomancer*, *Swan Sister*, *Trampoline*, *The Infinite Matrix*, *The Journal of Pulse-Pounding Narratives*, and elsewhere, and have recently been collected in *Bittersweet Creek*.

About "The Voluntary State," he says:

" 'The Voluntary State' was written as a submission piece for the 2003 Sycamore Hill Writers Conference, where all of the attendees gave me insightful and useful advice.

"Specifically, Jonathan Lethem and Jeffrey Ford both identified a lot of places for improvement to the, yes, pretty messy manuscript I turned in, as did my fellow nominee Andy Duncan and workshop corunner John Kessel. I owe all those guys a lot.

"Even more, I owe thanks to these three incomparable people: Richard Burner, Kelly Link, and Karen Joy Fowler. There's more critical acumen in that one sentence than I could begin to describe to you. Not to mention character, grace, talent, generosity, and kindness.

"After the first round of post Syc Hill rewrites, I sent the story to Ellen Datlow, who agreed to publish it with the proviso that I clarify some things. Over the last few years, I've started making more and more demands of the people who read my fiction, and Ellen pointed out places where clarity had been sacrificed to my own bullheaded notions of art.

"So I sent the story to Ted Chiang, one of the smartest writers. (I started to put some kind of clause on the end of that sentence like '. . . in the field' or '. . . I've ever met,' but I think I should probably let it stand.) See, I was trying a runaround. I was going to prove, to myself at least, that the story could be "got" as it was. Ted expressed confusion over some passages. Friends, when Ted Chiang doesn't get something you've written, it's not because your readers aren't as clever as you are.

"It went back to Ellen and it came back to me and it went back to Ellen and it came back to me. Ellen kept pushing me to get it closer and closer to what she thought it could be, and eventually I realized that what Ellen thought it could be is pretty much what it should be. Thanks, Ellen.

"All of those people did all of that work for me and that story, and I thank them for it.

"But of course, none of them did a damned thing compared to the person who essentially started the story in the first place, the person who said, in response to my whining that I didn't have anything to write about, 'There's a car on top of a hill. The door's open. There's nobody in it. Now shut up.'

"So most of all, thanks to my wife, Gwenda Bond. This is where the 'without whom' goes, but I can't think of anything to put afterward, because I can't think of anything I'd do or be without her."

THE VOLUNTARY STATE

CHRISTOPHER ROWE

Soma had parked his car in the trailhead lot above Governor's Beach. A safe place, usually, checked regularly by the Tennessee Highway Patrol and surrounded on three sides by the limestone cliffs that plunged down into the Gulf of Mexico.

But today, after his struggle up the trail from the beach, he saw that his car had been attacked. The driver's side window had been kicked in.

Soma dropped his pack and rushed to his car's side. The car shied away from him, backed to the limit of its tether before it recognized him and turned, let out a low, pitiful moan.

"Oh, car," said Soma, stroking the roof and opening the passenger door. "Oh, car, you're hurt." Then Soma was rummaging through the emergency kit, tossing aside flares and bandages, finally, *finally* finding the glass salve. Only after he'd spread the ointment over the shattered window and brushed the glass shards out onto the gravel, only after he'd sprayed the whole door down with analgesic aero, only then did he close his eyes, access call signs, drop shields. He opened his head and used it to call the police.

In the scant minutes before he saw the cadre of blue and white bicycles angling in from sunward, their bubblewings pumping furiously, he gazed down the beach at Nashville. The cranes the Governor had ordered grown to dredge the harbor would go dormant for the winter soon—already their acres-broad leaves were tinged with orange and gold.

"Soma-With-The-Paintbox-In-Printer's-Alley," said voices from above. Soma turned to watch the policemen land. They all spoke simultaneously in the sing-song chant of law enforcement. "Your car will be healed at taxpayers' expense." Then the ritual words, "And the wicked will be brought to justice."

Efficiency and order took over the afternoon as the threatened rain began to fall. One of the 144 Detectives manifested, Soma and the policemen all looking about as they felt the weight of the Governor's servant inside their heads. It brushed aside the thoughts of one of the Highway Patrolmen and rode him, the man's movements becoming slightly less fluid as he was mounted and steered. The Detective filmed Soma's statement.

"I came to sketch the children in the surf," said Soma. He opened his daypack for the soapbubble lens, laid out the charcoal and pencils, the sketchbook of boughten paper bound between the rusting metal plates he'd scavenged along the middenmouth of the Cumberland River.

"Show us, show us," sang the Detective.

Soma flipped through the sketches. In black and gray, he'd drawn the floating lures that crowded the shallows this time of year. Tiny, naked babies most of them, but also some little girls in one-piece bathing suits and even one fat prepubescent boy clinging desperately to a deflating beach ball and turning horrified, pleading eyes on the viewer.

"Tssk, tssk," sang the Detective, percussive. "Draw filaments on those babies, Soma Painter. Show the lines at their heels."

Soma was tempted to show the Detective the artistic licenses tattooed around his wrists in delicate salmon inks, to remind the intelligence which authorities had purview over which aspects of civic life, but bit his tongue, fearful of a For-the-Safety-of-the-Public proscription. As if there were a living soul in all of Tennessee who didn't know that the children who splashed in the surf were nothing but extremities, nothing but lures growing from the snouts of alligators crouching on the sandy bottoms.

The Detective summarized. "You were here at your work, you parked legally, you paid the appropriate fee to the meter, you saw nothing, you informed the authorities in a timely fashion. Soma-With-The-Paintbox-In-Printer's-Alley, the Tennessee Highway Patrol applauds your citizenship."

The policemen had spread around the parking lot, casting cluenets and staring back through time. But they all heard their cue, stopped what they were doing, and broke into a raucous cheer for Soma. He accepted their adulation graciously.

Then the Detective popped the soapbubble camera and plucked the film from the air before it could fall. It rolled up the film, chewed it up thoughtfully, then dismounted the policeman, who shuddered and fell against Soma. So Soma did not at first hear what the others had begun to chant, didn't decipher it until he saw what they were encircling. Something was caught on the wispy thorns of a nodding thistle growing at the edge of the lot.

"Crow's feather," the policemen chanted. "Crow's feather Crow's feather Crow's feather."

And even Soma, licensed for art instead of justice, knew what the fluttering bit of black signified. His car had been assaulted by Kentuckians.

Soma had never, so far as he recalled, painted a self-portrait. But his disposition was melancholy, so he might have taken a few visual notes of his trudge back to Nashville if he'd thought he could have shielded the paper from the rain.

Soma Between the Sea and the City, he could call a painting like that. Or, if he'd decided to choose that one clear moment when the sun had shone through the towering slate clouds, *Soma Between Storms.*

Either image would have shown a tall young man in a broad-brimmed hat, black pants cut off at the calf, yellow jersey unsealed to show a thin chest. A young man, sure, but not a young man used to long walks. No helping that; his car would stay in the trailhead lot for at least three days.

The mechanic had arrived as the policemen were leaving, galloping up the gravel road on a white mare marked with red crosses. She'd swung from the saddle and made sympathetic clucking noises at the car even before she greeted Soma, endearing herself to auto and owner simultaneously.

Scratching the car at the base of its aerial, sussing out the very spot the car best liked attention, she'd introduced herself. "I am Jenny-With-Grease-Beneath-Her-Fingernails," she'd said, but didn't seem to be worried about it because she ran her free hand through unfashionably short cropped blond hair as she spoke.

She'd whistled for her horse and began unpacking the saddlebags.

"I have to build a larger garage than normal for your car, Soma Painter, for it must house me and my horse during the convalescence. But don't worry, my licenses are in good order. I'm bonded by the city and the state. This is all at taxpayers' expense."

Which was a very great relief to Soma, poor as he was. With friends even poorer, none of them with cars, and so no one to hail out of the Alley to his rescue, and now this long, wet trudge back to the city.

Soma and his friends did not live uncomfortable lives, of course. They had dry spaces to sleep above their studios, warm or cool in response to the season and even clean if that was the proclivity of the individual artist, as was the case with Soma. A clean, warm or cool, dry space to sleep. A good space to work and a more than ample opportunity to sell his paintings and drawings, the Alley being one of the *other* things the provincials did when they visited Nashville. Before they went to the great vaulted Opera House or after.

All that and even a car, sure, freedom of the road. Even if it wasn't so free because the car was not *really* his, gift of his family, product of their ranch. Both of them, car and artist, product of that ranching life Soma did his best to forget.

If he'd been a little closer in time to that ranching youth, his legs might not have ached so. He might not have been quite so miserable to be lurching down the gravel road toward the city, might have been sharp-eyed enough to still *see* a city so lost in the fog, maybe sharp-eared enough to have heard the low hoots and caws that his assailants used to organize themselves before they sprang from all around him—down from tree branches, up from ditches, out from the undergrowth.

And there was a Crow raiding party, the sight stunning Soma motionless. "This only happens on television," he said.

The caves and hills these Kentuckians haunted unopposed were a hundred miles and more north and east, across the shifting skirmish line of a border. Kentuckians couldn't be here, so far from the frontier stockades at Fort Clarksville and Barren Green.

But here they definitely were, hopping and calling, scratching the gravel with their clawed boots, blinking away the rain when it trickled down behind their masks and into their eyes.

A Crow clicked his tongue twice and suddenly Soma was the center of much activity. Muddy hands forced his mouth open and a

paste that first stung then numbed was swabbed around his mouth and
nose. His wrists were bound before him with rough hemp twine.
Even frightened as he was, Soma couldn't contain his astonishment.
"Smoke rope!" he said.

The squad leader grimaced, shook his head in disgust and disbelief. "Rope and cigarettes come from two completely different varieties of plants," he said, his accent barely decipherable. "Vols are so
fucking stupid."

Then Soma was struggling through the undergrowth himself, alter-
nately dragged and pushed and even half-carried by a succession of
Crow Brothers. The boys were running hard, and if he was a burden
to them, then their normal speed must have been terrifying. Someone
finally called a halt, and Soma collapsed.

The leader approached, pulling his mask up and wiping his face.
Deep red lines angled down from his temples, across his cheekbones,
ending at his snub nose. Soma would have guessed the man was forty
if he'd seen him in the Alley dressed like a normal person in jersey
and shorts.

Even so exhausted, Soma wished he could dig his notebook and a
bit of charcoal out of the daypack he still wore, so that he could capture some of the savage countenances around him.

The leader was just staring at Soma, not speaking, so Soma broke
the silence. "Those scars"—the painter brought up his bound hands,
traced angles down either side of his own face—"are they ceremonial? Do they indicate your rank?"

The Kentuckians close enough to hear snorted and laughed. The
man before Soma went through a quick, exaggerated pantomime of
disgust. He spread his hands, why-me-lording, then took the beaked
mask off the top of his head and showed Soma its back. Two leather
bands crisscrossed its interior, supporting the elaborate superstructure
of the mask and preventing the full weight of it, Soma saw, from bearing down on the wearer's nose. He looked at the leader again, saw
him rubbing at the fading marks.

"Sorry," said the painter.

"It's okay," said the Crow. "It's the fate of the noble savage to be
misunderstood by effete city dwellers."

Soma stared at the man for a minute. He said, "You guys must
watch a lot of the same TV programs as me."

The leader was looking around, counting his boys. He lowered his mask and pulled Soma to his feet. "That could be. We need to go."

It developed that the leader's name was Japheth Sapp. At least that's what the other Crow Brothers called out to him from where they loped along ahead or behind, circled farther out in the brush, scrambled from limb to branch to trunk high above.

Soma descended into a reverie space, sing-songing subvocally and supervocally (and being hushed down by Japheth hard then). He guessed in a lucid moment that the paste the Kentuckians had dosed him with must have some sort of will-sapping effect. He didn't feel like he could open his head and call for help; he didn't even want to. But *"I will take care of you,"* Athena was always promising. He held onto that and believed that he wasn't panicking because of the Crows' drugs, sure, but also because he would be rescued by the police soon. *"I will take care of you."* After all, wasn't that one of the Governor's slogans, clarifying out of the advertising flocks in the skies over Nashville during Campaign?

It was good to think of these things. It was good to think of the sane capital and forget that he was being kidnapped by aliens, by Indians, by toughs in the employ of a rival Veronese merchant family.

But then the warchief of the marauding band was throwing him into a gully, whistling and gesturing, calling in all his boys to dive into the wash, to gather close and throw their cloaks up and over their huddle.

"What's up, boss?" asked the blue-eyed boy Soma had noticed earlier, crouched in the mud with one elbow somehow dug into Soma's ribs.

Japheth Sapp didn't answer but another of the younger Crow Brothers hissed, "THP even got a bear in the air!"

Soma wondered if a bear meant rescue from this improbable aside. Not that parts of the experience weren't enjoyable. It didn't occur to Soma to fear for his health, even when Japheth knocked him down with a light kick to the back of the knees after the painter stood and brushed aside feathered cloaks for a glimpse of the sky.

There *was* a bear up there. And yes, it was wearing the blue and white.

"I want to see the bear, Japheth," said a young Crow. Japheth shook his head, said, "I'll take you to Willow Ridge and show you the black bears that live above the Green River when we get back home, Lowell. That bear up there is just a robot made out of balloons and possessed by a demon, not worth looking at unless you're close enough to cut her."

With all his captors concentrating on their leader or on the sky, Soma wondered if he might be able to open his head. As soon as he thought it, Japheth Sapp wheeled on him, stared him down.

Not looking at any one of them, Japheth addressed his whole merry band. "Give this one some more paste. But be careful with him; we'll still need this vol's head to get across the Cumberland, even after we bribe the bundle bugs."

Soma spoke around the viscous stuff the owl-feathered endomorph was spackling over the lower half of his face. "Bundle bugs work for the city and are above reproach. Your plans are ill-laid if they depend on corrupting the servants of the Governor."

More hoots, more hushings, then Japheth said, "If bundle bugs had mothers, they'd sell them to me for half a cask of Kentucky bourbon. And we brought more than half a cask."

Soma knew Japheth was lying—this was a known tactic of neo-anarchist agitator hero figures. "I know you're lying," said Soma. "It's a known tactic of—"

"Hush hush, Soma Painter. I like you—this you—but we've all read the Governor's curricula. You'll see that we're too sophisticated for your models." Japheth gestured and the group broke huddle. Outrunners ran out and the main body shook off cramps. "And I'm not an anarchist agitator. I'm a lot of things, but not that."

"Singer!" said a young Crow, scampering past.

"I play out some weekends, he means; I don't have a record contract or anything," Japheth said, pushing Soma along himself now.

"Welder!" said another man.

"Union-certified," said Japheth. "That's my day job, working at the border."

More lies, knew Soma. "I suppose Kentuckians built the Girding Wall, then?"

Everything he said amused these people greatly. "Not just Kentuckians, vol, the whole rest of the world. Only we call it the containment field."

"Agitator, singer, welder," said the painter, the numbness spreading deeper than it had before, affecting the way he said words and the way he chose them.

"Assassin," rumbled the Owl, the first thing Soma had heard the burly man say.

Japheth was scrambling up a bank before Soma. He stopped and twisted. His foot corkscrewed through the leaf mat and released a humid smell. He looked at the Owl, then hard at Soma, reading him.

"You're doped up good now, Soma Painter. No way to open that head until we open it for you. So, sure, here's some truth for you. We're not just here to steal her things. We're here to break into her mansion. We're here to kill Athena Parthenus, Queen of Logic and Governor of the Voluntary State of Tennessee."

Jenny-With-Grease-Beneath-Her-Fingernails spread fronds across the parking lot, letting the high green fern leaves dry out before she used the mass to make her bed. Her horse watched from above the half-door of its stall. Inside the main body of the garage, Soma's car slept, lightly anesthetized.

"Just enough for a soft cot, horse," said Jenny. "All of us we'll sleep well after this hard day."

Then she saw that little flutter. One of the fronds had a bit of feather caught between some leaves, and yes, it was coal black, midnight blue, reeking of the north. Jenny sighed, because her citizenship was less faultless than Soma's, and policemen disturbed her. But she opened her head and stared at the feather.

A telephone leapt off a tulip poplar a little ways down the road to Nashville. It squawked through its brief flight and landed with inelegant weight in front of Jenny. It turned its beady eyes on her.

"Ring," said the telephone.

"Hello," said Jenny.

Jenny's Operator sounded just like Jenny, something else that secretly disturbed her. Other people's Operators sounded like television stars or famous Legislators or like happy cartoon characters, but Jenny was in that minority of people whose Operators and Teachers always sounded like themselves. Jenny remembered a slogan from Campaign, "My voice is yours."

"The Tennessee Highway Patrol has plucked one already, Jenny Healer." The voice from the telephone thickened around Jenny and began pouring through her ears like cold syrup. "But we want a sample of this one as well. Hold that feather, Jenny, and open your head a little wider."

❁

Now, here's the secret of those feathers. The one Jenny gave to the police and the one the cluenets had caught already. The secret of those feathers, and the feathers strung like look-here flags along the trails down from the Girding Wall, and even of the Owl feathers that had pushed through that fence and let the outside in. All of them were oily with intrigue. Each had been dipped in potent *math,* the autonomous software developed by the Owls of the Bluegrass.

Those feathers were hacks. They were lures and false attacks. Those feathers marked the way the Kentuckians didn't go.

The math kept quiet and still as it floated through Jenny's head, through the ignorable defenses of the telephone and the more considerable, but still avoidable, rings of barbed wire around Jenny's Operator. The math went looking for a Detective or even a Legislator if one were to be found not braying in a pack of its brethren, an unlikely event.

The math stayed well clear of the Commodores in the Great Salt Lick ringing the Parthenon. It was sly math. Its goals were limited, realizable. It marked the way they didn't go.

❁

The Crows made Soma carry things. "You're stronger than you think," one said and loaded him up with a sloshing keg made from white oak staves. A lot of the Crows carried such, Soma saw, and others carried damp, muddy burlap bags flecked with old root matter and smelling of poor people's meals.

Japheth Sapp carried only a piece of paper. He referred to it as he huddled with the Owl and the blue-eyed boy, crouched in a dry stream bed a few yards from where the rest of the crew were hauling out their goods.

Soma had no idea where they were at this point, though he had a vague idea that they'd described an arc above the northern suburbs and the conversations indicated that they were now heading toward the capital, unlikely as that sounded. His head was still numb and soft inside, not an unpleasant situation, but not one that helped his already shaky geographical sense.

He knew what time it was, though, when the green fall of light speckling the hollow they rested in shifted toward pink. Dull as his mind was, he recognized that and smiled.

The clouds sounded the pitch note, then suddenly a great deal was happening around him. For the first time that day, the Crows' reaction to what they perceived to be a crisis didn't involve Soma being poked somewhere or shoved under something. So he was free to sing the anthem while the Crows went mad with activity.

The instant the rising bell tone fell out of the sky, Japheth flung his mask to the ground, glared at a rangy redheaded man, and bellowed, "Where's my timekeeper? You were supposed to remind us!"

The man didn't have time to answer though, because like all of them he was digging through his pack, wrapping an elaborate crenellated set of earmuffs around his head.

The music struck up, and Soma began.

"Tonight we'll remake Tennessee, every night we remake Tennessee . . ."

It was powerfully odd that the Kentuckians didn't join in the singing, and that none of them were moving into the roundel lines that a group this size would normally be forming during the anthem.

Still, it might have been stranger if they had joined in.

"Tonight we'll remake Tennessee, every night we remake Tennessee . . ."

There was a thicket of trumpet flowers tucked amongst a stand of willow trees across the dry creek, so the brass was louder than Soma was used to. Maybe they were farther from the city than he thought. Aficionados of different musical sections tended to find places like this and frequent them during anthem.

"Tonight we'll remake Tennessee, every night we remake Tennessee . . ."

Soma was happily shuffling through a solo dance, keeping one eye on a fat raccoon that was bobbing its head in time with the music as it turned over stones in the stream bed, when he saw that the young Crow who wanted to see a bear had started keeping time as well, raising and lowering a clawed boot. The Owl was the first of the outlanders who spied the tapping foot.

"Tonight we'll remake Tennessee, every night we remake Tennessee . . ."

Soma didn't feel the real connection with the citizenry that anthem usually provided on a daily basis, didn't feel his confidence and vigor improve, but he blamed that on the drugs the Kentuckians had given him. He wondered if those were the same drugs they were using on the Crow who now feebly twitched beneath the weight of the Owl, who had wrestled him to the ground. Others pinned down the dancing Crow's arms and legs and Japheth brought out a needle and injected the poor soul with a vast syringe full of some milky brown substance that had the consistency of honey. Soma remembered that he knew the dancing Crow's name. Japheth Sapp had called the boy Lowell.

"Tonight we'll remake Tennessee, every night we remake Tennessee . . ."

The pink light faded. The raccoon waddled into the woods. The trumpet flowers fell quiet and Soma completed the execution of a pirouette.

The redheaded man stood before Japheth wearing a stricken and haunted look. He kept glancing to one side, where the Owl stood over the Crow who had danced. "Japheth, I just lost track," he said. "It's so hard here, to keep track of things."

Japheth's face flashed from anger through disappointment to something approaching forgiveness. "It is. It's hard to keep track. Everybody fucks up sometime. And I think we got the dampeners in him in time."

Then the Owl said, "Second shift now, Japheth. Have to wait for the second round of garbage drops to catch our bundle bug."

Japheth grimaced, but nodded. "We can't move anyway, not until we know what's going to happen with Lowell," he said, glancing at the unconscious boy. "Get the whiskey and the food back into the cache. Set up the netting. We're staying here for the night."

Japheth stalked over to Soma, fists clenched white.

"Things are getting clearer and clearer to you, Soma Painter, even if you think things are getting harder and harder to understand. Our motivations will open up things inside you."

He took Soma's chin in his left hand and tilted Soma's face up. He waved his hand to indicate Lowell.

"There's one of mine. There's one of my motivations for all of this."

Slowly, but with loud lactic cracks, Japheth spread his fingers wide.

"I fight her, Soma, in the hope that she'll not clench up another mind. I fight her so that minds already bound might come unbound."

In the morning, the dancing Crow boy was dead.

Jenny woke near dark, damp and cold, curled up in the gravel of the parking lot. Her horse nickered. She was dimly aware that the horse had been neighing and otherwise emanating concern for some time now, and it was this that had brought her up to consciousness.

She rolled over and climbed to her feet, spitting to rid her mouth of the metal Operator taste. A dried froth of blood coated her nostrils and upper lip, and she could feel the flaky stuff in her ears as well. She looked toward the garage and saw that she wasn't the only one rousing.

"Now, you get back to bed," she told the car.

Soma's car had risen up on its back wheels and was peering out the open window, its weight resting against the force-grown wall, bulging it outward.

Jenny made a clucking noise, hoping to reassure her horse, and walked up to the car. She was touched by its confusion and concern.

She reached for the aerial. "You should sleep some more," she said, "and not worry about me. The Operators can tell when you're being uncooperative is all, even when *you* didn't know you were being uncooperative. Then they have to root about a bit more than's comfortable to find the answers they want."

Jenny coaxed the car down from the window, wincing a little at the sharp echo pains that flashed in her head and ears. "Don't tell your owner, but this isn't the first time I've been called to question. Now, to bed."

The car looked doubtful, but obediently rolled back to the repair bed that grew from the garage floor. It settled in, grumbled a bit, then switched off its headlights.

Jenny walked around to the door and entered. She found that the water sacs were full and chilled and drew a long drink. The water tasted faintly of salt. She took another swallow, then dampened a rag with a bit more of the tangy stuff to wipe away the dried blood. Then she went to work.

The bundle bugs crawled out of the city, crossed Distinguished Opposition Bridge beneath the watching eye of bears floating overhead, then described a right-angle turn along the levy to their dumping grounds. Soma and the Kentuckians lay hidden in the brushy wasteland at the edge of the grounds, waiting.

The Owl placed a hand on Japheth's shoulder, pointing at a bundle bug just entering the grounds. Then the Owl rose to his knees and began worming his way between the bushes and dead appliances.

"Soma Painter," whispered Japheth. "I'm going to have to break your jaw in a few minutes and cut out as many of her tentacles as we can get at, but we'll knit it back up as soon as we cross the river."

Soma was too far gone in the paste to hold both of the threats in his mind at the same time. A broken jaw, Crows in the capital. He concentrated on the second.

"The bears will scoop you up and drop you in the Salt Lick," Soma said. "Children will climb on you during Campaign and Legislators will stand on your shoulders to make their stump speeches."

"The bears will not see us, Soma."

"The bears watch the river and the bridges, 'and—"

" '—and their eyes never close,' " finished Japheth. "Yes, we've seen the commercials."

A bundle bug, a large one at forty meters in length, reared up over them, precariously balanced on its rearmost set of legs. Soma said, "They're very good commercials," and the bug crashed down over them all.

Athena's data realm mirrored her physical realm. One-to-one constructs mimicked the buildings and the citizenry, showed who was riding and who was being ridden.

In that numerical space, the Kentuckians' math found the bridge. The harsh light of the bears floated above. Any bear represented a statistically significant portion of the Governor herself, and from the point of view of the math, the pair above Distinguished Opposition Bridge looked like miniature suns, casting probing rays at the marching bundle bugs, the barges floating along the Cumberland, and even into the waters of the river itself, illuminating the numerical analogs of the dangerous things that lived in the muddy bottom.

Bundle bugs came out of the city, their capacious abdomens distended with the waste they'd ingested along their routes. The math could see that the bug crossing through the bears' probes right now had a lot of restaurants on its itinerary. The beams pierced the dun-colored carapace and showed a riot of uneaten jellies, crumpled cups, soiled napkins.

The bugs marching in the opposite direction, emptied and ready for reloading, were scanned even more carefully than their outward-bound kin. The beam scans were withering, complete, and exceedingly precise.

The math knew that precision and accuracy are not the same thing.

"Lowell's death has set us back further than we thought," said Japheth, talking to the four Crows, the Owl, and, Soma guessed, to the bundle bug they inhabited. Japheth had detailed off the rest of the raiding party to carry the dead boy back north, so there was plenty of room where they crouched.

The interior of the bug's abdomen was larger than Soma's apartment by a factor of two and smelled of flowers instead of paint thinner. Soma's apartment, however, was not an alcoholic.

"This is good, though, good good." The bug's voice rang from every direction at once. "I'm scheduled down for a rest shift. You-uns was late and missed my last run, and now we can all rest and drink good whiskey. Good good."

But none of the Kentuckians drank any of the whiskey from the casks they'd cracked once they'd crawled down the bug's gullet. Instead, every half hour or so, they poured another gallon into one of the damp fissures that ran all through the interior. Bundle bugs abdomens weren't designed for digestion, just evacuation, and it was the circulatory system that was doing the work of carrying the bourbon to the bug's brain.

Soma dipped a finger into an open cask and touched finger to tongue. "Bourbon burns!" he said, pulling his finger from his mouth.

"Burns good!" said the bug. "Good good."

"We knew that not all of us were going to be able to actually enter the city—we don't have enough outfits, for one thing—but six is a bare minimum. And since we're running behind, we'll have to wait out tonight's anthem in our host's apartment."

"Printer's Alley is two miles from the Parthenon," said the Owl, nodding at Soma.

Japheth nodded. "I know. And I know that those might be the two longest miles in the world. But we expected hard walking."

He banged the curving gray wall he leaned against with his elbow. "Hey! Bundle bug! How long until you start your shift?"

A vast and disappointed sigh shuddered through the abdomen. "Two more hours, bourbon man," said the bug.

"Get out your gear, cousin," Japheth said to the Owl. He stood and stretched, motioned for the rest of the Crows to do the same. He turned toward Soma. "The rest of us will hold him down."

Jenny had gone out midmorning, when the last of the fog was still burning off the bluffs, searching for low-moisture organics to feed the garage. She'd run its reserves very low, working on one thing and another until quite late in the night.

As she suspected from the salty taste of the water supply, the filters in the housings between the taproots and the garage's plumbing array were clogged with silt. She'd blown them out with pressurized air—no need to replace what you can fix—and reinstalled them one, two, three. But while she was blowing out the filters, she'd heard a whine she didn't like in the air compressor, and when she'd gone to check it she found it panting with effort, tongue hanging out onto the workbench top where it sat.

And then things went as these things go, and she moved happily from minor maintenance problem to minor maintenance problem—wiping away the air compressor's crocodile tears while she stoned the motor brushes in its A/C motor, then replacing the fusible link in the garage itself. "Links are so easily fusible," she joked to her horse when she rubbed it down with handfuls of the sweet-smelling fern fronds she'd intended for her own bed.

And all the while, of course, she watched the little car, monitoring the temperatures at its core points and doing what she could to coax the broken window to reknit in a smooth, steady fashion. Once, when the car awoke in the middle of the night making colicky noises, Jenny had to pop the hood, where she found that the points needed to be pulled and regapped. They were fouled with the viscous residue of the analgesic aero the owner had spread about so liberally.

She tsked. The directions on the labels clearly stated that the nozzle was to be pointed *away* from the engine compartment. Still, hard to fault Soma Painter's goodhearted efforts. It was an easy fix, and she would have pulled the plugs during the tune-up she had planned for the morning anyway.

So, repairings and healings, lights burning and tools turning, and when she awoke to the morning tide sounds the garage immediately began flashing amber lights at her wherever she turned. The bellygrumble noises it floated from the speakers worried the horse, so she set out looking for something to put in the hoppers of the hungry garage.

When she came back, bearing a string-tied bundle of dried wood and a half bucket of old walnuts some gatherer had wedged beneath an overhang and forgotten at least a double handful of autumns past, the car was gone.

Jenny hurried to the edge of the parking lot and looked down the road, though she couldn't see much. This time of year the morning fog turned directly into the midday haze. She could see the city, and bits of road between trees and bluff line, but no sign of the car.

The garage pinged at her, and she shoved its breakfast into the closest intake. She didn't open her head to call the police—she hadn't yet fully recovered from yesterday afternoon's interview. She was even hesitant to open her head the little bit she needed to access her own garage's security tapes. But she'd built the garage, and either built or rebuilt everything in it, so she risked it.

She stood at her workbench, rubbing her temple, as a see-through Jenny and a see-through car built themselves up out of twisted light. Light Jenny put on a light rucksack, scratched the light car absently on the roof as she walked by, and headed out the door. Light Jenny did not tether the car. Light Jenny did not lock the door.

"Silly light Jenny," said Jenny.

As soon as light Jenny was gone, the little light car rolled over to the big open windows. It popped a funny little wheelie and caught itself on the sash, the way it had yesterday when it had watched real Jenny swim up out of her government dream.

The light car kept one headlight just above the sash for a few minutes, then lowered itself back to the floor with a bounce (real Jenny had aired up the tires first thing, even before she grew the garage).

The light car revved its motor excitedly. Then, just a gentle tap on the door, and it was out in the parking lot. It drove over to the steps leading down to the beach, hunching its grill down to the ground. It circled the lot a bit, snuffling here and there, until it found whatever it was looking for. Before it zipped down the road toward Nashville, it circled back round and stopped outside the horse's stall. The light car opened its passenger door and waggled it back and forth a time or two. The real horse neighed and tossed its head at the light car in a friendly fashion.

Jenny-With-Grease-Beneath-Her-Fingernails visited her horse with the meanest look that a mechanic can give a horse. The horse snickered. "You laugh, horse," she said, opening the tack locker, "but we still have to go after it."

Inside the bundle bug, there was some unpleasantness with a large glass-and-pewter contraption of the Owl's. The Crow Brothers held Soma as motionless as they could, and Japheth seemed genuinely sorry when he forced the painter's mouth open much wider than Soma had previously thought possible. "You should have drunk more of the whiskey," said Japheth. There was a loud, wet, popping sound, and Soma shuddered, stiffened, fainted.

"Well, that'll work best for all of us," said Japheth. He looked up at the Owl, who was peering through a lens polished out of a semi-precious gemstone, staring down into the painter's gullet.

"Have you got access?"

The Owl nodded.

"Talk to your math," said the Crow.

The math had been circling beneath the bridge, occasionally dragging a curiosity-begat string of numbers into the water. Always low-test numbers, because invariably whatever lived beneath the water snatched at the lines and sucked them down.

The input the math was waiting for finally arrived in the form of a low hooting sound rising up from the dumping grounds. It was important that the math not know which bundle bug the sound emanated from. There were certain techniques the bears had developed for teasing information out of recalcitrant math.

No matter. The math knew the processes. It had the input. It spread itself out over the long line of imagery the bundle bugs yielded up to the bears. It affected its changes. It lent clarity.

Above, the bears did their work with great precision.

Below, the Kentuckians slipped into Nashville undetected.

Soma woke to find the Kentuckians doing something terrible. When he tried to speak, he found that his face was immobilized by a mask of something that smelled of the docks but felt soft and gauzy.

The four younger Crows were dressed in a gamut of jerseys and shorts colored in the hotter hues of the spectrum. Japheth was struggling into a long, jangly coat hung with seashells and old capacitors.

But it was the Owl that frightened Soma the most. The broad-chested man was dappled with opal stones from collarbones to ankles and wore nothing else save a breechcloth cut from an old newspaper. Soma moaned, trying to attract their attention again.

The blue-eyed boy said, "Your painter stirs, Japheth."

But it was the Owl who leaned over Soma, placed his hand on Soma's chin and turned his head back and forth with surprising gentleness. The Owl nodded, to himself Soma guessed, for none of the Crows reacted, then peeled the bandages off Soma's face.

Soma took a deep breath, then said, "Nobody's worn opals for months! And those shorts," he gestured at the others, "Too much orange! Too much orange!"

Japheth laughed. "Well, we'll be tourists in from the provinces, then, not princes of Printer's Alley. Do *I* offend?" He wriggled his shoulders, set the shells and circuits to clacking.

Soma pursed his lips, shook his head. "Seashells and capacitors are timeless," he said.

Japheth nodded. "That's what it said on the box." Then, "Hey! Bug! Are we to market yet?"

"It's hard to say, whiskey man," came the reply. "My eyes are funny."

"Close enough. Open up."

The rear of the beast's abdomen cracked, and yawned wide. Japheth turned to his charges. "You boys ready to play like vols?"

The younger Crows started gathering burlap bundles. The Owl hoisted a heavy rucksack, adjusted the flowers in his hat, and said, "Wacka wacka ho."

In a low place, horizon bounded by trees in every direction, Jenny and her horse came on the sobbing car. From the ruts it had churned up in the mud, Jenny guessed it had been there for some time, driving back and forth along the northern verge.

"Now what have you done to yourself?" she asked, dismounting. The car turned to her and shuddered. Its front left fender was badly dented, and its hood and windshield were a mess of leaves and small branches.

"Trying to get into the woods? Cars are for roads, car." She brushed some muck off the damaged fender.

"Well, that's not too bad, though. This is all cosmetic. Why would a car try to go where trees are? See what happens?"

The horse called. It had wandered a little way into the woods and was standing at the base of a vast poplar. Jenny reached in through the passenger's window of the car, avoiding the glassy knitting blanket on the other side, and set the parking brake. "You wait here."

She trotted out to join her horse. It was pawing at a small patch of ground. Jenny was a mechanic and had no woodscraft, but she could see the outline of a cleft-toed sandal. Who would be in the woods with such impractical footwear?

"The owner's an artist. An artist looking for a shortcut to the Alley, I reckon," said Jenny. "Wearing funny artist shoes."

She walked back to the car, considering. The car was pining. Not unheard of, but not common. It made her think better of Soma Painter that his car missed him so.

"Say, horse. Melancholy slows car repair. I think this car will convalesce better in its own parking space."

The car revved.

"But there's the garage still back at the beach," said Jenny.

She turned things over and over. "Horse," she said, "you're due three more personal days this month. If I release you for them now, will you go fold up the garage and bring it to me in the city?"

The horse tossed its head enthusiastically.

"Good. I'll drive with this car back to the Alley, then—" But the horse was already rubbing its flanks against her.

"Okay, okay." She drew a tin of salve from her tool belt, dipped her fingers in it, then ran her hands across the horse's back. The red crosses came away in her hands, wriggling. "The cases for these are in my cabinet," she said, and then inspiration came.

"Here, car," she said, and laid the crosses on its hood. They wriggled around until they were at statute-specified points along the doors and roof. "Now you're an ambulance! Not a hundred percent legal, maybe, but this way you can drive fast and whistle siren-like."

The car spun its rear wheels but couldn't overcome the parking brake. Jenny laughed. "Just a minute more. I need you to give me a ride into town."

She turned to speak to the horse, only to see it already galloping along the coast road. "Don't forget to drain the water tanks before you fold it up!" she shouted.

The bundles that were flecked with root matter, Soma discovered, were filled with roots. Carrots and turnips, a half dozen varieties of potatoes, beets. The Kentuckians spread out through the Farmer's Market, trading them by the armload for the juices and gels that the rock monkeys brought in from their gardens.

"This is our secondary objective," said Japheth. "We do this all the time, trading doped potatoes for that shit y'all eat."

"You're poisoning us?" Soma was climbing out of the paste a little, or something. His thoughts were shifting around some.

"Doped with nutrients, friend. Forty ain't old outside Tennessee. Athena doesn't seem to know any more about human nutrition than she does human psychology. Hey, we're trying to *help* you people."

Then they were in the very center of the market, and the roar of the crowds drowned out any reply Soma might make.

Japheth kept a grip on Soma's arm as he spoke to a gray old monkey. "Ten pounds, right?" The monkey was weighing a bundle of carrots on a scale.

"Okay," grunted the monkey. "Okay, man. Ten pounds I give you . . . four blue jellies."

Soma was incredulous. He'd never developed a taste for them himself, but he knew that carrots were popular. Four blue jellies was an insulting trade. But Japheth said, "Fair enough," and pocketed the plastic tubes the monkey handed over.

"You're no trader," said Soma, or started to, but heard the words slur out of him in an unintelligible mess of vowels. *One spring semester, when he'd already been a TA for a year, he was tapped to work on the interface. No more need for scholarships.*

"Painter!" shouted Japheth.

Soma looked up. There was a Crow dressed in Alley haute couture standing in front of him. He tried to open his head to call the Tennessee Highway Patrol. He couldn't find his head.

"Give him one of these yellow ones," said a monkey. "They're good for fugues."

"Painter!" shouted Japheth again. The grip on Soma's shoulder was like a vise.

Soma struggled to stand under his own power. "I'm forgetting something."

"Hah!" said Japheth, "You're remembering. Too soon for my needs, though. Listen to me. Rock monkeys are full voluntary citizens of Tennessee."

The outlandishness of the statement shocked Soma out of his reverie and brought the vendor up short.

"Fuck you, man!" said the monkey.

"No, no," said Soma, then said by rote, "Tennessee is a fully realized postcolonial state. The land of the rock monkeys is an autonomous partner-principality within our borders, and while the monkeys are our staunch allies, their allegiance is not to our Governor, but to their king."

"Yah," said the monkey. "Long as we get our licenses and pay the tax machine. Plus, who the jelly cubes going to listen to besides the monkey king, huh?"

Soma marched Japheth to the next stall. "Lot left in there to wash out yet," Japheth said.

"I wash every day," said Soma, then fell against a sloshing tray of juice containers. *The earliest results were remarkable.*

A squat man covered with black gems came up to them. The man who'd insulted the monkey said, "You might have killed too much of it; he's getting kind of wonky."

The squat man looked into Soma's eyes. "We can stabilize him easy enough. There are televisions in the food court."

Then Soma and Japheth were drinking hot rum punches and watching a newsfeed. There was a battle out over the Gulf somewhere, Commodores mounted on bears darted through the clouds, lancing Cuban zeppelins.

"The Cubans will never achieve air superiority," said Soma, and it felt right saying it.

Japheth eyed him wearily. "I need you to keep thinking that for now, Soma Painter," he said quietly. "But I hope sometime soon you'll know that Cubans don't live in a place called the Appalachian Archipelago, and that the salty reach out there isn't the Gulf of Mexico."

The bicycle race results were on then, and Soma scanned the lists, hoping to see his favorites' names near the top of the general classifications.

"That's the Tennessee River, dammed up by your Governor's hubris."

Soma saw that his drink was nearly empty and heard that his friend Japheth was still talking. "What?" he asked, smiling.

"I asked if you're ready to go to the Alley," said Japheth.

"Good good," said Soma.

The math was moving along minor avenues, siphoning data from secondary and tertiary ports when it sensed her looming up. It re-
searched ten thousand thousand escapes but rejected them all when it
perceived that it had been subverted, that it was inside her now, becoming part of her, that it *is primitive in materials but clever clever in architecture and there have been blindings times not seen places to root out root
out all of it check again check one thousand more times all told all told eat it
all up all the little bluegrass math is absorbed*

"The Alley at night!" shouted Soma. "Not like where you're from,
eh, boys?"

A lamplighter's stalk legs eased through the little group. Soma saw
that his friends were staring up at the civil servant's welding mask
head, gaping openmouthed as it turned a spigot at the top of a tree
and lit the gas with a flick of its tongue.

"Let's go to my place!" said Soma. "When it's time for anthem
we can watch the parade from my balcony. I live in one of the lofts
above the Tyranny of the Anecdote."

"Above what?" asked Japheth.

"It's a tavern. They're my landlords," said Soma. "Vols are so
fucking stupid."

But that wasn't right.

Japheth's Owl friend fell to his knees and vomited right in the
street. Soma stared at the jiggling spheres in the gutter as the man
choked some words out. "She's taken the feathers. She's looking for
us now."

Too much rum punch, thought Soma, thought it about the Owl
man and himself and about all of Japheth's crazy friends.

"Soma, how far now?" asked Japheth.

Soma remembered his manners. "Not far," he said.

And it wasn't, just a few more struggling yards, Soma leading the
way and Japheth's friends half-carrying, half-dragging their drunken
friend down the Alley. Nothing unusual there. Every night in the Alley was Carnival.

Then a wave at the bouncer outside the Anecdote, then up the steps, then sing "Let me in, let me in!" to the door, and finally all of them packed into the cramped space.

"There," said the sick man, pointing at the industrial sink Soma had installed himself to make brush cleaning easier. *Brushes . . . where were his brushes, his pencils, his notes for the complexity seminar?*

"Towels, Soma?"

"What? Oh, here let me get them." Soma bustled around, finding towels, pulling out stools for the now silent men who filled his room.

He handed the towels to Japheth. "Was it something he ate?" Soma asked.

Japheth shrugged. "Ate a long time ago, you could say. Owls are as much numbers as they are meat. He's divesting himself. Those are ones and zeroes washing down your drain."

The broad man—hadn't he been broad?—the scrawny man with opals falling off him said, "We can only take a few minutes. There are unmounted Detectives swarming the whole city now. What I've left in me is too deep for their little minds, but the whole sphere is roused and things will only get tighter. Just let me—" He turned and retched into the sink again. "Just a few minutes more until the singing."

Japheth moved to block Soma's view of the Owl. He nodded at the drawings on the wall. "Yours?"

The blue-eyed boy moved over to the sink, helped the Owl ease to the floor. Soma looked at the pictures. "Yes, mostly. I traded for a few."

Japheth was studying one charcoal piece carefully, a portrait. "What's this one?"

The drawing showed a tall, thin young man dressed in a period costume, leaning against a mechanical of some kind, staring intently out at the viewer. Soma didn't remember drawing it, specifically, but knew what it must be.

"That's a caricature. I do them during Campaign for the provincials who come into the city to vote. Someone must have asked me to draw him and then never come back to claim it."

And he remembered trying to remember. He remembered asking his hand to remember when his head wouldn't.

"I'm . . . what did you put in me?" Soma asked. There was moisture on his cheeks, and he hoped it was tears.

The Owl was struggling up to his feet. A bell tone sounded from the sky and he said, "Now, Japheth. There's no time."

"Just a minute more," snapped the Crow. "What did *we* put in

you? You . . ." Japheth spat. "While you're remembering, try and remember this. You *chose* this! All of you chose it!"

The angry man wouldn't have heard any reply Soma might have
made, because it was then that all of the Kentuckians clamped their
ears shut with their odd muffs. To his surprise, they forced a pair onto
Soma as well.

Jenny finally convinced the car to stop wailing out its hee-haw pitch
when they entered the maze of streets leading to Printer's Alley. The
drive back had been long, the car taking every northern side road,
backtracking, looping, even trying to enter the dumping grounds at
one point before the bundle bugs growled them away. During anthem, while Jenny drummed her fingers and forced out the words, the
car still kept up its search, not even pretending to dance.

So Jenny had grown more and more fascinated by the car's behav-
ior. She had known cars that were slavishly attached to their owners
before, and she had known cars that were smart—almost as smart as
bundle bugs, some of them—but the two traits never seemed to go
together. "Cars are dogs or cars are cats," her Teacher had said to explain the phenomenon, another of the long roll of enigmatic state-
ments that constituted formal education in the Voluntary State.

But here, now, here was a bundle bug that didn't seem to live up
to those creatures' reputations for craftiness. The car had been following the bug for a few blocks—Jenny only realized that after the car,
for the first time since they entered the city proper, made a turn *away*
from the address painted on its name tag.

The bug was a big one, and was describing a gentle career down
Commerce Street, drifting from side to side and clearly ignoring the
traffic signals that flocked around its head in an agitated cloud.

"Car, we'd better get off this street. Rogue bugs are too much for
the THP. If it doesn't self-correct, a Commodore is likely to be
rousted out from the Parthenon." Jenny sometimes had nightmares
about Commodores.

The car didn't listen—though it was normally an excellent
listener—but accelerated toward the bug. The bug, Jenny now saw,
had stopped in front of a restaurant and cracked its abdomen. Dump-
ster feelers had started creeping out of the interstices between thorax
and head when the restaurateur charged out, beating at the feelers
with a broom. "Go now!" the man shouted, face as red as his vest and

leggings. "I told you twice already! You pick up here Chaseday! Go! I
already called your supervisor, bug!"

The bug's voice echoed along the street. "No load? Good good."
Its sigh was pure contentment, but Jenny had no time to appreciate it.
The car sped up, and Jenny covered her eyes, anticipating a collision.
But the car slid to a halt with bare inches to spare, peered into the
empty cavern of the bug's belly, then sighed, this one not content at
all.

"Come on, car," Jenny coaxed. "He must be at home by now.
Let's just try your house, okay?"

The car beeped and executed a precise three-point turn. As they
turned off Commerce and climbed the viaduct that arced above the
Farmer's Market, Jenny caught a hint of motion in the darkening sky.
"THP bicycles, for sure," she said. "Tracking your bug friend."

At the highest point on the bridge, Jenny leaned out and looked
down into the controlled riot of the Market. Several stalls were doing
brisk business, and when Jenny saw why, she asked the car to stop,
then let out a whistle.

"Oi! Monkey!" she shouted. "Some beets up here!"

Jenny loved beets.

*signals from the city center subsidiaries routing reports and recommendations
increase percentages dedicated to observation and prediction dispatch commodore downcycle biological construct extra-parametrical lower authority*

"It's funny that I don't know what it means, though, don't you think,
friends?" Soma was saying this for perhaps the fifth time since they
began their walk. "*Church* Street. *Church*. Have you ever heard that
word anywhere else?"

"No," said the blue-eyed boy.

The Kentuckians were less and less talkative the farther the little
group advanced west down Church Street. It was a long, broad avenue, but rated for pedestrians and emergency vehicles only. Less a
street, really, than a linear park, for there were neither businesses nor
apartments on either side, just low gray government buildings, slate-
colored in the sunset.

The sunset. That was why the boulevard was crowded, as it was
every night. As the sun dropped down, down, down it dropped be-

hind the Parthenon. At the very instant the disc disappeared behind the sand-colored edifice, the Great Salt Lick self-illuminated and the flat acres of white surrounding the Parthenon shone with a vast, icy light.

The Lick itself was rich with the minerals that fueled the Legislators and Bears, but the white light emanating from it was sterile. Soma noticed that the Crows' faces grew paler and paler as they all got closer to its source. *His work was fascinating, and grew more so as more and more disciplines began finding ways to integrate their fields of study into a meta-architecture of science. His department chair co-authored a paper with an expert in animal husbandry, of all things.*

The Owl held Soma's head as the painter vomited up the last of whatever was in his stomach. Japheth and the others were making reassuring noises to passersby. "Too much monkey wine!" they said, and, "We're in from the provinces, he's not used to such rich food!" and, "He's overcome by the sight of the Parthenon!"

Japheth leaned over next to the Owl. "Why's it hitting him so much harder than the others?"

The Owl said, "Well, we've always taken them back north of the border. This poor fool we're dragging ever closer to the glory of his owner. I couldn't even guess what's trying to fill up the empty spaces I left in him—but I'm pretty sure whatever's rushing in isn't all from her."

Japheth cocked an eyebrow at his lieutenant. "I think that's the most words I've ever heard you say all together at once."

The Owl smiled, another first, if that sad little half grin counted as a smile. "Not a lot of time left for talking. Get up now, friend painter."

The Owl and Japheth pulled Soma to his feet. "What did you mean," Soma asked, wiping his mouth with the back of his hand, " 'the glory of his owner'?"

"Governor," said Japheth. "He said, 'the glory of his Governor,' " and Japheth swept his arm across, and yes, there it was, the glory of the Governor.

Church Street had a slight downward grade in its last few hundred yards. From where they stood, they could see that the street ended at the spectacularly defined border of the Great Salt Lick, which served as legislative chambers in the Voluntary State. At the center of the lick stood the Parthenon, and while no normal citizens walked the salt just then, there was plenty of motion and color.

Two bears were lying facedown in the Lick, bobbing their heads as they took in sustenance from the ground. A dozen or more Legislators slowly unambulated, their great slimy bodies leaving trails of gold or silver depending on their party affiliation. One was engulfing one of the many salt-white statues that dotted the grounds, gaining a few feet of height to warble its slogan songs from. And, unmoving at the corners of the rectangular palace in the center of it all, four Commodores stood.

They were tangled giants of rust, alike in their towering height and in the oily bathyspheres encasing the scant meat of them deep in their torsos, but otherwise each a different silhouette of sensor suites and blades, each with a different complement of articulated limbs or wings or wheels.

"Can you tell which ones they are?" Japheth asked the blue-eyed boy, who had begun murmuring to himself under his breath, eyes darting from Commodore to Commodore.

> *"Ruby-eyed Sutcliffe, stomper, smasher,*
> *Tempting Nguyen, whispering, lying,*
> *Burroughs burrows, up from the underground . . ."*

The boy hesitated, shaking his head. "Northeast corner looks kind of like Praxis Dale, but she's supposed to be away West, fighting the Federals. Saint Sandalwood's physical presence had the same profile as Dale's, but we believe he's gone, consumed by Athena after their last sortie against the containment field cost her so much."

"I'll never understand why she plays at politics with her subordinates when she *is* her subordinates," said Japheth.

The Owl said, "That's not as true with the Commodores as with a lot of the . . . inhabitants. I think it *is* Saint Sandalwood; she must have reconstituted him, or part of him. And remember his mnemonic?"

"*Sandalwood staring,*" sang the blue-eyed boy.

"*Inside and outside,*" finished Japheth, looking the Owl in the eye. "Time then?"

"Once we're on the Lick I'd do anything she told me, even empty as I am," said the Owl. "Bind me."

Then the blue-eyed boy took Soma by the arm, kept encouraging him to take in the sights of the Parthenon, turning his head away from where the Crows were wrapping the Owl in grapevines. They took the Owl's helmet from a rucksack and seated it, cinching the cork seals at the neck maybe tighter than Soma would have thought was comfortable.

Two of the Crows hoisted the Owl between them, his feet stumbling some. Soma saw that the eyeholes of the mask had been blocked with highly reflective tape.

Japheth spoke to the others. "The bears won't be in this; they'll take too long to stand up from their meal. Avoid the Legislators, even their trails. The THP will be on the ground, but won't give you any trouble. You boys know why you're here."

The two Crows holding the Owl led him over to Japheth, who took him by the hand. The blue-eyed boy said, "We know why we're here, Japheth. We know why we were born."

And suddenly as that, the four younger Crows were gone, fleeing in every direction except back up Church Street.

"Soma Painter," said Japheth. "Will you help me lead this man on?"

Soma was taken aback. While he knew of no regulation specifically prohibiting it, traditionally no one actually trod the Lick except during Campaign.

"We're going into the Salt Lick?" Soma asked.

"We're going into the Parthenon," Japheth answered.

As they crossed Church Street from the south, the car suddenly stopped.

"Now what, car?" said Jenny. Church Street was her least favorite thoroughfare in the capital.

The car snuffled around on the ground for a moment, then, without warning, took a hard left and accelerated, siren screeching. Tourists and sunset gazers scattered to either side as the car and Jenny roared toward the glowing white horizon.

The Owl only managed a few yards under his own power. He slowed, then stumbled, and then the Crow and the painter were carrying him.

"What's wrong with him?" asked Soma.

They crossed the verge onto the salt. They'd left the bravest sightseers a half-block back.

"He's gone inside himself," said Japheth.

"Why?" asked Soma.

Japheth half laughed. "You'd know better than me, friend."

It was then that the Commodore closest to them took a single step forward with its right foot, dragged the left a dozen yards in the same direction, and then, twisting, fell to the ground with a thunderous crash.

"Whoo!" shouted Japheth. "The harder they fall! We'd better start running now, Soma!"

Soma was disappointed, but unsurprised, to see that Japheth did not mean run *away*.

There was only one bear near the slightly curved route that Japheth picked for them through the harsh glare. Even light as he was, purged of his math, the Owl was still a burden and Soma couldn't take much time to marvel at the swirling colors in the bear's plastic hide.

"Keep up, Soma!" shouted the Crow. Ahead of them, two of the Commodores had suddenly turned on one another and were landing terrible blows. Soma saw a tiny figure clinging to one of the giants' shoulders, saw it lose its grip, fall, and disappear beneath an ironshod boot the size of a bundle bug.

Then Soma slipped and fell himself, sending all three of them to the glowing ground and sending a cloud of the biting crystal salt into the air. One of his sandaled feet, he saw, was coated in gold slime. They'd been trying to outflank one Legislator only to stumble on the trail of another.

Japheth picked up the Owl, now limp as a rag doll, and with a grunt heaved the man across his shoulders. "Soma, you should come on. We might make it." *It's not a hard decision to make at all. How can you not make it? At first he'd needed convincing, but then he'd been one of those who'd gone out into the world to convince others. It's not just history; it's after history.*

"Soma!"

Japheth ran directly at the unmoving painter, the deadweight of the Owl across his shoulders slowing him. He barreled into Soma, knocking him to the ground again, all of them just missing the unknowing Legislator as it slid slowly past.

"Up, up!" said Japheth. "Stay behind it, so long as it's moving in the right direction. I think my boys missed a Commodore." His voice was very sad.

The Legislator stopped and let out a bellowing noise. Fetid steam began rising from it. Japheth took Soma by the hand and pulled him along, through chaos. One of the Commodores, the first to fall, was motionless on the ground, two or three Legislators making their way along its length. The two who'd fought lay locked in one another's grasp, barely moving and glowing hotter and hotter. The only standing Commodore, eyes like red suns, seemed to be staring just behind them.

As it began to sweep its gaze closer, Soma heard Japheth say, "We got closer than I would have bet."

Then Soma's car, mysteriously covered with red crosses and wailing at the top of its voice, came to a sliding, crunching stop in the salt in front of them.

Soma didn't hesitate, but threw open the closest rear door and pulled Japheth in behind him. When the three of them—painter, Crow, Owl—were stuffed into the rear door, Soma shouted, "Up those stairs, car!"

In the front seat, there was a woman whose eyes seemed as large as saucers.

commodores faulting headless people in the lick protocols compel reeling in, strengthening, temporarily abandoning telepresence locate an asset with a head asset with a head located

Jenny-With-Grease-Beneath-Her-Fingernails was trying not to go crazy. Something was pounding at her head, even though she hadn't tried to open it herself. Yesterday, she had been working a remote repair job on the beach, fixing a smashed window. Tonight, she was hurtling across the Great Salt Lick, Legislators and bears and *Commodores* acting in ways she'd never seen or heard of.

Jenny herself acting in ways she'd never heard of. Why didn't she just pull the emergency brake, roll out of the car, wait for the THP? Why did she just hold on tighter and pull down the sunscreen so she could use the mirror to look into the backseat?

It *was* three men. She hadn't been sure at first. One appeared to be unconscious and was dressed in some strange getup, a helmet of some kind completely encasing his head. She didn't know the man in the capacitor jacket, who was craning his head out the window, trying to see something above them. The other one though, she recognized.

"Soma Painter," she said. "Your car is much better, though it has missed you terribly."

The owner just looked at her glaze-eyed. The other one pulled himself back in through the window, a wild glee on his face. He rapped the helmet of the prone man and shouted, "Did you hear that? The unpredictable you prophesied! And it fell in our favor!"

Soma worried about his car's suspension, not to mention the tires, when it slalomed through the legs of the last standing Commodore and bounced up the steeply cut steps of the Parthenon. *He hadn't had a direct hand in the subsystems design—by the time he'd begun to develop the cars, Athena was already beginning to take over a lot of the details. Not all of them, though; he couldn't blame her for the guilt he felt over twisting his animal subjects into something like onboard components.*

But the car made it onto the platform inside the outer set of columns, seemingly no worse for wear. The man next to him—Japheth, his name was Japheth and he was from Kentucky—jumped out of the car and ran to the vast, closed counterweighted bronze doors.

"It's because of the crosses. We're in an emergency vehicle according to their protocols." That was the mechanic, Jenny, sitting in the front seat and trying to stanch a nosebleed with a greasy rag. "I can hear the Governor," she said.

Soma could hear Japheth raging and cursing. He stretched the Owl out along the backseat and climbed out of the car. Japheth was pounding on the doors in futility, beating his fists bloody, spinning, spitting. He caught sight of Soma.

"*These* weren't here before!" he said, pointing to two silver columns that angled up from the platform's floor, ending in flanges on the doors themselves. "The doors aren't locked, they're just sealed by these fucking cylinders!" Japheth was shaking. "Caw!" he cried. "Caw!"

"What's he trying to do?" asked the woman in the car.

Soma brushed his fingers against his temple, trying to remember. "I think he's trying to remake Tennessee," he said.

The weight of a thousand cars on her skull, the hoofbeats of a thousand horses throbbing inside her eyes, Jenny was incapable of making any rational decision. So, irrationally, she left the car. She stumbled over to the base of one of the silver columns. When she tried to catch herself on it, her hand slid off.

"Oil," she said. "These are just hydraulic cylinders." She looked around the metal sheeting where the cylinder disappeared into the platform, saw the access plate. She pulled a screwdriver from her belt and used it to remove the plate.

The owner was whispering to his car, but the crazy man had come over to her. "What are you doing?" he asked.

"I don't know," she said, but she meant it only in the largest sense. Immediately, she was thrusting her wrists into the access plate, playing the licenses and government bonds at her wrists under a spray of light, murmuring a quick apology to the machinery. Then she opened a long vertical cut down as much of the length of the hydraulic hose as she could with her utility blade.

Fluid exploded out of the hole, coating Jenny in the slick, dirty green stuff. The cylinders collapsed.

The man next to Jenny looked at her. He turned and looked at Soma-With-The-Paintbox-In-Printer's-Alley and at Soma's car.

"We must have had a pretty bad plan," he said, then rushed over to pull the helmeted figure from the backseat.

❈

breached come home all you commodores come home cancel emergency designation on identified vehicle and downcycle now jump in jump in jump in

❈

Jenny could not help Soma and his friend drag their burden through the doors of the temple, but she staggered through the doors. She had only seen Athena in tiny parts, in the mannequin shrines that contained tiny fractions of the Governor.

Here was the true and awesome thing, here was the forty-foot-tall sculpture—armed and armored—attended by the broken remains of her frozen marble enemies. Jenny managed to lift her head and look past sandaled feet, up cold golden raiment, past tart painted cheeks to the lapis lazuli eyes.

Athena looked back at her. Athena leapt.

Inside Jenny's head, inside so small an architecture, there was no more room for Jenny-With-Grease-Beneath-Her-Fingernails. Jenny fled.

❈

Soma saw the mechanic, the woman who'd been so kind to his car, fall to her knees, blood gushing from her nose and ears. He saw Japheth laying out the Owl like a sacrifice before the Governor. *He'd been among the detractors, scoffing at the idea of housing the main armature in such a symbol-potent place.*

Behind him, his car beeped. The noise was barely audible above the screaming metal sounds out in the Lick. The standing Commodore was swiveling its torso, turning its upper half toward the Parthenon. Superheated salt melted in a line slowly tracking toward the steps.

Soma trotted back to his car. He leaned in and *remembered the back door, the Easter egg he hadn't documented.* A twist on the ignition housing, then press in, and the key sank into the column. The car shivered.

"Run home as fast you can, car. Back to the ranch with your kin. Be fast, car, be clever."

The car woke up. It shook off Soma's ownership and closed its little head. It let out a surprised beep and then fled with blazing speed, leaping down the steps, over the molten salt, and through the storm, bubblewinged bicycles descending all around. The Commodore began another slow turn, trying to track it.

Soma turned back to the relative calm inside the Parthenon. Athena's gaze was baleful, but he couldn't feel it. The Owl had ripped the ability from him. The Owl lying before Japheth, defenseless against the knife Japheth held high.

"Why?" shouted Soma.

But Japheth didn't answer him, instead diving over the Owl in a somersault roll, narrowly avoiding the flurry of kicks and roundhouse blows being thrown by Jenny. Her eyes bugged and bled. More blood flowed from her ears and nostrils, but still she attacked Japheth with relentless fury.

Japheth came up in a crouch. The answer to Soma's question came in a slurred voice from Jenny. Not Jenny, though. Soma knew the voice, remembered it from somewhere, and it wasn't Jenny's.

"there is a bomb in that meat soma-friend a knife a threat an eraser"

Japheth shouted at Soma. "You get to decide again! Cut the truth out of him!" He gestured at the Owl with his knife.

Soma took in a shuddery breath. "So free with lives. One of the reasons we climbed up."

Jenny's body lurched at Japheth, but the Crow dropped onto the polished floor. Jenny's body slipped when it landed, the soles of its shoes coated with the same oil as its jumpsuit.

"My Owl cousin died of asphyxiation at least ten minutes ago, Soma," said Japheth. "Died imperfect and uncontrolled." Then, dancing backward before the scratching thing in front of him, Japheth tossed the blade in a gentle underhanded arc. It clattered to the floor at Soma's feet.

All of the same arguments.

All of the same arguments.

Soma picked up the knife and looked down at the Owl. The fight before him, between a dead woman versus a man certain to die soon, spun on. Japheth said no more, only looked at Soma with pleading eyes.

Jenny's body's eyes followed the gaze, saw the knife in Soma's hand.

"you are due upgrade soma-friend swell the ranks of commodores you were 96th percentile now 99th

soma-with-the-paintbox-in-printer's-alley the voluntary state of tennessee applauds your citizenship"

But it wasn't the early slight, the denial of entry to the circle of highest minds. Memories of before *and* after, decisions made by him and for him, sentiences and upgrades decided by fewer and fewer and then one; one who'd been a *product,* not a builder.

Soma plunged the knife into the Owl's unmoving chest and sawed downward through the belly with what strength he could muster. The skin and fat fell away along a seam straighter than he could ever cut. The bomb—the knife, the eraser, the threat—looked like a tiny white balloon. He pierced it with the killing tip of the Kentuckian's blade.

A nova erupted at the center of the space where math and Detectives live. A wave of scouring numbers washed outward, spreading all across Nashville, all across the Voluntary State to fill all the space within the containment field.

The 144 Detectives evaporated. The King of the Rock Monkeys, nothing but twisted light, fell into shadow. The Commodores fell immobile, the ruined biology seated in their chests went blind, then deaf, then died.

And singing Nashville fell quiet. Ten thousand thousand heads slammed shut and ten thousand thousand souls fell insensate, unsupported, in need of revival.

North of the Girding Wall, alarms began to sound.

At the Parthenon, Japheth Sapp gently placed the tips of his index and ring fingers on Jenny's eyelids and pulled them closed.

Then the ragged Crow pushed past Soma and hurried out into the night. The Great Salt Lick glowed no more, and even the lights of the city were dimmed, so Soma quickly lost sight of the man. But then the cawing voice rang out once more. "We only hurt the car because we had to."

Soma thought for a moment, then said, "So did I."

But the Crow was gone, and then Soma had nothing to do but wait. He had made the only decision he had left in him. He idly watched as burning bears floated down into the sea. A striking image, but he had somewhere misplaced his paints.

Anne McCaffrey has been one of the best-known and best-selling writers in science fiction for more than forty years, having published dozens of books, including *The Dragonriders of Pern, To Ride Pegasus, Crystal Singer, Killashandra, The White Dragon, All the Weyrs of Pern, The Renegades of Pern, Decision on Doona,* and many, many others. She won a Hugo Award in 1968 for her novella "Weyr Search," a Nebula Award in 1969 for her novella "Dragonrider," and in 2005 was named the recipient of SFFWA's prestigious Grand Master Award, acknowledging her lifetime of achievement in the field.

In recognition of her appointment as SFFWA's newest Grand Master, we're pleased to be able to bring you a heartfelt appreciation of Anne McCaffrey by McCaffrey's longtime friend and collaborator, Jody Lynn Nye, followed by one of McCaffrey's best-known and most acclaimed stories.

Jody Lynn Nye lists her main career activity as "spoiling cats." She lives northwest of Chicago with two of the above and her husband, author and packager Bill Fawcett. She has published thirty books, including six contemporary fantasies, four SF novels, four novels in collaboration with Anne McCaffrey, including *The Ship Who Won*; edited a humorous anthology about mothers, *Don't Forget Your Spacesuit, Dear!*; and written over eighty short stories. Her latest books are *The Lady and the Tiger*, third in her *Taylor's Ark* series, *Strong Arm Tactics*, first in the Wolfe Pack series, and *Class Dis-Mythed*, cowritten with Robert Asprin.

GRAND MASTER ANNE McCAFFREY: AN APPRECIATION

JODY LYNN NYE

owe a lot to my friend Barbara for introducing me to Anne Mc-Caffrey. In Barbara's home I admired a couple of beautiful prints on the wall, all lacy and medieval in style, depicting a pretty girl with lots of dark, wavy hair surrounded by tiny flying dragons. "Those are the covers from *Dragonsong* and *Dragonsinger*," she said. "You mean, you haven't read them? Oh, you have to. But you should really start with *Dragonflight*."

So I did. The Pern books grabbed me from the very first line, and never let go. They were about dragons. I had always been fascinated by dragons. These weren't just any dragons; they were *scientifically plausible* dragons. The best part was, instead of being terrifying predators, they were mankind's ally. If you had one of these dragons, it belonged to you and no one else, a powerful, telepathic friend whose voice only you could hear, and who loved you and protected you before all other people, against the compelling danger of the mindless Thread. What a terrific image to offer to readers who often felt vulnerable and lost in the real world. And the survival-oriented nature of the society meant that this treat was not available to just a few, but to thousands of would-be dragonriders, making it desirably inclusive to those dreamers who read Anne's books.

The attraction of Anne McCaffrey's books does not by any means end with dragons. Her human characters are people whom you could actually know and would want to hang around with. Here were men who were real men and—thank heaven!—women who were *real* women. Unlike many of her early male contemporaries' female characters, Anne's women are strong and effective. They are never cardboard cutouts devoid of feelings or thoughts, curvaceous cuties who scream and faint and need to be rescued by their big, strong hero companions, or thinly disguised men in skirts. Her heroines do quite a lot of their own rescuing, thank you. Lessa of Pern takes the initiative to save the world at nearly the cost of her own life and the life of the only fertile female dragon left on the planet. She is an original, complex personality, prickly, intelligent, quick-witted and strong-minded, yet tender toward her beloved Ramoth. Killashandra Ree holds her own in a dangerous world where only the strong survive for long, and only the talented make money. Helva, the Ship Who Sang, plies the spaceways with impunity, knowing that she belongs there.

Even so-called spear-carriers in Anne's books are so well drawn, responding to situations as actual people would, not just as the appropriately acting agent for the MacGuffin that would solve the world-threatening problem that is at the heart of any good science fiction story. Her characters' strength to face challenges was not only to be found in the robust and muscular, but in those who were gentle and meek. There is danger, but there is also love. Anne has said in the past that her books are romances with a little science fiction wrapped around them. Her readers revel in the relationships as much as they do in the adventures and problems that must be solved for the characters to survive.

But wait, as the infomercials say, there's more! Most of Anne's worlds touch the wish-fulfillment reflex in us. Imagine a job in which perfect pitch and musical talent is the key to limitless wealth, instead of second seat in the flute section. Imagine near-immortality and unfettered freedom even for those considered hopelessly physically handicapped. Imagine a humanlike species in whom the legend of the unicorn comes true. Imagine being able to communicate telepathically from star system to star system. Anne has brought us so many different dreams, and all we need to do to step into them is turn to the first page.

Anne claims in her biographies to have written her first novel in Latin class. Furtive fiction writing certainly seems to have been a far better use of her time than learning declensions or reading Cicero's orations in the original. Even if by her current standards the early book is unreadable, it was the first step in developing the style that her readers have come to know and cherish.

The elevation of Anne McCaffrey to the status of Grand Master is recognition by the wide and diverse community of her fellow science fiction writers of the excellence of her writing, but not everyone knows what a wonderful person she is as well. Anne is generous, both professionally and personally. She gives the credit to the legendary editor John Campbell for suggesting that she write about dragons. She also said at the Nebula banquet when she was given the Grand Master award that Andre Norton told her to write about a white dragon, one with special abilities, which gave rise to Anne's first *New York Times* best seller, *The White Dragon*.

Quite a number of her fans whom I asked found Anne's work in much the same manner I did: through a friend who wanted to share the pleasure of a cracking good read. Others were handed the books by parents or older siblings. More came across it in bookstores, libraries, and PXs (she has a huge readership in the military). But no matter where they met Anne's worlds they all find that true treasure a writer can give her readers: escape in her books from their daily lives. Many feel as if they know her characters, and would like to live in some of her worlds, most notably Pern.

There is a reason Anne McCaffrey doesn't just have readers; she has fans . . . and friends. Her fans appreciate Anne not only for her writing, but for her approachability. She has a warm, open heart and great strength of character. Her knack for making anyone feel at home in her presence encourages even the most tongue-tied fan to open up and say what he or she spent far too much time nervously contemplating in that long autograph line, and to be devoted ever afterward to her. Anne's fans have bonded with her and with one another to form an extended family. Except for a few "universes" that include *Star Trek* and *Star Wars,* there are probably more organized groups of Anne's readers than any other writer's. They have formed a mutually supportive community that is as full of talent, good humor, and hospitality to strangers as the lady herself. They keep in touch with one another, such communication greatly enhanced by the development of the Internet, share fiction set in her worlds, have hatching parties, exchange recipes, make costumes and write songs that celebrate facets of the complex worlds that Anne has created.

Readers also applaud the inclusive nature of her work. Women are given starring roles, yet men are in no means given short shrift. Her heroes are every bit as glamorous as her heroines. The door is open to every kind of human being. Gay groups applaud the presence of green riders on Pern, male riders chosen by female dragons who participate in the complex, energetic (and occasionally violent) mating ritual with other riders, also male, while their dragons are similarly engaged. No Earth-based racial group is excluded from being part of an adventure. *Dragonsdawn* specifically treats with the many cultures who made up the landing party that settled Pern. Psychic ability, such as that described in the Talents series, knows no racial boundaries.

Anne has, in the last fifteen or so years, allowed several junior authors, myself included, the privilege of sharing her spotlight by allowing further episodes to be written in a number of her established worlds, and in one case she created a series that has been collaborative since it began (*The Powers That Be*). I and my co-collaborators (we've each worked with Anne but not yet with one another) all have reason to be grateful to her, not only for the boost appearing on a cover with her has given our careers, but for the advice and encouragement she's always given to us. She's invited us into her home and made us feel part of the family. I learned a lot from her that I believe made my independent work better. I am also proud to be a friend of someone whom I admire so much.

In the next pages you will find a story that touches on Anne's humanity, insight, and quick wit. Enjoy the fiction, but enjoy too knowing that the warmth that pervades all Anne's characters and worlds is a reflection of someone who could have been the heroine herself, and to many of us, she really is.

Here's a classic tale by Grand Master Anne McCaffrey, one of the earliest science fiction stories to deal with cyborgs and the Posthuman Condition—and still one of the best. (Helva's further adventures can be found in *The Ship Who Sang*; *Partner-Ship*, written with Margaret Ball; *The Ship Who Searched*, with Mercedes R. Lackey; *The City Who Fought*, with S. M. Stirling; *The Ship Who Won*, with Jody Lynn Nye; *The Ship Avenged*, with S. M. Stirling; *The Ship Who Saved the Worlds*, with Jody Lynn Nye; *The Ship Errant*, by Jody Lynn Nye; and *The City and the Ship*, by S. M. Stirling.)

THE SHIP WHO SANG

ANNE McCAFFREY

She was born a thing and as such would be condemned if she failed to pass the encephalograph test required of all newborn babies. There was always the possibility that though the limbs were twisted, the mind was not, that though the ears would hear only dimly, the eyes see vaguely, the mind behind them was receptive and alert.

The electro-encephalogram was entirely favorable, unexpectedly so, and the news was brought to the waiting, grieving parents. There was the final, harsh decision: to give their child euthanasia or permit it to become an encapsulated "brain," a guiding mechanism in any one of a number of curious professions. As such, their offspring would suffer no pain, live a comfortable existence in a metal shell for several centuries, performing unusual service to Central Worlds.

She lived and was given a name, Helva. For her first three vegetable months she waved her crabbed claws, kicked weakly with her clubbed feet and enjoyed the usual routine of the infant. She was not alone for there were three other such children in the big city's special nursery. Soon they all were removed to Central Laboratory School where their delicate transformation began.

One of the babies died in the initial transferral but of Helva's "class," seventeen thrived in the metal shells. Instead of kicking feet, Helva's neural responses started her wheels; instead of grabbing with hands, she manipulated mechanical extensions. As she matured, more and more neural synapses would be adjusted to operate other mechanisms that went into the maintenance and running of a space ship. For Helva was destined to be the "brain" half of a scout ship, partnered with a man or a woman, whichever she chose, as the mobile half. She would be among the elite of her kind. Her initial intelligence tests registered above normal and her adaptation index was unusually high. As long as her development within her shell lived up to expectations, and there were no side-effects from the pituitary tinkering, Helva would live a rewarding, rich and unusual life, a far cry from what she would have faced as an ordinary, "normal" being.

However, no diagram of her brain patterns, no early I.Q. tests recorded certain essential facts about Helva that Central must eventually learn. They would have to bide their official time and see, trusting that the massive doses of shell-psychology would suffice her, too, as the necessary bulwark against her unusual confinement and the pressures of her profession. A ship run by a human brain could not run rogue or insane with the power and resources Central had to build into their scout ships. Brain ships were, of course, long past the experimental stages. Most babes survived the techniques of pituitary manipulation that kept their bodies small, eliminating the necessity of transfers from smaller to larger shells. And very, very few were lost when the final connection was made to the control panels of ship or industrial combine. Shell people resembled mature dwarfs in size whatever their natal deformities were, but the well-oriented brain would not have changed places with the most perfect body in the Universe.

So, for happy years, Helva scooted around in her shell with her classmates, playing such games as Stall, Power-Seek, studying her lessons in trajectory, propulsion techniques, computation, logistics, mental hygiene, basic alien psychology, philology, space history, law, traffic, codes: all the et ceteras that eventually became compounded into a reasoning, logical, informed citizen. Not so obvious to her, but of more importance to her teachers, Helva ingested the precepts of her conditioning as easily as she absorbed her nutrient fluid. She would one day be grateful to the patient drone of the sub-conscious-level instruction.

Helva's civilization was not without busy, do-good associations, exploring possible inhumanities to terrestrial as well as extraterrestrial citizens. One such group got all incensed over shelled "children" when Helva was just turning fourteen. When they were forced to, Central Worlds shrugged its shoulders, arranged a tour of the Laboratory Schools and set the tour off to a big start by showing the members' case histories, complete with photographs. Very few committees ever looked past the first few photos. Most of their original objections about "shells" were overridden by the relief that these hideous (to them) bodies *were* mercifully concealed.

Helva's class was doing Fine Arts, a selective subject in her crowded program. She had activated one of her microscopic tools which she would later use for minute repairs to various parts of her control panel. Her subject was large—a copy of the Last Supper—and her canvas, small—the head of a tiny screw. She had tuned her sight to the proper degree. As she worked she absentmindedly crooned, producing a curious sound. Shell people used their own vocal cords and diaphragms but sound issued through microphones rather than mouths. Helva's hum then had a curious vibrancy, a warm, dulcet quality even in its aimless chromatic wanderings.

"Why, what a lovely voice you have," said one of the female visitors.

Helva "looked" up and caught a fascinating panorama of regular, dirty craters on a flaky pink surface. Her hum became a gurgle of surprise. She instinctively regulated her "sight" until the skin lost its cratered look and the pores assumed normal proportions.

"Yes, we have quite a few years of voice training, madam," remarked Helva calmly. "Vocal peculiarities often become excessively irritating during prolonged intra-stellar distances and must be eliminated. I enjoyed my lessons."

Although this was the first time that Helva had seen unshelled people, she took this experience calmly. Any other reaction would have been reported instantly.

"I meant that you have a nice singing voice . . . dear," the lady amended.

"Thank you. Would you like to see my work?" Helva asked, politely. She instinctively sheered away from personal discussions but she filed the comment away for further meditation.

"Work?" asked the lady.

"I am currently reproducing the Last Supper on the head of a screw."

"O, I say," the lady twittered.

Helva turned her vision back to magnification and surveyed her copy critically.

"Of course, some of my color values do not match the old Master's and the perspective is faulty but I believe it to be a fair copy."

The lady's eyes, unmagnified, bugged out.

"Oh, I forget," and Helva's voice was really contrite. If she could have blushed, she would have. "You people don't have adjustable vision."

The monitor of this discourse grinned with pride and amusement as Helva's tone indicated pity for the unfortunate.

"Here, this will help," suggested Helva, substituting a magnifying device in one extension and holding it over the picture.

In a kind of shock, the ladies and gentlemen of the committee bent to observe the incredibly copied and brilliantly executed Last Supper on the head of a screw.

"Well," remarked one gentleman who had been forced to accompany his wife, "the good Lord can eat where angels fear to tread."

"Are you referring, sir," asked Helva politely, "to the Dark Age discussions of the number of angels who could stand on the head of a pin?"

"I had that in mind."

"If you substitute 'atom' for 'angel,' the problem is not insoluble, given the metallic content of the pin in question."

"Which you are programed to compute?"

"Of course."

"Did they remember to program a sense of humor, as well, young lady?"

"We are directed to develop a sense of proportion, sir, which contributes the same effect."

The good man chortled appreciatively and decided the trip was worth his time.

If the investigation committee spent months digesting the thoughtful food served them at the Laboratory School, they left Helva with a morsel as well.

"Singing" as applicable to herself required research. She had, of course, been exposed to and enjoyed a music appreciation course which had included the better known classical works such as "Tristan und Isolde," "Candide," "Oklahoma," "Nozze de Figaro," the atomic age singers, Eileen Farrell, Elvis Presley and Geraldine Todd, as well as the curious rhythmic progressions of the Venusians, Capellan visual chromatics and the sonic concerti of the Altairians. But "singing" for any shell person posed considerable technical difficulties to be overcome. Shell people were schooled to examine every aspect of a problem or situation before making a prognosis. Balanced properly between optimism and practicality, the nondefeatist attitude of the shell people led them to extricate themselves, their ships and personnel, from bizarre situations. Therefore to Helva, the problem that she couldn't open her mouth to sing, among other restrictions, did not bother her. She would work out a method, by-passing her limitations, whereby she could sing.

She approached the problem by investigating the methods of sound reproduction through the centuries, human and instrumental. Her own sound production equipment was essentially more instrumental than vocal. Breath control and the proper enunciation of vowel sounds within the oral cavity appeared to require the most development and practice. Shell people did not, strictly speaking, breathe. For their purposes, oxygen and other gases were not drawn from the surrounding atmosphere through the medium of lungs but sustained artificially by solution in their shells. After experimentation, Helva discovered that she could manipulate her diaphragmic unit to sustain tone. By relaxing the throat muscles and expanding the oral cavity well into the frontal sinuses, she could direct the vowel sounds into the most felicitous position for proper reproduction through her throat microphone. She compared the results with tape recordings of modern singers and was not unpleased although her own tapes had a peculiar quality about them, not at all unharmonious, merely unique. Acquiring a repertoire from the Laboratory library was no problem to one trained to perfect recall. She found herself able to sing any role and any song which struck her fancy. It would not have occurred to her that it was curious for a female to sing bass, baritone, tenor, alto, mezzo, soprano and coloratura as she pleased. It was, to Helva, only a matter of the correct reproduction and diaphragmic control required by the music attempted.

If the authorities remarked on her curious avocation they did so among themselves. Shell people were encouraged to develop a hobby so long as they maintained proficiency in their technical work.

On the anniversary of her sixteenth year in her shell, Helva was unconditionally graduated and installed in her ship, the XH-834. Her permanent titanium shell was recessed behind an even more indestructible barrier in the central shaft of the scout ship. The neural, audio, visual and sensory connections were made and sealed. Her extendibles were diverted, connected or augmented and the final, delicate-beyond-description brain taps were completed while Helva remained anesthetically unaware of the proceedings. When she awoke, she *was* the ship. Her brain and intelligence controlled every function from navigation to such loading as a scout ship of her class needed. She could take care of herself and her ambulatory half, in any situation already recorded in the annals of Central Worlds and any situation its most fertile minds could imagine.

Her first actual flight, for she and her kind had made mock flights on dummy panels since she was eight, showed her complete mastery of the techniques of her profession. She was ready for her great adventures and the arrival of her mobile partner.

There were nine qualified scouts sitting around collecting base pay the day Helva was commissioned. There were several missions which demanded instant attention but Helva had been of interest to several department heads in Central for some time and each man was determined to have her assigned to *his* section. Consequently no one had remembered to introduce Helva to the prospective partners. The ship always chose its own partner. Had there been another "brain" ship at the Base at the moment, Helva would have been guided to make the first move. As it was, while Central wrangled among itself, Robert Tanner sneaked out of the pilots' barracks, out to the field and over to Helva's slim metal hull.

"Hello, anyone at home?" Tanner wisecracked.

"Of course," replied Helva logically, activating her outside scanners. "Are you my partner?" she asked hopefully, as she recognized the Scout Service uniform.

"All you have to do is ask," he retorted hopefully.

"No one has come. I thought perhaps there were no partners available and I've had no directives from Central."

Even to herself Helva sounded a little self-pitying but the truth was she was lonely, sitting on the darkened field. Always she had had the company of other shells and more recently, technicians by the score. The sudden solitude had lost its momentary charm and become oppressive.

"No directives from Central is scarcely a cause for regret, but there happen to be eight other guys biting their fingernails to the quick just waiting for an invitation to board you, you beautiful thing."

Tanner was inside the central cabin as he said this, running appreciative fingers over her panel, the scout's gravity-couch, poking his head into the cabins, the galley, the head, the pressured-storage compartments.

"Now, if you want to give Central a shove and do *us* a favor all in one, call up the Barracks and let's have a ship-warming partner-picking party. Hmmmm?"

Helva chuckled to herself. He was so completely different from the occasional visitors or the various Laboratory technicians she had encountered. He was so gay, so assured, and she was delighted by his suggestion of a partner-picking party. Certainly it was not against anything in her understanding of regulations.

"Cencom, this is XH-834. Connect me with Pilot Barracks."

"Visual?"

"Please."

A picture of lounging men in various attitudes of boredom came on her screen.

"This is XH-834. Would the unassigned scouts do me the favor of coming aboard?"

Eight figures galvanized into action, grabbing pieces of wearing apparel, disengaging tape mechanisms, disentangling themselves from bedsheets and towels.

Helva dissolved the connection while Tanner chuckled gleefully and settled down to await their arrival.

Helva was engulfed in an unshell-like flurry of anticipation. No actress on her opening night could have been more apprehensive, fearful or breathless. Unlike the actress, she could throw no hysterics, china objects d'art or greasepaint to relieve her tension. She could, of course, check her stores for edibles and drinks, which she did, serving Tanner from the virgin selection of her commissary.

Scouts were colloquially known as "brawns" as opposed to their ship "brains." They had to pass as rigorous a training program as the brains and only the top one percent of each contributory world's highest scholars were admitted to Central Worlds Scout Training Program. Consequently the eight young men who came pounding up the gantry into Helva's hospitable lock were unusually fine-looking, intelligent, well-co-ordinated and adjusted young men, looking forward to a slightly drunken evening, Helva permitting, and all quite willing to do each other dirt to get possession of her.

Such a human invasion left Helva mentally breathless, a luxury she thoroughly enjoyed for the brief time she felt she should permit it. She sorted out the young men. Tanner's opportunism amused but did not specifically attract her; the blond Nordsen seemed too simple; dark-haired Al-atpay had a kind of obstinacy with which she felt no compassion: Mir-Ahnin's bitterness hinted an inner darkness she did not wish to lighten although he made the biggest outward play for her attention. Hers was a curious courtship—this would be only the first of several marriages for her, for brawns retired after 75 years of service, or earlier if they were unlucky. Brains, their bodies safe from any deterioration, served 200 years, and were then permitted to decide for themselves if they wished to continue. Helva had actually spoken to one shell person three hundred and twenty-two years old. She had been so awed by the contact she hadn't presumed to ask the personal questions she had wanted to.

Her choice did not stand out from the others until Tanner started to sing a scout ditty, recounting the misadventures of the bold, dense, painfully inept Billy Brawn. An attempt at harmony resulted in cacophony and Tanner wagged his arms wildly for silence.

"What we need is a roaring good lead tenor. Jennan, besides palming aces, what do you sing?"

"Sharp," Jennan replied with easy good humor.

"If a tenor is absolutely necessary, I'll attempt it," Helva volunteered.

"My good *woman*," Tanner protested.

"Sound your 'A,' " laughed Jennan.

Into the stunned silence that followed the rich, clear, high "A," Jennan remarked quietly, "Such an A, Caruso would have given the rest of his notes to sing."

It did not take them long to discover her full range.

"All Tanner asked for was one roaring good lead tenor," Jennan complained jokingly, "and our sweet mistress supplies us an entire repertory company. The boy who gets this ship will go far, far, far."

"To the Horsehead Nebulae?" asked Nordsen, quoting an old Central saw.

"To the Horsehead Nebulae and back, we shall make beautiful music," countered Helva, chuckling.

"Together," Jennan amended. "Only you'd better make the music and with my voice, I'd better listen."

"I rather imagined it would be I who listened," suggested Helva.

Jennan executed a stately bow with an intricate flourish of his crush-brimmed hat. He directed his bow toward the central control pillar where Helva *was*. Her own personal preference crystallized at that precise moment and for that particular reason: Jennan, alone of the men, had addressed his remarks directly at her physical presence, regardless of the fact that he knew she could pick up his image wherever he was in the ship and regardless of the fact that her body was behind massive metal walls. Throughout their partnership, Jennan never

failed to turn his head in her direction no matter where he was in re-
lation to her. In response to this personalization, Helva at that moment and from then on always spoke to Jennan only through her
central mike, even though that was not always the most efficient
method.

Helva didn't know that she fell in love with Jennan that evening.
As she had never been exposed to love or affection, only the drier
cousins, respect and admiration, she could scarcely have recognized
her reaction to the warmth of his personality and consideration. As a
shell-person, she considered herself remote from emotions largely
connected with physical desires.

"Well, Helva, it's been swell meeting you," said Tanner suddenly,
as she and Jennan were arguing about the Baroque quality of "Come
All Ye Sons of Art." "See you in space some time, you lucky dog, Jennan. Thanks for the party, Helva."

"You don't have to go so soon?" pleaded Helva, realizing belat-
edly that she and Jennan had been excluding the others.

"Best man won," Tanner said, wryly. "Guess I'd better go get a
tape on love ditties. May need 'em for the next ship, if there're any
more at home like you."

Helva and Jennan watched them leave, both a little confused.

"Perhaps Tanner's jumping to conclusions?" Jennan asked.

Helva regarded him as he slouched against the console, facing her
shell directly. His arms were crossed on his chest and the glass he held
had been empty for some time. He was handsome, they all were; but
his watchful eyes were unwary, his mouth assumed a smile easily, his
voice (to which Helva was particularly drawn) was resonant, deep and
without unpleasant overtones or accent.

"Sleep on it, Helva. Call me in the morning if it's your op."

She called him at breakfast, after she had checked her choice
through Central. Jennan moved his things aboard, received their joint
commission, had his personality and experience file locked into her
reviewer, gave her the co-ordinates of their first mission and the XH-
834 officially became the JH-834.

Their first mission was a dull but necessary crash priority (Medical
got Helva), rushing a vaccine to a distant system plagued with a viru-
lent spore disease. They had only to get to Spica as fast as possible.

After the initial, thrilling forward surge of her maximum speed,

Helva realized her muscles were to be given less of a workout than her brawn on this tedious mission. But they did have plenty of time for exploring each other's personalities. Jennan, of course, knew what Helva was capable of as a ship and partner, just as she knew what she could expect from him. But these were only facts and Helva looked forward eagerly to learning that human side of her partner which could not be reduced to a series of symbols. Nor could the give and take of two personalities be learned from a book. It has to be experienced.

"My father was a scout, too, or is that programed?" began Jennan their third day out.

"Naturally."

"Unfair, you know. You've got all my family history and I don't know one blamed thing about yours."

"I've never known either," Helva confided. "Until I read yours, it hadn't occurred to me I must have one, too, some place in Central's files."

Jennan snorted. "Shell psychology!"

Helva laughed. "Yes, and I'm even programed against curiosity about it. You'd better be, too."

Jennan ordered a drink, slouched into the gravity couch opposite her, put his feet on the bumpers, turning himself idly from side to side on the gimbals.

"Helva—a made-up name . . ."

"With a Scandinavian sound."

"You aren't blond," Jennan said positively.

"Well, then, there're dark Swedes."

"And blond Turks and this one's harem is limited to one."

"Your woman in purdah, yes, but you can comb the pleasure houses—" Helva found herself aghast at the edge to her carefully trained voice.

"You know," Jennan interrupted her, deep in some thought of his own, "my father gave me the impression he was a lot more married to his ship, the Silvia, than to my mother. I know I used to think Silvia was my grandmother. She was a low number so she must have been a great-great-grandmother at least. I used to talk to her for hours."

"Her registry?" asked Helva, unwitting of the jealousy for everyone and anyone who had shared his hours.

"422. I think she's TS now. I ran into Tom Burgess once."

Jennan's father had died of a planetary disease, the vaccine for which his ship had used up in curing the local citizens.

"Tom said he'd got mighty tough and salty. You lose your sweetness and I'll come back and haunt you, girl," Jennan threatened.

Helva laughed. He startled her by stamping up to the control panel, touching it with light, tender fingers.

"I *wonder* what you look like," he said softly, wistfully.

Helva had been briefed about this natural curiosity of scouts. She didn't know anything about herself and neither of them ever would or could.

"Pick any form, shape and shade and I'll be yours obliging," she countered as training suggested.

"Iron Maiden, I fancy blondes with long tresses," and Jennan pantomined Lady Godiva–like tresses. "Since you're immolated in titanium, I'll call you Brunehilda, my dear," and he made his bow.

With a chortle, Helva launched into the appropriate aria just as Spica made contact.

"What'n'ell's that yelling about? Who are you? And unless you're Central Worlds Medical go away. We've got a plague with no visiting privileges."

"My ship is singing, we're the JH–834 of Worlds and we've got your vaccine. What are our landing co-ordinates?"

"Your *ship* is singing?"

"The greatest S.A.T.B. in organized space. Any request?"

The JH–834 delivered the vaccine but no more arias and received immediate orders to proceed to Leviticus IV. By the time they got there, Jennan found a reputation awaiting him and was forced to defend the 834's virgin honor.

"I'll stop singing," murmured Helva contritely as she ordered up poultices for this third black eye in a week.

"You will not," Jennan said through gritted teeth. "If I have to black eyes from here to the Horsehead to keep the snicker out of the title, we'll be the ship who sings."

After the "ship who sings" tangled with a minor but vicious narcotic ring in the Lesser Magallenics, the title became definitely respectful. Central was aware of each episode and punched out a "special interest" key on JH–834's file. A first-rate team was shaking down well.

Jennan and Helva considered themselves a first-rate team, too, after their tidy arrest.

"Of all the vices in the universe, I *hate* drug addiction," Jennan remarked as they headed back to Central Base. "People can go to hell quick enough without that kind of help."

"Is that why you volunteered for Scout Service? To redirect traffic?"

"I'll bet my official answer's on your review."

"In far too flowery wording. 'Carrying on the traditions of my family which has been proud of four generations in Service' if I may quote you your own words."

Jennan groaned. "I was *very* young when I wrote that and I certainly hadn't been through Final Training and once I was in Final Training, my pride wouldn't let me fail. . . ."

"As I mentioned, I used to visit Dad on board the Silvia and I've a very good idea she might have had her eye on me as a replacement for my father because I had had massive doses of scout-oriented propaganda. It took. From the time I was seven, I was going to be a scout or else." He shrugged as if deprecating a youthful determination that had taken a great deal of mature application to bring to fruition.

"Ah, so? Scout Sahir Silan on the JS-422 penetrating into the Horsehead Nebulae?"

Jennan chose to ignore her sarcasm. "With *you*, I may even get that far but even with Silvia's nudging *I* never day-dreamed myself *that* kind of glory in my wildest flights of fancy. I'll leave the whoppers to your agile brain henceforth. I have in mind a smaller contribution to Space History."

"So modest?"

"No. Practical. We also serve, et cetera." He placed a dramatic hand on his heart.

"Glory hound!" scoffed Helva.

"Look who's talking, my Nebulae-bound friend. At least I'm not greedy. There'll only be one hero like my dad at Parsaea, but I *would* like to be remembered for some kudo. Everyone does. Why else do or die?"

"Your father died on his way back from Parsaea, if I may point out a few cogent facts. So he could never have known he was a hero for damming the flood with his ship. Which kept Parsaean colony from being abandoned. Which gave them a chance to discover the anti-paralytic qualities of Parsaea. Which *he* never knew."

"*I* know," said Jennan softly.

Helva was immediately sorry for the tone of her rebuttal. She knew very well how deep Jennan's attachment to his father had been. On his review a note was made that he had rationalized his father's loss with the unexpected and welcome outcome of the Affair at Parsaea.

"Facts are not human, Helva. My father was and so am I. And *basically,* so are you. Check over your dial, 834. Amid all the wires attached to you is a heart, an underdeveloped human heart. Obviously!"

"I apologize, Jennan," she said contritely.

Jennan hesitated a moment, threw out his hands in acceptance and then tapped her shell affectionately.

"If they ever take us off the milkruns, we'll make a stab at the Nebulae, huh?"

As so frequently happened in the Scout Service, within the next hour they had orders to change course, not to the Nebulae, but to a recently colonized system with two habitable planets, one tropical, one glacial. The sun, named Ravel, had become unstable; the spectrum was that of a rapidly expanding shell, with absorption lines rapidly displacing toward violet. The augmented heat of the primary had already forced evacuation of the nearer world, Daphnis. The pattern of spectral emissions gave indication that the sun would sear Chloe as well. All ships in the vicinity were to report to Disaster Headquarters on Chloe to effect removal of the remaining colonists.

The JH-834 obediently presented itself and was sent to outlying areas on Chloe to pick up scattered settlers who did not appear to appreciate the urgency of the situation. Chloe, indeed, was enjoying the first temperatures above freezing since it had been flung out of its parent. Since many of the colonists were religious fanatics who had settled on rigorous Chloe to fit themselves for a life of pious reflection, Chloe's abrupt thaw was attributed to sources other than a rampaging sun.

Jennan had to spend so much time countering specious arguments that he and Helva were behind schedule on their way to the fourth and last settlement. Helva jumped over the high range of jagged peaks that surrounded and sheltered the valley from the former raging snows as well as the present heat. The violent sun with its flaring corona was just beginning to brighten the deep valley.

"They'd better grab their toothbrushes and hop aboard," Helva commented. "HQ says speed it up."

"All women," remarked Jennan in surprise as he walked down to meet them. "Unless the men on Chloe wear furred skirts."

"Charm 'em but pare the routine to the bare essentials. And turn on your two-way private."

Jennan advanced smiling, but his explanation was met with absolute incredulity and considerable doubt as to his authenticity. He groaned inwardly as the matriarch paraphrased previous explanations of the warming sun.

"Revered mother, there's been an overload on that prayer circuit and the sun is blowing itself up in one obliging burst. I'm here to take you to the spaceport at Rosary—"

"That Sodom?" The worthy woman glowered and shuddered disdainfully at his suggestion. "We thank you for your warning but we have no wish to leave our cloister for the rude world. We must go about our morning meditation which has been interrupted—"

"It'll be permanently interrupted when that sun starts broiling. You must come now," Jennan said firmly.

"Madame," said Helva, realizing that perhaps a female voice might carry more weight in this instance than Jennan's very masculine charm.

"Who spoke?" cried the nun, startled by the bodiless voice.

"I, Helva, the ship. Under my protection you and your sisters-in-faith may enter safely and be unprofaned by association with a male. I will guard you and take you safely to a place prepared for you."

The matriarch peered cautiously into the ship's open port.

"Since only Central Worlds is permitted the use of such ships, I acknowledge that you are not trifling with us, young man. However, we are in no danger here."

"The temperature at Rosary is now 99°," said Helva. "As soon as the sun's rays penetrate directly into this valley, it will also be 99°, and it is due to climb to approximately 180° today. I notice your buildings are made of wood with moss chinking. Dry moss. It should fire around noontime."

The sunlight was beginning to slant into the valley through the peaks and the fierce rays warmed the restless group behind the matriarch. Several opened the throats of their furry parkas.

"Jennan," said Helva privately to him, "our time is very short."

"I can't leave them, Helva. Some of those girls are barely out of their teens."

"Pretty, too. No wonder the matriarch doesn't want to get in."

"Helva."

"It will be the Lord's will," said the matriarch stoutly and turned her back squarely on rescue.

"To burn to death?" shouted Jennan as she threaded her way through her murmuring disciples.

"They want to be martyrs? Their opt, Jennan," said Helva dispassionately. "*We* must leave and that is no longer a matter of option."

"How can I leave, Helva?"

"Parsaea?" Helva flung tauntingly at him as he stepped forward to grab one of the women. "You can't drag them *all* aboard and we don't have time to fight it out. Get on board, Jennan, or I'll have you on report."

"They'll die," muttered Jennan dejectedly as he reluctantly turned to climb on board.

"You can risk only so much," Helva said sympathetically. "As it is we'll just have time to make a rendezvous. Lab reports a critical speed-up in spectral evolution."

Jennan was already in the airlock when one of the younger women, screaming, rushed to squeeze in the closing port. Her action set off the others and they stampeded through the narrow opening. Even crammed back to breast, there was not enough room inside. Jennan broke out spacesuits for the three who would have to remain with him in the airlock. He wasted valuable time explaining to the matriarch that she must put on the suit because the airlock had no independent oxygen or cooling units.

"We'll be caught," said Helva grimly to Jennan on their private connection. "We've lost 18 minutes in this last-minute rush. I am now overloaded for maximum speed and I must attain maximum speed to outrun the heat-wave."

"Can you lift? We're suited."

"Lift? Yes," she said, doing so. "Run? I stagger."

Jennan, bracing himself and the women, could feel her sluggishness as she blasted upward. Heartlessly, Helva applied thrust as long as she could, despite the fact that the gravitational force mashed her cabin passengers brutally and crushed two fatally. It was a question of saving as many as possible. The only one for whom she had any concern was Jennan and she was in desperate terror about his safety. Airless and uncooled, protected by only one layer of metal, not three, the airlock was not going to be safe for the four trapped there, despite their spacesuits. These were only the standard models, not built to withstand the excessive heat to which the ship would be subjected.

Helva ran as fast as she could but the incredible wave of heat from the explosive sun caught them halfway to cold safety.

She paid no heed to the cries, moans, pleas and prayers in her cabin. She listened only to Jennan's tortured breathing, to the missing throb in his suit's purifying system and the sucking of the overloaded cooling unit. Helpless, she heard the hysterical screams of his three companions as they writhed in the awful heat. Vainly, Jennan tried to calm them, tried to explain they would soon be safe and cool if they could be still and endure the heat. Undisciplined by their terror and torment, they tried to strike out at him despite the close quarters. One flailing arm became entangled in the leads to his power pack and the damage was quickly done. A connection, weakened by heat and the dead weight of the arm, broke.

For all the power at her disposal, Helva was helpless. She watched as Jennan fought for his breath, as he turned his head beseechingly toward *her*, and died.

Only the iron conditioning of her training prevented Helva from swinging around and plunging back into the exploding sun. Numbly she made rendezvous with the refugee convoy. She obediently transferred her burned, heat-prostrated passengers to the assigned transport.

"I will retain the body of my scout and proceed to the nearest base for burial," she informed Central dully.

"You will be provided escort," was the reply.

"I have no need of escort," she demurred.

"Escort is provided, XH-834," she was told curtly.

The shock of hearing Jennan's initial severed from her call number cut off her half-formed protest. Stunned, she waited by the transport until her screens showed the arrival of two other slim brain ships. The cortege proceeded homeward at unfunereal speeds.

"834? The ship who sings?"

"I have no more songs."

"Your scout was Jennan?"

"I do not wish to communicate."

"I'm 422."

"Silvia?"

"Silvia died a long time ago. I'm 422. Currently MS," the ship rejoined curtly. "AH-640 is our other friend, but Henry's not listening in. Just as well—he wouldn't understand it if you wanted to turn rogue. But I'd stop *him* if he tried to delay you."

"Rogue?" the term snapped Helva out of her apathy.

"Sure. You're young. You've got power for years. Skip. Others have done it. 732 went rogue two years ago after she lost her scout on a mission to that white dwarf. Hasn't been seen since."

"I never heard about rogues," gasped Helva.

"As it's exactly the thing we're conditioned against, you sure wouldn't hear about it in school, my dear," 422 said.

"Break conditioning?" cried Helva, anguished, thinking of the white, white furious hot heart of the sun she had just left.

"For you I don't think it would be hard at the moment," 422 said quietly, her voice devoid of her earlier cynicism. "The stars are out there, winking."

"Alone?" cried Helva from her heart.

"Alone!" 422 confirmed bleakly.

Alone with all of space and time. Even the Horsehead Nebulae would not be far enough away to daunt her. Alone with a hundred years to live with her memories and nothing . . . nothing more.

"Was Parsaea worth it?" she asked 422 softly.

"Parsaea?" 422 came back, surprised. "With his father? Yes. We were there, at Parsaea when we were needed. Just as you . . . and his son . . . were at Chloe. When you were needed. The crime is always not knowing where need is and not being there."

"But *I* need *him*. Who will supply my need?" said Helva bitterly. . . .

"834," said 422 after a day's silent speeding. "Central wishes your report. A replacement awaits your opt at Regulus Base. Change course accordingly."

"A replacement?" That was certainly not what she needed . . . a reminder inadequately filling the void Jennan left. Why, her hull was barely cool of Chloe's heat. Atavistically, Helva wanted time to mourn Jennan.

"Oh, none of them are impossible if *you're* a good ship," 422 remarked philosophically. "And it is just what you need. The sooner the better."

"You told them I wouldn't go rogue, didn't you?" Helva said heavily.

"The moment passed you even as it passed me after Parsaea, and before that, after Glen Arhur, and Betelgeuse."

"We're conditioned to go on, aren't we? We *can't* go rogue. You were testing."

"Had to. Orders. Not even Psycho knows why a rogue occurs. Central's very worried, and so, daughter, are your sister ships. I asked to be your escort. I . . . don't want to lose you both."

In her emotional nadir, Helva could feel a flood of gratitude for Silvia's rough sympathy.

"We've all known this grief, Helva. It's no consolation but if we couldn't feel with our scouts, we'd only be machines wired for sound."

Helva looked at Jennan's still form stretched before her in its shroud and heard the echo of his rich voice in the quiet cabin.

"Silvia! I *couldn't* help him," she cried from her soul.

"Yes, dear. I know," 422 murmured gently and then was quiet.

The three ships sped on, wordless, to the great Central Worlds base at Regulus. Helva broke silence to acknowledge landing instructions and the officially tendered regrets.

The three ships set down simultaneously at the wooded edge where Regulus' gigantic blue trees stood sentinel over the sleeping dead in the small Service cemetery. The entire Base complement approached with measured step and formed an aisle from Helva to the burial ground. The honor detail, out of step, walked slowly into her cabin. Reverently they placed the body of her dead love on the wheeled bier, covered it honorably with the deep blue, star-splashed flag of the Service. She watched as it was driven slowly down the living aisle which closed in behind the bier in last escort.

Then, as the simple words of interment were spoken, as the atmosphere planes dipped wings in tribute over the open grave, Helva found voice for her lonely farewell.

Softly, barely audible at first, the strains of the ancient song of evening and requiem swelled to the final poignant measure until black space itself echoed back the sound of the song the ship sang.

Eileen Gunn is not a prolific writer, but her stories are well worth waiting for, and are relished (and eagerly anticipated) by a small but select group of knowledgeable fans who know that she has a twisted perspective on life unlike anyone else's, and a strange and pungent sense of humor all her own. She has made several sales to *Asimov's Science Fiction,* as well as to markets such as *Amazing, Proteus, Tales by Moonlight,* and *Alternate Presidents,* and has been a Nebula and Hugo finalist several times. She is the editor and publisher of the jazzy and eclectic electronic magazine *The Infinite Matrix* (www.infinite matrix.net), and the chairman of the board of the Clarion West writers workshop. Her first short-story collection, *Stable Strategies and Others,* came out in 2004; in addition to containing the Nebula-winning story that follows, the collection as a whole has been short-listed for the Philip K. Dick Award and for the James Tiptree, Jr., Memorial Awards. Gunn is presently at work on a biography of the late Avram Davidson. After brief periods of exile in Brooklyn and San Francisco, she is now back in Seattle, Washington, where she had formerly resided for many years, much to the relief of the other inhabitants.

On "Coming to Terms," this year's Nebula winner in the short-story category, she says:

"For a long time I've wanted to write a story about the emotional life of objects, and perhaps this is that story. As I have mentioned elsewhere, I started this story after helping Avram Davidson's son Ethan pack up his father's books and papers after Avram's death. I finished it after the deaths of my own parents, and after packing up their possessions.

"Avram's books and papers were copiously and idiosyncratically annotated: in some sense, they knew that they would be read by someone other than himself after his death, and they reached out to that reader. I found this a very affecting experience, and it influenced me to take on the task of writing Avram's biography. However, although Avram inspired this story, the characters in it are not Avram or his son. Nor are they me, except in the sense that all a writer's characters are in some way a reflection of herself.

"I ran this by several workshops and many tolerant friends. Thank you all: Your efforts bore some fruit."

COMING TO TERMS

EILEEN GUNN

The life leaked out of the old man. He lay in bed for more than a month, in hospital and nursing home, in worlds of pain. He fought first for control of his death, then for control of his life once more. Toward the end he gave up his desire for control, as much as he was able. He still issued every visitor a list of tasks, but he knew he had no control over whether those tasks got done.

So, painstakingly, he combed the thatch of the past. He returned to the old mysteries and puzzles, and reflected at length on the lives and motivations of people long dead. He constructed theories to explain the petty cruelties of childhood bullies. He made plans to purchase a small house, to reclaim his land in Guatemala, to publish essays, fiction, fragments of prose. He ate bananas and rye bread and institutional meals, and put his teeth in when visitors stopped by. He resolved not to worry about things he couldn't fix, and struggled to keep that resolution.

Then the muscles of his heart, exhausted after three billion beats and weakened by pneumonia, diabetes, and the stress of a choleric temperament, paused just for a moment, and could not resume. A nurse called for help and, with a team of aides, brought him back. He squeezed her hand, his heart failed again, and they let him go. The tenuous flow of electrochemical impulses that made up his nervous system slowed and ceased, and the order that he had imposed on the universe started to disintegrate, releasing heat.

His body cooled. A mortician came and removed it. A nurse's aide gathered his belongings together, threw out a few unimportant scraps of paper, put the rest in a plastic bag. The bed was remade: someone was waiting for it.

Friends came to visit, and found him gone. The news traveled, a spasm of regret at the disappearance of a keen mind, a brilliant wit, a generous friend. Kindnesses postponed would not be realized. Harsh words, whatever the source or reason, could not be unsaid.

He died with a book newly released, an essay in the current issue of a popular journal, a story to appear shortly in a well-known magazine. He left a respectable amount of work and a stack of unpublished manuscripts made more marketable by the fact of his death. For days after he died, his friends continued to receive his cards and letters.

After the passage of several weeks, his daughter, sorry about her father's death but not pleased at having to shoulder the responsibility, came from out of state to pack up his papers and books and to dispose, somehow, of the rest of his belongings. She unlocked the door and let herself into the silent, stale-smelling apartment.

The old man's spirit was still strong; he had always put its stamp on everything of consequence in his possession.

An umbrella with the handle carved into the shape of a goose's head leaned against the wall inside the door. A tag hung from the neck. It read, in her father's handwriting: "The kind gift of Arthur Detweiler, whom I met in the public library reading room on a rainy March afternoon."

She looked around the cramped two-room apartment. There were slippery piles of manuscripts and writing supplies. Heaps of clothes, towels, dirty dishes. A scattering of loose CDs across the top of his desk. Stacks of books, books, books.

She had never been there before. Her father had moved, not long before his death, to this last remote way station in a lifetime of wandering. Too new to the old man to be called his home, the small flat was clearly in disarray. Some belongings were in cardboard boxes, still unpacked from his last move or the one before that.

She had a fleeting thought that perhaps someone had broken in, to rifle her father's few belongings, and had put them in the boxes to take them away. At his previous place, a kid with a knife had come in and demanded forty bucks from his wallet. It made her angry, the idea of somebody coming in and rooting through her father's stuff, while he lay dying in the hospital. But then, she thought, it doesn't matter. He took no money with him, and he surely didn't leave much behind.

What he had had of value was his mind and his persistence and his writing skills, and those, actually, he *had* taken with him.

The cleanup seemed daunting, too much for her to deal with all at once. Maybe she'd make herself a cup of tea first. If there was tea.

In the kitchen, scraps of paper were taped on surfaces, stuck into openings, poked into canisters. A torn piece of lined yellow paper, taped to the front of the refrigerator, read, "This big refrigerator! What for? I'm an old man, I don't cook."

You didn't cook when you were younger, either, thought the daughter. A hotdog when she came for lunch, Chinese if she stayed for dinner. When she was a teenager, trying to create a normal life for this wayward parent, she had tried cooking meals for him when she came to visit, but he wasn't patient with her mistakes.

On the stove, a piece of paper was stuck on the front of the clock, obscuring the face: "Ignore this clock. The clocks on stoves are always wrong."

Squares of paper were taped all over the stove:

"Mornings, I make myself a pot of coffee, if my stomach permits."

"A deep fat fryer! What are they trying to do, kill me?"

"The oven needs cleaning. My mother used to get down on her hands and knees and clean the oven every week. She baked her own bread, and put a hot meal on the table every night. She made us oatmeal in the mornings, none of this toasted-twinkies instant-breakfast stuff. She sewed all her own clothes, and my sister's as well. She's been dead thirty-five years, and I miss her still."

The young woman sighed. In thirty-five years, would she miss her father? Maybe you miss people more as you get older—but she'd come to terms with his absence many years before.

When he had moved across the country, in search of a job or a woman, she had completely lost the sense of being his child, of being under his protection. She didn't miss him yet: it didn't seem that he was gone, just that he'd moved on.

She filled a small saucepan with water and put it on to boil, then opened the door of the cabinet next to the stove: a tin of baking powder, a package of cardboard salt-and-pepper shakers, vinegar, spices. . . .

She moved an herb-jar, and a piece of yellow paper wafted down. "The odor of wild thyme, Pliny tells us, drives away snakes. Dionysius of Syracuse, on the other hand, thinks it an aphrodisiac. The Egyptians, I am told, used the herb for embalming, so I may yet require the whole of this rather large packet."

She reached behind the herbs and grabbed a box of tea bags, a supermarket house brand. Better than nothing. Written on the box: "My mother drank Red Rose tea all her days, and I used to wonder how she could abide it when the world was full of aromatic teas with compelling names: Lapsang Souchong, Gunpowder, Russian Caravan. I keep this box for guests with unadventurous palates. There is *good* tea in the canister marked 'Baking Powder.' Don't ask why."

She pulled down the baking powder tin. There was a tiny yellow note stuck to the inside of the lid. In miniature script, it said, "The famous green tea of Uji, where there is a temple to Inari, attended by mossy stone foxes wearing red bibs." Her father had spent several years in Japan studying Zen. The experience had not made him, in her opinion, calmer, more accepting, more in tune with the universe, or any of those other things she thought Eastern religions were supposed to do.

A teaball? She opened the drawer below the counter. There were no notes in it, but there was a bamboo tea strainer among the knives and spatulas. She picked it up. Written on the handle, in spidery black ink, were the words, "Leaks like a sieve."

Sitting in the worn easychair in the living room of the small apartment, a mug of green tea balanced on the arm, she took stock of the situation. The lease was up in a week, and she had no intention of paying another month's rent on the place. Best to get the books sorted and packed up first, then look through the other stuff to see what she might want to sell and what she'd give to the Goodwill. She didn't plan to keep much. Had he really read all these books?

She had liked to read when she was a kid. But reading took so much time, all of it spent inside someone else's head. Movies and tv, you could watch them with other people. That's what it boiled down to: how much time you wanted to be all alone by yourself, with just a book for company.

There in her father's apartment, she could see how much his life had been about books and the company they provided. It wasn't just that he created books—in some way, books created him. Who he was was the sum of the books he had read and the books he had written. And now, all that was left was the books. And herself.

When she was younger, she had seen the books, both the ones he read and the ones he wrote, as rivals for her father's affection. She had abdicated the competition long ago.

A mammoth unabridged dictionary sat, closed, on the desk, next to the typewriter. *Webster's Third New International Dictionary*. She opened it. The binding was broken, and the cover flopped open to the title page. The editor's name was starred in red ink, and her father's handwriting sprawled across the bottom of the page. "Dr. Gove had been my freshman English teacher at New York University on the old mainland campus, circa 1940. He told me I was the most promising freshman he had ever taught," it said in red. Below that, in black: "My attempts to re-establish contact with him have come to nought."

Later, in a cheap, plastic-covered copy of *Webster's Ninth New Collegiate,* on the page crediting the editorial staff, she found an inscription in red: "Re: P. B. Gove?" and, again in black, "P. B. Gove is dead."

So was her father. So would she be eventually, all the flotsam of her life left for someone else to clean up. With that in mind, the little yellow notes made sense. Like his books, they were a way for her father to extend his lifespan, they were hooks that would reach into someone else's life after he was gone.

There was a pile of empty boxes in the bedroom—the very boxes these books had come out of? She dragged several into the living room and started putting books into them. One box for books she'd keep, another for books she'd sell, a third for completely worthless books, for the Goodwill.

There were a lot of books to sell. She checked them warily for yellow notes, and found only marginalia. Her father carried on a dialogue with every book he read, sometimes arguing points of fact, sometimes just interrupting the author's train of thought with reminiscences of his own.

"Disembarking from a troop carrier was not as easy as this description implies."

"When I was in Samarkand in 1969, this mosque was open to the public. The majolica tiles of the iwan were among the most glorious I've seen anywhere."

"1357 is the most often cited date for this battle, but in fact it un-doubtedly occurred in 1358."

She frowned at the tiny scribblings. They would certainly reduce the book's resale value. Why on earth had her father written all over these valuable books? It seemed to show a lack of respect.

She opened Samuel Pepys's *Diaries,* read her father's lengthy in-scription on the inside. "Books are memory," it said. "They remem-ber their contents and pass them on. They keep track of who claims ownership, who they were given by and for what occasion. They me-diate, in their margins, disagreements between reader and author." Her father's books, it seemed, were charged with enormous responsi-bility. Could they mediate a decade of emptiness between him and her? Can you make peace with someone after they're dead?

As she worked, something puzzled her. The bookshelves, usually the most orderly part of any place her father lived, were in quite a bit of disarray. There were gaps in between the books, but few books by the bed or on his desk. In the bathroom she found only a book on the Greek alphabet, one on Islamic architecture, and Volume Ed–Fu of the *Encyclopedia Britannica, Eleventh Edition,* in an inexpensive cloth binding. What was missing? Again, she wondered if someone had dis-turbed her father's things.

The next few days did not pass quickly, but they passed. She finished her father's Japanese tea and ate crackers from a package she had found unopened in the cupboard. She called in pizza. She drank too much Diet Pepsi.

She boxed letters and manuscripts for a library in Kansas that was willing to accept her father's papers. She found many photographs of people she did not know, but there were some that meant something to her.

A Polaroid of her mother, maybe twenty years old, in a ridiculous orange dress and heavy leather boots. Another of her father, already a middle-aged man, holding her as a baby. Their faces held nothing, ap-parently, but hope for the future.

A cheap folding frame that held a blurry shot of her father as a child, napping on the lawn in front of an apartment house, paired with a shot of herself in a similar pose. They did look alike, she thought, skinny little kids with cropped, curly dark hair. Funny of him to notice that.

She found a tiny photo, only an inch square, of her father during World War II. He was a skinny teenager in camo pants and a helmet, striking a pose with a machine gun, and a similar photo of another young guy: on the back it said, "Woody Herald—killed on Guadalcanal." She'd never heard of Woody Herald, but her father had carried that photo around with him for fifty years.

She sorted books, but she read them too. She was not getting as much done as she wanted. There were so many books that he'd written in, and she was reading them all out of order.

She knew this was so, because he dated his annotations. She could, conceivably, put the books in order, and read her father's moods and interests as they rolled out before her. Maybe Woody Herald was somewhere in the notes. Maybe she and her mother were in there as well.

She continued to find yellow notes. In the top drawer of his bureau, her father kept old wallets, watches that didn't work and cufflinks—a dozen boxes of cufflinks. When do you suppose, she thought, he wore French cuffs? She opened a box at random. There was a yellow note inside: "It used to be that you could tell the age and social position of a man from his cufflinks. Nowdays you have to look at his entire shirt. If he's wearing one."

At first annoyed with her father having written in the books, she felt, the more she read, that he was sharing himself in the books in a way he never had in life. Perhaps she should keep them: turned loose into the world—sold or given away—they lost meaning, broke loose from their rightful place. For whom had he written the notes, she wondered. For herself? How would he know she would read them? She found herself putting any book that he'd written in aside, to ship home rather than to sell, even if she wasn't interested in the book itself.

By the evening of the third day, she was exhausted, with many books still left unsorted. It should have been larger now than the others, but somehow the pile of books to get rid of was the smallest.

The Physics of Time Asymmetry. Keep it or not? She opened the book: it was dense with equations proving that time doesn't run backwards. Her father couldn't possibly have understood this, she thought.

She put it back in the stack. Why did he own this book? She sank into the easy chair, put her feet up on the footstool, and allowed herself to doze off, just for a bit.

She was awakened by a sound on the other side of the room, a noise at the window. The pane slid open and a small, faun-like child slipped in. She was so much larger than he was that she was more surprised than afraid. Was this who had disturbed her father's papers? This might have been a neighborhood kid that her father had chatted with, given candy to. The thought bothered her. What kind of a child, so young, would steal from the dead?

The room was lit only by the streetlight outside. He silently moved through the dark, avoiding the places where, she knew, there were boxes of books and piles of trash. He went to the shelf of her father's work, which she had yet to pack, and picked up a book, opened it, and started leafing through it, turning each page separately. What is he looking for, she wondered. It was too dark to read. She watched him from the shadows, the darkest part of the dark room, as he went through each book in turn, page by page. Finally, she spoke.

"Whatever you're looking for, it's not there."

He turned, his eyes huge and bright even in the dark. She got up from the chair and moved toward him. "What are you doing? How can you see?"

Close-cut, loosely curly dark hair, large dark eyes. He was slight, maybe nine years old, and he looked oddly familiar. Had she seen him lurking about outside?

"Who are you?"

The boy stood motionless, like a mouse or a chipmunk when it knows you're watching. She moved closer. "Don't be afraid. What were you looking for?" He didn't seem to breathe. "Did you take the other books?" Not a sound. His eyes caught light and threw it back.

Was he mute? Could he hear her?

Without warning, he leaped onto her like a monkey, knocking her over, kicking, clawing and biting, grabbing for her eyes. At first she fought just to get him off her, but it was a hard fight. So small a child to fight so fiercely. He pressed down on her windpipe, and suddenly she felt real fear. Summoning a strength she didn't know she had, she brought her arms up between his and pushed them outward at the elbows, breaking his grip on her throat and shoving him off-balance. She pushed him off her, and knocked him flat, face down to the carpet, then rolled over on top of him. She realized that he had stopped struggling. Wary, she pulled up his head by the hair and realized that it flopped loosely. She had broken his neck. She got up, knelt beside him. He wasn't just unconscious. He was dead, and he looked smaller than ever.

Is there something you're supposed to do? She should call the police. She hadn't meant to kill him. Would they believe her? Why wouldn't they? She stood up, staggering. How could she undo it? What should she have done differently?

Afraid to turn on the light, she moved cautiously across the dark room to the kitchen. She filled a glass of water from the tap and gulped it down. She stood there for a minute, two minutes. Then she went back into the living room. She would call the police.

She went over to the dead child. In the dark, the body could barely be distinguished from the stacks of books sorted out on the floor. It still looked oddly familiar, like her father as a child, she thought. That photo of him asleep on the lawn.

There was a piece of yellow paper near the child's head. She picked it up.

"Chekhov wrote, 'Only fools and charlatans know and understand everything.'"

"Agreed," she said. "But is it possible to know and understand *anything?* Is the past always gone? Is it possible to make peace with the dead?"

She knelt down by the body. Did it look like her father? Did it look like herself? There was no answer. There was no body. There were only stacks and stacks of books.

She reached down and picked one up from the pile that had been the child. *The Physics of Time Asymmetry*. She picked up the pen, opened the book, and wrote on the flyleaf. "For reasons unknown to physics, time runs only in one direction. The mind and the heart, curiously, transcend time."

New writer Benjamin Rosenbaum has made sales to *The Magazine of Fantasy & Science Fiction, Asimov's Science Fiction, Argosy, The Infinite Matrix, Strange Horizons, Harper's, McSweeney's, Lady Churchill's Rosebud Wristlet*, and elsewhere. He has been a party clown, a day care worker on a kibbutz in the Galilee, a student in Italy, a stay-at-home dad, and a programmer for Silicon Valley start-ups, the U.S. government, online fantasy games, and the Swiss banks of Zurich. Recently returned from a long stay in Switzerland, he now lives with his family in Falls Church, Virginia. He has a Web site at: http://home.datacomm.ch/benrose.

About "Embracing-the-New," he says:

"'Embracing-the-New' coalesced out of a lot of strands. The religion of the Godly is loosely based on vodoun (a.k.a voodoo)—I've always been fascinated by vodoun's model of the self—the idea of the little everyday self, the *petit bon ange*, and the greater self, the *gros bon ange* . . . and by the practical usefulness of the idea of inviting the loa to 'ride' you, supplying you with traits and characteristics you might otherwise not have.

"The idea of memory symbiotes came from reading Richard Dawkins's *The Selfish Gene* and thinking about mutualism, and how mutualism might interact with intelligence. A lot of Dawkins-inspired speculation ended up on this story's cutting-room floor (such as ways in which the Ghennungs and their hosts might not always be entirely aligned, and how Ghennungs might have the incentive to "lie," by reporting false memories . . .). Maybe in a sequel . . .

"A definite influence on the story was Orson Scott Card's *How to Write Science Fiction and Fantasy*, which outlines why it's usually a bad idea to write a story with all aliens, without any humans. I find that the opposite of any good writing advice is usually also good advice.

"I came to Clarion West in 2001 with a lot of notes on the world of this story, but no story. The plot and emotional core came out of an exercise assigned to us the very first evening by my hero Octavia Butler. (I stayed up all night writing it, very annoyed at being goaded into writing a story so quickly, instead of being able to rely on trunk stories. I guess it worked out all right, though, so I'm grateful now to Leslie and Neile.) I got excellent feedback on the story from all sixteen of my fellow CW2KL-ers, Octavia, and the other instructors. And Gardner Dozois saved the story by having me cut a scene (of Vru's crime and flight) that I'd ill-advisedly added in a weak moment of succumbing to the mantra 'show, don't tell.'

"Not everything I write is this Old Skool—I feel like this story could have come straight out of the pages of a 1963 issue of *Amazing*. I'm oddly proud of that."

EMBRACING-THE-NEW

BENJAMIN ROSENBAUM

The sun blazed, the wagon creaked and shuddered. Vru crouched near the master's canopy, his fur dripping with sweat. His Ghennungs crawled through his fur, seeking shade. Whenever one uprooted itself from his body, breaking their connection, he felt the sudden loss of memories, like a limb being torn away.

Not for the first time, Vru was forced to consider his poverty. He had only five Ghennungs. Three had been with him from birth; another had been his father's first; and the oldest had belonged to both his father and his grandfather. Once, when both of the older Ghennungs pulled their fangs out of him to shuffle across his belly, sixty years of memory—working stone, making love to his grandmother and his mother, worrying over apprenticeships and duels—were gone, and he had the strange and giddy feeling of knowing only his body's own twenty years.

"Vile day," Khancriterquee said. The ancient godcarver, sprawled on a pile of furs under the canopy, gestured with a claw. "Vile sun. Boy! There's cooling oil in the crimson flask. Smear some on me, and mind you don't spill any."

Vru found the oil and smeared it across his master's ancient flesh. Khancriterquee was bloated; in patches, his fur was gone. He stank like dead beasts rotting in the sun. Vru's holding-hands shuddered to touch him. The master was dying, and when he died, Vru's certain place in the world would be gone.

Around Khancriterquee's neck, as around Vru's, Delighting-in-Beauty hung from a leather cord: the plump, smooth, laughing goddess, twenty-seven tiny Ghennungs dancing upon her, carved in hard gray stone. Khancriterquee had carved both copies. How strange, that the goddess of beauty would create herself through his ugly, bloated flesh!

Khancriterquee's bloodshot eyes twitched open. "You are not a godcarver," he croaked.

Vru held still. What had he done wrong? The master was vain—had he noticed Vru's disgust? Would Khancriterquee send him back to his father's house in disgrace, to herd fallowswine, to never marry—hoping, when his own body was decrepit, to find some nephew who would take pity on him and accept a few of his memories?

"Do you know why we have won these territories?" the master asked. Pushing aside the curtains, he gestured over the wagon's side at the blasted red crags around them.

"We defeat the Godless in battle because the gods favor us, master," Vru recited.

Khancriterquee snorted. "It is not that the gods favor us. It is that we favor the gods."

Vru did not understand, and bent to massage the master's flesh. Khancriterquee pushed Vru's holding-hands away with a claw and, wheezing, sat up. He stared at Vru with disgust.

Vru realized that he was clicking his claws together, and forced himself to stop. The master watched him—remembering Vru's every twitch into the Ghennungs the journeymen would soon carry.

Vru pulled himself erect. "Master, there is something I have never understood."

Khancriterquee's eyes glittered with interest, or suspicion. "Ask," he said.

"How can the Godless really be godless?"

The master frowned.

"I mean, how can someone without a god not go mad when he takes new Ghennungs?" Vru remembered the day he had taken Delighting-in-Beauty as his goddess, to be the organizing devotion of his life. As the doctors had gently separated the Ghennungs from his father's cooling corpse in the Great Hall below, he had wanted to cling to childhood, wanted to wait before choosing a god. But the priest had lectured him sternly—for without a god, a person would just be a shifting collection of memories. The allegiances, desires, and opinions of his various Ghennungs would be at war, and he would be buffeted like a rowboat in a hundred-years' storm.

"Ah, my apprentice is ambitious," Khancriterquee whispered.

"The master is old and weak. Perhaps the apprentice should attend the high military councils in my stead. Perhaps he should learn the secrets of our war against the Godless—"

"Master, I meant no—"

"The Godless do not trade Ghennungs," Khancriterquee said.

"What?"

"Perhaps at a very young age they do," Khancriterquee said, waving his holding-hands, "or they trade certain very specific skills only, without other memories, using some kind of mutilated Ghennungs. We are not certain. But in general, when they die"—he paused, watching Vru's reaction—"their Ghennungs are destroyed. That is why we win the battles. Their greatest soldier is only as old as his body."

Vru suddenly felt sick; bitter, stinging fluids from his stomach sputtered into his throat. The Godless intentionally murdered themselves when their bodies died!

"Now I will tell you why you are not a godcarver, if the ambitious apprentice has time to listen," Khancriterquee said. He tapped the Delighting-in-Beauty around Vru's neck with his claw. "Carving copies, so that the people will not forget their gods and go mad, is nothing. It is time for you to carve a new god, as I did when I carved Fearless-in-Justice, as my grandfather did with Delighting-in-Beauty." He lay back on the furs and closed his eyes. "It will be a monument, to be unveiled at the Festival of Hrsh. You will use this new green stone."

Vru watched in silence as the master slept. He could hear his own heart beating.

None of Khancriterquee's journeymen had been allowed to create a god, not even Turmca. Why let an apprentice? To embarrass and spite the journeymen—to punish their eager impatience for Khancriterquee's death? Or did the master think Vru had that much talent?

*

The Bereft worked in the new mines, carving the green stone from the cliff face. Their fur had been shaved, because of the heat. Many of them had bloody claws, torn by the stone. Vru tried to look away. He had rarely seen so many Bereft. Their bodies were muscular, powerful . . . and naked of Ghennungs. It was horrible, yet there was something about those empty expanses of skin that called to him, like a field of untrodden snow.

The green stone glittered, embedded in the gray rock. Khancriterquee had been yelling at the foreman all day. Why use the idiot Bereft? They understood enough to be useful in the older mines, with the older gray stone. But this wonderful new green stone, in which so much detail would be possible—the perfect stone for gods, won from the Godless—was difficult to extract, and they were incapable of learning to do it. They had ruined every large piece so far.

"They are useless! Useless!" Khancriterquee screamed at the foreman. "Why could you not get real people?"

"It's mining," said the foreman stubbornly. "Real people won't do this work, holy one."

"Vru! Useless boy! Standing around like one of the Bereft yourself!" Hatred glittered in the master's eyes. "Bring that one to me," he said, motioning to a great Bereft body working dully in the nearby stone, cracking precious nodes of it into two with every swipe of its claws.

Vru led it to the master. It was docile; he only had to touch it lightly with his claws, on its strange, bare flesh. The Bereft panted softly as it walked. Its claws were torn, and it looked hungry. Vru wanted to embrace its mighty body in his holding-hands, murmur words of comfort in its ear—insane, stupid thoughts, which he tried to ignore.

"Bend its head over to me," Khancriterquee croaked.

Vru pushed it down to kneel by his master. Was the master going to whisper something to it? How could that help?

As the foreman stood nearby, dancing angrily from one foot to another, Khancriterquee slid his ancient claws against the soft fur of the Bereft's neck. The Bereft stared solemnly, fearfully, back. Straining and grunting, Khancriterquee closed his claws, tearing through the skin. The Bereft jerked, shuddered, and let out a piercing scream; the foreman, cursing, rushed forward; and then there was a snap and the head of the Bereft rolled from its body, which collapsed onto the ground. Blood poured onto Khancriterquee.

"Are you mad?" yelled the foreman, forgetting himself. Then terror came over his face and he dropped to the ground, burying his face in the dust. "Holiness, please . . ." he moaned.

The master chuckled, pleased perhaps that his body's old claws were still capable of killing. He clacked them together. The blood was black. Then he scowled. "Bring me some real people to work this mine." he said. "These abominations are worse than useless."

Vru vomited onto the dust.

"You need whole stone for your monument!" the master said. "Stupid boy. Now clean me."

The green stone was a miracle. On a calm blue day a month later, with whorls of fog skating across the ground and drifting into the sky, Vru stood in the sculpting pit of Khancriterquee's compound, before the monolith brought from the mines. Carving it was like a dream of power; it sang under his claws and under the hammer and file in his holding-hands.

For the last weeks he had returned to the dormitory only for the evening meal and to sleep. This work was altogether different from the work of making copies of the gods. Khancriterquee had been right; until now, Vru had never been a godcarver, only a copyist. Now, a new god was taking shape beneath his claws.

When Vru looked at the new god, he felt as if he had a thousand Ghennungs, with memories as old as the Ghennungs of the Oracle. He would never, himself, poor castle-builder's ninth son, dare to sculpt anything so shocking and so true. It was a god working through him, he knew, but not Delighting-in-Beauty; a new god, a god only he knew, was using his claws to birth itself into the green stone.

The god, he had decided, was called Embracing-the-New. It was a terrible and wonderful statue. In it, a person naked of Ghennungs, like one of the Bereft or a banished criminal, stooped to touch a Ghennung upon the ground with his claw; gently, a caress. Vru knew that in the next moment, the person would take up the Ghennung in his holding-hands and bring it to his chest: the Ghennung would sink its fangs into him, finding blood and nerves; and the sweet rush of memories would burn into the person's consciousness: the first thoughts, the new identity.

Vru looked down at his holding-hands; they were shaking. He did not feel tired; he felt like singing. But it had been twenty-nine hours since he had rested. He could not risk a mistake.

He pulled a cloth over the god, and walked up the trail toward the dormitory. As he left the sculpting pit, the embrace of the god faded, and weariness crept through his limbs. He could barely keep his claws up.

As he passed through the empty spring pavilion, a shadow moved ahead of him. He stopped. From the darkness, he heard ragged breathing.

"Who's there?" he said.

Turmca the journeyman stepped out into the daylight.

Vru relaxed. "You frightened me, Turmca!" he said. Even as he spoke, he noticed that Turmca was not wearing Delighting-in-Beauty around his neck, but Fearless-in-Justice, the soldier god. "Why are you—?"

The journeyman took a shuddering step toward him. His eyes were strange, vacant. Was he drunk? "How are you, Vru?" he asked. "How is your *work?*" Turmca's claws snapped together, and he jerked as if surprised at his own movement.

"Are you well, Turmca?" Vru asked, taking a step backward.

"How kind of you to ask," said Turmca, taking uneven steps forward. Vru moved backward into the pavilion's yard. Turmca was smaller than Vru, but well fed, with muscles from years of godcarving.

"I wanted to ask you," Vru said, "Turmca, when the master, ah, passes away, would you, have you considered taking me on? I would be grateful if—"

Turmca barked out loud, shuddering laughter. He bent over, put his claws against his eyes, and his body shook. Then he looked up at Vru.

"They all go to you," Turmca said.

Vru blinked.

"Khancriterquee said so to the Master Singer. I overheard. You will bear all his Ghennungs. He does not want his memories weakened and dispersed among the journeymen, or rather, he says, that is not what Delighting-in-Beauty wants."

"Turmca, that's insane. I don't have the talent. . . ."

Turmca's claws snapped open. They gleamed, newly cleaned and sharpened. "Talent! You fool! He doesn't choose you for your talent! He chooses you because of your five feeble Ghennungs and your weak, malleable nature. He wants to live on as himself, that's all! Your memories will be no trouble to him!"

Turmca's right foot slid back, and his holding-hands came in to cover the Ghennungs on his chest. Vru had seen that stance before, when his brother Viruarg was drilling. It was a soldier's stance.

"Turmca—"

Vru leapt backward as Turmca struck, but too slow—the points of a claw opened gashes in his side. Vru had not fought since he was a child playing thakka in a dirt field. He bent low and then lunged forward, checking Turmca's claws and trying to slam his body into him. But Turmca spun away, and his holding-hands darted out to smack against Vru's ear fronds. Vru's legs gave way and he collapsed to the ground, pain washing through him.

Turmca wasn't fighting like an amateur: he must have borrowed or rented Ghennungs from a solider. He wasn't drunk. His glazed look was that of one who has not integrated his Ghennungs, who has a battle in his soul. But he was united enough in his desire to kill Vru.

"Get up, Vru," barked Turmca, and it was a soldier's voice, the voice of a follower of Fearless-in-Justice, who wanted a kill with honor. And then in a gentler voice, the voice of the journeyman instructing a young apprentice: "I'll make this quick."

Vru felt exhaustion flooding through him, singing in his muscles. If he cried out for help, he knew Turmca would kill him and be gone before help came. He heard Turmca's feet scuffing cautiously toward where he lay on the sand. Goddess, help me, he prayed.

But it was not Delighting-in-Beauty who helped him—it must have been the new god, Embracing-the-New, who wanted to be carved, for he did something that Vru could not, would never do. Embracing-the-New picked Vru's body up and flung it at Turmca, and Vru's claw lashed out and severed the cord that held Fearless-in-Justice around Turmca's neck. Turmca, godless, screamed. Vru grabbed the god as it fell and threw it into the darkness of the pavilion. Turmca's claws reached for Vru, but his body turned and lurched after his god. Vru ran to the master's compound.

Vru returned from a week of fasting on the day of the Festival of Hrsh. He was weak, but he felt purified, ready for his task. When Embracing-the-New was unveiled, he would finally win honor for his family.

He sat on the stage, next to Khancriterquee. In front of them stood the monument, hidden by a cloth. Vru longed to see Embracing-the-New, but he could not, until the god was revealed. Suddenly he wondered what the people would see. A Bereft or a criminal as a god, reaching for a forbidden Ghennung! If the god had not carved it through his hands, he would be appalled himself. He trembled—what if they did not see the hand of the god? What if he had carved heresy? He tried to focus on Delighting-in-Beauty, to let her center him as a potter centers clay upon the wheel. But his head swam with images. The strong and lovely Bereft who had worked the green stone; the bloody head, rolling in the dust of the mine pit. The Godless and their strange, evil customs. He imagined the Bereft of his statue, reaching out to greet them. He sat stiffly, his head full of strange thoughts, until it was time.

The priest was calling him. He jerked out of his seat, stumbled across the stage. All around, the audience strained forward. A few people hushed children, then all was still. He reached up and pulled the cloth from Embracing-the-New, and a cry went up from the crowd.

But it was not Embracing-the-New.

The form was the same; it was his own block of green stone that he had lovingly carved. But into the figure's flesh were carved the distinct bulges of Ghennungs: seventeen Ghennungs, a new number for a new god. And the reaching claw was not caressing a fallen Ghennung; it was crushing a tiny Godless soldier with his claws aflame.

In the stone were the bold, smooth strokes of the master's hand.

The people applauded. Vru turned to look at Khancriterquee.

The master's jaws were drawn up into a satisfied, indulgent smirk. I added that which you forgot, his eyes said. It was not bad work, but the message was not correct. I corrected it.

What does it matter, Vru imagined Khancriterquee saying. What does it matter? He gazed at Vru smugly. You have proved yourself worthy of me. Soon this body will collapse, and you will carry my Ghennungs. All my memories, all my power. We will be one person. And then we will carve as Delighting-in-Beauty guides our hand.

Vru could smell, faintly, the decaying odor of Khancriterquee's skin from where he stood. The master was dying, but the master would not die. He would not even change much. Vru knew his five weak Ghennungs would be no match for Khancriterquee's sixteen, his own memories dim whispers in a roaring. Some would perhaps be weeded out, for twenty-one is too many for even a young body to carry. Something might remain: Vru's industriousness, perhaps, his love of textures in the stone. But when he thought of Khancriterquee cutting off the head of the Bereft in the mines, it would be sixteen loud voices of satisfaction, perhaps three of weak dismay.

He should be happy. His god was Delighting-in-Beauty. Why should he not rejoice that the greatest godcarver of the Godly would work with his muscles, his claws, creating grandeur? What did it

matter if his memories were dissipated? He remembered seeing himself as a mewling baby in his mother's holding-hands: a ninth, un-
wanted son. He remembered stroking his mother's brow as she held
the infant. "There will be no inheritance for him," she had said. "We
will find something," he had said. "Perhaps the priesthood. He will
have one of my Ghennungs." "Two," Mother had said. He had
scowled down at the crying, wan baby and thought, two? For this
scrawny fish?

Vru endured the applause and shuffled back to sit beside Khancriterquee. The stench was overpowering.

This scrawny fish will never make a soldier, his father had
thought.

I would rather be Godless, Vru realized. I would rather die once,
and then fully, than become Khancriterquee.

"Let the verdict of the Oracle be pronounced for all to hear," cried
the herald. "The crime is treason, heresy, and attempted desertion to
the enemy. The body is not at fault, and will be spared, but is unfit
to bear memory. Let it be banished to the wilds. Generous is the
Oracle."

They held him, but Vru would not struggle. He was limp and
sweaty. He looked at his chest; how strange not to see Delighting-in-
Beauty there. He felt like a child again.

He kept seeing the false Embracing-the-New, as he had left it,
with its Ghennungs broken off. Had he killed a god? But it was a false
god, a monstrosity!

The doctors teased a Ghennung from his flesh. He watched as it
burned in the brazier, twitching. A strange, hissing scream came from
it. Fear filled his guts like a balloon expanding. They took another
Ghennung, the one that had been his grandfather's. What had his
grandmother looked like? He could only remember her old. How
sad, how sad. She had surely been beautiful young. Hadn't he often
said so?

They took another. He needed a god, a god to center him. But he
could not think of Delighting-in-Beauty. He had betrayed her. He
thought of Embracing-the-New, the real Embracing-the-New, the
figure bereft reaching for hope. Yes, he thought. They took another
Ghennung. It blackened and twisted in the fire. Vru, he thought. My

name is Vru. They reached for the last Ghennung. Embracing-the-New, he thought, the body of green stone. Remember.

The beast stood in the courtyard. The wind was cool, the forest smelled like spring. There would be hunting there. Others were holding him. They smelled like his clan, so he did not attack. They let him go.

He looked around. There was one horrible old one who stank, who looked angry, or sad. The others brandished claws, shouted. He hissed back and brandished his claws. But there were too many to fight. He ran.

He headed for the forest. It smelled like spring. There would be hunting there.

Lois McMaster Bujold was born in Columbus, Ohio, in 1949; she now lives in Minneapolis. She started writing for professional publication in 1982. Her first three SF novels were all published in 1986 by Baen Books. Bujold went on to write the Nebula-winning *Falling Free* (1988) and many other books featuring her popular character Miles Naismith Vorkosigan, his family, friends, and enemies. The series includes three Hugo Award–winning novels; readers interested in learning more about the far-flung Vorkosigan clan are encouraged to start with the omnibus *Cordelia's Honor*. Bujold's books have been translated into nineteen languages, and have also found audio and e-book editions. In 2001 came a new fantasy, *The Curse of Chalion,* which garnered a Mythopoeic Award for Adult Fantasy. *Paladin of Souls,* a sequel in the same world, followed in 2003, and won the Locus and Hugo awards, and now has won a Nebula Award as well. A third volume, *The Hallowed Hunt,* will be out from Eos/HarperCollins in June 2005. A fan-run Web site devoted to her work, *The Bujold Nexus,* may be found at www.dendarii.com.

About *Paladin of Souls,* this year's Nebula winner in the novel category, she says:

"Ista dy Chalion, the heroine of *Paladin of Souls,* started out as a minor (if pivotal) character in *The Curse of Chalion,* my first book in this fantasy world. She had enormous gravitational pull—every scene she appeared in seemed to tilt toward her—but she could not be that tale's central focus. The last scene of that book included a sort of promissory note that I would get back to her properly, give her her own story and her own journey of learning and redemption.

"If *Chalion* dealt with the concerns of the goddess the Daughter of Spring, in this world's five-part and decidedly nondualistic pantheon, Ista's book hinged on the ambiguous god called the Bastard, not coincidentally the god of all things out of season, which Ista surely is. It was a lot of fun to write an older heroine—Ista is about forty—who doesn't get shuffled off to the sidelines. (Well, all right, forty doesn't look old to me now, but this was based on an era of shorter life spans.) It also allowed me to draw on a much broader range of life experiences than for a younger protagonist. Ista at last finds her own place to stand, stepping away from the constrained patterns imposed upon her by her place in her society, which is a theme pertinent to any age."

LOIS McMASTER BUJOLD

I sta leaned forward between the crenellations atop the gate tower, the stone gritty beneath her pale hands, and watched in numb exhaustion as the final mourning party cleared the castle gate below. Their horses' hooves scraped on the old cobblestones, and their good-byes echoed in the portal's vaulting. Her earnest brother, the provincar of Baocia, and his family and retinue were last of the many to leave, two full weeks after the divines had completed the funeral rites and ceremonies of the interment.

Dy Baocia was still talking soberly to the castle warder, Ser dy Ferrej, who walked at his stirrup, grave face upturned, listening to the stream, no doubt, of final instructions. Faithful dy Ferrej, who had served the late Dowager Provincara for all the last two decades of her long residence here in Valenda. The keys of the castle and keep glinted from the belt at his stout waist. Her mother's keys, which Ista had collected and held, then turned over to her older brother along with all the other papers and inventories and instructions that a great lady's death entailed. And that he had handed back for permanent safekeeping not to his sister, but to good, old, honest dy Ferrej. Keys to lock out all danger . . . and, if necessary, Ista in.

It's only habit, you know. I'm not mad anymore, really.

It wasn't as though she wanted her mother's keys, nor her mother's life that went with them. She scarcely knew what she wanted. She knew what she feared—to be locked up in some dark, narrow place by people who loved her. An enemy might drop his guard, weary of his task, turn his back; love would never falter. Her fingers rubbed restlessly on the stone.

Dy Baocia's cavalcade filed off down the hill through the town and was soon lost from her view among the crowded red-tiled roofs. Dy Ferrej, turning back, walked wearily in through the gate and out of sight.

The chill spring wind lifted a strand of Ista's dun hair and blew it across her face, catching on her lip; she grimaced and tucked it back into the careful braiding wreathing her head. Its tightness pinched her scalp.

The weather had warmed these last two weeks, too late to ease an old woman bound to her bed by injury and illness. If her mother had not been so old, the broken bones would have healed more swiftly, and the inflammation of the lungs might not have anchored itself so deeply in her chest. If she had not been so fragile, perhaps the fall from the horse would not have broken her bones in the first place. If she had not been so fiercely willful, perhaps she would not have been on that horse at all at her age . . . Ista looked down to find her fingers bleeding, and hid them hastily in her skirt.

In the funeral ceremonies, the gods had signed that the old lady's soul had been taken up by the Mother of Summer, as was expected and proper. Even the gods would not dare violate her views on protocol. Ista imagined the old Provincara ordering heaven, and smiled a little grimly.

And so I am alone at last.

Ista considered the empty spaces of that solitude, its fearful cost. Husband, father, son, and mother had all filed down to the grave ahead of her in their turn. Her daughter was claimed by the royacy of Chalion in as tight an embrace as any grave, and as little likely to return from her high place, five gods willing, as the others from their low ones. *Surely I am done.* The duties that had defined her, all accomplished. Once, she had been her parents' daughter. Then great, unlucky Ias's wife. Her children's mother. At the last, her mother's keeper. *Well, I am none of these things now.*

Who am I, when I am not surrounded by the walls of my life? When they have all fallen into dust and rubble?

Well, she was still Lord dy Lutez's murderer. The last of that little, secret company left alive, now. *That* she had made of herself, and that she remained.

She leaned between the crenellations again, the stone abrading the lavender sleeves of her court mourning dress, catching at its silk threads. Her eye followed the road in the morning light, starting from the stones below and flowing downhill, through the town, past the

river . . . and where? All roads were one road, they said. A great net
across the land, parting and rejoining. All roads ran two ways. They
said, *I want a road that does not come back.*

A frightened gasp behind her jerked her head around. One of her
lady attendants stood on the battlement with her hand to her lips, eyes
wide, breathing heavily from her climb. She smiled with false cheer.
"My lady. I've been seeking you everywhere. Do . . . do come away
from that edge, now . . ."

Ista's lips curled in irony. "Content you. I do not yearn to meet
the gods face-to-face this day." *Or on any other. Never again.* "The gods
and I are not on speaking terms."

She suffered the woman to take her arm and stroll with her as if
casually along the battlement toward the inner stairs, careful, Ista
noted, to take the outside place, between Ista and the drop. *Content
you, woman. I do not desire the stones.*

I desire the road.

The realization startled, almost shocked her. It was a new thought.
A new thought, me? All her old thoughts seemed as thin and ragged as
a piece of knitting made and ripped out and made and ripped out
again until all the threads were frayed, growing ever more worn, but
never larger. But how could *she* gain the road? Roads were made for
young men, not middle-aged women. The poor orphan boy packed
his sack and started off down the road to seek his heart's hope . . . a
thousand tales began that way. She was not poor, she was not a boy,
and her heart was surely as stripped of all hope as life and death could
render it. *I am an orphan now, though. Is that not enough to qualify me?*

They turned the corner of the battlement, making toward the
round tower containing the narrow, winding staircase that gave onto
the inner garden. Ista cast one last glance out across the scraggly
shrubs and stunted trees that crept up to the curtain wall of the castle.
Up the path from the shallow ravine, a servant towed a donkey loaded
with firewood, heading for the postern gate.

In her late mother's flower garden, Ista slowed, resisting her attendant's urgent hand upon her arm, and mulishly took to a bench in the
still-bare rose arbor. "I am weary," she announced. "I would rest here
for a time. You may fetch me tea."

She could watch her lady attendant turning over the risks in her
mind, regarding her high charge untrustingly. Ista frowned coldly.
The woman dropped a curtsey. "Yes, my lady. I'll tell one of the
maids. And I'll be *right back.*"

I expect you will. Ista waited only till the woman had rounded the corner of the keep before she sprang to her feet and ran for the postern gate.

The guard was just letting the servant and his donkey through. Ista, head high, sailed out past them without turning round. Pretending not to hear the guard's uncertain, "My lady . . . ?" she walked briskly down the steepening path. Her trailing skirts and billowing black velvet vest-cloak snagged on weeds and brambles as she passed, like clutching hands trying to hold her back. Once out of sight among the first trees, her steps quickened to something close to a run. She had used to run down this path to the river, when she was a girl. Before she was anybody's anything.

She was no girl now, she had to concede. She was winded and trembling by the time the river's gleam shone through the vegetation. She turned and strode along the bank. The path still held its remembered course to the old footbridge, across the water, and up again to one of the main roads winding around the hill to—or from—the town of Valenda.

The road was muddy and pocked with hoofprints; perhaps her brother's party had just passed on its way to his provincial seat of Taryoon. He had spent much of the past two weeks attempting to persuade her to accompany him there, promising her rooms and attendants in his palace, under his benign and protective eye, as though she had not rooms and attendants and prying eyes enough here. She turned in the opposite direction.

Court mourning and silk slippers were no garb for a country road. Her skirts swished around her legs as though she were trying to wade through high water. The mud sucked at her light shoes. The sun, climbing the sky, heated her velvet-clad back, and she broke into an unladylike sweat. She walked on, feeling increasingly uncomfortable and foolish. This was madness. This was just the sort of thing that got women locked up in towers with lack-witted attendants, and hadn't she had enough of that for one lifetime? She hadn't a change of clothes, a plan, any money, not so much as a copper vaida. She touched the jewels around her neck. *There's money.* Yes, too much value—what country-town moneylender could match for them? They were not a resource; they were merely a target, bait for bandits.

The rumble of a cart drew her eyes upward from picking her way along the puddles. A farmer drove a stout cob, hauling a load of ripe manure for spreading on his fields. He turned his head to stare dumfounded at the apparition of her on his road. She returned him a regal nod—after all, what other kind could she offer? She nearly laughed out loud, but choked back the unseemly noise and walked on. Not looking back. Not daring to.

She walked for over an hour before her tiring legs, dragging the weight of her dress, stumbled at last to a halt. She was close to weeping from the frustration of it all. *This isn't working. I don't know how to do this. I never had a chance to learn, and now I am too old.*

Horses again, galloping, and a shout. It flashed across her mind that among the other things she had failed to provision herself with was a weapon, even so much as a belt knife, to defend herself from assault. She pictured herself matched against a swordsman, any swordsman, with any weapon she could possibly pick up and swing, and snorted. It made a short scene, hardly likely to be worth the bother.

She glanced back over her shoulder and sighed. Ser dy Ferrej and a groom pounded down the road in her wake, the mud splashing from their horses' hooves. She was not, she thought, quite fool enough or mad enough to wish for bandits instead. Maybe that was the trouble; maybe she just wasn't crazed *enough*. True derangement stopped at no boundaries. Mad enough to wish for what she was not mad enough to grasp—now there was a singularly useless lunacy.

Guilt twinged in her heart at the sight of dy Ferrej's red, terrified, perspiring face as he drew up by her side. "Royina!" he cried. "My lady, what are you doing out here?" He almost tumbled from his saddle, to grasp her hands and stare into her face.

"I grew weary of the sorrows of the castle. I decided to take a walk in the spring sunshine to solace myself."

"My lady, you have come over five miles! This road is quite unfit for you—"

Yes, and I am quite unfit for it.

"No attendants, no guards—five gods, consider your station and your safety! Consider my gray hairs! You have stood them on end with this start."

"I do apologize to your gray hairs," said Ista, with a little real contrition. "They do not deserve the toil of me, nor does the remainder of you either, good dy Ferrej. I just . . . wanted to take a walk."

"Tell me next time, and I will arrange—"

"By myself."

"You are the dowager royina of all Chalion," stated dy Ferrej firmly. "You are Royina Iselle's own *mother*, for the five gods' sake. You cannot go skipping off down the road like a country wench."

Ista sighed at the thought of being a skipping country wench, and not tragic Ista anymore. Though she did not doubt country wenches had their tragedies, too, and much less poetic sympathy for them than did royinas. But there was nothing to be gained by arguing with him in the middle of the road. He made the groom give up his horse, and she acquiesced to being loaded aboard it. The skirts of this dress were not split for riding, and they bunched uncomfortably around her legs as she felt for the stirrups. Ista frowned again as the groom took the reins from her and made to lead her mount.

Dy Ferrej leaned across his saddle bow to grasp her hand, in consolation for the tears standing in her eyes. "I know," he murmured kindly. "Your lady mother's death is a great loss for us all."

I finished weeping for her weeks ago, dy Ferrej. She had sworn once to neither weep nor pray ever again, but she had forsworn herself on both oaths in those last dreadful days in the sickroom. After that, nei-the weeping nor praying had seemed to have any point. She decided not to trouble the castle warder's mind with the explanation that she wept now for herself, and not in sorrow but in a sort of rage. Let him take her as a little unhinged by bereavement; bereavement passed.

Dy Ferrej, quite as tired out as she by the past weeks of grief and guests, did not trouble her with further conversation, and the groom did not dare. She sat her plodding horse and let the road roll up again beneath her like a carpet being put away, denied its use. What was her use now? She chewed her lip and stared between her horse's bobbing ears.

After a time, its ears flickered. She followed its snorting glance to see another cavalcade approaching down a connecting road, some dozen or two riders on horses and mules. Dy Ferrej rose in his stir-rups and squinted, but then eased back in his saddle at the sight of the four outriders clad in the blue tunics and gray cloaks of soldier-brothers of the Daughter's Order, whose mandate encompassed the safe conveyance of pilgrims on the road. As the party rode closer, it could be seen that its members included both men and women, all decked out in the colors of their chosen gods, or as close as their wardrobes could manage, and that they wore colored ribbons on their sleeves in token of their holy destinations.

The two parties reached the joining of the roads simultaneously, and dy Ferrej exchanged reassuring nods with the soldier-brothers, stolid conscientious fellows like himself. The pilgrims stared in speculation at Ista in her fine somber clothes. A stout, red-faced older woman—*she's not any older than I am, surely*—offered Ista a cheery smile. After an uncertain moment, Ista's lips curved up in response, and she returned her nod. Dy Ferrej had placed his horse between the pilgrims and Ista, but his shielding purpose was defeated when the stout woman reined her horse back and kneed it into a trot to come up around him.

"The gods give you a good day, lady," the woman puffed. Her fat piebald horse was overburdened with stuffed saddlebags and yet more bags tied to them with twine and bouncing as precariously as its rider. It dropped back to a walk, and she caught her breath and straightened her straw hat. She wore Mother's greens in somewhat mismatched dark hues proper to a widow, but the braided ribbons circling her sleeve marched down in a full rank of five: blue wound with white, green with yellow, red with orange, black with gray, and white twined with cream.

After a moment's hesitation, Ista nodded again. "And you."

"We are pilgrims from around Baocia," the woman announced invitingly. "Traveling to the shrine of the miraculous death of Chancellor dy Jironel, in Taryoon. Well, except for the good Ser dy Brauda over there." She nodded toward an older man in subdued browns wearing a red-and-orange favor marking allegiance to the Son of Autumn. A more brightly togged young man rode by his side, who leaned forward to frown quellingly around him at the green-clad woman. "He's taking his boy, over there—isn't he a pretty lad, now, eh?"

The boy recoiled and stared straight ahead, growing flushed as if to harmonize with the ribbons on his sleeve; his father was not successful in suppressing a smile.

"—up to Cardegoss to be invested in the Son's Order, like his papa before him, to be sure. The ceremony is to be performed by the holy general, the Royse-Consort Bergon himself! I'd so like to see *him*. They say he's a handsome fellow. That Ibran seashore he comes from is supposed to be good for growing fine young men. I shall have to find some reason to pray in Cardegoss myself, and give my old eyes that treat."

"Indeed," said Ista neutrally at this anticipatory, but on the whole accurate, description of her son-in-law.

"I am Caria of Palma. I was wife of a saddler there, most lately. Widow, now. And you, good lady? Is this surly fellow your husband, then?"

The castle warder, listening with obvious disapproval to such familiarity, made to pull his horse back and fend off the tiresome woman, but Ista held up her hand. "Peace, dy Ferrej." He raised his brows, but shrugged and held his tongue.

Ista continued to the pilgrim, "I am a widow of . . . Valenda."

"Ah, indeed? Why, and so am I," the woman returned brightly. "My first man was of there. Though I've buried three husbands altogether." She announced this as though it were an achievement. "Oh, not all together, of course. One at a time." She cocked her head in curiosity at Ista's high mourning colors. "Did you just bury yours, then, lady? Pity. No wonder you look so sad and pale. Well, dear, it's a hard time, especially with the first, you know. At the beginning you want to die—I know I did—but that's just fear talking. Things will come about again, don't you worry."

Ista smiled briefly and shook her head in faint disagreement, but was not moved to correct the woman's misapprehension. Dy Ferrej was clearly itching to depress the creature's forwardness by announcing Ista's rank and station, and by implication his own, and perhaps driving her off, but Ista realized with a little wonder that she found Caria amusing. The widow's burble did not displease her, and she didn't want her to stop.

There was, apparently, no danger of that. Caria of Palma pointed out her fellow pilgrims, favoring Ista with a rambling account of their stations, origins, and holy goals; and if they rode sufficiently far out of earshot, with opinions of their manners and morals thrown in gratis. Besides the amused veteran dedicat of the Son of Autumn and his blushing boy, the party included four men from a weavers' fraternity who went to pray to the Father of Winter for a favorable outcome of a lawsuit; a man wearing the ribbons of the Mother of Summer, who prayed for the safety of a daughter nearing childbirth; and a woman whose sleeve sported the blue and white of the Daughter of Spring, who prayed for a husband for *her* daughter. A thin woman in finely cut green robes of an acolyte of the Mother's Order, with a maid and two servants of her own, turned out to be neither midwife nor physician, but a comptroller. A wine merchant rode to give thanks and redeem his pledge to the Father for his safe return with his caravan, almost lost the previous winter in the snowy mountain passes to Ibra.

The pilgrims within hearing, who had evidently been riding with Caria for some days now, rolled their eyes variously as she talked on, and on. An exception was an obese young man in the white garb, grimed from the road, of a divine of the Bastard. He rode along quietly with a book open atop the curve of his belly, his muddy white mule's reins slack, and glanced up only when he came to turn a page, blinking nearsightedly and smiling muzzily.

The Widow Caria peered at the sun, which had topped the sky. "I can hardly wait to get to Valenda. There is a famous inn where we are to eat that specializes in the most delicious roast suckling pigs." She smacked her lips in anticipation.

"There is such an inn in Valenda, yes," said Ista. She had never eaten there, she realized, not in all her years of residence.

The Mother's comptroller, who had been one of the widow's more pained involuntary listeners, pursed her mouth in disapproval. "I shall take no meat," she announced. "I made a vow that no gross flesh would cross my lips upon this journey."

Caria leaned over and muttered to Ista, "If she'd made a vow to swallow her pride, instead of her salads, it would have been more to the point for a pilgrimage, I'm thinking." She sat up again, grinning; the Mother's comptroller sniffed and pretended not to have heard.

The merchant with the Father's gray-and-black ribbons on his sleeve remarked as if to the air, "I'm sure the gods have no use for pointless chatter. We should be using our time better—discussing high-minded things to prepare our minds for prayer, not our bellies for dinner."

Caria leered at him, "Aye, or lower parts for better things still? And you ride with the Father's favor on your sleeve, too! For shame."

The merchant stiffened. "That is *not* the aspect of the god to which I intend—or need—to pray, I assure you, madam!"

The divine of the Bastard glanced up from his book and murmured peaceably, "The gods rule all parts of us, from top to toe. There is a god for everyone, and every part."

"*Your* god has notably low tastes," observed the merchant, still stung.

"None who open their hearts to any one of the Holy Family shall be excluded. Not even the priggish." The divine bowed over his belly at the merchant.

Caria gave a cheerful crack of laughter; the merchant snorted indignation, but desisted. The divine returned to his book.

Caria whispered to Ista, "I like that fat fellow, I do. Doesn't say much, but when he speaks, it's to the point. Bookish men usually have no patience with me, and I surely don't understand *them*. But that one does have lovely manners. Though I do think a man should get him a wife, and children, and do the work that pays for them, and not go haring off after the gods. Now, I have to admit, my dear second husband didn't—work, that is—but then, he drank. Drank himself to death eventually, to the relief of all who knew him, five gods rest his spirit." She signed herself, touching forehead, lip, navel, groin, and heart, spreading her hand wide over her plump breast. She pursed her lips, raised her chin and her voice, and called curiously, "But now I think on it, you've never told us what you go to pray for, Learned."

The divine placed his finger on his page and glanced up. "No, I don't think I have," he said vaguely.

The merchant said, "All you called folk pray to meet your god, don't you?"

"I have often prayed for the goddess to touch *my* heart," said the Mother's comptroller. "It is my highest spiritual goal to see Her face-to-face. Indeed, I often think I have felt Her, from time to time."

Anyone who desires to see the gods face-to-face is a great fool, thought Ista. Although that was not an impediment, in her experience.

"You don't have to pray to do that," said the divine. "You just have to die. It's not hard." He rubbed his second chin. "In fact, it's unavoidable."

"To be god-touched in *life*," corrected the comptroller coolly. "*That* is the great blessing we all long for."

No, it's not. If you saw the Mother's face right now, woman, you would drop weeping in the mud of this road and not get up for days. Ista became aware that the divine was squinting at her in arrested curiosity.

Was *he* one of the god-touched? Ista possessed some practice at spotting them. The reverse also held true, unfortunately. Or perhaps that calf-like stare was just shortsightedness. Discomforted, she frowned back at him.

He blinked apologetically and said to her, "In fact, I travel on business for my order. A dedicat in my charge came by chance across a little stray demon possessed by a ferret. I take it to Taryoon for the archdivine to return to the god with proper ceremony."

He twisted around to his capacious saddlebags and rummaged therein, trading the book for a small wicker cage. A lithe gray shape turned within it.

"Ah-ha! So that's what you've been hiding in there!" Caria rode closer, wrinkling her nose. "It looks like any other ferret to me." The creature stood up against the side of the cage and twitched its whiskers at her.

The fat divine turned in his saddle and held up the cage to Ista's view. The animal, circling, froze in her frown; for just a moment, its beady eyes glittered back with something other than animal intelligence. Ista regarded it dispassionately. The ferret lowered its head and backed away until it could retreat no farther. The divine gave Ista a curious sidelong look.

"Are you sure the poor thing isn't just sick?" said Caria doubtfully.

"What do you think, lady?" the divine asked Ista.

You know very well it has a real demon. Why do you ask me? "Why—I think the good archdivine will certainly know what it is and what to do with it."

The divine smiled faintly at this guarded reply. "Indeed, it is not much of a demon." He tucked the cage away again. "I wouldn't name it more than a mere elemental, small and unformed. It hasn't been long in the world, I'd guess, and so is little likely to tempt men to sorcery."

It did not tempt Ista, certainly, but she understood his need to be discreet. Acquiring a demon made one a sorcerer much as acquiring a horse made one a rider, but whether skilled or poor was a more open question. Like a horse, a demon could run away with its master. Unlike a horse, there was no dismounting. To a soul's peril; hence the Temple's concern.

Caria made to speak again, but the path to the castle split off at that point, and dy Ferrej reined his horse aside. The widow of Palma converted whatever she'd been about to say to a cheery farewell wave, and dy Ferrej escorted Ista firmly off the road.

He glanced back over his shoulder as they started down the bank into the trees. "Vulgar woman. I'll wager she has not a pious thought in her head! She uses her pilgrimage only to shield her holiday-making from the disapproval of her relatives and get herself a cheap armed escort on the road."

"I believe you are entirely right, dy Ferrej." Ista glanced back over her shoulder at the party of pilgrims advancing down the main road. The Widow Caria was now coaxing the divine of the Bastard to sing hymns with her, though the one she was suggesting more resembled a drinking song.

"She had not one man of her own family to support her," dy Ferrej continued indignantly. "I suppose she can't help the lack of a husband, but you'd think she could scare up a brother or son or at least a nephew. I'm sorry you had to be exposed to that, Royina."

A not entirely harmonious but thoroughly good-natured duet rose behind them, fading with distance.

"I'm not," said Ista. A slow smile curved her lips. *I'm not.*

Andy Duncan made his first sale, to *Asimov's Science Fiction,* in 1997, and quickly made others, to *Starlight, SCI FICTION, Amazing, Science Fiction Age, Dying For It, Realms of Fantasy,* and *Weird Tales,* as well as several more sales to *Asimov's.* By the beginning of the new century, he was widely recognized as one of the most individual, quirky, and flavorful new voices on the scene today. His story "The Executioner's Guild" was on both the Final Nebula Ballot and the final ballot for the World Fantasy Award in 2000, and in 2001 he *won* two World Fantasy Awards, for his story "The Pottawatomie Giant," and for his landmark first collection, *Beluthahatchie and Other Stories.* His most recent book is an anthology coedited with F. Brett Cox, *Crossroads: Tales of the Southern Literary Fantastic.* Coming up is a new collection, *Alabama Curiosities.* A graduate of the Clarion West writers' workshop in Seattle, he was born in Batesberg, South Carolina, and now lives in Northport, Alabama, with his wife, Sydney, where he edits *Overdrive* magazine, "The Voice of the American Trucker."

About "Zora and the Zombie," he says:

"My stories 'Beluthahatchie,' 'Lincoln in Frogmore,' and 'Daddy Mention and the Monday Skull' are all homages to the great Zora Neale Hurston, but 'Zora and the Zombie' is my first attempt to base a character on Zora herself.

"I long had been fascinated by Zora's brief account, in her 1937 book *Tell My Horse,* of her encounter with the Zombie Felicia Felix-Mentor, and by the photo of Felix-Mentor that she snapped in that hospital yard. For years, whenever Zora crossed my mind, I would think, 'One day I'll write a story about Zora and the Zombie.' When I finally realized that was the title, I was able to begin.

"My wife, Sydney, loves this story but not the title, which she thinks belongs on a pulp horror story. I think it's fitting, though, because the story is less about the Zombies of Haiti than about Zombies as they were adopted and adapted by U.S. pop culture in the 1930s and 1940s—by Zora, yes, but also by the contributors to *Weird Tales* and its rival 'shudder pulps.' So I like that the title would have fit the contents page of, say, *Terror Tales*. Now that the story has been nominated for a Stoker Award, my first such nomination, I wonder to what extent the title caught the attention of the Horror Writers Association!

"A note for the copy editors in the house: I capitalized Zombie because Zora did, partially out of her respect for this elect group of Haitians and partially, I suspect, to emphasize the alliteration of the word with her name—for in the reader's mind she's never Hurston, always Zora.

"I have been stunned to realize, since the story was published, that many of its readers had never heard of Zora before. I hope my story inspires even a few of them to go read her, but if I had known at the outset that I would be making introductions, I likely wouldn't have dared write the story at all!

"Thanks to everyone at the Sycamore Hill Writers Conference who helped me with this story, especially L. Timmel Duchamp, Karen Joy Fowler, and Kelly Link for their enthusiasm; to Ellen Datlow for publishing it in *SCI FICTION*; to Kelly Link and Gavin Grant for reprinting it in *The Year's Best Fantasy and Horror*; to John Kessel for too many reasons to list; and to Sydney for more reasons still."

ANDY DUNCAN

"**W**hat is the truth?" the houngan shouted over the drums. The mambo, in response, flung open her white dress. She was naked beneath. The drummers quickened their tempo as the mambo danced among the columns in a frenzy. Her loose clothing could not keep pace with her kicks, swings, and swivels. Her belt, shawl, kerchief, dress floated free. The mambo flung herself writhing onto the ground. The first man in line shuffled forward on his knees to kiss the truth that glistened between the mambo's thighs.

Zora's pencil point snapped. Ah, shit. Sweat-damp and jostled on all sides by the crowd, she fumbled for her penknife and burned with futility. Zora had learned just that morning that the Broadway hoofer and self-proclaimed anthropologist Katherine Dunham, on her Rosenwald fellowship to Haiti—the one that rightfully should have been Zora's—not only witnessed this very truth ceremony a year ago, but for good measure underwent the three-day initiation to become Mama Katherine, bride of the serpent god Damballa—the heifer!

Three nights later, another houngan knelt at another altar with a platter full of chicken. People in the back began to scream. A man with a terrible face flung himself through the crowd, careened against people, spread chaos. His eyes rolled. The tongue between his teeth drooled blood. "He is mounted!" the people cried. "A loa has made him his horse." The houngan began to turn. The horse crashed into him. The houngan and the horse fell together, limbs entwined. The chicken was mashed into the dirt. The people moaned and sobbed.

Zora sighed. She had read this in Herskovitz, and in Johnson, too. Still, maybe poor fictional Tea Cake, rabid, would act like this. In the pandemonium she silently leafed to the novel section of her notebook. "Somethin' got after me in mah sleep, Janie," she had written. "Tried tuh choke me tuh death."

Another night, another compound, another pencil. The dead man sat up, head nodding forward, jaw slack, eyes bulging. Women and men shrieked. The dead man lay back down and was still. The mambo pulled the blanket back over him, tucked it in. Perhaps tomorrow, Zora thought, I will go to Pont Beudet, or to Ville Bonheur. Perhaps something new is happening there.

"Miss Hurston," a woman whispered, her heavy necklace clanking into Zora's shoulder. "Miss Hurston. Have they shared with you what was found a month ago? Walking by daylight in the Ennery road?"

Dr. Legros, chief of staff at the hospital at Gonaives, was a good-looking mulatto of middle years with pomaded hair and a thin mustache. His three-piece suit was all sharp creases and jutting angles, like that of a paper doll, and his handshake left Zora's palm powder dry. He poured her a belt of raw white clairin, minus the nutmeg and peppers that would make it palatable to Guede, the prancing black-clad loa of derision, but breathtaking nonetheless, and as they took dutiful medicinal sips his small talk was all big, all politics: whether Mr. Roosevelt would be true to his word that the Marines would never be back; whether Haiti's good friend Senator King of Utah had larger ambitions; whether America would support President Vincent if the grateful Haitians were to seek to extend his second term beyond the arbitrary date technically mandated by the Constitution. But his eyes—to Zora, who was older than she looked and much older than she claimed—posed an entirely different set of questions. He seemed to view Zora as a sort of plenipotentiary from Washington and only reluctantly allowed her to steer the conversation to the delicate subject of his unusual patient.

"It is important for your countrymen and your sponsors to understand, Miss Hurston, that the beliefs of which you speak are not the beliefs of civilized men, in Haiti or elsewhere. These are Negro beliefs, embarrassing to the rest of us, and confined to the canaille—

to the, what is the phrase, the backwater areas, such as your American South. These beliefs belong to Haiti's past, not her future."

Zora mentally placed the good doctor waistcoat-deep in a backwater area of Eatonville, Florida, and set gators upon him. "I understand, Dr. Legros, but I assure you I'm here for the full picture of your country, not just the Broadway version, the tomtoms and the shouting. But in every ministry, veranda, and salon I visit, why, even in the office of the director-general of the Health Service, what is all educated Haiti talking about but your patient, this unfortunate woman Felicia Felix-Mentor? Would you stuff my ears, shelter me from the topic of the day?"

He laughed, his teeth white and perfect and artificial. Zora, self-conscious of her own teeth, smiled with her lips closed, chin down. This often passed for flirtation. Zora wondered what the bright-eyed Dr. Legros thought of the seductive man-eater Erzulie, the most "un-civilized" loa of all. As she slowly crossed her legs, she thought: Huh! What's Erzulie got on Zora, got on me?

"Well, you are right to be interested in the poor creature," the doctor said, pinching a fresh cigarette into his holder while looking neither at it nor at Zora's eyes. "I plan to write a monograph on the subject myself, when the press of duty allows me. Perhaps I should apply for my own Guggenheim, eh? Clement!" He clapped his hands. "Clement! More clairin for our guest, if you please, and mangoes when we return from the yard."

As the doctor led her down the central corridor of the ginger-bread Victorian hospital, he steered her around patients in creeping wicker wheelchairs, spat volleys of French at cowed black women in white, and told her the story she already knew, raising his voice whenever passing a doorway through which moans were unusually loud.

"In 1907, a young wife and mother in Ennery town died after a brief illness. She had a Christian burial. Her widower and son grieved for a time, then moved on with their lives, as men must do. *Empty this basin immediately! Do you hear me, woman? This is a hospital, not a chickenhouse!* My pardon. Now we come to a month ago. The Haitian Guard received reports of a madwoman accosting travelers near Ennery. She made her way to a farm and refused to leave, became violently agitated by all attempts to dislodge her. The owner of this family farm was summoned. He took one look at this poor creature and said, 'My God, it is my sister, dead and buried nearly thirty years.' Watch your step, please."

He held open a French door and ushered her onto a flagstone veranda, out of the hot, close, blood-smelling hospital into the hot, close outdoors, scented with hibiscus, goats, charcoal, and tobacco in bloom. "And all the other family members, too, including her husband and son, have identified her. And so one mystery was solved, and in the process, another took its place."

In the far corner of the dusty, enclosed yard, in the sallow shade of an hourglass grove, a sexless figure in a white hospital gown stood huddled against the wall, shoulders hunched and back turned, like a child chosen It and counting.

"That's her," said the doctor.

As they approached, one of the hourglass fruits dropped onto the stony ground and burst with a report like a pistol firing, not three feet behind the huddled figure. She didn't budge.

"It is best not to surprise her," the doctor murmured, hot clairin breath in Zora's ear, hand in the small of her back. "Her movements are . . . unpredictable." As yours are not, Zora thought, stepping away.

The doctor began to hum a tune that sounded like

> Mama don't want no peas no rice
> She don't want no coconut oil
> All she wants is brandy
> Handy all the time

but wasn't. At the sound of his humming, the woman—for woman she was; Zora would resist labeling her as all Haiti had done—sprang forward into the wall with a fleshy smack, as if trying to fling herself face first through the stones, then sprang backward with a half-turn that set her arms to swinging without volition, like pendulums. Her eyes were beads of clouded glass. The broad lumpish face around them might have been attractive had its muscles displayed any of the tension common to animal life.

In her first brush with theater, years before, Zora had spent months scrubbing bustles and darning epaulets during a tour of that damned *Mikado*—may Gilbert and Sullivan both lose their heads— and there she learned that putty cheeks and false noses slide into grotesquerie by the final act. This woman's face likewise seemed to have been sweated beneath too long.

All this Zora registered in a second, as she would a face from an elevated train. The woman immediately turned away again, snatched down a slim hourglass branch and slashed the ground, back and forth, as a machete slashes through cane. The three attached fruits blew up, *bang bang bang,* seeds clouding outward, as she flailed the branch in the dirt.

"What is she doing?"

"She sweeps," the doctor said. "She fears being caught idle, for idle servants are beaten. In some quarters." He tried to reach around the suddenly nimble woman and take the branch.

"Nnnnn," she said, twisting away, still slashing the dirt.

"Behave yourself, Felicia. This visitor wants to speak with you."

"Please leave her be," Zora said, ashamed because the name Felicia jarred when applied to this wretch. "I didn't mean to disturb her."

Ignoring this, the doctor, eyes shining, stopped the slashing movements by seizing the woman's skinny wrist and holding it aloft. The patient froze, knees bent in a half-crouch, head averted as if awaiting a blow. With his free hand, the doctor, still humming, still watching the woman's face, pried her fingers from the branch one by one, then flung it aside, nearly swatting Zora. The patient continued saying "Nnnnn, nnnnn, nnnnn" at metronomic intervals. The sound lacked any note of panic or protest, any communicative tonality whatsoever, was instead a simple emission, like the whistle of a turpentine cooker.

"Felicia?" Zora asked.

"Nnnnn, nnnnn, nnnnn."

"My name is Zora, and I come from Florida, in the United States."

"Nnnnn, nnnnn, nnnnn."

"I have heard her make one other noise only," said the doctor, still holding up her arm as if she were Joe Louis, "and that is when she is bathed or touched with water—a sound like a mouse that is trod upon. I will demonstrate. Where is that hose?"

"No need for that!" Zora cried. "Release her, please."

The doctor did so. Felicia scuttled away, clutched and lifted the hem of her gown until her face was covered and her buttocks bared. Zora thought of her mother's wake, where her aunts and cousins had greeted each fresh burst of tears by flipping their aprons over their heads and rushing into the kitchen to mewl together like nestlings. Thank God for aprons, Zora thought. Felicia's legs, to Zora's surprise, were ropy with muscle.

"Such strength," the doctor murmured, "and so untamed. You realize, Miss Hurston, that when she was found squatting in the road, she was as naked as all mankind."

A horsefly droned past.

The doctor cleared his throat, clasped his hands behind his back, and began to orate, as if addressing a medical society at Columbia. "It is interesting to speculate on the drugs used to rob a sentient being of her reason, of her will. The ingredients, even the means of administration, are most jealously guarded secrets."

He paced toward the hospital, not looking at Zora, and did not raise his voice as he spoke of herbs and powders, salves and cucumbers, as if certain she walked alongside him, unbidden. Instead she stooped and hefted the branch Felicia had wielded. It was much heavier than she had assumed, so lightly had Felicia snatched it down. Zora tugged at one of its twigs and found the dense, rubbery wood quite resistant. Lucky for the doctor that anger seemed to be among the emotions cooked away. What emotions were left? Fear remained, certainly. And what else?

Zora dropped the branch next to a gouge in the dirt that, as she glanced at it, seemed to resolve itself into the letter M.

"Miss Hurston?" called the doctor from halfway across the yard. "I beg your pardon. You have seen enough, have you not?"

Zora knelt, her hands outstretched as if to encompass, to contain, the scratches that Felicia Felix-Mentor had slashed with the branch. Yes, that was definitely an M, and that vertical slash could be an I, and that next one—

MI HAUT MI BAS

Half high, half low?

Dr. Boas at Barnard liked to say that one began to understand a people only when one began to think in their language. Now, as she knelt in the hospital yard, staring at the words Felicia Felix-Mentor had left in the dirt, a phrase welled from her lips that she had heard often in Haiti but never felt before, a Creole phrase used to mean "So be it," to mean "Amen," to mean "There you have it," to mean whatever one chose it to mean but always conveying a more or less resigned acquiescence to the world and all its marvels.

"Ah bo bo," Zora said.

"Miss Hurston?" The doctor's dusty wingtips entered her vision, stood on the delicate pattern Zora had teased from the dirt, a pattern that began to disintegrate outward from the shoes, as if they produced a breeze or tidal eddy. "Are you suffering perhaps the digestion? Often the peasant spices can disrupt refined systems. Might I have Clement bring you a soda? Or"—and here his voice took on new excitement—"could this be perhaps a feminine complaint?"

"No, thank you, doctor," Zora said as she stood, ignoring his out-
stretched hand. "May I please, do you think, return tomorrow with
my camera?"

She intended the request to sound casual but failed. Not in *Dum-
balla Calls,* not in *The White King of La Gonave,* not in *The Magic Island,* not in any best-seller ever served up to the Haiti-loving
American public had anyone ever included a photograph of a Zombie.

As she held her breath, the doctor squinted and glanced from
Zora to the patient and back, as if suspecting the two women of col-
lusion. He loudly sucked a tooth. "It is impossible, madame," he said.
"Tomorrow I must away to Port-de-Paix, leaving at dawn and not re-
turning for—"

"It must be tomorrow!" Zora blurted, hastily adding, "because the
next day I have an appointment in . . . Petionville." To obscure that
slightest of pauses, she gushed, "Oh, Dr. Legros," and dimpled his tai-
lored shoulder with her forefinger. "Until we have the pleasure of
meeting again, surely you won't deny me this one small token of your
regard?"

Since she was a sprat of thirteen sashaying around the gatepost in
Eatonville, slowing Yankees aboil for Winter Park or Sunken Gardens
or the Weeki Wachee with a wink and a wave, Zora had viewed sexuality, like other talents, as a bank of backstage switches to be flipped
separately or together to achieve specific effects—a spotlight glare, a
thunderstorm, the slow, seeping warmth of dawn. Few switches were
needed for everyday use, and certainly not for Dr. Legros, who was
the most everyday of men.

"But of course," the doctor said, his body ready and still. "Dr.
Belfong will expect you, and I will ensure that he extend you every
courtesy. And then, Miss Hurston, we will compare travel notes on
another day, n'est-ce pas?"

As she stepped onto the veranda, Zora looked back. Felicia Felix-
Mentor stood in the middle of the yard, arms wrapped across her
torso as if chilled, rocking on the balls of her calloused feet. She was
looking at Zora, if at anything. Behind her, a dusty flamingo high-
stepped across the yard.

❦

Zora found signboards in Haiti fairly easy to understand in French,
but the English ones were a different story. As she wedged herself into

a seat in the crowded tap-tap that rattled twice a day between Go-naives and Port-au-Prince, she found herself facing a stern injunction above the grimy, cracked windshield: "Passengers Are Not Permitted To Stand Forward While the Bus Is Either at a Standstill or Approach-ing in Motion."

As the bus lurched forward, tires spinning, gears grinding, the driver loudly recited: "Dear clients, let us pray to the Good God and to all the most merciful martyrs in heaven that we may be delivered safely unto our chosen destination. Amen."

Amen, Zora thought despite herself, already jotting in her note-book. The beautiful woman in the window seat beside her shifted sideways to give Zora's elbow more room, and Zora absently flashed her a smile. At the top of the page she wrote, "Felicia Felix-Mentor," the hyphen jagging upward from a pothole. Then she added a ques-tion mark and tapped the pencil against her teeth.

Who had Felicia been, and what life had she led? Where was her family? Of these matters, Dr. Legros refused to speak. Maybe the family had abandoned its feeble relative, or worse. The poor woman may have been brutalized into her present state. Such things happened at the hands of family members, Zora knew.

Zora found herself doodling a shambling figure, arms out-stretched. Nothing like Felicia, she conceded. More like Mr. Karloff's monster. Several years before, in New York to put together a Broad-way production that came to nothing, Zora had wandered, depressed and whimsical, into a Times Square movie theater to see a foolish horror movie titled "White Zombie." The swaying sugar cane on the poster ("She was not dead . . . She was not alive . . . WHAT WAS SHE?") suggested, however spuriously, Haiti, which even then Zora hoped to visit one day. Bela Lugosi in Mephistophelean whiskers proved about as Haitian as Fannie Hurst, and his Zombies, stalking bug-eyed and stiff-legged around the tatty sets, *all* looked white to Zora, so she couldn't grasp the urgency of the title, whatever Lugosi's designs on the heroine. Raising Zombies just to staff a sugar mill, moreover, struck her as wasted effort, since many a live Haitian (or Floridian) would work a full Depression day for as little pay as any Zombie and do a better job too. Still, she admired how the movie Zombies walked mindlessly to their doom off the parapet of Lugosi's castle, just as the fanatic soldiers of the mad Haitian King Henri Christophe were supposed to have done from the heights of the Citadel LaFerriere.

But suppose Felicia *were* a Zombie—in Haitian terms, anyway? Not a supernaturally revived corpse, but a sort of combined kidnap and poisoning victim, released or abandoned by her captor, her bocor, after three decades.

Supposedly, the bocor stole a victim's soul by mounting a horse backward, facing the tail, and riding by night to her house. There he knelt on the doorstep, pressed his face against the crack beneath the door, bared his teeth, and *sssssssst!* He inhaled the soul of the sleeping woman, breathed her right into his lungs. And then the bocor would have marched Felicia (so the tales went) past her house the next night, her first night as a Zombie, to prevent her ever recognizing it or seeking it again.

Yet Felicia *had* sought out the family farm, however late. Maybe something had gone wrong with the spell. Maybe someone had fed her salt—the hair-of-the-dog remedy for years-long Zombie hangovers. Where, then, was Felicia's bocor? Why hold her prisoner all this time, but no longer? Had he died, setting his charge free to wander? Had he other charges, other Zombies? How had Felicia become both victim and escapee?

"And how do you like your Zombie, Miss Hurston?"

Zora started. The beautiful passenger beside her had spoken.

"I beg your pardon!" Zora instinctively shut her notebook. "I do not believe we have met, Miss . . . ?"

The wide-mouthed stranger laughed merrily, her opalescent earrings shimmering on her high cheekbones. One ringlet of brown hair spilled onto her forehead from beneath her kerchief, which like her tight-fitting, high-necked dress was an ever-swirling riot of color. Her heavy gold necklace was nearly lost in it. Her skin was two parts cream to one part coffee. Antebellum New Orleans would have been at this woman's feet, in private, behind latched shutters.

"Ah, I knew you did not recognize me, Miss Hurston." Her accent made the first syllable of "Hurston" a prolonged purr. "We met in Archahaie, in the hounfort of Dieu Donnez St. Leger, during the rite of the fishhook of the dead." She bulged her eyes and sat forward slack-jawed, then fell back, clapping her hands with delight, ruby ring flashing, at her passable imitation of a dead man.

"You may call me Freida. It is I, Miss Hurston, who first told you of the Zombie Felix-Mentor."

Their exchange in the sweltering crowd had been brief and confused, but Zora could have sworn that her informant that night had been an older, plainer woman. Still, Zora probably hadn't looked her best, either. The deacons and mothers back home would deny it, but many a worshipper looked better outside church than in.

Zora apologized for her absentmindedness, thanked this— Freida?—for her tip, and told her some of her hospital visit. She left out the message in the dirt, if message it was, but mused aloud:

"Today we lock the poor woman away, but who knows? Once she may have had a place of honor, as a messenger touched by the gods."

"No, no, no, no, no, no, no," said Freida in a forceful singsong. "No! The gods did not take her powers away." She leaned in, became conspiratorial. "Some *man,* and only a man, did that. You saw. You know."

Zora, teasing, said, "Ah, so you have experience with men."

"None more," Freida stated. Then she smiled. "Ah bo bo. That is night talk. Let us speak instead of daylight things."

The two women chatted happily for a bouncing half-hour, Freida questioning and Zora answering—talking about her Haiti book, the sights of New York, the smell of the turpentine harvest in the Florida pines. It was good to be questioned herself for a change, after collecting from others all the time. The tap-tap jolted along, ladling dust equally onto all who shared the road: mounted columns of Haitian Guards, shelf-hipped laundresses, half-dead donkeys laden with guinea-grass. The day's shadows lengthened.

"This is my stop," said Freida at length, though the tap-tap showed no signs of slowing, and no stop was visible through the windows, just dense palm groves to either side. Where a less graceful creature would merely have stood, Freida rose, then turned and edged toward the aisle, facing not the front but, oddly, the back of the bus. Zora swiveled in her seat to give her more room, but Freida pressed against her anyway, thrust her pelvis forward against the older woman's bosom. Zora felt Freida's heat through the thin material. Above, Freida flashed a smile, nipped her own lower lip, and chuckled as the pluck of skin fell back into place.

"I look forward to our next visit, Miss Hurston."

"And where might I call on you?" Zora asked, determined to follow the conventions.

Freida edged past and swayed down the aisle, not reaching for the handgrips. "You'll find me," she said, over her shoulder.

Zora opened her mouth to say something but forgot what. Directly in front of the bus, visible through the windshield past Freida's shoulder, a charcoal truck roared into the roadway at right angles. Zora braced herself for the crash. The tap-tap driver screamed with everyone else, stamped the brakes and spun the wheel. With a hellish screech, the bus slewed about in a cloud of dirt and dust that darkened the sunlight, crusted Zora's tongue, and hid the charcoal truck from view. For one long, delirious, nearly sexual moment, the bus tipped sideways. Then it righted itself with a tooth-loosening *slam* that shattered the windshield. In the silence, Zora heard someone sobbing, heard the engine's last faltering cough, heard the front door slide open with its usual clatter. She righted her hat in order to see. The tap-tap and the charcoal truck had come to rest a foot away from one another, side by side and facing opposite directions. Freida, smiling, unscathed, kerchief still angled just·so, sauntered down the corridor between the vehicles, one finger trailing along the side of the truck, tracking the dust like a child. She passed Zora's window without looking up, and was gone.

"She pulled in her horizon like a great fish-net. Pulled it from around the waist of the world and draped it over her shoulder. So much of life in its meshes! She called in her soul to come and see."

Mouth dry, head aching from the heat and from the effort of reading her own chicken-scratch, Zora turned the last page of the manuscript, squared the stack and looked up at her audience. Felicia sat on an hourglass root, a baked yam in each hand, gnawing first one, then the other.

"That's the end," Zora said, in the same soft, nonthreatening voice with which she had read her novel thus far. "I'm still unsure of the middle," she continued, setting down the manuscript and picking up the Brownie camera, "but I know this is the end, all right, and that's something."

As yam after yam disappeared, Felicia's eyes registered nothing. No matter. Zora always liked to read her work aloud as she was writing, and Felicia was as good an audience as anybody. She was, in fact, the first audience this particular book had had.

While Zora had no concerns whatsoever about sharing her novel with Felicia, she was uncomfortably aware of the narrow Victorian casements above, and felt the attentive eyes of the dying and the mad. On the veranda, a bent old man in a wheelchair mumbled to himself, half-watched by a nurse with a magazine.

In a spasm of experiment, Zora had salted the yams, to no visible effect. This Zombie took salt like an editor took whiskey.

"I'm not in your country to write a novel," Zora told her chewing companion. "Not officially. I'm being paid just to do folklore on this trip. Why, this novel isn't even set in Haiti, ha! So I can't tell the foundation about this quite yet. It's our secret, right, Felicia?"

The hospital matron had refused Zora any of her good china, grudgingly piling bribe-yams onto a scarred gourd-plate instead. Now, only two were left. The plate sat on the ground, just inside Felicia's reach. Chapter by chapter, yam by yam, Zora had been reaching out and dragging the plate just a bit nearer herself, a bit farther away from Felicia. So far, Felicia had not seemed to mind.

Now Zora moved the plate again, just as Felicia was licking the previous two yams off her fingers. Felicia reached for the plate, then froze, when she registered that it was out of reach. She sat there, arm suspended in the air.

"Nnnnn, nnnnn, nnnnn," she said.

Zora sat motionless, cradling her Brownie camera in her lap.

Felicia slid forward on her buttocks and snatched up two yams— choosing to eat them where she now sat, as Zora had hoped, rather than slide backward into the shade once more. Zora took several pictures in the sunlight, though none of them, she later realized, managed to penetrate the shadows beneath Felicia's furrowed brow, where the patient's sightless eyes lurked.

"Zombies!" came an unearthly cry. The old man on the veranda was having a spasm, legs kicking, arms flailing. The nurse moved quickly, propelled his wheelchair toward the hospital door. "I made them all Zombies! Zombies!"

"Observe my powers," said the mad Zombie-maker King Henri Christophe, twirling his stage mustache and leering down at the beautiful young(ish) anthropologist who squirmed against her snakeskin bonds. The mad king's broad white face and syrupy accent suggested Budapest. At his languid gesture, black-and-white legions of Zombies both black and white shuffled into view around the papier-mâché cliff and marched single file up the steps of the balsa parapet, and over. None cried out as he fell. Flipping through his captive's notebook, the king laughed maniacally and said, "I never knew you wrote this! Why, this is *good!*" As Zombies toppled behind him like ninepins, their

German Expressionist shadows scudding across his face, the mad king began hammily to read aloud the opening passage of *Imitation of Life*.

Zora woke in a sweat.

The rain still sheeted down, a ceremonial drumming on the slate roof. Her manuscript, a white blob in the darkness, was moving sideways along the desktop. She watched as it went over the edge and dashed itself across the floor with a sound like a gust of wind. So the iguana had gotten in again. It loved messing with her manuscript. She should take the iguana to New York, get it a job at Lippincott's. She isolated the iguana's crouching, bowlegged shape in the drumming darkness and lay still, never sure whether iguanas jumped and how far and why.

Gradually she became aware of another sound nearer than the rain: someone crying.

Zora switched on the bedside lamp, found her slippers with her feet and reached for her robe. The top of her writing desk was empty. The manuscript must have been top-heavy, that's all. Shaking her head at her night fancies, cinching her belt, yawning, Zora walked into the corridor and nearly stepped on the damned iguana as it scuttled just ahead of her, claws clack-clack-clacking on the hardwood. Zora tugged off her left slipper and gripped it by the toe as an unlikely weapon as she followed the iguana into the great room. Her housekeeper, Lucille, lay on the sofa, crying two-handed into a handkerchief. The window above her was open, curtains billowing, and the iguana escaped as it had arrived, scrambling up the back of the sofa and out into the hissing rain. Lucille was oblivious until Zora closed the sash, when she sat up with a start.

"Oh, Miss! You frightened me! I thought the Sect Rouge had come."

Ah, yes, the Sect Rouge. That secret, invisible mountain-dwelling cannibal cult, their distant nocturnal drums audible only to the doomed, whose blood thirst made the Klan look like the Bethune-Cookman board of visitors, was Lucille's most cherished night terror. Zora had never had a housekeeper before, never wanted one, but Lucille "came with the house," as the agent had put it. It was all a package: mountainside view, Sect Rouge paranoia, hot and cold running iguanas.

"Lucille, darling, whatever is the matter? Why are you crying?"

A fresh burst of tears. "It is my faithless husband, madame! My Etienne. He has forsaken me . . . for Erzulie!" She fairly spat the name, as a wronged woman in Eatonville would have spat the infamous name of Miss Delpheeny.

Zora had laid eyes on Etienne only once, when he came flushed and hatless to the back door to show off his prize catch, grinning as widely as the dead caiman he held up by the tail. For his giggling wife's benefit, he had tied a pink ribbon around the creature's neck, and Zora had decided then that Lucille was as lucky a woman as any.

"There, there. Come to Zora. Here, blow your nose. That's better. You needn't tell me any more, if you don't want to. Who is this Erzulie?"

Zora had heard much about Erzulie in Haiti, always from other women, in tones of resentment and admiration, but she was keen for more.

"Oh, madame, she is a terrible woman! She has every man she wants, all the men, and . . . and some of the women, too!" This last said in a hush of reverence. "No home in Haiti is safe from her. First she came to my Etienne in his dreams, teasing and tormenting his sleep until he cried out and spent himself in the sheets. Then she troubled his waking life, too, with frets and ill fortune, so that he was angry with himself and with me all the time. Finally I sent him to the houngan, and the houngan said, 'Why do you ask me what this is? Any child could say to you the truth: You have been chosen as a consort of Erzulie.' And then he embraced my Etienne, and said: 'My son, your bed above all beds is now the one for all men to envy.' Ah, madame, religion is a hard thing for women!"

Even as she tried to console the weeping woman, Zora felt a pang of writerly conscience. On the one hand, she genuinely wanted to help; on the other hand, everything was material.

"Whenever Erzulie pleases, she takes the form that a man most desires, to ride him as dry as a bean husk, and to rob his woman of comfort. Oh, madame! My Etienne has not come to my bed in . . . in . . . *twelve days!*" She collapsed into the sofa in a fresh spasm of grief, buried her head beneath a cushion and began to hiccup. Twelve whole days, Zora thought, my my, as she did her own dispiriting math, but she said nothing, only patted Lucille's shoulder and cooed.

Later, while frying an egg for her dejected, red-eyed housekeeper, Zora sought to change the subject. "Lucille. Didn't I hear you say the other day, when the postman ran over the rooster, something like, 'Ah, the Zombies eat well tonight!' "

"Yes, madame, I think I did say this thing."

"And last week, when you spotted that big spider web just after putting the ladder away, you said, 'Ah bo bo, the Zombies make extra work for me today.' When you say such things, Lucille, what do you mean? To what Zombies do you refer?"

"Oh, madame, it is just a thing to say when small things go wrong. Oh, the milk is sour, the Zombies have put their feet in it, and so on. My mother always says it, and her mother too."

Soon Lucille was chatting merrily away about the little coffee girls and the ritual baths at Saut d'Eau, and Zora took notes and drank coffee, and all was well. Ah bo bo!

The sun was still hours from rising when Lucille's chatter shut off mid-sentence. Zora looked up to see Lucille frozen in terror, eyes wide, face ashen.

"Madame . . . Listen!"

"Lucille, I hear nothing but the rain on the roof."

"Madame," Lucille whispered, "the rain has stopped."

Zora set down her pencil and went to the window. Only a few drops pattered from the eaves and the trees. In the distance, far up the mountain, someone was beating the drums—ten drums, a hundred, who could say? The sound was like thunder sustained, never coming closer but never fading either.

Zora closed and latched the shutters and turned back to Lucille with a smile. "Honey, that's just man-noise in the night, like the big-mouthing on the porch at Joe Clarke's store. You mean I never told you about all the lying that men do back home? Break us another egg, Cille honey, and I'll tell *you* some things."

Box 128-B
Port-au-Prince, Haiti

November 20, 1936

Dr. Henry Allen Moe, Sec.
John Simon Guggenheim Memorial Foundation
551 Fifth Avenue
New York, N.Y.

Dear Dr. Moe,

I regret to report that for all my knocking and ringing and dust-raising, I have found no relatives of this unfortunate Felix-

Mentor woman. She is both famous and unknown. All have heard of her and know, or think they know, the two-sentence outline of her "story," and have their own fantasies about her, but can go no further. She is the Garbo of Haiti. I would think her a made-up character had I not seen her myself, and taken her picture as . . . evidence? A photograph of the Empire State Building is evidence, too, but of what? That is for the viewer to say.

I am amused of course, as you were, to hear from some of our friends and colleagues on the Haiti beat their concerns that poor Zora has "gone native," has thrown away the WPA and Jesse Owens and the travel trailer and all the other achievements of the motherland to break chickens and become an initiate in the mysteries of the Sect Rouge. Lord knows, Dr. Moe, I spent twenty-plus years in the Southern U.S., beneath the constant gaze of every First Abyssinian Macedonian African Methodist Episcopal Presbyterian Pentecostal Free Will Baptist Assembly of God of Christ of Jesus with Signs Following minister, mother, and deacon, all so full of the spirit they look like death eating crackers, and in all that time I never once came down with even a mild case of Christianity. I certainly won't catch the local disease from only six months in Haiti . . .

Obligations, travel and illness—"suffering perhaps the digestion," thank you, Dr. Legros—kept Zora away from the hospital at Gonaives for some weeks. When she finally did return, she walked onto the veranda to see Felicia, as before, standing all alone in the quiet yard, her face toward the high wall. Today Felicia had chosen to stand on the sole visible spot of green grass, a plot of soft imprisoned turf about the diameter of an Easter hat. Zora felt a deep satisfaction upon seeing her—this self-contained, fixed point in her traveler's life.

To reach the steps, she had to walk past the mad old man in the wheelchair, whose nurse was not in sight today. Despite his sunken cheeks, his matted eyelashes, his patchy tufts of white hair, Zora could see he must have been handsome in his day. She smiled as she approached.

He blinked and spoke in a thoughtful voice. "I will be a Zombie soon," he said.

That stopped her. "Excuse me?"

"Death came for me many years ago," said the old man, eyes bright, "and I said, No, not me, take my wife instead. And so I gave her up as a Zombie. That gained me five years, you see. A good bargain. And then, five years later, I gave our oldest son. Then our daughter. Then our youngest. And more loved ones, too, now all Zombies, all. There is no one left. No one but me." His hands plucked at the coverlet that draped his legs. He peered all around the yard. "I will be a Zombie soon," he said, and wept.

Shaking her head, Zora descended the steps. Approaching Felicia from behind, as Dr. Legros had said that first day, was always a delicate maneuver. One had to be loud enough to be heard but quiet enough not to panic her.

"Hello, Felicia," Zora said.

The huddled figure didn't turn, didn't budge, and Zora, emboldened by long absence, repeated the name, reached out, touched Felicia's shoulder with her fingertips. As she made contact, a tingling shiver ran up her arm and down her spine to her feet. Without turning, Felicia emerged from her crouch. She stood up straight, flexed her shoulders, stretched her neck, and spoke.

"Zora, my friend!"

Felicia turned and was not Felicia at all, but a tall, beautiful woman in a short white dress. Freida registered the look on Zora's face and laughed.

"Did I not tell you that you would find me? Do you not even know your friend Freida?"

Zora's breath returned. "I know you," she retorted, "and I know that was a cruel trick. Where is Felicia? What have you done with her?"

"Whatever do you mean? Felicia was not mine to give you, and she is not mine to take away. No one is owned by anyone."

"Why is Felicia not in the yard? Is she ill? And why are you here? Are you ill as well?"

Freida sighed. "So many questions. Is this how a book gets written? If Felicia were not ill, silly, she would not have been here in the first place. Besides." She squared her shoulders. "Why do you care so about this . . . powerless woman? This woman who let some man lead her soul astray, like a starving cat behind an eel-barrel?" She stepped close, the heat of the day coalescing around. "Tell a woman of power your book. Tell *me* your book," she murmured. "Tell *me* of the mule's funeral, and the rising waters, and the buzzing pear-tree, and young Janie's secret sigh."

Zora had two simultaneous thoughts, like a moan and a breath interlaced: *Get out of my book!* and *My God, she's jealous!*

"Why bother?" Zora bit off, flush with anger. "You think you know it by heart already. And besides," Zora continued, stepping forward, nose to nose, "there are powers other than yours."

Freida hissed, stepped back as if pattered with stove-grease.

Zora put her nose in the air and said, airily, "I'll have you know that Felicia is a writer, too."

Her mouth a thin line, Freida turned and strode toward the hospital, thighs long and taut beneath her gown. Without thought, Zora walked, too, and kept pace.

"If you must know," Freida said, "your writer friend is now in the care of her family. Her son came for her. Do you find this so remarkable? Perhaps the son should have notified you, hmm?" She winked at Zora. "He is quite a muscular young man, with a taste for older women. Much, *much* older women. I could show you where he lives. I have been there often. I have been there more than he knows."

"How dependent you are," Zora said, "on men."

As Freida stepped onto the veranda, the old man in the wheelchair cringed and moaned. "Hush, child," Freida said. She pulled a nurse's cap from her pocket and tugged it on over her chestnut hair.

"Don't let her take me!" the old man howled. "She'll make me a Zombie! She will! A Zombie!"

"Oh, pish," Freida said. She raised one bare foot and used it to push the wheelchair forward a foot or so, revealing a sensible pair of white shoes on the flagstones beneath. These she stepped into as she wheeled the chair around. "Here is your bocor, Miss Hurston. What use have I for a Zombie's cold hands? Au revoir, Miss Hurston. Zora. I hope you find much to write about in my country . . . however you limit your experiences."

Zora stood at the foot of the steps, watched her wheel the old man away over the uneven flagstones.

"Erzulie," Zora said.

The woman stopped. Without turning, she asked, "What name did you call me?"

"I called you a true name, and I'm telling you that if you don't leave Lucille's Etienne alone, so the two of them can go to hell in their own way, then I . . . well, then I will forget all about you, and you will never be in my book."

Freida pealed with laughter. The old man slumped in his chair. The laughter cut off like a radio, and Freida, suddenly grave, looked down. "They do not last any time, do they?" she murmured. With a forefinger, she poked the back of his head. "Poor pretty things." With a sigh, she faced Zora, gave her a look of frank appraisal, up and down. Then she shrugged. "You are mad," she said, "but you are fair." She backed into the door, shoved it open with her behind, and hauled the dead man in after her.

The tap-tap was running late as usual, so Zora, restless, started out on foot. As long as the road kept going downhill and the sun stayed over yonder, she reasoned, she was unlikely to get lost. As she walked through the countryside, she sang and picked flowers and worked on her book in the best way she knew to work on a book, in her own head, with no paper and indeed no words, not yet. She enjoyed the caution signs on each curve—"La Route Tue et Blesse," or, literally, "The Road Kills And Injures."

She wondered how it felt, to walk naked along a roadside like Felicia Felix-Mentor. She considered trying the experiment, when she realized that night had fallen. (And where was the tap-tap, and all the other traffic, and why was the road so narrow?) But once shed, her dress, her shift, her shoes would be a terrible armful. The only efficient way to carry clothes, really, was to wear them. So thinking, she plodded, footsore, around a sharp curve and nearly ran into several dozen hooded figures in red, proceeding in the opposite direction. Several carried torches, all carried drums, and one had a large, mean-looking dog on a rope.

"Who comes?" asked a deep male voice. Zora couldn't tell which of the hooded figures had spoken, if any.

"Who wants to know?" she asked.

The hoods looked at one another. Without speaking, several reached into their robes. One drew a sword. One drew a machete. The one with the dog drew a pistol, then knelt to murmur into the dog's ear. With one hand he scratched the dog between the shoulder blades, and with the other he gently stroked its head with the moon-gleaming barrel of the pistol. Zora could hear the thump and rustle of the dog's tail wagging in the leaves.

"Give us the words of passage," said the voice, presumably the sword-wielder's, as he was the one who pointed at Zora for emphasis. "Give them to us, woman, or you will die, and we will feast upon you."

"She cannot know the words," said a woman's voice, "unless she too has spoken with the dead. Let us eat her."

Suddenly, as well as she knew anything on the round old world, Zora knew exactly what the words of passage were. Felicia Felix-Mentor had given them to her. *Mi haut, mi bas.* Half high, half low. She could say them now. But she would not say them. She would believe in Zombies, a little, and in Erzulie, perhaps, a little more. But she would not believe in the Sect Rouge, in blood-oathed societies of men. She walked forward again, of her own free will, and the red-robed figures stood motionless as she passed among them. The dog whimpered. She walked down the hill, hearing nothing behind but a growing chorus of frogs. Around the next bend she saw the distant lights of Port-au-Prince and, much nearer, a tap-tap idling in front of a store. Zora laughed and hung her hat on a caution sign. Between her and the bus, the moonlit road was flecked with tiny frogs, distinguished from bits of gravel and bark only by their leaping, their errands of life. Ah bo bo! She called in her soul to come and see.

Kathi Maio was the film editor of *Sojourner* for many years, and for the last fifteen years has been the film columnist for *The Magazine of Fantasy & Science Fiction*. She contributed the film essays to *Nebula Awards 29, Nebula Awards 30,* and *Nebula Awards 31,* and is the author of two books of film essays, *Feminist in the Dark* and *Popcorn & Sexual Politics*. She lives in Malden, Massachusetts.

KATHI MAIO

SF and fantasy fans have been known to grumble about the dearth of quality films in the genre. I've been known to grouse about that topic myself. But as I sit down to write this particular essay, taking a quick overview of the year in film, I find myself in a glass-half-full frame of mind.

After all, we may see a shortage of really first-rate science fiction films each year, but the same could be said of historical dramas or romantic comedies. With the field of SF and fantasy, at least Hollywood usually delivers a healthy *quantity* of movies in the genre. (The same could certainly not be said of detective and mystery films—another popular culture formula of which I am quite fond.) Make enough films of a particular type, and you're bound to produce a few treasures. And so it was in 2004.

Oh, yes, there were plenty of disastrous exercises in the cinematic arts that year. And one or two actually cultivated a theme of disaster. Of these, most notable was *The Day After Tomorrow*. A climatological variation on the big, brash, FX-loaded blockbuster wannabes Roland Emmerich has been cultivating since *Independence Day* (1996), *Day After Tomorrow* fast-forwards our fears of global warming into a full-fledged ice age. And accomplishes it all practically overnight.

The media pundit and activist response to the movie was actually more entertaining than the film itself. Environmentalists (including former VP—or was that president?—Al Gore) tried to use the movie as talking points to warn of dangerous real-life scenarios. Meanwhile, conservative commentators pointed to the film as an example of the vast left-wing conspiracy that is Hollywood. (Ironic, that, since the film was released by Fox.)

It was all puffery and hype, but at least it was out-of-the-ordinary puffery and hype. In this case, the film needed all the help it could get.

Although the subject matter of the film is undeniably powerful, its exploration left much to be desired. Written by director Emmerich, along with Jeffrey Nachmanoff, the movie does CGI snow, water, and ice quite well. It's the human story that fails to capture much interest. Which is a shame, since the film stars Dennis Quaid as the scientist, Jack Hall, who tried to warn the world, and Jake Gyllenhaal as his estranged school-age son, Sam. Both are fine actors, but they can do little here except look worried and determined as they slog through water and snow.

In keeping with Emmerich's filmic mannerisms, we know that most of the extras in the movie are destined for a Popsicle fate. And we know that a few of Jack Hall's colleagues and buddies will perish bravely. We can also predict that, counter to all logic, Hall and his offspring will survive and rebond as father and child. Even mom (a physician played by the totally wasted Sela Ward) survives in this one, after rejecting her first chance at rescue to stay at the cold, dark hospital with a half-blind, cancer-ridden child. It's just the kind of plot device thrown in to tug at our heartstrings. Yet it is so calculated that it is incapable of actually touching us.

As long as you expect nothing more than hackneyed humanity from a millennial disaster film, *The Day After Tomorrow* doesn't fail completely. The same can't be said of some of the other films labeled disasters for completely different reasons.

One such movie was *Van Helsing,* a film made out of more spare parts than the Frankenstein monster—which just happens to be one of the many requisitioned characters to appear in it.

Writer/director Stephen Sommers was clearly hoping that lots of classic monsters (including Dracula and his brides, Frankenstein, and Mr. Hyde) and nonstop action would make some money. And it did. It just didn't make for a good movie.

Star Hugh Jackman, in the title role, and Kate Beckinsale, as his partner in Vatican-sponsored vampire hunting, never connect with each other or their audience. Even so, Sommers leads them through their battering paces in pointed pursuit of a *Van Helsing* sequel. Whether this will happen is still unclear. Perhaps if we all wear garlic and carry a power crossbow we can ward off another such film.

I don't mean to dismiss sequels as automatic stinkers, however. As per usual, several of the SF and fantasy films of 2004 fell into this category. And, all in all, the sequels were better movies than the majority of original films of the same period.

Most lauded of the sequels was the final installment in the *Lord of the Rings* trilogy, *The Return of the King*. Although actually a 2003 release, since it won the 2004 Nebula for best script, I am compelled to mention it here. But what is there left to say about this film that won more Oscars and other awards than you could shake a sword at?

Certainly director Peter Jackson and his coscreenwriters Fran Walsh and Phillippa Boyens did an amazing job with a monumental task of adapting Tolkien's dense, multiplotted, and war-intensive novel. The CGI effects were remarkable, but no more impressive than the way the writing and editing layered and crosscut the many story threads as to maintain emotional contrast and energy in a very complex and long film.

That said, to my mind, *Return of the King* was actually the weakest of the three films in the trilogy. Too many plotlines were given short shrift so as to leave plenty of time for the perpetual battle sequences. Why is Eowyn standing next to Faramir at the end of the film? Those who never read the novels (and there *are* one or two such viewers) wouldn't have a clue. A few more of these character-enriching areas should have been explored. If the filmmakers needed to save screen time, they could have lopped off a few of the movie's extra endings.

Perhaps I am just in the mood to be a naysayer. Dare I opine that screenwriter Steve Kloves and director Alfonso Cuaron did just as good of a job adapting another whopping big novel called *Harry Potter and the Prisoner of Azkaban*? Oh, there are still problems with expunged plot elements here. And such antics can annoy fans of the novel as well as possibly confuse those who haven't read the adapted source material. Nevertheless, this third, beautifully moody and atmospheric film in the Potter series shows that the young wizard's maturation saga still has the power to delight young and old alike. (Although Richard Harris's Dumbledore is sorely missed!)

Another sequel that can be enthusiastically enjoyed by both children and adults is *Shrek 2*. With Shrek and his now ogre-ish bride happily married, where's the conflict? It emanates from Fiona's royal parents (that is to say, Shrek's horrified in-laws), of course. Then there's the numerous machinations of an avaricious fairy godmother with her own family agenda to promote. Besides little life lessons on self-acceptance—this time for Shrek as well as Fiona—the movie has plenty of cultural references, witty banter, and a few interesting new characters like Antonio Banderas spoofing his Zorro success as Puss in Boots.

Although the novelty of the characters is lost in *Shrek 2,* the film makes up for the loss with a ceaseless sense of fun and our continuing affection for the story's characters. The same could be said for another second in a series, *Spider-Man 2.* Although there is nothing cartoonish about the way return helmer Sam Raimi and screenwriter Alvin Sargent tell their comic book–inspired tale.

When we meet Peter Parker again, he is a student struggling to make a living, keep up with schoolwork, and still maintain his rigorous self-imposed duties as Spider-Man. Something's gotta give. For starters, Peter forgoes developing his relationship with his true love, Mary Jane. But as his life continues to unravel (and his powers become erratic, at best) Peter decides that it's his Spidey identity that needs to be jettisoned from his life.

Superherodom is not, however, easy to quit. So Spidey continues to battle his own demons, as well as a new unintentional supervillain, Doc Ock (well played by Alfred Molina).

Can *Spider-Man 2* be that rare sequel that isn't just as good, but is actually better than its predecessor? I think so. Sam Raimi's direction is even more assured and stylish than in the first outing. And Tobey Maguire's endearingly conflicted hero is someone we deeply care about and can easily relate to.

It's a little harder to identify another comic-book lead appearing in his first movie. He is a Dark Horse comic hero, created by Mike Mignola, called Hellboy. The film version, written and directed by the very talented Mexican director Guillermo del Toro, has to spend a great deal of time on story background and setup, but never loses the audience for a minute. It seems that during World War II, Nazis, Rasputin, and several scary assorted cronies had attempted to open up a portal to hell in order to summon all manner of dark forces forth in aid of the Third Reich. A plucky band of Allied foes, including a paranormal scientist named Trevor "Broom" Bruttenholm, manage to foil the plot. But not before the gates of hell opened long enough for a red monkey-ish devil baby to pass through. Broom saves and raises the creature.

Decades later, Broom (John Hurt) is still fighting the good fight against dark forces. And he is now aided by his adult adopted son, Hellboy (Ron Perlman), along with government agents and other, shall we say, unusual cohorts.

The plot of *Hellboy* is both complicated and simple. It's your basic good versus evil (and I mean *way* evil) story. The difference between *Hellboy* and, say, *Van Helsing* is that the action isn't unrelenting. We are given a chance to breathe, soak up the fantastical atmosphere, and learn to care for the characters. Notable among these is the titular hero. Hellboy looks bizarre, and often sounds like something out of a hard-boiled detective pulp. Yet there is a melancholy gentleness about him, too. (Clearly, this was the perfect role for Mr. Perlman!)

You wouldn't expect a big red guy with a club fist and horn stumps on his forehead to be a romantic hero. But when you see Hellboy with Liz Sherman (Selma Blair), his even more melancholic and pyrokinetic sweetheart, you realize that's exactly what he is.

A movie that so deftly mixes action, horror, comedy, and romance deserves a wide audience and, yes, even a sequel. Not so other comic-book heroes to launch onto screens in 2004.

One of the biggest duds in this category is the Halle Berry vehicle, *Catwoman*. The screenplay by John Brancato, Michael Ferris, and John Rogers is an out-and-out mess. And the direction, by Pitof, is neither playful nor exciting. As for Ms. Berry, she is as beautiful as ever, but she is never able to find her character. She is never believably mousy as her ad designer true self. And although she looks mighty hot in dominatrix leather, her superhero alter ego never really convinces, either.

Bouncing off of walls is a nice trick, but having a personality and a purpose is even more important. As for *Catwoman*'s predictable romance with a generic cop (Benjamin Bratt), it is about as emotionally involving as one of those cans of tuna her confused character gobbles down.

The utter failure of *Catwoman* in 2004 as well as other high-profile projects like 2005's *Elektra* have caused some to speculate upon the impracticality of the female action hero as a box-office draw. Although it's true that the base audience for superhero action movies is probably adolescent and male, I doubt that the reason *Catwoman* failed is that young men don't really want to see empowered kick-ass women. *Catwoman* failed because it was a bad movie.

If the writers and directors of Hollywood (also mostly male) can ever create a good movie with a convincing female action hero, I predict that audiences of all genders and ages will embrace it. But for now, the female-centered fantasy films that are released tend to be of the gentler and more romantic variety.

In 2004, one of these starred *Elektra* and *Alias* star Jennifer Garner. Clearly wanting a change of pace from kicking asses right and left, Ms. Garner made her romantic-comedy screen debut in a little, very *Big*-ish movie called *13 Going on 30*.

The film opens with a late-eighties pubescent lass named Jenna facing down her birthday, hoping to be accepted by her school's clique of popular girls. Her best friend and would-be suitor, Matt, tries to tell her to stay original, but she wants only to be cool. When her party turns into a humiliating disaster, Matt's gift of wishing dust allows her to jump past the awkward years and become "thirty, flirty, and thriving."

She's got the career and the wardrobe and the sexy boyfriend. But somewhere during that time leap, Jenna lost her soul. And the rest of the movie consists of our heroine peeling back the bitchy, glam career gal, and refinding her inner child, as well as her first boyfriend (adult Matt, played by Mark Ruffalo).

Screenwriters Josh Goldsmith and Cathy Yuspa (who also did a number on the modern working woman in their 2000 fantasy, *What Women Want*) don't make it clear how sweet young Jenna became the harridan her coworkers perceive her to be. Perhaps just growing up and becoming successful is enough to make a woman into a treacherous, adulterous, secretary-terrorizing shrew.

If Jenna's time-warp character makes little sense, luckily no one told Jennifer Garner. She has charm to burn, and a knack for physical comedy. She almost makes the movie work. Almost.

An even better fantasy with a female hero can be found in a fractured fairy tale called *Ella Enchanted,* starring another equally appealing actor, Anne Hathaway. Given the "gift" of obedience by a very inept fairy shortly after her birth, the plot consists of Ella's quest to get the curse lifted and to save her home from the cruel control of her evil stepmother and her two nasty stepsisters. Of course, a prince comes into play, along with his power-hungry uncle (played, in a nice twist, by the *Princess Bride*'s leading man, Cary Elwes). Into the mix goes oppressed ethnic groups (in this case, giants and elves), who find an able champion in Ella.

It's all undeniably silly, and quite entertaining. Forget about *Catwoman*. Here's real girl power.

Girls and boys, and teens of all description, are obviously the target audiences for many fantasy films. In 2004, there were a wide array of films pitched to the young. Some, like *Lemony Snicket's A Series of*

Unfortunate Events, had a built-in audience. Yet in the case of that film, written by *Men in Black II*'s Robert Gordon from three of the best-selling children's books, the ready-made audience was likely disappointed. Although the opening and closing animated sequences were a perfect match, not so the live action. The problem is partially tone. But in large part the issue is the film's big-name star, Jim Carrey. Histrionic without being particularly humorous, Carrey was probably urged by director Brad Silberling to ham it up to his heart's content. Alas, this ends up being a disservice to the film as whole, and to the development of the Baudelaire orphans in particular.

A Series of Unfortunate Events is less than good, but at least it's not as bad as *Scooby-Doo 2: Monsters Unleashed,* an idiotic little tale for the teenybopper set. It's not even worth mentioning, except that as I watched I realized that the biggest problem the film had was that it was trying to bring a cartoon to life. Which begs the question, why would anyone *want* a cartoon brought to life? Similar ruminations came to mind while watching another 2004 feature, *The Polar Express.* Directed and cowritten (with William Broyles, Jr.) by fantasy and science fiction master Robert Zemeckis, the film is considered a breakthrough in "performance capture"—the translation of human action into computer animation. It was supposed to be magical, but it gave me the creeps.

This holiday yarn about a train visit to Santa is populated by children with crossed, cold eyes, and a flat emotional affect to match their dull unnatural skin tones. It's kiddies and Kris Kringle in the Land of the Living Dead!

Perhaps I'm just a reactionary. But I don't want anyone to make my cartoons real. I embrace the artificiality and otherworldness of animation. But I still want a full-length cartoon to have something to say about real life.

Such is the case with one of the best films of the year, *The Incredibles.* Written and directed by Brad Bird, *The Incredibles* was the filmmaker's first foray into computer animation, following his brilliant 1999 drawn animation feature, *The Iron Giant.* When I first heard that one of the great last hopes for traditional animation had gone over to computer graphics, I was dismayed. Would he make his family of forcibly retired superheroes too "realistic"? Not a chance!

Although Bird made full use of technology's talent for achieving deeply detailed environments and textures, he never lost sight of the power of out-and-out fantasy. His Parr family, lead by Mr. Incredible

(Craig T. Nelson) and Elastigirl (Holly Hunter) look like plastic action figures and not at all like flesh-and-blood people. But that doesn't mean that Bird isn't able to express fully human emotions through his characters.

In fact, amidst the exciting save-the-world adventure story, this amiable little cartoon says a great deal about the dangers of mediocrity and hero worship, and provides plenty of subtle commentary on family dynamics, gender roles, and countless other aspects of modern life.

Although Brad Bird seems to have found the perfect way to inject humanity into synthetically produced art, other filmmakers are still feeling their way—especially as they work to have live actors interact with CGI environments and characters.

One of the most ambitious films to tackle this challenge is Kerry Conran's *Sky Captain and the World of Tomorrow*. Conran's small cast of actors worked almost entirely in a blue-screen environment. Later, some eighty visual effects wizards created the astounding two thousand effects shots that would provide the backdrop and most of the set for the live action.

Visually, *Sky Captain* is a remarkable achievement. Conran admits that he "stole" from everything from comic books to B science fiction films to *Citizen Kane*. The resulting World of Tomorrow is a glowing and ominous art deco wonder. The story is slightly less inspiring. For although Angelina Jolie shines as a cocky, no-nonsense British squadron commander, Jude Law and Gwyneth Paltrow sometimes seem a bit lost in their retro roles and their artificial sets.

Since Will Smith seemingly has enough swagger to dominate any movie, you might think that he would have an easier time in *I, Robot*. But he, too, has a tough time holding his own. The CGI robotic lead, Sonny (injected with the voice and on-set performance of actor Alan Tudyk) is actually far and away the most interesting character in the film.

I, Robot is one of those movies that requires a total disconnect from its literary forebears. If you expect the film to have any resemblance to Isaac Asimov's important collection of linked stories, or in any way deal with philosophical and psychological conundrums posed by those stories, you are bound to be completely outraged by the movie directed by Alex Proyas and written by Jeff Vintar and Akiva Goldsman. However, if you can just watch it as a well-crafted, dumb summer flick, then *I, Robot* actually entertains—at least until its very limp ending.

It is hard to be quite that merciful with another summer movie, the Frank Oz/Paul Rudnick remake of the *Stepford Wives*. The movie is such a mishmash of styles and tones and messages—played, badly, for satiric comedy instead of suspense—that you wonder what anyone involved could have been thinking. The film can't even decide whether the titular spouses have been replaced by robots or not. A result of filmmaking by committee and focus group, the movie is a complete failure.

For a more intriguing movie, made up of four short films, I would recommend *Robot Stories*. Directed and written by Greg Pak, this independent feature hit the film festival circuit in 2002, but didn't receive limited theatrical release until 2004.

Although the individual shorts vary in quality and the small budget often shows, this is nonetheless an impressive collection that uses our interactions with robots, holograms, and even toys as a means of exploring our common humanity.

Indie features are often willing to explore ideas in an uncompromising way that major studio releases are unwilling to match. Such is the case with a first feature, shot on a budget of just seven thousand dollars, which ended up winning the grand jury prize at 2004 Sundance, and also received the Alfred P. Sloan Foundation prize for science-related film. The movie is called *Primer,* and it was written, directed, edited, and scored by self-taught filmmaker Shane Carruth—who also stars in one of the two lead roles.

Primer is the story of two friends—techie nerds who run a secondary business out of a garage—who stumble upon a scientific discovery related to time travel. The film explores the process of innovation and the limits of trust, and its greatest strength might also be its greatest weakness. Carruth refuses to talk down to his audience or sacrifice the reality of his character's lives. Therefore, his characters speak in jargon, finishing each other's thoughts from long association.

If the constant tech-talk fragments don't drive you insane, you will likely enjoy *Primer,* despite the ever more confusing time loops and the wholly unsatisfying conclusion.

The way past and future intersect and how memory and experience inform every aspect of our lives are themes that even a couple of studio-released films were willing to tackle in 2004. And although one was more successful than the other, they both get points for not being the same old, same old.

The Butterfly Effect's title comes from the proposition that the flutter of a butterfly in one part of the globe can cause a typhoon half a world away. The feature, written and directed by Eric Bress, is not, however, an examination of chaos theory. Rather, it's the repeating story of a young man who inherited a talent (or, rather, a curse) to fast-rewind his life in the hopes of making things better. Specifically, young Evan (Ashton Kutcher) wants desperately to save his childhood love, Kayleigh (Amy Smart) from various ruinous fates.

Butterfly Effect touches on lots of interesting ideas—notably the disastrous impacts of child abuse on the victim and those around them—but it can't quite keep its story line together. And although Ashton Kutcher is an affable young man, he doesn't quite have the gravitas to handle the challenging central role of Evan.

Acting duties are not, however, an issue in one of the finest movies of the year, *Eternal Sunshine of the Spotless Mind*. The film stars Jim Carrey (who, for once, actually plays his character instead of doing his manic shtick) and the equally gifted Kate Winslet. They both give splendid performances in a film that is fully worthy of their performance skills.

Director Michel Gondry was inspired by the idea of artist friend Pierre Bismuth to send cards to people telling them they'd been erased from someone else's memory. He shared this idea with friend and collaborator, screenwriter Charlie Kaufman, and the result is a film about a mismatched (or are they perfect for each other?) couple named Joel and Clementine. What happens when, in the middle of a breakup, they both seek the services of a scientist, Dr. Howard Mierzwiak (Tom Wilkinson) who maps and expunges memories from the human brain?

Therein lies the tale.

Set against Joel's erasure procedure, viewers get to haunt Joel's evaporating remembrance, witnessing all that was terrible and enriching in his liaison with the offbeat Clementine.

The film clearly tells us that memories—even painful ones—are essential to our lives. And relationships—even ones that disintegrate—are treasures worth preserving.

Low-tech and luminous, seeing *Eternal Sunshine* is a memory to savor, as well.

Mike Resnick is one of the best-selling authors in science fiction, and one of the most prolific. His many novels include *Santiago, The Dark Lady, Stalking the Unicorn, Birthright: The Book of Man, Paradise, Ivory, Soothsayer, Oracle, Lucifer Jones, Purgatory, Inferno, A Miracle of Rare Design, The Widowmaker, The Soul Eater, A Hunger in the Soul,* and *The Return of Santiago.* His award-winning short fiction has been gathered in the collections *Will the Last Person to Leave the Planet Please Turn off the Sun?, An Alien Land, Kirinyaga, A Safari of the Mind,* and *Hunting the Snark and Other Short Novels.* In the last decade or so, he has become almost as prolific as an anthologist, producing, as editor, *Inside the Funhouse: 17 SF stories about SF, Whatdunits, More Whatdunits,* and *Shaggy B.E.M. Stories*; a long string of anthologies coedited with Martin H. Greenberg—*Alternate Presidents, Alternate Kennedys, Alternate Warriors, Aladdin: Master of the Lamp, Dinosaur Fantastic, By Any Other Fame, Alternate Outlaws, Sherlock Holmes in Orbit, Stars: Stories Based on the Songs of Janis Ian* (edited with Janis Ian), *New Voices in Science Fiction, Men Writing Science Fiction as Women,* and *Women Writing Science Fiction as Men,* among others. He won the Hugo Award in 1989 for *Kirinyaga.* He won another Hugo Award in 1991 for another story in the Kirinyaga series, "The Manumouki," and another Hugo and Nebula in 1995 for his novella "Seven Views of Olduvai Gorge." His most recent book is a new anthology, *I, Alien,* and coming up are two new novels, *Starship Mutiny* and *A Gathering of Widowmakers.* He lives with his wife, Carol, in Cincinnati, Ohio.

Of "Travels with My Cats," he says:

"Every now and then I read a book or see a movie that I remember fondly from my youth. If I encountered them for the first time as an adult, I would probably be quite critical of them—but they carry a lot of my emotional baggage with them. I wanted to *be* the author, or the cowboy, or the detective, and if that author or hero was a woman, the younger version of me probably fell a little bit in love with her.

"As an atheist I believe that such immortality as I achieve will not come in Heaven or Hell, but will last only for the time it takes someone to read one of my books or stories after I am dead, that for as long as it takes them to read it I'll be alive again in some ill-defined and mystical way.

"I took those two concepts—the fondly remembered books of my youth, and my idiosyncratic notion of immortality—and came up with 'Travels with My Cats.' I think it's one of my best, and I thank the SFFWA membership for agreeing, at least to the extent that it made the final ballot.

"Writing is a form of immortality. If you don't believe in an afterlife, it's comforting to think that long after you're dead, some vital part of you will be alive again for the length of time that someone picks up one of your books and reads it. I've heard other writers say it often enough; I've occasionally said it myself.

"I thought that it might be interesting to write a story about it, not from the writer's point of view, but rather from the viewpoint of someone who fondly remembers a cherished volume, one that changed his life, or at least made it a little more tolerable, and was written by an author he can never know, someone who died before he was born—as I wish I could have met a couple of authors who had profound influences on me when I was first starting to read.

"Hence 'Travels with My Cats.' I thought this was a pretty good story when I was writing it, and I'm delighted that the membership agrees with me."

MIKE RESNICK

found it in the back of a neighbor's garage. They were retiring and moving to Florida, and they'd put most of their stuff up for sale rather than pay to ship it south.

I was eleven years old, and I was looking for a Tarzan book, or maybe one of Clarence Mulford's Hopalong Cassidy epics, or perhaps (if my mother was looking the other way) a forbidden Mickey Spillane novel. I found them, too—and then the real world intruded. They were 50 cents each (and a whole dollar for *Kiss Me Deadly*), and all I had was a nickel.

So I rummaged some more, and finally found the only book that was in my price range. It was called *Travels with My Cats,* and the author was Miss Priscilla Wallace. Not Priscilla, but Miss Priscilla. For years I thought Miss was her first name.

I thumbed through it, hoping it at least had some photos of half-naked native girls hidden in its pages. There weren't any pictures at all, just words. I wasn't surprised; somehow I had known that an author called Miss wasn't going to plaster naked women all over her book.

I decided that the book itself felt too fancy and feminine for a boy who was trying out for the Little League later in the day—the letters on the cover were somehow raised above the rest of the surface, the endpapers were an elegant satin, the boards were covered with a russet, velvet-like cloth, and it even had a bookmark, which was a satin ribbon attached to the binding. I was about to put it back when it fell open to a page that said that this was Number 121 of a Limited Printing of 200.

That put a whole new light on things. My very own limited edition for a nickel—how could I say No? I brought it to the front of the garage, dutifully paid my nickel, and waited for my mother to finish looking (she always looked, never shopped—shopping implied parting with money, and she and my father were Depression kids who never bought what they could rent cheaper, or, better yet, borrow for free).

That night I was faced with a major decision. I didn't want to read a book called *Travels with My Cats* by a woman called Miss, but I'd spent my last nickel on it—well, the last until my allowance came due again next week—and I'd read all my other books so often you could almost see the eyetracks all over them.

So I picked it up without much enthusiasm, and read the first page, and then the next—and suddenly I was transported to Kenya Colony and Siam and the Amazon. Miss Priscilla Wallace had a way of describing things that made me wish I was there, and when I finished a section I felt like I'd *been* there.

There were cities I'd never heard of before, cities with exotic names like Maracaibo and Samarkand and Addis Ababa, some with names like Constantinople that I couldn't even find on the map.

Her father had been an explorer, back in the days when there still *were* explorers. She had taken her first few trips abroad with him, and he had undoubtedly given her a taste for distant lands. (My own father was a typesetter. How I envied her!)

I had half hoped the African section would be filled with rampaging elephants and man-eating lions, and maybe it was—but that wasn't the way she saw it. Africa may have been red of tooth and claw, but to her it reflected the gold of the morning sun, and the dark, shadowy places were filled with wonder, not terror.

She could find beauty anywhere. She would describe two hundred flower sellers lined up along the Seine on a Sunday morning in Paris, or a single frail blossom in the middle of the Gobi Desert, and somehow you knew that each was as wondrous as she said.

And suddenly I jumped as the alarm clock started buzzing. It was the first time I'd ever stayed up for the entire night. I put the book away, got dressed for school, and hurried home after school so that I could finish it.

I must have read it six or seven more times that year. I got to the point where I could almost recite parts of it word-for-word. I was in love with those exotic faraway places, and maybe a little bit in love with the author, too. I even wrote her a fan letter addressed to "Miss Priscilla Wallace, Somewhere," but of course it came back.

Then, in the fall, I discovered Robert A. Heinlein and Louis L'Amour, and a friend saw *Travels with My Cats* and teased me about its fancy cover and the fact that it was written by a woman, so I put it on a shelf and over the years I forgot about it.

I never saw all those wonderful, mysterious places she wrote about. I never did a lot of things. I never made a name for myself. I never got rich and famous. I never married.

By the time I was forty, I was finally ready to admit that nothing unusual or exciting was ever likely to happen to me. I'd written half of a novel that I was never going to finish or sell, and I'd spent twenty years looking fruitlessly for someone I could love. (That was Step One; Step Two—finding someone who could love me—would probably have been even more difficult, but I never got around to it.)

I was tired of the city, and of rubbing shoulders with people who had latched onto the happiness and success that had somehow eluded me. I was Midwestern born and bred, and eventually I moved to Wisconsin's North Woods, where the most exotic cities were small towns like Manitowoc and Minnaqua and Wausau—a far cry from Macau and Marrakech and the other glittering capitals of Priscilla Wallace's book.

I worked as a copy editor for one of the local weekly newspapers—the kind where getting the restaurant and real estate ads right was more important than spelling the names in the news stories correctly. It wasn't the most challenging job in the world, but it was pleasant enough, and I wasn't looking for any challenges. Youthful dreams of triumph had gone the way of youthful dreams of love and passion; at this late date, I'd settled for tranquility.

I rented a small house out on a little nameless lake, some fifteen miles out of town. It wasn't without its share of charm: it had an old-fashioned veranda, with a porch swing that was almost as old as the house. A pier for the boat I didn't own jutted out into the lake, and there was even a water trough for the original owner's horses. There was no air-conditioning, but I didn't really need it—and in the winter I'd sit by the fire, reading the latest paperback thriller.

It was on a late summer's night, with just a bit of a Wisconsin chill in the air, as I sat next to the empty fireplace, reading about a rip-roaring gun-blazing car chase through Berlin or Prague or some other city I'll never see, that I found myself wondering if this was my future: a lonely old man, spending his evenings reading pop fiction by a fireplace, maybe with a blanket over his legs, his only companion a tabby cat. . . .

And for some reason—probably the notion of the tabby—I remembered *Travels with My Cats*. I'd never owned a cat, but *she* had; there had been two of them, and they'd gone everywhere with her.

I hadn't thought of the book for years. I didn't even know if I still had it. But for some reason, I felt an urge to pick it up and look through it.

I went to the spare room, where I kept all the stuff I hadn't unpacked yet. There were maybe two dozen boxes of books. I opened the first of them, then the next. I rummaged through Bradburys and Asimovs and Chandlers and Hammetts, dug deep beneath Ludlums and Amblers and a pair of ancient Zane Grays—and suddenly there it was, as elegant as ever. My one and only Limited Numbered Edition.

So, for the first time in perhaps thirty years, I opened the book and began reading it. And found myself just as captivated as I had been the first time. It was every bit as wonderful as I remembered. And, as I had done three decades ago, I lost all track of the time and finished it just as the sun was rising.

I didn't get much work done that morning. All I could do was think about those exquisite descriptions and insights into worlds that no longer existed—and then I began wondering if Priscilla Wallace herself still existed. She'd probably be a very old lady, but maybe I could update that old fan letter and finally send it.

I stopped by the local library at lunchtime, determined to pick up everything else she had written. There was nothing on the shelves or in their card file. (They were a friendly old-fashioned rural library; computerizing their stock was still decades away.)

I went back to the office and had my computer run a search on her. There were thirty-seven distinct and different Priscilla Wallaces. One was an actress in low-budget movies. One taught at Georgetown University. One was a diplomat stationed in Bratislava. One was a wildly successful breeder of show poodles. One was the youthful mother of a set of sextuplets in South Carolina. One was an inker for a Sunday comic strip.

And then, just when I was sure the computer wouldn't be able to find her, the following came up on my screen:

"Wallace, Priscilla, b. 1892, d. 1926. Author of one book: *Travels with My Cats*."

1926. So much for fan letters, then or now; she'd died decades before I'd been born. Even so, I felt a sudden sense of loss, and of resentment—resentment that someone like that had died so young, and that all her unlived years had been taken by people who would never see the beauty that she found everywhere she went.

People like me.

There was also a photo. It looked like a reproduction of an old sepia-toned tintype, and it showed a slender, auburn-haired young woman with large dark eyes that seemed somehow sad to me. Or maybe the sadness was my own, because I knew she would die at thirty-four and all that passion for life would die with her. I printed up a hard copy, put it in my desk drawer, and took it home with me at the end of the day. I don't know why. There were only two sentences on it. Somehow a life—any life—deserved more than that. Especially one that could reach out from the grave and touch me and make me feel, at least while I was reading her book, that maybe the world wasn't quite as dull and ordinary as it seemed to me.

That night, after I heated up a frozen dinner, I sat down by the fireplace and picked up *Travels with My Cats* again, just thumbing through it to read my favorite passages here and there. There was the one about the stately procession of elephants against the backdrop of snow-capped Kilimanjaro, and another about the overpowering perfume of the flowers as she walked through the gardens of Versailles on a May morning. And then, toward the end, there was what had become my favorite of all:

"There is so much yet to see, so much still to do, that on days like this I wish I could live forever. I take comfort in the heartfelt belief that long after I am gone, I will be alive again for as long as someone picks up a copy of this book and reads it."

It *was* a comforting belief, certainly more immortality than I ever aspired to. I'd made no mark, left no sign by which anyone would know I'd ever been here. Twenty years after my death, maybe thirty at most, no one would ever know that I'd even existed, that a man named Ethan Owens—my name; you've never encountered it before, and you doubtless never will again—lived and worked and died here, that he tried to get through each day without doing anyone any harm, and that was the sum total of his accomplishments.

Not like her. Or maybe very much like her. She was no politi-cian, no warrior queen. There were no monuments to her. She wrote a forgotten little travel book and died before she could write another. She'd been gone for more than three-quarters of a century. Who re-membered Priscilla Wallace?

I poured myself a beer and began reading again. Somehow, the more she described each exotic city and primal jungle, the less exotic and primal they felt, the more they seemed like an extension of home. As often as I read it, I couldn't figure out how she managed to do that.

I was distracted by a clattering on the veranda. *Damned raccoons are getting bolder every night,* I thought—but then I heard a very distinct *meow.* My nearest neighbor was a mile away, and that seemed a long way for a cat to wander, but I figured the least I could do was go out and look, and if it had a collar and a tag I'd call its owner. And if not, I'd shoo it away before it got into the wrong end of a disagreement with the local raccoons.

I opened the door and stepped out onto the veranda. Sure enough, there was a cat there, a small white one with a couple of tan markings on its head and body. I reached down to pick it up, and it backed away a couple of steps.

"I'm not going to hurt you," I said gently.

"He knows that," said a feminine voice. "He's just shy."

I turned—and there she was, sitting on my porch swing. She made a gesture, and the cat walked across the veranda and jumped up onto her lap.

I'd seen that face earlier in the day, staring at me in sepia tones. I'd studied it for hours, until I knew its every contour.

It was *her.*

"It's a beautiful night, isn't it?" she said as I kept gaping at her. "And quiet. Even the birds are asleep." She paused. "Only the cicadas are awake, serenading us with their symphonies."

I didn't know what to say, so I just watched her and waited for her to vanish.

"You look pale," she noted after a moment.

"You look real," I finally managed to croak.

"Of course I do," she replied with a smile. "I *am* real."

"You're Miss Priscilla Wallace, and I've spent so much time think-ing about you that I've begun hallucinating."

"Do I look like an hallucination?"

"I don't know," I admitted. "I don't think I've ever had one before, so I don't know what they look like—except that obviously they look like you." I paused. "They could look a lot worse. You have a beautiful face."

She laughed at that. The cat jumped, startled, and she began stroking it gently. "I do believe you're trying to make me blush," she said.

"*Can* you blush?" I asked, and then of course wished I hadn't.

"Of course I can," she replied, "though I had my doubts after I got back from Tahiti. The things they *do* there!" Then, "You were reading *Travels with My Cats,* weren't you?"

"Yes, I was. It's been one of my most cherished possessions since I was a child."

"Was it a gift?" she asked.

"No, I bought it myself."

"That's very gratifying."

"It's very gratifying to finally meet the author who's given me so much pleasure," I said, feeling like an awkward kid all over again.

She looked puzzled, as if she was about to ask a question. Then she changed her mind and smiled again. It was a lovely smile, as I had known it would be.

"This is very pretty property," she said. "Is it yours all the way up to the lake?"

"Yes."

"Does anyone else live here?"

"Just me."

"You like your privacy," she said. It was a statement, not a question.

"Not especially," I answered. "That's just the way things worked out. People don't seem to like me very much."

Now why the hell did I tell you that? I thought. *I've never even admitted it to myself.*

"You seem like a very nice person," she said. "I find it difficult to believe that people don't like you."

"Maybe I overstated the case," I admitted. "Mostly they don't notice me." I shifted uncomfortably. "I didn't mean to unburden myself on you."

"You're all alone. You have to unburden yourself to *someone,*" she replied. "I think you just need a little more self-confidence."

"Perhaps."

She stared at me for a long moment. "You keep looking like you're expecting something terrible to happen."

"I'm expecting you to disappear."

"Would that be so terrible?"

"Yes," I said promptly. "It would be."

"Then why don't you simply accept that I'm here? If you're wrong, you'll know it soon enough."

I nodded. "Yeah, you're Priscilla Wallace, all right. That's exactly the kind of answer she'd give."

"You know who *I* am. Perhaps you'll tell me who *you* are?"

"My name is Ethan Owens."

"Ethan," she repeated. "That's a nice name."

"You think so?"

"I wouldn't say so if I didn't." She paused. "Shall I call you Ethan, or Mr. Owens?"

"Ethan, by all means. I feel like I've known you all my life." I felt another embarrassing admission coming on. "I even wrote you a fan letter when I was a kid, but it came back."

"I would have liked that," she said. "I never once got a fan letter. Not from anyone."

"I'm sure hundreds of people wanted to write. Maybe they couldn't find your address either."

"Maybe," she said dubiously.

"In fact, just today I was thinking about sending it again."

"Whatever you wanted to say, you can tell me in person." The cat jumped back down onto the veranda. "You look very uncomfortable perched on the railing like that, Ethan. Why don't you come and sit beside me?"

"I'd like that very much," I said, standing up. Then I thought it over. "No, I'd better not."

"I'm thirty-two years old," she said in amused tones. "I don't need a chaperone."

"Not with me, you don't," I assured her. "Besides, I don't think we have them anymore."

"Then what's the problem?"

"The truth?" I said. "If I sit next to you, at some point my hip will press against yours, or perhaps I'll inadvertently touch your hand. And . . ."

"And what?"

"And I don't want to find out that you're not really here."

"But I am."

"I hope so," I said. "But I can believe it a lot easier from where I am."

She shrugged. "As you wish."

"I've had my wish for the night," I said.

"Then why don't we just sit and enjoy the breeze and the scents of the Wisconsin night?"

"Whatever makes you happy," I said.

"Being here makes me happy. Knowing my book is still being read makes me happy." She was silent for a moment, staring off into the darkness. "What's the date, Ethan?"

"April 17."

"I mean the year."

"2004."

She looked surprised. "It's been *that* long?"

"Since . . . ?" I said hesitantly.

"Since I died," she said. "Oh, I know I must have died a long time ago. I have no tomorrows, and my yesterdays are all so very long ago. But the new millennium? It seems"—she searched for the right word—"excessive."

"You were born in 1892, more than a century ago," I said.

"How did you know that?"

"I had the computer run a search on you."

"I don't know what a computer is," she said. Then, suddenly: "Do you also know when and how I died?"

"I know when, not how."

"Please don't tell me," she said. "I'm thirty-two, and I've just written the last page of my book. I don't know what comes next, and it would be wrong for you to tell me."

"All right," I said. Then, borrowing her expression, "As you wish."

"Promise me."

"I promise."

Suddenly the little white cat tensed and looked off across the yard.

"He sees his brother," said Priscilla.

"It's probably just the raccoons," I said. "They can be a nuisance."

"No," she insisted. "I know his body language. That's his brother out there."

And sure enough, I heard a distinct *meow* a moment later. The white cat leaped off the veranda and headed toward it.

"I'd better go get them before they become completely lost," said Priscilla, getting to her feet. "It happened once in Brazil, and I didn't find them for almost two days."

"I'll get a flashlight and come with you," I said.

"No, you might frighten them, and it wouldn't do to have them run away in strange surroundings." She stood up and stared at me. "You seem like a very nice man, Ethan Owens. I'm glad we finally met." She smiled sadly. "I just wish you weren't so lonely."

She climbed down to the yard and walked off into the darkness before I could lie and tell her I led a rich full life and wasn't lonely at all. Suddenly I had a premonition that she wasn't coming back. "Will we meet again?" I called after her as she vanished from sight.

"That depends on you, doesn't it?" came her answer out of the darkness.

I sat on the porch swing, waiting for her to reappear with the cats. Finally, despite the cold night air, I fell asleep. I woke up when the sun hit the swing in the morning.

I was alone.

It took me almost half the day to convince myself that what had happened the night before was just a dream. It wasn't like any other dream I'd ever had, because I remembered every detail of it, every word she'd said, every gesture she'd made. Of course she hadn't really visited me, but just the same I couldn't get Priscilla Wallace out of my mind, so I finally stopped working and used my computer to try to learn more about her.

There was nothing more to be found under her name except for that single brief entry. I tried a search on *Travels with My Cats* and came up empty. I checked to see if her father had ever written a book about his explorations; he hadn't. I even contacted a few of the hotels she had stayed at, alone or with her father, but none of them kept records that far back.

I tried one line of pursuit after another, but none of them proved fruitful. History had swallowed her up almost as completely as it would someday swallow me. Other than the book, the only proof I had that she had ever lived was that one computer entry, consisting of ten words and two dates. Wanted criminals couldn't hide from the law any better than she'd hidden from posterity.

Finally I looked out the window and realized that night had fallen and everyone else had gone home. (There's no night shift on a weekly paper.) I stopped by a local diner, grabbed a ham sandwich and a cup of coffee, and headed back to the lake.

I watched the ten o'clock news on TV, then sat down and picked up her book again, just to convince myself that she really *had* lived once upon a time. After a couple of minutes I got restless, put the book back on a table, and walked out for a breath of fresh air.

She was sitting on the porch swing, right where she had been the night before. There was a different cat next to her, a black one with white feet and white circles around its eyes.

She noticed me looking at the cat. "This is Goggle," she said. "I think he's exceptionally well-named, don't you?"

"I suppose," I said distractedly.

"The white one is Giggle, because he loves getting into all sorts of mischief." I didn't say anything. Finally she smiled. "Which of them has your tongue?"

"You're back," I said at last.

"Of course I am."

"I was reading your book again," I said. "I don't think I've ever encountered anyone who loved life so much."

"There's so much to love!"

"For some of us."

"It's all around you, Ethan," she said.

"I prefer seeing it through your eyes. It was like you were born again into a new world each morning," I said. "I suppose that's why I kept your book, and why I find myself re-reading it—to share what you see and feel."

"You can feel things yourself."

I shook my head. "I prefer what *you* feel."

"Poor Ethan," she said sincerely. "You've never loved anything, have you?"

"I've tried."

"That isn't what I said." She stared at me curiously. "Have you ever married?"

"No."

"Why not?"

"I don't know." I decided I might as well give her an honest answer. "Probably because none of them ever measured up to you."

"I'm not that special," she said.

"To me you are. You always have been."

She frowned. "I wanted my book to enrich your life, Ethan, not ruin it."

"You didn't ruin it," I said. "You made it a little more bearable."

"I wonder . . ." she mused.

"About what?"

"My being here. It's puzzling."

"Puzzling is an understatement," I said. "Unbelievable is more the word for it."

She shook her head distractedly. "You don't understand. I remember last night."

"So do I—every second of it."

"That's not what I meant." She stroked the cat absently. "I was never brought back before last night. I wasn't sure then. I thought perhaps I forgot after each episode. But today I remember last night."

"I'm not sure I follow you."

"You can't be the only person to read my book since I died. Or even if you were, I've never been called back before, not even by you." She stared at me for a long moment. "Maybe I was wrong."

"About what?"

"Maybe what brought me here wasn't the fact that *I* needed to be read. Maybe it's because *you* so desperately need someone."

"I—" I began heatedly, and then stopped. For a moment it seemed like the whole world had stopped with me. Then the moon came out from behind a cloud, and an owl hooted off to the left.

"What is it?"

"I was about to tell you that I'm not that lonely," I said. "But it would have been a lie."

"It's nothing to be ashamed of, Ethan."

"It's nothing to brag about, either." There was something about her that made me say things I'd never said to anyone else, including myself. "I had such high hopes when I was a boy. I was going to love my work, and I was going to be good at it. I was going to find a woman to love and spend the rest of my life with. I was going to see all the places you described. Over the years I saw each of those hopes die. Now I settle for paying my bills and getting regular check-ups at the doctor's." I sighed deeply. "I think my life can be described as a fully-realized diminished expectation."

"You have to take risks, Ethan," she said gently.

"I'm not like you," I said. "I wish I was, but I'm not. Besides, there aren't any wild places left."

She shook her head. "That's not what I meant. Love involves risk. You have to risk getting hurt."

"I've *been* hurt," I said. "It's nothing to write home about."

"Maybe that's why I'm here. You can't be hurt by a ghost."

The hell I can't, I thought. Aloud I said: "*Are* you a ghost?"

"I don't feel like one."

"You don't look like one."

"How *do* I look?" she asked.

"As lovely as I always knew you were."

"Fashions change."

"But beauty doesn't," I said.

"That's very kind of you to say, but I must look very old-fashioned. In fact, the world I knew must seem primitive to you." Her face brightened. "It's a new millennium. Tell me what's happened."

"We've walked on the moon—and we've landed ships on Mars and Venus."

She looked up into the night sky. "The moon!" she exclaimed. Then: "Why are you here when you could be there?"

"I'm not a risk-taker, remember?"

"What an exciting time to be alive!" she said enthusiastically. "I always wanted to see what lay beyond the next hill. But *you*—you get to see what's beyond the next star!"

"It's not that simple," I said.

"But it will be," she persisted.

"Someday," I agreed. "Not during my lifetime, but someday."

"Then you should die with the greatest reluctance," she said. "I'm sure I did." She looked up at the stars, as if envisioning herself flying to each of them. "Tell me more about the future."

"I don't know anything about the future," I said.

"*My* future. Your present."

I told her what I could. She seemed amazed that hundreds of millions of people now traveled by air, that I didn't know anyone who didn't own a car, and that train travel had almost disappeared in America. The thought of television fascinated her; I decided not to tell her what a vast wasteland it had been since its inception. Color movies, sound movies, computers—she wanted to know all about them. She was eager to learn if zoos had become more humane, if *people* had become more humane. She couldn't believe that heart transplants were actually routine.

I spoke for hours. Finally I just got so dry I told her I was going to have to take a break for a couple of minutes while I went into the kitchen and got us some drinks. She'd never heard of Fanta or Dr Pepper, which is what I had, and she didn't like beer, so I made her an iced tea and popped open a Bud for me. When I brought them out to the porch she and Goggle were gone.

I didn't even bother looking for her. I knew she had returned to the *somewhere* from which she had come.

She was back again the next three nights, sometimes with one cat, sometimes with both. She told me about her travels, about her over-whelming urge to see what there was to see in the little window of time allotted us humans, and I told her about the various wonders she would never see.

It was strange, conversing with a phantom every night. She kept assuring me she was real, and I believed it when she said it, but I was still afraid to touch her and discover that she was just a dream after all. Somehow, as if they knew my fears, the cats kept their distance too; not once in all those evenings did either of them ever so much as brush against me.

"I wish I'd seen all the sights *they've* seen," I said on the third night, nodding toward the cats.

"Some people thought it was cruel to take them all over the world with me," replied Priscilla, absently running her hand over Goggle's back as he purred contentedly. "I think it would have been more cruel to leave them behind."

"None of the cats—these or the ones that came before—ever caused any problems?"

"Certainly they did," she said. "But when you love something, you put up with the problems."

"Yeah, I suppose you do."

"How do you know?" she asked. "I thought you said you'd never loved anything."

"Maybe I was wrong."

"Oh?"

"I don't know," I said. "Maybe I love someone who vanishes every night when I turn my back." She stared at me, and suddenly I felt very awkward. I shrugged uncomfortably. "Maybe."

"I'm touched, Ethan," she said. "But I'm not of this world, not the way you are."

"I haven't complained," I said. "I'll settle for the moments I can get." I tried to smile; it was a disaster. "Besides, I don't even know if you're real."

"I keep telling you I am."

"I know."

"What would you do if you *knew* I was?" she asked.

"Really?"

"Really."

I stared at her. "Try not to get mad," I began.

"I won't get mad."

"I've wanted to hold you and kiss you since the first instant I saw you on my veranda," I said.

"Then why haven't you?"

"I have this . . . this *dread* that if I try to touch you and you're not here, if I prove conclusively to myself that you don't exist, then I'll never see you again."

"Remember what I told you about love and risk?"

"I remember."

"And?"

"Maybe I'll try tomorrow," I said. "I just don't want to lose you yet. I'm not feeling that brave tonight."

She smiled, a rather sad smile I thought. "Maybe you'll get tired of reading me."

"Never!"

"But it's the same book all the time. How often can you read it?"

I looked at her, young, vibrant, maybe two years from death, certainly less than three. I knew what lay ahead for her; all she could see was a lifetime of wonderful experiences stretching out into the distance.

"Then I'll read one of your other books."

"I wrote others?" she asked.

"Dozens of them," I lied.

She couldn't stop smiling. "Really?"

"Really."

"Thank you, Ethan," she said. "You've made me very happy."

"Then we're even."

There was a noisy squabble down by the lake. She quickly looked around for her cats, but they were on the porch, their attention also attracted by the noise.

"Raccoons," I said.

"Why are they fighting?"

"Probably a dead fish washed up on the shore," I answered. "They're not much for sharing."

She laughed. "They remind me of some people I know." She paused. "Some people I *knew*," she amended.

"Do you miss them—your friends, I mean?"

"No. I had hundreds of acquaintances, but very few close friends. I was never in one place long enough to make them. It's only when I'm with you that I realize they're gone." She paused. "I don't quite understand it. I know that I'm here with you, in the new millennium—but I feel like I just celebrated my thirty-second birthday. Tomorrow I'll put flowers on my father's grave, and next week I set sail for Madrid."

"Madrid?" I repeated. "Will you watch them fight the brave bulls in the arena?"

An odd expression crossed her face. "Isn't that curious?" she said.

"Isn't what curious?"

"I have no idea what I'll do in Spain . . . but you've read all my books, so *you* know."

"You don't want me to tell you," I said.

"No, that would spoil it."

"I'll miss you when you leave."

"You'll pick up one of my books and I'll be right back here," she said. "Besides, I went more than seventy-five years ago."

"It gets confusing," I said.

"Don't look so depressed. We'll be together again."

"It's only been a week, but I can't remember what I did with my evenings before I started talking to you."

The squabbling at the lake got louder, and Giggle and Goggle began huddling together.

"They're frightening my cats," said Priscilla.

"I'll go break it up," I said, climbing down from the veranda and heading off to where the raccoons were battling. "And when I get back," I added, feeling bolder the farther I got from her, "maybe I'll find out just how real you are after all."

By the time I reached the lake, the fight was all but over. One large raccoon, half a fish in its mouth, glared at me, totally unafraid. Two others, not quite as large, stood about ten feet away. All three were bleeding from numerous gashes, but it didn't look as if any of them had suffered a disabling injury.

"Serves you right," I muttered.

I turned and started trudging back up to the house from the lake. The cats were still on the veranda, but Priscilla wasn't. I figured she'd stepped inside to get another iced tea, or perhaps use the bathroom—one more factor in favor of her not being a ghost—but when she didn't come out in a couple of minutes I searched the house for her.

She wasn't there. She wasn't anywhere in the yard, or in the old empty barn. Finally I went back and sat down on the porch swing to wait.

A couple of minutes later Goggle jumped up on my lap. I'd been idly petting him for a couple of minutes before I realized that he was real.

I bought some cat food in the morning. I didn't want to set it out on the veranda, because I was sure the raccoons would get wind of it and drive Giggle and Goggle off, so I put it in a soup bowl and placed it on the counter next to the kitchen sink. I didn't have a litter box, so I left the kitchen window open enough for them to come and go as they pleased.

I resisted the urge to find out any more about Priscilla with the computer. All that was really left to learn was how she'd died, and I didn't want to know. How *does* a beautiful, healthy, world-traveling woman die at thirty-four? Torn apart by lions? Sacrificed by savages? Victim of a disfiguring tropical disease? Mugged, raped, and killed in New York? Whatever it was, it had robbed her of half a century. I didn't want to think of the books she could have written in that time, but rather of the joy she could have felt as she traveled from one new destination to another. No, I very definitely didn't want to know how she died.

I worked distractedly for a few hours, then knocked off in mid-afternoon and hurried home. To her.

I knew something was wrong the moment I got out of my car. The porch swing was empty. Giggle and Goggle jumped off the veranda, raced up to me, and began rubbing against my legs as if for comfort.

I yelled her name, but there was no response. Then I heard a rustling inside the house. I raced to the door, and saw a raccoon climbing out through the kitchen window just as I entered.

The place was a mess. Evidently he had been hunting for food, and since all I had were cans and frozen meals, he just started ripping the house apart, looking for anything he could eat.

And then I saw it: *Travels with My Cats* lay in tatters, as if the raccoon had had a temper tantrum at the lack of food and had taken it out on the book, which I'd left on the kitchen table. Pages were ripped to shreds, the cover was in pieces, and he had even urinated on what was left.

I worked feverishly on it for hours, tears streaming down my face for the first time since I was a kid, but there was no salvaging it—and that meant there would be no Priscilla tonight, or any night until I found another copy of the book.

In a blind fury I grabbed my rifle and a powerful flashlight and killed the first six raccoons I could find. It didn't make me feel any better—especially when I calmed down enough to consider what she would have thought of my bloodlust.

I felt as if morning would never come. When it did, I raced to the office, activated my computer, and tried to find a copy of Priscilla's book at www.abebooks.com and www.bookfinder.com, the two biggest computerized clusters of used book dealers. There wasn't a single copy for sale.

I contacted some of the other book dealers I'd used in the past. None of them had ever heard of it.

I called the copyright division at the Library of Congress, figuring they might be able to help me. No luck: *Travels with My Cats* was never officially copyrighted; there was no copy on file. I began to wonder if I hadn't dreamed the whole thing, the book as well as the woman.

Finally I called Charlie Grimmis, who advertises himself as The Book Detective. He does most of his work for anthologists seeking rights and permissions to obscure, long-out-of-print books and stories, but he didn't care who he worked for, as long as he got his money.

It took him nine days and cost me six hundred dollars, but finally I got a definitive answer:

> Dear Ethan:
> You led me a merry chase. I'd have bet halfway through it that the book didn't exist, but you were right: evidently you did own a copy of a limited, numbered edition.
> *Travels with My Cats* was self-published by one Priscilla

Wallace (d. 1926), in a limited, numbered edition of 200. The printer was the long-defunct Adelman Press of Bridgeport, Connecticut. The book was never copyrighted or registered with the Library of Congress.

Now we get into the conjecture part. As near as I can tell, this Wallace woman gave about one hundred and fifty copies away to friends and relatives, and the final fifty were probably trashed after her death. I've checked back, and there hasn't been a copy for sale anywhere in the past dozen years. It's hard to get trustworthy records farther back than that. Given that she was an unknown, that the book was a vanity press job, and that it went only to people who knew her, the likelihood is that no more than fifteen or twenty copies still exist, if that many.
Best,
Charlie

When it's finally time to start taking risks, you don't think about it—you just do it. I quit my job that afternoon, and for the past year I've been criss-crossing the country, hunting for a copy of *Travels with My Cats*. I haven't found one yet, but I'll keep looking, no matter how long it takes. I get lonely, but I don't get discouraged.

Was it a dream? Was she a hallucination? A couple of acquaintances I confided in think so. Hell, I'd think so too—except that I'm not traveling alone. I've got two feline companions, and they're as real and substantial as cats get to be.

So the man with no goal except to get through another day finally has a mission in life, an important one. The woman I love died half a century too soon. I'm the only one who can give her back those years, if not all at once then an evening and a weekend at a time—but one way or another she's going to get them. I've spent all my yesterdays and haven't got a thing to show for them; now I'm going to start stockpiling her tomorrows.

Anyway, that's the story. My job is gone, and so is most of my money. I haven't slept in the same bed twice in close to four hundred days. I've lost a lot of weight, and I've been living in these clothes for longer than I care to think. It doesn't matter. All that matters is that I find a copy of that book, and someday I know I will.

Do I have any regrets?

Just one.

I never touched her. Not even once.

The Rhysling Awards are named after the Blind Singer of the Spaceways featured in Robert A. Heinlein's "The Green Hills of Earth." They are given each year by members of the Science Fiction Poetry Association in two categories, Best Short Poem and Best Long Poem.

This year, the 2005 Rhysling Award for Short Poem went to Roger Dutcher for "Just Distance," published in *Tales of the Unanticipated* 23. Roger Dutcher lives in Beloit, Wisconsin, where in addition to writing, he reads, gardens, and has been known to drink wine. He is the editor of *The Magazine of Speculative Poetry*, and a coeditor for poetry at the Hugo-nominated Web site *Strange Horizons*.

The 2005 Rhysling Award for Long Poem went to Theodora Goss for "Octavia Is Lost in the Hall of Masks," published in *Mythic Delirium* 8. Theodora Goss lives in Boston, where she is completing a Ph.D. in English literature. Her short stories and poems have appeared in a variety of magazines and anthologies, including *Alchemy, Polyphony, Realms of Fantasy, Strange Horizons, Mythic Delirium, The Lyric,* and *Lady Churchill's Rosebud Wristlet*. They have been reprinted in *The Year's Best Fantasy, The Year's Best Fantasy and Horror,* and *The Year's Best Science Fiction and Fantasy for Teens*. Her chapbook of short stories and poems, *The Rose in Twelve Petals & Other Stories,* is available from Small Beer Press, and a short story collection, *In the Forest of Forgetting,* is forthcoming from Prime Books.

Since 1978, the Science Fiction Poetry Association (SFPA) has served as a gathering place for writers with an interest in poetry that contains elements of science, science fiction, fantasy and horror, or any combination thereof. The SFPA publishes an annual *Rhysling An-*

thology containing each year's nominees for the association's Rhysling Awards, given to honor excellence in speculative poetry. Recently, the SFPA published *The Alchemy of Stars: Rhysling Award Winners Showcase,* which for the first time collects Rhysling Award—winning poems from 1978 to 2004 in one volume. As of this writing, annual membership dues for SFPA in the U.S. are eighteen dollars. For more information on how to become a member and/or to order SFPA's books, visit http://www.sfpoetry.com.

JUST DISTANCE

ROGER DUTCHER

"Just distance," she said.
"Not mad, not dislike, not hate;"
the moon is bright and the
Perseids meteors pale,
as I contemplate "distance."
The Earth, perfectly positioned,
would boil at closer than
93 million miles distant,
and freeze if farther away.
The moon moves our oceans
and its reflected light
suffuses our poetry and songs,
yet any closer and we would be
torn apart by its gravity.
Somewhere, Comet Swift-Tuttle
moves, cold and dirty.
Only briefly does the solar wind
cause it to flare into beauty,
then, as it moves away,
and the distance grows, it
enters again, its cold, long orbit
so far from the sun.
Yet the debris it leaves
produces this beauty and
each year I watch
as one by one
the meteors are consumed
in the distance they fall.
"Just distance," she said,
not realizing that distance is all,
and yet no distance is greater
than that between human hearts.

OCTAVIA IS LOST IN
THE HALL OF MASKS

THEODORA GOSS

The Mask of Inquiry asks: Why are you here, Octavia? The linens have been spread for the wedding feast. The glasses have been filled with yellow wine. A roasted pig lies in its bed of parsley, squabs lift their legs in paper caps between turnips carved to resemble roses. The wedding guests are waiting to toast the bride.

The Mask of Elegance says: The Duke sits beside an empty chair. There is a collar of Flanders lace beneath his receding chin, there is a boot of Spanish leather on his clubfoot. A ring of gold and onyx has slipped from his finger. His chin has dropped and his lips are slightly parted, as though to ask a question. Surely he is asking where you are, Octavia.

The Mask of Confusion says: A fly wanders over the breast of a Countess, and she does not brush it away. The pageboys lie with their legs tangled, like lovers.

The Mask of Propriety says: There is blood on the hem of your petticoat, which ought to be as white as snow, as bone, as virginity. There is blood on the hem of your dress, and blood on the seed pearls sewn in an arabesque across your train. There is blood beneath the fingernails of your right hand.

The Mask of Flattery says: You are beautiful tonight, Octavia. Your hair, piled on your head in ringlets, shines like a nest of little black snakes. Your eyes are the color of rusted coins, your neck the color of old ivory.

The Mask of Skepticism says: Yes, you are beautiful, like something dead.

The Mask of Nostalgia says: Ivy grows over the walls of your father's castle, leaves rustling where sparrows have made their nests. Bubbles appear on the surface of the moat, and you wonder what lies beneath the lily flowers. You dip your toes into the green water. A trout rises to the surface, flashing its dark iridescence, and then sinks again. In the distance, cowbells chime, low and irregular.

The moon rises.

Your shifts are laid in chests scented with lavender. Your bed is spread with sheets of ironed linen edged with lace. They are marked with a red spot from the first time blood ran between your legs.

The moon is touching the tops of the chestnut trees. You enter the grotto where you first lay down for the gamekeeper's boy.

The Mask of Seduction says: The thief is waiting for you in the forest. His lips are thick and the backs of his hands are covered with black hair. His grip will bruise your wrist, his filth will rub off on your body.

The Mask of Longing says: He will tickle the insides of your thighs with a knife.

The Mask of Perception says: The thief with eyes like the backs of mirrors was once the gamekeeper's boy.

The Mask of Accusation says: You have poisoned the wine, Octavia. You have poured a white powder into the glasses. The wedding guests have drunk in careful sips. How silently they sit, how very still.

You have stabbed the Duke, and licked the knife you stabbed him with. You have spit blood and saliva on his cheek. It runs down and stains his collar with a spot of red.

The Mask of Consequences says: The knife is still in your hand, Octavia. Put it to your wrist, peel back the skin as you would peel a damson plum.

The Mask of Fragmentation says: Your wrists are streaming away in red ribbons. Your dress falls like confetti. Your corset disintegrates, and moths of white silk flutter through the corridors. Your waist cracks, your torso crashes on the floor. Your hair writhes like little black snakes, then crawls into hidden corners. Your nose breaks, like the nose of an Attic statue. A breeze blows away your left ear.

Only your mouth remains. It parts and attempts to speak without teeth or palate or tongue, saying nothing, not even stirring the air.

VERNOR VINGE

Born in Waukesha, Wisconsin, Vernor Vinge now lives in San Diego, California, where he is an associate professor of math sciences at San Diego State University. He sold his first story, "Apartness," to *New Worlds* in 1965; it immediately attracted a good deal of attention, was picked up for Donald A. Wollheim and Terry Carr's collaborative *World's Best Science Fiction* anthology the following year, and still strikes me as one of the strongest stories of that entire period. Since this impressive debut, he has become a frequent contributor to *Analog*; he has also sold to *Orbit, Far Frontiers, If, Stellar,* and other markets. His novella "True Names," which is famous in Internet circles and among computer enthusiasts well outside of the usual limits of the genre, and is cited by some as having been the *real* progenitor of cyberpunk rather than William Gibson's *Neuromancer,* was a finalist for both the Nebula and Hugo awards in 1981. His novel *A Fire Upon the Deep,* one of the most epic and sweeping of modern Space Operas, won him a Hugo Award in 1993; its sequel, *A Deepness in the Sky,* won him another Hugo Award in 2000, and his novella "Fast Times at Fairmont High" won another Hugo in 2003 . . . and these days Vinge is regarded as one of the best of the American "hard science" writers, along with people such as Greg Bear and Gregory Benford. His other books include the novels *Tatja Grimm's World, The Witling, The Peace War* and *Marooned in Realtime* (which have been released in an omnibus volume as *Across Realtime*), and the collections *True Names and Other Dangers* and *Threats and Other Promises.* His most recent book is the massive collection *The Collected Stories of Vernor Vinge.*

About "The Cookie Monster," he says: [Warning: There are story spoilers in these comments.]

"Word for word, 'The Cookie Monster' may be the most difficult story-writing job of my career. I have a first draft that features Rob Lusk alone, locked in his apartment. For a long time, I couldn't imagine how to do better.

"Originally, I thought the story was about measures and

countermeasures related to safe AI. In the end, I think a more important point is that there are many innocent-seeming programming goals (perhaps including spam filtering, customer service, essay exam grading . . .) where true success would run head-on into Big Moral Issues."

THE COOKIE MONSTER

VERNOR VINGE

"**S**o how do you like the new job?"

Dixie Mae looked up from her keyboard and spotted a pimply face peering at her from over the cubicle partition. "It beats flipping burgers, Victor," she said.

Victor bounced up so his whole face was visible. "Yeah? It's going to get old awfully fast."

Actually, Dixie Mae felt the same way. But doing customer support at LotsaTech was a real job, a foot in the door at the biggest high-tech company in the world. "Gimme a break, Victor! This is our first day." Well, it was the first day not counting the six days of product familiarization classes. "If you can't take this, you've got the attention span of a cricket."

"That's a mark of intelligence, Dixie Mae. I'm smart enough to know what's not worth the attention of a first-rate creative mind."

Grr. "Then your first-rate creative mind is going to be out of its gourd by the end of the summer."

Victor smirked. "Good point." He thought a second, then continued more quietly, "But see, um, I'm doing this to get material for my column in the *Bruin*. You know, big headlines like 'The New Sweat-shops' or 'Death by Boredom.' I haven't decided whether to play it for laughs or go for heavy social consciousness. In any case,"—he lowered his voice another notch—"I'm bailing out of here, um, by the end of next week, thus suffering only minimal brain damage from the whole sordid experience."

"And you're not seriously helping the customers at all, huh, Victor? Just giving them hilarious misdirections?"

Victor's eyebrows shot up. "I'll have you know I'm being articulate and seriously helpful . . . at least for another day or two." The weasel grin crawled back onto his face. "I won't start being Bastard Consultant from Hell till right before I quit."

That figures. Dixie Mae turned back to her keyboard. "Okay, Victor. Meantime, how about letting me do the job I'm being paid for?"

Silence. Angry, insulted silence? No, this was more a leering, undressing-you-with-my-eyes silence. But Dixie Mae did not look up. She could tolerate such silence as long as the leerer was out of arm's reach.

After a moment, there was the sound of Victor dropping back into his chair in the next cubicle.

Ol' Victor had been a pain in the neck from the get-go. He was slick with words; if he wanted to, he could explain things as good as anybody Dixie Mae had ever met. At the same time, he kept rubbing it in how educated he was and what a dead-end this customer support gig was. Mr. Johnson—the guy running the familiarization course— was a great teacher, but smart-ass Victor had tested the man's patience all week long. Yeah, Victor really didn't belong here, but not for the reasons he bragged about.

It took Dixie Mae almost an hour to finish off seven more queries. One took some research, being a really bizarre question about Voxalot for Norwegian. Okay, this job would get old after a few days, but there was a virtuous feeling in helping people. And from Mr. Johnson's lectures, she knew that as long as she got the reply turned in by closing time this evening, she could spend the whole afternoon researching just how to make LotsaTech's vox program recognize Norwegian vowels.

Dixie Mae had never done customer support before this; till she took Prof. Reich's tests last week, her highest-paying job really had been flipping burgers. But like the world and your Aunt Sally, she had often been the *victim* of customer support. Dixie Mae would buy a new book or a cute dress, and it would break or wouldn't fit—and then when she wrote customer support, they wouldn't reply, or had useless canned answers, or just tried to sell her something more—all the time talking about how their greatest goal was serving the customer.

But now LotsaTech was turning all that around. Their top bosses had realized how important real humans were to helping real human customers. They were hiring hundreds and hundreds of people like

Dixie Mae. They weren't paying very much, and this first week had been kinda tough since they were all cooped up here during the crash intro classes.

But Dixie Mae didn't mind. "LotsaTech is a lot of Tech." Before, she'd always thought that motto was stupid. But LotsaTech was *big*; it made IBM and Microsoft look like minnows. She'd been a little nervous about that, imagining that she'd end up in a room bigger than a football field with tiny office cubicles stretching away to the horizon. Well, Building 0994 did have tiny cubicles, but her team was just fifteen nice people—leaving Victor aside for the moment. Their work floor had windows all the way around, a panoramic view of the Santa Monica mountains and the Los Angeles basin. And li'l ol' Dixie Mae Leigh had her a desk right beside one of those wide windows! *I'll bet there are CEOs who don't have a view as good as mine.* Here's where you could see a little of what the Lotsa in LotsaTech meant. Just outside of B0994 there were tennis courts and a swimming pool. Dozens of similar buildings were scattered across the hillside. A golf course covered the next hill over, and more company land lay beyond that. These guys had the money to buy the top off Runyon Canyon and plunk themselves down on it. And this was just the LA branch office.

Dixie Mae had grown up in Tarzana. On a clear day in the valley, you could see the Santa Monica mountains stretching off forever into the haze. They seemed beyond her reach, like something from a fairy tale. And now she was up here. Next week, she'd bring her binoculars to work, go over on the north slope, and maybe spot where her father still lived down there.

Meanwhile, back to work. The next six queries were easy, from people who hadn't even bothered to read the single page of directions that came with Voxalot. Letters like those would be hard to answer politely the thousandth time she saw them. But she would try—and today she practiced with cheerful specifics that stated the obvious and gently pointed the customers to where they could find more. Then came a couple of brain twisters. Damn. She wouldn't be able to finish those today. Mr. Johnson said "finish anything you start on the same day"—but maybe he would let her work on those first thing Monday morning. She really wanted to do well on the hard ones. Every day, there would be the same old dumb questions. But there would also be hard new questions. And eventually she'd get really, really good with Voxalot. More important, she'd get good about managing questions and organization. So what that she'd screwed the last seven years of her life and never made it through college? Little by little she would improve herself, till a few years from now her past stupidities wouldn't matter anymore. Some people had told her that such things weren't possible nowadays, that you really needed the college degree. But people had always been able to make it with hard work. Back in the twentieth century, lots of steno pool people managed it. Dixie Mae figured customer support was pretty much the same kind of starting point.

Nearby, somebody gave out a low whistle. Victor. Dixie Mae ignored him.

"Dixie Mae, you gotta see this."

Ignore him.

"I swear Dixie, this is a first. How did you do it? I got an incoming query for *you,* by name! Well, almost."

"What!? Forward it over here, Victor."

"No. Come around and take a look. I have it right in front of me."

Dixie Mae was too short to look over the partition. *Jeez.*

Three steps took her into the corridor. Ulysse Green poked her head out of her cubicle, an inquisitive look on her face. Dixie Mae shrugged and rolled her eyes, and Ulysse returned to her work. The sound of fingers on keys was like occasional raindrops (no Voxalots allowed in cubicle-land). Mr. Johnson had been around earlier, answering questions and generally making sure things were going okay. Right now he should be back in his office on the other side of the building; this first day, you hardly needed to worry about slackers. Dixie Mae felt a little guilty about making that a lie, but . . .

She popped into Victor's cubicle, grabbed a loose chair. "This better be good, Victor."

"Judge for yourself, Dixie Mae." He looked at his display. "Oops, I lost the window. Just a second." He dinked around with his mouse. "So, have you been putting your name on outgoing messages? That's the only way I can imagine this happening—"

"No. I have not. I've answered twenty-two questions so far, and I've been AnnetteG all the way." The fake signature was built into her "send" key. Mr. Johnson said this was to protect employee privacy and give users a feeling of continuity even though follow-up questions would rarely come to the original responder. He didn't have to say that it was also to make sure that LotsaTech support people would be interchangeable, whether they were working out of the service center in Lahore or Londonderry—or Los Angeles. So far, that had been one of Dixie Mae's few disappointments about this job; she could never have an ongoing helpful relationship with a customer.

So what the devil was this all about?

"Ah! Here it is." Victor waved at the screen. "What do you make of it?"

The message had come in on the help address. It was in the standard layout enforced by the query acceptance page. But the "previous responder field" was not one of the house sigs. Instead it was:

Ditzie May Lay

"Grow up, Victor."

Victor raised his hands in mock defense, but he had seen her expression, and some of the smirk left his face. "Hey, Dixie Mae, don't kill the messenger. This is just what came in."

"No way. The server-side script would have rejected an invalid responder name. You faked this."

For a fleeting moment, Victor looked uncertain. *Hah!* thought Dixie Mae. She had been paying attention during Mr. Johnson's lectures; she knew more about what was going on here than Victor-the-great-mind. And so his little joke had fallen flat on its rear end. But Victor regrouped and gave a weak smile. "It wasn't me. How would I know about this, er, nickname of yours?"

"Yes," said Dixie Mae, "it takes real genius to come up with such a clever play on words."

"Honest, Dixie Mae, it wasn't me. Hell, I don't even know how to use our form editor to revise header fields."

Now *that* claim had the ring of truth.

"What's happening?"

They looked up, saw Ulysse standing at the entrance to the cubicle.

Victor gave her a shrug. "It's Dit—Dixie Mae. Someone here at LotsaTech is jerking her around."

Ulysse came closer and bent to read from the display. "Yech. So what's the message?"

Dixie Mae reached across the desk and scrolled down the display.

The return address was lusting925@freemail.sg. The topic choice was "Voice Formatting." They got lots on that topic; Voxalot format control wasn't quite as intuitive as the ads would like you to believe.

But this was by golly *not* a follow-up on anything Dixie Mae had answered:

> Hey there, Honey Chile! I'll be truly grateful if you would tell me how to put the following into italics:
> "Remember the Tarzanarama tree house? The one you set on fire? If you'd like to start a much bigger fire, then figure out how I know all this. A big clue is that 999 is 666 spelled upside down."
> I've tried everything and I can't set the above proposition into indented italics—leastwise without fingering. Please help.
> Aching for some of your Southron Hospitality, I remain your very bestest fiend,
> —Lusting (for you deeply)

Ulysse's voice was dry: "So, Victor, you've figured how to edit incoming forms."

"God damn it, I'm innocent!"

"Sure you are." Ulysse's white teeth flashed in her black face. The three little words held a world of disdain.

Dixie Mae held up her hand, waving them both to silence. "I . . . don't know. There's something real strange about this mail." She stared at the message body for several seconds. A big ugly chill was growing in her middle. Mom and Dad had built her that tree house when she was seven years old. Dixie Mae had loved it. For two years she was Tarzana of Tarzana. But the name of the tree house— Tarzanarama—had been a secret. Dixie Mae had been nine years old when she torched that marvelous tree house. It had been a terrible accident. Well, a world-class temper tantrum, actually. But she had never meant the fire to get so far out of control. The fire had darn near burned down their real house, too. She had been a scarifyingly well-behaved little girl for almost two years after that incident.

Ulysse was giving the mail a careful read. She patted Dixie Mae on the shoulder. "Whoever this is, he certainly doesn't sound friendly."

Dixie Mae nodded. "This weasel is pushing every button I've got." Including her curiosity. Dad was the only living person that knew who had started the fire, but it was going on four years since he'd had any address for his daughter—and Daddy would never have taken this sex-creep, disrespecting tone.

Victor glanced back and forth between them, maybe feeling hurt that he was no longer the object of suspicion. "So who do you think it is?"

Don Williams craned his head over the next partition. "Who is what?"

Given another few minutes, and they'd have everyone on the floor with some bodily part stuck into Victor's cubicle.

Ulysse said, "Unless you're deaf, you know most of it, Don. Someone is messing with us."

"Well then, report it to Johnson. This is our first day, people. It's not a good day to get sidetracked."

That brought Ulysse down to earth. Like Dixie Mae, she regarded this LotsaTech job as her last real chance to break into a profession.

"Look," said Don. "It's already lunch time."—Dixie Mae glanced at her watch. It really was!—"We can talk about this in the cafeteria, then come back and give Great Lotsa a solid afternoon of work. And then we'll be done with our first week!" Williams had been planning a party down at his folks' place for tonight. It would be their first time off the LotsaTech campus since they took the job.

"Yeah!" said Ulysse. "Dixie Mae, you'll have the whole weekend to figure out who's doing this—and plot your revenge."

Dixie Mae looked again at the impossible "previous responder field." "I . . . don't know. This looks like it's something happening right here on the LotsaTech campus." She stared out Victor's picture window. It was the same view as from her cubicle, of course—but now she was seeing everything with a different mind set. Somewhere in the beautiful country-club buildings, there was a real sleaze ball. And he was playing guessing games with her.

Everybody was quiet for a second. Maybe that helped—Dixie Mae realized just what she was looking at: the next lodge down the hill. From here you could only see the top of its second story. Like all the buildings on the campus, it had a four-digit identification number made of gold on every corner. That one was Building 0999.

A big clue is that 999 is just 666 spelled upside down. "Jeez, Ulysse. Look: 999." Dixie Mae pointed down the hillside.

"It could be a coincidence."

"No, it's too pat." She glanced at Victor. This really was the sort of thing someone like him would set up. *But whoever wrote that letter just knew too much.* "Look, I'm going to skip lunch today and take a little walk around the campus."

"That's crazy," said Don. "LotsaTech is an open place, but we're not supposed to be wandering into other project buildings."

"Then they can turn me back."

"Yeah, what a great way to start out with the new job," said Don. "I don't think you three realize what a good deal we have here. I know that none of you have worked a customer support job before." He looked around challengingly. "Well I have. This is heaven. We've got our own friggin' offices, onsite tennis courts and health club. We're being treated like million-dollar system designers. We're being given all the time we need to give top-notch advice to the customers. What LotsaTech is trying to do here is revolutionary! And you dips are just going to piss it away." Another all-around glare. "Well, do what you want, but I'm going to lunch."

There was a moment of embarrassed silence. Ulysse stepped out of the cubicle and watched Don and others trickle away toward the stairs. Then she was back. "I'll come with you, Dixie Mae, but . . . have you thought Don may be right? Maybe you could just postpone this till next week?" Unhappiness was written all over her face. Ulysse was a lot like Dixie Mae, just more sensible.

Dixie Mae shook her head. She figured it would be at least fifteen minutes before her common sense could put on the brakes.

"I'll come, Dixie Mae," said Victor. "Yeah. . . . This could be an interesting story."

Dixie Mae smiled at Ulysse and reached out her hand. "It's okay, Ulysse. You should go to lunch." The other looked uncertain. "Really. If Mr. Johnson asks about me missing lunch, it would help if you were there to set him right about what a steady person I am."

"Okay, Dixie Mae. I'll do that." She wasn't fooled, but this way it really was okay.

Once she was gone, Dixie Mae turned back to Victor. "And you. I want a printed copy of that freakin' email."

❈

They went out a side door. There was a soft-drink and candy machine on the porch. Victor loaded up on "expeditionary supplies" and the two started down the hill.

"Hot day," said Victor, mumbling around a mouth full of chocolate bar.

"Yeah." The early part of the week had been all June Gloom. But the usual overcast had broken, and today was hot and sunny—and Dixie Mae suddenly realized how pleasantly air-conditioned life had been in the LotsaTech "sweatshop." Common sense hadn't yet reached the brakes, but it was getting closer.

Victor washed the chocolate down with a Dr. Fizz and flipped the can behind the oleanders that hung close along the path. "So who do you think is behind that letter? Really?"

"I don't *know,* Victor! Why do you think I'm risking my job to find out?"

Victor laughed. "Don't worry about losing the job, Dixie Mae. Heh. There's no way it could have lasted even through the summer." He gave his usual superior-knowledge grin.

"You're an idiot, Victor. Doing customer support *right* will be a billion dollar winner."

"Oh, maybe . . . if you're on the right side of it." He paused as if wondering what to tell her. "But for you, look: support costs money. Long ago, the Public Spoke about how much they were willing to pay." He paused, like he was trying to put together a story that she could understand. "Yeah . . . and even if you're right, your vision of the project is doomed. You know why?"

Dixie Mae didn't reply. His reason would be something about the crappy quality of the people who had been hired.

Sure enough, Victor continued: "I'll tell you why. And this is the surprise kink that's going to make my articles for the *Bruin* really shine: Maybe LotsaTech has its corporate heart in the right place. That would be surprising considering how they brutalized Microsoft. But maybe they've let this bizarre idealism go too far. Heh. For anything long-term, they've picked the wrong employees."

Dixie Mae kept her cool. "We took all sorts of psych tests. You don't think Professor Reich knows what he's doing?"

"Oh, I bet he knows what he's doing. But what if LotsaTech isn't using his results? Look at us. There are some—such as yours truly—who are way over-educated. I'm closing in on a master's degree in journalism; it's clear I won't be around for long. Then there's people like Don and Ulysse. They have the right level of education for customer support, but they're too smart. Yes, Ulysse talks about doing this job so well that her talent is recognized, and she is a diligent sort.

But I'll bet that even she couldn't last a summer. As for some of the others . . . well, may I be frank, Dixie Mae?"

What saved him from a fist in the face was that Dixie Mae had never managed to be really angry about more than one thing at once. "Please *do* be frank, Victor."

"You talk the same game plan as Ulysse—but I'll bet your multi-phasic shows you have the steadiness of mercury fulminate. Without this interesting email from Mr. Lusting, you might be good for a week, but sooner or later you'd run into something so infuriating that direct action was required—and you'd be bang out on your rear."

Dixie Mae pretended to mull this over. "Well, yes," she said. "After all, you're still going to be here next week, right?"

He laughed. "I rest my case. But seriously, Dixie Mae, this is what I mean about the personnel situation here. We have a bunch of bright and motivated people, but their motivations are all over the map, and most of their enthusiasm can't be sustained for any realistic span of time. Heh. So I guess the only rational explanation—and frankly, I don't think it would work—is that LotsaTech figures . . ."

He droned on with some theory about how LotsaTech was just looking for some quick publicity and a demonstration that high-quality customer support could win back customers in a big way. Then after they flushed all these unreliable new hires, they could throttle back into something cheaper for the long term.

But Dixie Mae's attention was far away. On her left was the familiar view of Los Angeles. To her right, the ridgeline was just a few hundred yards away. From the crest you could probably see down into the valley, even pick out streets in Tarzana. Someday, it would be nice to go back there, maybe prove to Dad that she could keep her temper and make something of herself. *All my life, I've been screwing up like today.* But that letter from "Lusting" was like finding a burglar in your bedroom. The guy knew too much about her that he shouldn't have known, and he had mocked her background and her family. Dixie Mae had grown up in Southern California, but she'd been born in Georgia—and she was proud of her roots. Maybe Daddy never realized that, since she was running around rebelling most of the time. He and Mom always said she'd eventually settle down. But then she fell in love with the wrong kind of person—and it was her folks who'd gone ballistic. Words Were Spoken. And even though things hadn't worked out with her new love, there was no way she could go back.

By then Mom had died. Now, *I swear I'm not going back to Daddy till I can show I've made something of myself*.

So why was she throwing away her best job in ages? She slowed to a stop, and just stood there in the middle of the walkway; common sense had finally gotten to the brakes. But they had walked almost all the way to 0999. Much of the building was hidden behind twisty junipers, but you could see down a short flight of stairs to the ground level entrance.

We should go back. She pulled the "Lusting" email out of her pocket and glared at it for a second. *Later. You can follow up on this later*. She read the mail again. The letters blurred behind tears of rage, and she dithered in the hot summer sunlight.

Victor made an impatient noise. "Let's go, kiddo." He pushed a chocolate bar into her hand. "Get your blood sugar out of the basement."

They went down the concrete steps to B0999's entrance. *Just a quick look*, Dixie Mae had decided.

Beneath the trees and the overhang, all was cool and shady. They peered through the ground floor windows, into empty rooms. Victor pushed open the door. The layout looked about the same as in their own building, except that B0999 wasn't really finished: There was the smell of Carpenter Nail in the air, and the lights and wireless nodes sat naked on the walls.

The place was occupied. She could hear people talking up on the main floor, what was cubicle-city back in B0994. She took a quick hop up the stairs, peeked in—no cubicles here. As a result, the place looked cavernous. Six or eight tables had been pushed together in the middle of the room. A dozen people looked up at their entrance.

"Aha!" boomed one of them. "More warm bodies. Welcome, welcome!"

They walked toward the tables. Don and Ulysse had worried about violating corporate rules and project secrecy. They needn't have bothered. These people looked almost like squatters. Three of them had their legs propped up on the tables. Junk food and soda cans littered the tables.

"Programmers?" Dixie Mae muttered to Victor.

"Heh. No, these look more like . . . graduate students."

The loud one had red hair snatched back in a ponytail. He gave Dixie Mae a broad grin. "We've got a couple of extra display flats. Grab some seating." He jerked a thumb toward the wall and a stack of folding chairs. "With you two, we may actually be able to finish today!"

Dixie Mae looked uncertainly at the display and keyboard that he had just lit up. "But what—"

"Cognitive Science 301. The final exam. A hundred dollars a question, but we have 107 bluebooks to grade, and Gerry asked mainly essay questions."

Victor laughed. "You're getting a hundred dollars for each bluebook?"

"For each question in each bluebook, man. But don't tell. I think Gerry is funding this out of money that LotsaTech thinks he's spending on research." He waved at the nearly empty room, in this nearly completed building.

Dixie Mae leaned down to look at the display, the white letters on a blue background. It was a standard bluebook, just like at Valley Community College. Only here the questions were complete nonsense, such as:

> 7. Compare and contrast cognitive dissonance in operant conditioning with Minsky-Loève attention maintenance. Outline an algorithm for constructing the associated isomorphism.

"So," said Dixie Mae, "what's cognitive science?"

The grin disappeared from the other's face. "Oh, Christ. You're not here to help with the grading?"

Dixie Mae shook her head. Victor said, "It shouldn't be too hard. I've had some grad courses in psych."

The redhead did not look encouraged. "Does anyone know this guy?"

"I do," said a girl at the far end of all the tables. "That's Victor Smaley. He's a journalism grad, and not very good at that."

Victor looked across the tables. "Hey, Mouse! How ya doing?"

The redhead looked beseechingly at the ceiling. "I do not need these distractions!" His gaze came down to the visitors. "Will you two just please go away?"

"No way," said Dixie Mae. "I came here for a reason. Someone—

probably someone here in Building 0999—is messing with our work in Customer Support. I'm going to find out who." *And give them some free dental work.*

"Look. If we don't finish grading the exam today, Gerry Reich's going to make us come back tomorrow and—"

"I don't think that's true, Graham," said a guy sitting across the table. "Prof. Reich's whole point was that we should not feel time pressure. This is an experiment, comparing time-bounded grading with complete individualization."

"Yes!" said Graham the redhead. "That's exactly why Reich would lie about it. 'Take it easy, make good money,' he says. But I'll bet that if we don't finish today, he'll screw us into losing the weekend."

He glared at Dixie Mae. She glared back. Graham was going to find out just what stubborn and willful really meant. There was a moment of silence and then—

"I'll talk to them, Graham." It was the woman at the far end of the tables.

"Argh. Okay, but not here!"

"Sure, we'll go out on the porch." She beckoned Dixie Mae and Victor to follow her out the side door.

"And hey," called Graham as they walked out, "don't take all day, Ellen. We need you here."

The porch on 0999 had a bigger junk-food machine than back at Customer Support. Dixie Mae didn't think that made up for no cafeteria, but Ellen Garcia didn't seem to mind. "We're only going to be here this one day. *I'm* not coming back on Saturday."

Dixie Mae bought herself a sandwich and soda and they all sat down on some beat-up lawn furniture.

"So what do you want to know?" said Ellen.

"See, Mouse, we're following up on the weirdest—"

Ellen waved Victor silent, her expression pretty much the same as all Victor's female acquaintances. She looked expectantly at Dixie Mae.

"Well, my name is Dixie Mae Leigh. This morning we got this email at our customer support address. It looks like a fake. And there are things about it that—" She handed over the hard copy.

Ellen's gaze scanned down. "Kind of fishy dates," she said to herself. Then she stopped, seeing the "To:" header. She glanced up at Dixie Mae. "Yeah, this is abuse. I used to see this kind of thing when

I was a Teaching Assistant. Some guy would start hitting on a girl in my class." She eyed Victor speculatively.

"Why does everybody suspect me?" he said.

"You should be proud, Victor. You have such a reliable reputation." She shrugged. "But actually, this isn't quite your style." She read on. "The rest is smirky lascivious, but otherwise it doesn't mean anything to me."

"It means a lot to *me*," said Dixie Mae. "This guy is talking about things that nobody should know."

"Oh?" She went back to the beginning and stared at the printout some more. "I don't know about secrets in the message body, but one of my hobbies is rfc9822 headers. You're right that this is all scammed up. The message number and ident strings are too long; I think they may carry added content."

She handed back the email. "There's not much more I can tell you. If you want to give me a copy, I could crunch on those header strings over the weekend."

"Oh. . . . Okay, thanks." It was more solid help than anyone had offered so far, but—"Look Ellen, the main thing I was hoping for was some clues here in Building 0999. The letter pointed me here. I run into . . . abusers sometimes, myself. I don't let them get away with it! I'd bet money that whoever this is, he's one of those graders." *And he's probably laughing at us right now.*

Ellen thought a second and then shook her head. "I'm sorry, Dixie Mae. I know these people pretty well. Some of them are a little strange, but they're not bent like this. Besides, we didn't know we'd be here till yesterday afternoon. And today we haven't had time for mischief."

"Okay," Dixie Mae forced a smile. "I appreciate your help." She would give Ellen a copy of the letter and go back to Customer Support, just slightly better off than if she had behaved sensibly in the first place.

Dixie Mae started to get up, but Victor leaned forward and set his notepad on the table between them. "That email had to come from somewhere. Has anyone here been acting strange, Mousy?"

Ellen glared at him, and after a second he said, "I mean 'Ellen.' You know I'm just trying to help out Dixie Mae here. Oh yeah, and maybe get a good story for the *Bruin*."

Ellen shrugged. "Graham told you; we're grading on the side for Gerry Reich."

"Huh." Victor leaned back. "Ever since I've been at UCLA, Reich has had a reputation for being an operator. He's got big government contracts and all this consulting at LotsaTech. He tries to come across as a one-man supergenius, but actually it's just money, um, buying lots and lots of peons. So what do you think he's up to?"

Ellen shrugged. "Technically, I bet Gerry is misusing his contacts with LotsaTech. But I doubt if they care; they really like him." She brightened. "And I approve of what Prof. Reich is doing with this grading project. When I was a TA, I wished there was some way that I could make a day-long project out of reading each student's exam. That was an impossible wish; there was just never enough time. But with his contacts here at LotsaTech, Gerry Reich has come close to doing it. He's paying some pretty sharp grad students very good money to grade and comment on every single essay question. Time is no object, he's telling us. The students in these classes are going to get really great feedback."

"This guy Reich keeps popping up," said Dixie Mae. "He was behind the testing program that selected Victor and me and the others for customer support."

"Well, Victor's right about him. Reich is a manipulator. I know he's been running tests all this week. He grabbed all of Olson Hall for the operation. We didn't know what it was for until afterwards. He nailed Graham and the rest of our gang for this one-day grading job. It looks like he has all sorts of projects."

"Yeah, we took our tests at Olson Hall, too." There had been a small upfront payment, and hints of job prospects. . . . And Dixie Mae had ended up with maybe the best job offer she'd ever had. "But we did that last week."

"It can't be the same place. Olson Hall is a gym."

"Yes, that's what it looked like to me."

"It was used for the NCAA eliminations last week."

Victor reached for his notepad. "Whatever. We gotta be going, Mouse."

"Don't 'Mouse' me, Victor! The NCAA elims were the week of 4 June. I did Gerry's questionnaire yesterday, which was Thursday, 14 June."

"I'm sorry, Ellen," said Dixie Mae. "Yesterday was Thursday, but it was the 21st of June."

Victor made a calming gesture. "It's not a big deal."

Ellen frowned, but suddenly she wasn't arguing. She glanced at her watch. "Let's see your notepad, Victor. What date does it say?"

"It says, June . . . huh. It says June 15."

Dixie Mae looked at her own watch. The digits were so precise, and a week wrong: Fri Jun 15 12:31:18 PDT 2012. "Ellen, I looked at my watch before we walked over here. It said June 22nd."

Ellen leaned on the table and took a close look at Victor's notepad. "I'll bet it did. But both your watch and the notepad get their time off the building utilities. Here you're getting set by our local clock—and you're getting the truth."

Now Dixie Mae was getting mad. "Look, Ellen. Whatever the time service says, I would not have made up a whole extra week of my life." All those product-familiarization classes.

"No, you wouldn't." Ellen brought her heels back on the edge of her chair. For a long moment, she didn't say anything, just stared through the haze at the city below.

Finally she said: "You know, Victor, you should be pleased."

"Why is that?" suspiciously.

"You may have stumbled into a real, world-class news story. Tell me. During this extra week of life you've enjoyed, how often have you used your phone?"

Dixie Mae said, "Not at all. Mr. Johnson—he's our instructor—said that we're deadzoned till we get through the first week."

Ellen nodded. "So I guess they didn't expect the scam to last more than a week. See, we are not deadzoned here. LotsaTech has a pretty broad embargo on web access, but I made a couple of phone calls this morning."

Victor gave her a sharp look. "So where do you think the extra week came from?"

Ellen hesitated. "I think Gerry Reich has gone beyond where the UCLA human subjects committee would ever let him go. You guys probably spent one night in drugged sleep, being pumped chock full of LotsaTech product trivia."

"Oh! You mean . . . Just-in-Time Training?" Victor tapped away at his notepad. "I thought that was years away."

"It is if you play by the FDA's rules. But there are meds and treatments that can speed up learning. Just read the journals and you'll see that in another year or two, they'll be a scandal as big as sports drugs ever were. I think Gerry has just jumped the gun with something that is very, *very* effective. You have no side-effects. You have all sorts of new, specialized knowledge—even if it's about a throwaway topic.

And apparently you have detailed memories of life experience that *never* happened."

Dixie Mae thought back over the last week. There had been no strangeness about her experience at Olson Hall: the exams, the job interview. True, the johns were fantastically clean—like a hospital, now that she thought about it. She had only visited them once, right after she accepted the job offer. And then she had . . . done what? Taken a bus directly out to LotsaTech . . . without even going back to her apartment? After that, everything was clear again. She could remember jokes in the Voxalot classes. She could remember meals, and late night talks with Ulysse about what they might do with this great opportunity. "It's brainwashing," she finally said.

Ellen nodded. "It looks like Gerry has gone way, way too far on this one."

"And he's stupid, too. Our team is going to a party tonight, downtown. All of a sudden, there'll be sixteen people who'll know what's been done to them. We'll be mad as—" Dixie Mae noticed Ellen's pitying look.

"Oh." So tonight instead of partying, their customer support team would be in a drugged stupor, *un*remembering the week that never was. "We won't remember a thing, will we?"

Ellen nodded. "My guess is you'll be well-paid, with memories of some one-day temp job here at LotsaTech."

"Well, that's not going to happen," said Victor. "I've got a story and I've got a grudge. I'm not going back."

"We have to warn the others."

Victor shook his head. "Too risky."

Dixie Mae gave him a glare.

Ellen Garcia hugged her knees for a moment. "If this were just you, Victor, I'd be sure you were putting me on." She looked at Dixie Mae for a second. "Let me see that email again."

She spread it out on the table. "LotsaTech has its share of defense and security contracts. I'd hate to think that they might try to shut us up if they knew we were onto them." She whistled an ominous tune. "Paranoia rages. . . . Have you thought that this email might be someone trying to tip you off about what's going on?"

Victor frowned. "Who, Ellen?" When she didn't answer, he said, "So what do you think we should do?"

Ellen didn't look up from the printout. "Mainly, try not to act like idiots. All we really know is that someone has played serious games with your heads. Our first priority is to get us all out of LotsaTech, with you guys free of medical side-effects. Our second priority is to blow the whistle on Gerry or . . ." She was reading the mail headers again, ". . . or whoever is behind this."

Dixie Mae said, "I don't think we know enough not to act like idiots."

"Good point. Okay, I'll make a phone call, an innocuous message that should mean something to the police if things go really bad. Then I'll talk to the others in our grading team. We won't say anything while we're still at LotsaTech, but once away from here we'll scream long and loud. You two . . . it might be safest if you just lie low till after dark and we graders get back into town."

Victor was nodding.

Dixie Mae pointed at the mystery email. "What was it you just noticed, Ellen?"

"Just a coincidence, I think. Without a large sample, you start seeing phantoms."

"Speak."

"Well, the mailing address, 'lusting925@freemail.sg.' Building 0925 is on the hill crest thataway."

"You can't see that from where we started."

"Right. It's like 'Lusting' had to get you *here* first. And that's the other thing. Prof. Reich has a senior graduate student named Rob Lusk."

Lusk? Lusting? The connection seemed weak to Dixie Mae. "What kind of a guy is he?"

"Rob's not a particularly friendly fellow, but he's about two sigmas smarter than the average grad student. He's the reason Gerry has the big reputation for hardware. Gerry has been using him for five or six years now, and I bet Rob is getting desperate to graduate." She broke off. "Look. I'm going to go inside and tell Graham and the others about this. Then we'll find a place for you to hide for the rest of the day."

She started toward the door.

"I'm not going to hide out," said Dixie Mae.

Ellen hesitated. "Just till closing time. You've seen the rent-a-cops at the main gate. This is not a place you can simply stroll out of. But my group will have no trouble going home this evening. As soon as we're off-site, we'll raise such a stink that the press and police will be back here. You'll be safe at home in no time."

Victor was nodding. "Ellen's right. In fact, it would be even better if we don't spread the story to the other graders. There's no telling—"

"I'm not going to hide out!" Dixie Mae looked up the hill. "I'm going to check out 0925."

"That's crazy, Dixie Mae! You're guaranteed safe if you just hide till the end of the work day—and then the cops can do better investigating than anything you could manage. You do what Ellen says!"

"No one tells me what to do, Victor!" said Dixie Mae, while inside she was thinking, *Yeah, what I'm doing is a little bit like the plot of a cheap game: teenagers enter haunted house, and then split up to be murdered in pieces . . .*

But Ellen Garcia was making assumptions, too. Dixie Mae glared at both of them. "I'm following up on this email."

Ellen gave her a long look. Whether it was contemptuous or thoughtful wasn't clear. "Just wait for me to tell Graham, okay?"

Twenty minutes later, the three of them were outdoors again, walking up the long grade toward Building 0925.

Graham the Red might be a smart guy, but he turned out to be a fool, too. He was sure that the calendar mystery was just a scam cooked up by Dixie Mae and Victor. Ellen wasn't that good at talking to him—and the two customer support winkies were beneath his contempt. Fortunately, most of the other graders had been willing to listen. One of them also poked an unpleasant hole in all their assumptions: "So if it's that serious, wouldn't Gerry have these two under surveillance? You know, the Conspiracy Gestapo could arrive any second." There'd been a moment of apprehensive silence as everyone waited the arrival of bad guys with clubs.

In the end, everyone including Graham had agreed to keep their mouths shut till after work. Several of them had friends they made cryptic phone calls to, just in case. Dixie Mae could tell that most of them tilted toward Ellen's point of view, but however smart they were, they really didn't want to cross Graham.

Ellen, on the other hand, was *persona non grata* for trying to mess up Graham's schedule. She finally lost her temper with the redheaded jerk.

So now Ellen, Victor, and Dixie Mae were on the yellow brick road—in this case, the asphalt econo-cart walkway—leading to Building 0925.

The LotsaTech campus was new and underpopulated, but there *were* other people around. Just outside of 0999, they ran into a trio of big guys wearing gray blazers like the cops at the main entrance. Victor grabbed Dixie Mae's arm. "Just act natural," he whispered.

They ambled past, Victor giving a gracious nod. The three hardly seemed to notice.

Victor released Dixie Mae's arm. "See? You just have to be cool."

Ellen had been walking ahead. She dropped back so they were three abreast. "Either we're being toyed with," she said, "or they haven't caught on to us."

Dixie Mae touched the email in her pocket. "Well, *somebody* is toying with us."

"You know, that's the biggest clue we have. I still think it could be somebody trying to—"

Ellen fell silent as a couple of management types came walking the other way. These paid them even less attention than the company cops had.

"—it could be somebody trying to help us."

"I guess," said Dixie Mae. "More likely it's some sadist using stuff they learned while I was drugged up."

"Ug. Yeah." They batted around the possibilities. It was strange. Ellen Garcia was as much fun to talk to as Ulysse, even though she had to be about five times smarter than either Ulysse or Dixie Mae.

Now they were close enough to see the lower windows of 0925. This place was a double-sized version of 0999 or 0994. There was a catering truck pulled up at the ground level. Beyond a green- tinted windbreak they could see couples playing tennis on the courts south of the building.

Victor squinted. "Strange. They've got some kind of blackout on the windows."

"Yeah. We should at least be able to see the strip lights in the ceiling."

They drifted off the main path and walked around to where they wouldn't be seen from the catering truck. Even up close, down under the overhang, the windows looked just like those on the other buildings. But it wasn't just dark inside. There was nothing but blackness. The inside of the glass was covered with black plastic like they put on closed storefronts.

Victor whipped out his notepad.

"No phone calls, Victor."

"I want to send out a live report, just in case someone gets really mad about us being here."

"I told you, they've got web access embargoed. Besides, just calling from here would trigger 911 locator logic."

"Just a short call, to—"

He looked up and saw that the two women were standing close. "—ah, okay. I'll just use it as a local cam."

Dixie Mae held out her hand. "Give me the notepad, Victor. We'll take the pictures."

For a moment it looked like he was going to refuse. Then he saw how her other hand was clenched into a fist. And maybe he remembered the lunchtime stories she had told during the week. *The week that never was?* Whatever the reason, he handed the notepad over to her. "You think I'm working for the bad guys?" he said.

"No," Dixie Mae said (65 percent truthfully, but declining), "I just don't think you'll always do what Ellen suggests. This way we'll get the pictures, but safely." *Because of my superior self-control. Yeah.*

She started to hand the notepad to Ellen, but the other shook her head. "Just keep a record, Dixie Mae. You'll get it back later, Victor."

"Oh. Okay, but I want first xmit rights." He brightened. "You'll be my cameragirl, Dixie. Just come back on me anytime I have something important to say."

"Will do, Victor." She panned the notepad camera in a long sweep, away from him.

No one bothered them as they walked halfway around the ground floor. The blackout job was very thorough, but just as at buildings 0994 and 0999, there was an ordinary door with an old-fashioned card swipe.

Ellen took a closer look. "We disabled the locks on 0999 just for the fun of it. Somehow I don't think these black-plastic guys are that easygoing."

"I guess this is as far as we go," said Victor.

Dixie Mae stepped close to the door and gave it push. There was no error beep, no alarms. The door just swung open.

Looks of amazement were exchanged.

Five seconds later they were still standing at the open doorway. What little they could see looked like your typical LotsaTech ground floor. "We should shut the door and go back," said Victor. "We'll be caught red-handed standing here."

"Good point." Ellen stepped inside, followed perforce by Victor, and then Dixie Mae taking local video.

"Wait! Keep the door open, Dixie Mae."

"Jeez."

"This is like an airlock!" They were in a tiny room. Above waist height, its walls were clear glass. There was another door on the fat end of the little room.

Ellen walked forward. "I had a summer job at Livermore last year. They have catch boxes like this. You walk inside easy enough—and then there are armed guards all around, politely asking you if you're lost." There were no guards visible here. Ellen pressed on the inner door. Locked. She reached up to the latch mechanism. It looked like cheap plastic. "This should not work," she said, even as she fiddled at it.

They could hear voices, but from upstairs. Down here, there was no one to be seen. Some of the layout was familiar, though. If this had been Building 0994, the hallway on the right would lead to restrooms, a small cafeteria, and a temporary dormitory.

Ellen hesitated and stood listening. She looked back at them. "That's strange. That sounds like . . . Graham!"

"Can you just break the latch, Ellen?" *We should go upstairs and strangle the two-faced weasel with his own ponytail.*

Another sound. A door opening! Dixie Mae looked past Ellen and saw a guy coming out of the men's room. Dixie Mae managed to grab Victor, and the two of them dropped behind the lower section of the holding cell.

"Hey, Ellen," said the stranger, "you look a bit peaked. Is Graham getting on your nerves, too?"

Ellen gave a squeaky laugh. "Y-yeah . . . so what else is new?"

Dixie Mae twisted the notepad and held it so the camera eye looked through the glass. In the tiny screen, she could see that the stranger was smiling. He was dressed in tee-shirt and knee-pants and he had some kind of glittering badge on a loop around his neck.

Ellen's mouth opened and shut a couple of times, but nothing came out. *She doesn't know this guy from Adam.*

The stranger was still clueless, but—"Hey, where's your badge?"

"Oh . . . damn. I must have left in the john," said Ellen. "And now I've locked myself out."

"You know the rules," he said, but his tone was not threatening. He did something on his side of the door. It opened and Ellen stepped through, blocking the guy's view of what was behind her.

"I'm sorry. I, uh, I got flustered."

"That's okay. Graham will eventually shut up. I just wish he'd pay more attention to what the professionals are asking of him."

Ellen nodded. "Yeah, I hear you!" Like she was really, really agreeing with him.

"Y'see, Graham's not splitting the topics properly. The idea is to be both broad *and* deep."

Ellen continued to make understanding noises. The talkative stranger was full of details about some sort of a NSA project, but he was totally ignorant of the three intruders.

There were light footsteps on the stairs, and a familiar voice. "Michael, how long are you going to be? I want to—" The voice cut off in a surprised squeak.

On the notepad display, Dixie Mae could see two brown-haired girls staring at each other with identical expressions of amazement. They sidled around each other for a moment, exchanging light slaps. It wasn't fighting . . . it was as if each thought the other was some kind of trick video. *Ellen Garcia, meet Ellen Garcia.*

The stranger—Michael?—stared with equal astonishment, first at one Ellen and then the other. The Ellens made inarticulate noises just loud enough to interrupt each other and make them even more upset.

Finally Michael said, "I take it you don't have a twin sister, Ellen?"

"No!" said both.

"So one of you is an impostor. But you've spun around so often now that I can't tell who is the original. Ha." He pointed at one of the Ellens. "Another good reason for having security badges."

But Ellen and Ellen were ignoring everyone except themselves. Except for their chorus of "No!", their words were just mutual interruptions, unintelligible. Finally, they hesitated and gave each other a nasty smile. Each reached into her pocket. One came out with a dollar coin, and the other came out empty.

"Ha! I've got the token. Deadlock broken." The other grinned and nodded. Dollar-coin Ellen turned to Michael. "Look, we're both real. And we're both only-children."

Michael looked from one to the other. "You're certainly not clones, either."

"Obviously," said the token holder. She looked at the other Ellen and asked, "Fridge-rot?"

The other nodded and said, "In April I made that worse." And both of them laughed.

Token holder: "Gerry's exam in Olson Hall?"

"Yup."

Token holder: "Michael?"

"After that," the other replied, and then she blushed. After a second the token holder blushed, too.

Michael said dryly, "And you're not perfectly identical."

Token holder Ellen gave him a crooked smile. "True. I've never seen you before in my life." She turned and tossed the dollar coin to the other Ellen, left hand to left hand.

And now that Ellen had the floor. She was also the version wearing a security badge. Call her NSA Ellen. "As far as I—we—can tell, we had the same stream of consciousness up through the day we took Gerry Reich's recruitment exam. Since then, we've had our own lives. We've even got our own new friends." She was looking in the direction of Dixie Mae's camera.

Grader Ellen turned to follow her gaze. "Come on out, guys. We can see your camera lens."

Victor and Dixie Mae stood and walked out of the security cell.

"A right invasion you are," said Michael, and he did not seem to be joking.

NSA Ellen put her hand on his arm. "Michael, I don't think we're in Kansas anymore."

"Indeed! I'm simply dreaming."

"Probably. But if not"—she exchanged glances with grader Ellen—"maybe we should find out what's been done to us. Is the meeting room clear?"

"Last I looked. Yes, we're not likely to be bothered in there." He led them down a hallway toward what was simply a janitor's closet back in Building 0994.

Michael Lee and NSA Ellen were working on still another of Professor Reich's projects. "Y'see," said Michael, "Professor Reich has a contract with my colleagues to compare our surveillance software with what intense human analysis might accomplish."

"Yes," said NSA Ellen, "the big problem with surveillance has always been the enormous amount of stuff there is to look at. The spook agencies use lots of automation and have lots of great specialists—people like Michael here—but they're just overwhelmed. Anyway, Gerry had the idea that even though that problem can't be solved, maybe a team of spooks and graduate students could at least estimate how much the NSA programs are missing."

Michael Lee nodded. "We're spending the entire summer looking at 1300 to 1400 UTC 10 June 2012, backwards and forwards and up and down, but on just three narrow topic areas."

Grader Ellen interrupted him. "And this is your first day on the job, right?"

"Oh, no. We've been at this for almost a month now." He gave a little smile. "My whole career has been the study of contemporary China. Yet this is the first assignment where I've had enough time to look at the data I'm supposed to pontificate upon. It would be a real pleasure if we didn't have to enforce security on these rambunctious graduate students."

NSA Ellen patted him on the shoulder. "But if it weren't for Michael here, I'd be as frazzled as poor Graham. One month down and two months to go."

"You think it's *August?*" said Dixie Mae.

"Yes, indeed." He glanced at his watch. "The 10 August it is."

Grader Ellen smiled and told him the various dates the rest of them thought today was.

"It's some kind of drug hallucination thing," said Victor. "Before we thought it was just Gerry Reich's doing. Now I think it's the government torquing our brains."

Both Ellens look at him; you could tell they both knew Victor from way back. But they seemed to take what he was saying seriously. "Could be," they both said.

"Sorry," grader Ellen said to NSA Ellen. "You've got the dollar."

"You could be right, Victor. But cognition is my—our—specialty. We two are something way beyond normal dreaming or hallucinations."

"Except *that* could be illusion, too," said Victor.

"Stuff it, Victor," said Dixie Mae. "If it's *all* a dream, we might as well give up." She looked at Michael Lee. "What is the government up to?"

Michael shrugged. "The details are classified, but it's just a post hoc survey. The isolation rules seem to be something that Professor Reich has worked out with my agency."

NSA Ellen flicked a glance at her double. The two had a brief and strange conversation, mostly half-completed words and phrases. Then NSA Ellen continued, "Mr. Renaissance Man Gerry Reich seems to be at the center of everything. He used some standard personality tests to pick out articulate, motivated people for the customer support job. I bet they do a very good job on their first day."

Yeah. Dixie Mae thought of Ulysse. And of herself.

NSA Ellen continued, "Gerry filtered out another group—graduate students in just the specialty for grading all his various exams and projects."

"We only worked on one exam," said grader Ellen. But she wasn't objecting. There was an odd smile on her face, the look of someone who has cleverly figured out some very bad news.

"And then he got a bunch of government spooks and CS grads for this surveillance project that Michael and I are on."

Michael looked mystified. Victor looked vaguely sullen, his own theories lying trampled somewhere in the dust. "But," said Dixie Mae, "your surveillance group has been going for a month, you say . . ."

Victor: "And the graders *do* have phone contact with the outside!"

"I've been thinking about that," said grader Ellen. "I made three phone calls today. The third was after you and Dixie Mae showed up. That was voicemail to a friend of mine at MIT. I was cryptic, but I tried to say enough that my friend would raise hell if I disappeared. The others calls were—"

"Voicemail, too?" asked NSA Ellen.

"One was voicemail. The other call was to Bill Richardson. We had a nice chat about the party he's having Saturday. But Bill—"

"Bill took Reich's 'job test' along with the rest of us!"

"Right."

Where this was heading was worse than Victor's dream theory. "S-so what has been done to us?" said Dixie Mae.

Michael's eyes were wide, though he managed a tone of dry understatement: "Pardon a backward Han language specialist. You're thinking we're just personality uploads? I thought that was science fiction."

Both Ellens laughed. One said, "Oh, it *is* science fiction, and not just the latest *Kywrack* episode. The genre goes back almost a century."

The other: "There's Sturgeon's Microcosmic God.'"

The first: "That would be rich; Gerry beware then! But there's also Pohl's 'Tunnel Under the World.'"

"Cripes. We're toast if that's the scenario."

"Okay, but how about Varley's 'Overdrawn at the Memory Bank'?"

"How about Wilson's *Darwinia?*"

"Or Moravec's 'Pigs in Cyberspace'?"

"Or Galouye's *Simulacron-3?*"

"Or Vinge's deathcubes?"

Now that the "twins" were not in perfect synch, their words were a building, rapid-fire chorus, climaxing with:

"Brin's 'Stones of Significance'!"

"Or *Kiln People!*"

"No, it couldn't be that." Abruptly they stopped, and nodded at each other. A little bit grimly, Dixie Mae thought. In all, the conversation was just as inscrutable as their earlier self-interrupted spasms.

Fortunately, Victor was there to rescue pedestrian minds. "It doesn't matter. The fact is, uploading is *only* sci-fi. It's worse than faster-than-light travel. There's not even a theoretical basis for uploads."

Each Ellen raised her left hand and made a faffling gesture. "Not exactly, Victor."

The token holder continued, "I'd say there is a *theoretical* basis for saying that uploads are theoretically possible." They gave a lopsided smile. "And guess who is responsible for that? Gerry Reich. Back in 2005, way before he was famous as a multi-threat genius, he had a couple of papers about upload mechanisms. The theory was borderline kookiness and even the simplest demo would take far more processing power than any supercomputer of the time."

"Just for a one-personality upload."

"So Gerry and his Reich Method were something of a laughingstock."

"After that, Gerry dropped the idea—just what you'd expect, considering the showman he is. But now he's suddenly world-famous, successful in half a dozen different fields. I think something happened. *Somebody* solved his hardware problem for him."

Dixie Mae stared at her email. "Rob Lusk," she said, quietly.

"Yup," said grader Ellen. She explained about the mail.

Michael was unconvinced. "I don't know, E-Ellen. Granted, we have an extraordinary miracle here"—gesturing at both of them—"but speculating about cause seems to me a bit like a sparrow trying to understand the 405 Freeway."

"No," said Dixie Mae, and they all looked back her way. She felt so frightened and so angry—but of the two, angry was better: "Somebody has *set us up!* It started in those superclean restrooms in Olson Hall—"

"Olson Hall," said Michael. "You were there too? The lavs smelled like a hospital! I remember thinking that just as I went in, but—hey, the next thing I remember is being on the bus, coming up here."

Like a hospital. Dixie Mae felt rising panic. "M-maybe we're all that's left." She looked at the twins. "This uploading thing, does it kill the originals?"

It was kind of a showstopper question; for a moment everyone was silent. Then the token holder said, "I—don't think so, but Gerry's papers were mostly theoretical."

Dixie Mae beat down the panic; rage did have its uses. *What can we know from here on the inside?* "So far we know of more than thirty of us who took the Olson Hall exams and ended up here. If we were all murdered, that'd be hard to cover up. Let's suppose we still have a life." Inspiration: "And maybe there are things we can figure! We have three of Reich's experiments to compare. There are differences, and they tell us things." She looked at the twins. "You've already figured this out, haven't you? The Ellen we met first is grading papers—just a one-day job, she's told. But I'll bet that every night, when they think they're going home—Lusk or Reich or whoever is doing this just turns them off, and *cycles them back* to do some other 'one-day' job."

"Same with our customer support," said Victor, a grudging agreement.

"Almost. We had six days of product familiarization, and then our first day on the job. We were all so enthusiastic. You're right, Ellen, on our first day we are great!" *Poor Ulysse, poor me; we thought we were going somewhere with our lives.* "I'll bet we disappear tonight, too."

Grader Ellen was nodding. "Customer-support-in-a-box, restarted and restarted, so it's always fresh."

"But there are still problems," said the other one. "Eventually, the lag in dates would tip you off."

"Maybe, or maybe the mail headers are automatically forged."

"But internal context could contradict—"

"Or maybe Gerry has solved the cognitive haze problem—" The two were off into their semi-private language.

Michael interrupted them. "Not everybody is recycled. The

point of our net-tracking project is that we spend the entire summer studying just one hour of network traffic."

The twins smiled. "So you think," said the token holder. "Yes, in this building we're not rebooted after every imaginary day. Instead, they run us the whole 'summer'—minutes of computer time instead of seconds?—to analyze one hour of network traffic. And then they run us again, on a different hour. And so on and on."

Michael said, "I can't imagine technology that powerful."

The token holder said, "Neither can I really, but—"

Victor interrupted with, "Maybe this is the *Darwinia* scenario. You know: we're just the toys of some superadvanced intelligence."

"No!" said Dixie Mae. "Not superadvanced. Customer support and net surveillance are valuable things in our own real world. Whoever's doing this is just getting slave labor, run really, really fast."

Grader Ellen glowered. "And grading his exams for him! That's the sort of thing that shows me it's really Gerry behind this. He's making chumps of all of us, and rerunning us before we catch on or get seriously bored."

NSA Ellen had the same expression, but a different complaint: "We *have* been seriously bored here."

Michael nodded. "Those from the government side are a patient lot; we've kept the graduate students in line. We can last three months. But it does . . . rankle . . . to learn that the reward for our patience is that we get to do it all over again. Damn. I'm sorry, Ellen."

"But now we know!" said Dixie Mae.

"And what good does it do you?" Victor laughed. "So you guessed this time. But at the end of the microsecond day, poof, it's reboot time and everything you've learned is gone."

"Not *this* time." Dixie Mae looked away from him, down at her email. The cheap paper was crumpled and stained. *A digital fake, but so are we.* "I don't think we're the only people who've figured things out." She slid the printout across the table, toward grader Ellen. "You thought it meant Rob Lusk was in this building."

"Yeah, I did."

"Who's Rob Lusk?" said Michael.

"A weirdo," NSA Ellen said absently. "Gerry's best grad student." Both Ellens were staring at the email.

"The 0999 reference led Dixie Mae to my grading team. Then I pointed out the source address."

"lusting925@freemail.sg?"

"Yes. And that got us here."

"But there's no Rob Lusk here," said NSA Ellen. "Huh! I like these fake mail headers."

"Yeah. They're longer than the whole message body!"

Michael had stood to look over the Ellens' shoulders. Now he reached between them to tap the message. "See there, in the middle of the second header? That looks like Pinyin with the tone marks written in-line."

"So what does it *say?*"

"Well, if it's Mandarin, it would be the number 'nine hundred and seventeen.'"

Victor was leaning forward on his elbows. "That has to be coincidence. How could Lusting know just who we'd encounter?"

"Anybody know of a Building 0917?" said Dixie Mae.

"I don't," said Michael. "We don't go out of our building except to the pool and tennis courts."

The twins shook their heads. "I haven't seen it . . . and right now I don't want to risk an intranet query."

Dixie Mae thought back to the LotsaTech map that had been in the welcome-aboard brochures. "If there is such a place, it would be farther up the hill, maybe right at the top. I say we go up there."

"But—" said Victor.

"Don't give me that garbage about waiting for the police, Victor, or about not being idiots. This *isn't* Kansas anymore, and this email is the only clue we have."

"What should we tell the people here?" said Michael.

"Don't tell them anything! We just sneak off. We want the operation here to go on normally, so Gerry or whoever doesn't suspect."

The two Ellens looked at each other, a strange, sad expression on their faces. Suddenly they both started singing "Home on the Range," but with weird lyrics:

> *"Oh, give me a clone*
> *Of my own flesh and bone*
> *With—"*

They paused and simultaneously blushed. "What a dirty mind that man Garrett had."

"Dirty but deep." NSA Ellen turned to Michael, and she seemed to blush even more. "Never mind, Michael. I think . . . you and I should stay here.

"No, wait," said Dixie Mae. "Where we're going we may have to convince someone that this crazy story is true. You Ellens are the best evidence we have."

The argument went round and round. At one point, Dixie Mae noticed with wonder that the two Ellens actually seemed to be arguing against each other.

"We don't know enough to decide," Victor kept whining.

"We have to do something, Victor. We *know* what happens to you and me if we sit things out till closing time this afternoon."

In the end Michael did stay behind. He was more likely to be believed by his government teammates. If the Ellens and Dixie Mae and Victor could bring back some real information, maybe the NSA group could do some good.

"We'll be a network of people trying to break this wheel of time." Michael was trying to sound wryly amused, but once he said the words he was silent, and none of the others could think of anything better to say.

Up near the hilltop, there were not nearly as many buildings, and the ones that Dixie Mae saw were single story, as though they were just entrances to something *under* the hills. The trees were stunted and the grass yellower.

Victor had an explanation. "It's the wind. You see this in lots of exposed land near the coast. Or maybe they just don't water very much up here."

An Ellen—from behind, Dixie Mae couldn't tell which one— said, "Either way, the fabrication is awesome."

Right. A fabrication. "That's something I don't understand," said Dixie Mae. "The best movie fx don't come close to this. How can their computers be this good?"

"Well for one thing," said the other Ellen, "cheating is a lot easier when you're also simulating the observers."

"Us."

"Yup. Everywhere you look, you see detail, but it's always at the center of your focus. We humans don't keep everything we've seen and everything we know all in mind at the same time. We have millions

of years of evolution invested in ignoring almost everything, and con-
juring sense out of nonsense."

Dixie Mae looked southward into the haze. It was all so real: the
dry hot breeze, the glint of aircraft sliding down the sky toward LAX,
the bulk of the Empire State Building looming up from the skyscrap-
ers at the center of downtown.

"There are probably dozens of omissions and contradictions
around us every second, but unless they're brought together in our attention all at once we don't notice them."

"Like the time discrepancy," said Dixie Mae.

"Right! In fact, the biggest problem with all our theories is not
how we could be individually duped, but how the fraud could work
with many communicating individuals all at once. That takes hardware beyond anything that exists, maybe a hundred liters of Bose
condensate."

"Some kind of quantum computer breakthrough," said Victor.

Both Ellens turned to look at him, eyebrows raised.

"Hey, I'm a journalist. I read it in the *Bruin* science section."

The twins' reply was something more than a monologue and less
than a conversation:

"Well . . . even so, you have a point. In fact, there were rumors
this spring that Gerry had managed to scale Gershenfeld's coffee cup
coherence scheme."

"Yeah, how he had five hundred liters of Bose condensate at room
temperature."

"But those stories started way after he had already become Mr.
Renaissance Man. It doesn't make sense."

We're not the first people hijacked. "Maybe," said Dixie Mae, "maybe
he started out with something simple, like a single superspeed human.
Could Gerry run a single upload with the kind of supercomputers we
have nowadays?"

"Well, that's more conceivable than this . . . *oh*. Okay, so an isolated genius was used to do a century or so of genius work on quantum computing. That sounds like the deathcube scenario. If it were
me, after a hundred years of being screwed like that, I'd give Gerry
one hell of a surprise."

"Yeah, like instead of a cure for cancer, he'd get airborne rabies
targeted on the proteome of scumbag middle-aged male CS profs."

The twins sounded as bloody-minded as Dixie Mae.

They walked another couple of hundred yards. The lawn degenerated into islands of crabgrass in bare dirt. The breeze was a hot whistling along the ridgeline. The twins stopped every few paces to look closely, now at the vegetation, now at a guide sign along the walkway. They were mumbling at each other about the details of what they were seeing, as if they were trying to detect inconsistencies:

". . . really, really good. We agree on everything we see."

"Maybe Gerry is saving cycles, running us as cognitive subthreads off the same process."

"Ha! No wonder we're still so much in synch."

Mumble, mumble. "There's really a lot we can infer—"

"—once we accept the insane premise of all this."

There was still no "Building 0917," but what buildings they did see had lower and lower numbers: 0933, 0921. . . .

A loud group of people crossed their path just ahead. They were singing. They looked like programmers.

"Just be cool," an Ellen said softly. "That conga line is straight out of the LotsaTech employee motivation program. The programmers have onsite parties when they reach project milestones."

"More victims?" said Victor. "Or AIs?"

"They might be victims. But I'll bet all the people we've seen along this path are just low-level scenery. There's nothing in Reich's theories that would make true AIs possible."

Dixie Mae watched the singers as they drifted down the hillside. This was the third time they had seen something-like-people on the walkway. "It doesn't make sense, Ellen. We think we're just—"

"Simulation processes."

"Yeah, simulation processes, inside some sort of super super-computer. But if that's true, then whoever is behind this should be able to spy on us better than any Big Brother ever could in the real world. We should've been caught and rebooted the minute we began to get suspicious."

Both Ellens started to answer. They stopped, then interrupted each other again.

"Back to who's-got-the-token," one said, holding up the dollar coin. "Dixie Mae, that is a mystery, but not as big as it seems. If Reich is using the sort of upload and simulation techniques I know about, then what goes on inside our minds can't be interpreted directly. Thoughts are just too idiosyncratic, too scattered. If we are simulations in a large quantum computer, even environment probes would be hard to run."

"You mean things like spy cameras?"

"Yes. They would be hard to implement, since in fact they would be snooping on the state of our internal imagery. All this is complicated by the fact that we're probably running thousands of times faster than real time. There are maybe three ways that Gerry could snoop: he could just watch team output, and if it falls off, he'd know that something had gone wrong—and he might reboot on general principles."

Suddenly Dixie Mae was very glad that they hadn't taken more volunteers on this hike.

"The second snoop method is just to look at things we write or the output of software we explicitly run. I'll bet that anything that we perceive as linear text *is* capable of outside interpretation." She looked at Victor. "That's why no note-taking." Dixie Mae still had his notepad.

"It's kinda stupid," said Victor. "First it was no pictures and now not even notes."

"Hey, look!" said the Ellens. "B0917!" But it wasn't a building, just a small sign wedged among the rocks.

They scrambled off the asphalt onto a dirt path that led directly up the hillside.

Now they were so near the hill crest that the horizon was just a few yards away. Dixie Mae couldn't see any land beyond. She remembered a movie where poor slobs like themselves got to the edge of the simulation . . . and found the wall at the end of their universe. But they took a few more steps and she could see over the top. There was a vista of further, lower hills, dropping down into the San Fernando Valley. Not quite hidden in the haze she could see the familiar snakey line of Highway 101. Tarzana.

Ellen and Ellen and Victor were not taking in the view. They were staring at the sign at the side of the path. Fifteen feet beyond that was a construction dig. There were building supplies piled neatly along the edge of the cut, and a robo-Cat parked on the far side. It might have been the beginning of the construction of a standard-model LotsaTech building . . . except that in the far side of the pit, almost hidden in shadows, there was a circular metal plug, like a bank vault door in some old movie.

"I have this theory," said the token holder. "If we get through that door, we may find out what your email is all about."

"Yup." The twins bounced down a steeply cut treadway into the pit. Dixie Mae and Victor scrambled after them, Victor clumsily bumping into her on the way down. The bottom of the pit was like nothing before. There were no windows, no card swipe. And up close, Dixie Mae could see that the vault door was pitted and scratched.

"They're mixing metaphors," said the token holder. "This entrance looks older than the pit."

"It looks old as the hills," Dixie Mae said, running her hand over the uneven metal—and half expecting to feel weirdo runes. "Somebody is trying to give us clues . . . or somebody is a big sadist. So what do we do? Knock a magic knock?"

"Why not?" The two Ellens took her tattered email and laid it out flat on the metal of the door. They studied the mail headers for a minute, mumbling to each other. The token holder tapped on the metal, then pushed.

"Together," they said, and tapped out a random something, but perfectly in synch.

That had all the effect you'd expect of tapping your fingers on ten tons of dead steel.

The token holder handed the email back to Dixie Mae. "You try something."

But what? Dixie Mae stepped to the door. She stood there, feeling clueless. Off to the side, almost hidden by the curve of the metal plug, Victor had turned away.

He had the notepad.

"Hey!" She slammed him into the side of the pit. Victor pushed her away, but by then the Ellens were on him. There was a mad scramble as the twins tried to do all the same things to Victor. Maybe that confused him. Anyway, it gave Dixie Mae a chance to come back and punch him in the face.

"I got it!" One of the twins jumped back from the fighting. She had the notepad in her hands.

They stepped away from Victor. He wasn't going to get his notepad back. "So, Ellen," said Dixie Mae, not taking her eyes off the sprawled figure, "what was that third method for snooping on us?"

"I think you've already guessed. Gerry could fool some idiot into uploading as a spy." She was looking over her twin's shoulder at the notepad screen.

Victor picked himself up. For a moment he looked sullen, and then the old superior smile percolated across his features. "You're crazy. I just want to break this story back in the real world. Don't you think that if Reich were using spies, he'd just upload himself?"

"That depends."

The one holding the notepad read aloud: "You just typed in: '925 999 994 know, reboot.' That doesn't sound like journalism to me, Victor."

"Hey, I was being dramatic." He thought for a second, and then laughed. "It doesn't matter anymore! I got the warning out. You won't remember any of this after you're rebooted."

Dixie Mae stepped toward him. "And you won't remember that I broke your neck."

Victor tried to look suave and jump backwards at the same time. "In fact, I *will* remember, Dixie Mae. See, once you're gone, I'll be merged back into my body in Doc Reich's lab."

"And we'll be dead again!"

Ellen held up the notepad. "Maybe not as soon as Victor thinks. I notice he never got past the first line of his message; he never pressed return. Now, depending on how faithfully this old notepad's hardware is being emulated, his treason is still trapped in a local cache— and Reich is still clueless about us."

For a moment, Victor looked worried. Then he shrugged. "So you get to live the rest of this run, maybe corrupt some other projects—ones a lot more important than you. On the other hand, I did learn about the email. When I get back and tell Doc Reich, he'll know what to do. You won't be going rogue in the future."

Everyone was silent for a second. The wind whistled across the yellow-blue sky above the pit.

And then the twins gave Victor the sort of smile he had bestowed on them so often. The token holder said, "I think your mouth is smarter than you are, Victor. You asked the right question a second ago: Why doesn't Gerry Reich upload himself to be the spy? Why does he have to use you?"

"Well," Victor frowned. "Hey, Doc Reich is an important man. He doesn't have time to waste with security work like this."

"Really, Victor? He can't spare even a copy of himself?"

Dixie Mae got the point. She closed in on Victor. "So how many times have *you* been merged back into your original?"

"This is my first time here!" Everybody but Victor laughed, and he rushed on, "But I've *seen* the merge done!"

"Then why won't Reich do it for *us?*"

"Merging is too expensive to waste on work threads like you," but now Victor was not even convincing himself.

The Ellens laughed again. "Are you really a UCLA journalism grad, Victor? I thought they were smarter than this. So Gerry showed you a re-merge, did he? I bet that what you actually saw was a lot of equipment and someone going through very dramatic convulsions. And then the 'subject' told you a nice story about all the things he'd seen in our little upload world. And all the time they were laughing at you behind their hands. See, Reich's upload theory depends on having a completely regular target. I know that theory: the merge problem—loading onto an existing mind—is exponential in the neuron count. There's no way back, Victor."

Victor was backing away from them. His expression flickered between superior sneer and stark panic. "What you think doesn't matter. You're just going to be rebooted at 5 P.M. And you don't know everything." He began fiddling with the fly zipper on his pants. "You see, I—*I* can escape!"

"Get him!"

Dixie Mae was closest. It didn't matter.

There was no hazy glow, no sudden popping noise. She simply fell through thin air, right where Victor had been standing.

She picked herself up and stared at the ground. Some smudged footprints were the only sign Victor had been there. She turned back to the twins. "So he could re-merge after all?"

"Not likely," said the token holder. "Victor's zipper was probably a thread self-terminate mechanism."

"His *pants zipper?*"

They shrugged. "I dunno. To leak out? Gerry has a perverse sense of humor." But neither twin looked amused. They circled the spot where Victor had left and kicked unhappily at the dirt. The token holder said, "Cripes. Nothing in Victor's life became him like the leaving it. I don't think we have even till '5 P.M.' now. A thread terminate signal is just the sort of thing that would be easy to detect from the outside. So Gerry won't know the details, but he—"

"—or his equipment—"

"—will soon know there is a problem and—"

"—that it's probably a security problem."

"So how long do we have before we lose the day?" said Dixie Mae.

"If an emergency reboot has to be done manually, we'll probably hit 5 P.M. first. If it's automatic, well, I know you won't feel insulted if the world ends in the middle of a syllable."

"Whatever it is, I'm going to use the time." Dixie Mae picked her email up from where it lay by the vault entrance. She waved the paper at the impassive steel. "I'm not going back! I'm here and I want some explanations!"

Nothing.

The two Ellens stood there, out of ideas and looking unhappy—or maybe that amounted to the same thing.

"I'm not giving up," Dixie Mae said to them, and pounded on the metal.

"No, I don't think you are," said the token holder. But now they were looking at her strangely. "I think we—*you* at least—must have been through this before."

"Yeah. And I must have messed up every time."

"No . . . I don't think so." They pointed at the email that she held crumpled in her hand. "Where do you think all those nasty secrets come from, Dixie Mae?"

"How the freakin' heck do I know? That's the whole reason I—" And then she felt smart and stupid at the same time. She leaned her head against the shadowed metal. "Oh. Oh oh *oh!*"

She looked down at the email hard-copy. The bottom part was torn, smeared, almost illegible. No matter; *that* part she had memorized. The Ellens had gone over the headers one by one. *But now we shouldn't be looking for technical secrets or grad student inside jokes. Maybe we should be looking for numbers that mean something to Dixie Mae Leigh.*

"If there were uploaded souls guarding the door, what you two have already done ought to be enough. I think you're right. It's some pattern I'm supposed to tap on the door." If it didn't work, she'd try something else, and keep trying till 5 P.M. or whenever she was suddenly back in Building 0994, so happy to have a job with potential. . . .

The tree house in Tarzana. Dixie Mae had been into secret codes then. Her childish idea of crypto. She and her little friends used a tap code for sending numbers. It hadn't lasted long, because Dixie Mae was the only one with the patience to use it. But—

"That number, '7474,' " she said.

"Yeah? Right in the middle of the fake message number?"

"Yes. Once upon a time, I used that as a password challenge. You know, like 'Who goes there' in combat games. The rest of the string could be the response."

The Ellens looked at each. "Looks too short to be significant," they said.

Then they both shook their heads, disagreeing with themselves. "Try it, Dixie Mae."

Her "numbers to taps" scheme had been simple, but for a moment she couldn't remember it. She held the paper against the vault and glared at the numbers. *Ah.* Carefully, carefully, she began tapping out the digits that came after "7474." The string was much longer than anything her childhood friends would have put up with. It was longer than anything she herself would have used.

"Cool," said the token holder. "Some kind of hex gray code?"

Huh? "What do you expect, Ellen? I was only eight years old."

They watched the door.

Nothing.

"Okay, on to Plan B," *and then to C and D and E, etc, until our time ends.*

There was the sound of something very old breaking apart. The vault door shifted under Dixie Mae's hand and she jumped back. The curved plug slowly turned, and turned, and turned. After some seconds, the metal plug thudded to the ground beside the entrance . . . and they were looking down an empty corridor that stretched off into the depths.

For the first quarter mile, no one was home. The interior decor was *not* LotsaTech standard. Gone were the warm redwood veneers and glow strips. Here fluorescent tube lights were mounted in the acoustic tile ceiling, and the walls were institutional beige.

"This reminds me of the basement labs in Norman Hall," said one Ellen.

"But there are *people* in Norman Hall," said the other. They were both whispering.

And here there were stairways that led only down. And down and down.

Dixie Mae said, "Do you get the feeling that whoever is here is in for the long haul?"

"Huh?"

"Well, the graders in B0999 were in for a day, and they thought they had real phone access to the outside. My group in Customer Support had six days of classes and then probably just one more day, where we answered queries—and we had no other contact with the outside."

"Yes," said NSA Ellen. "My group had been running for a month, and we were probably not going to expire for another two. We were officially isolated. No phones, no email, no weekends off. The longer the cycle time, the more isolation. Otherwise, the poor suckers would figure things out."

Dixie Mae thought for a second. "Victor really didn't want us to get this far. Maybe—" *Maybe, somehow, we can make a difference.*

They passed a cross corridor, then a second one. A half-opened door showed them an apparent dormitory room. Fresh bedding sat neatly folded on a mattress. Somebody was just moving in?

Ahead there was another doorway, and from it they could hear voices, argument. They crept along, not even whispering.

The voices were making words: "—is a year enough time, Rob?"

The other speaker sounded angry. "Well, it's got to be. After that, Gerry is out of money and I'm out of time."

The Ellens waved Dixie Mae back as she started for the door. Maybe they wanted to eavesdrop for a while. *But how long do we have before time ends?* Dixie Mae brushed past them and walked into the room.

There were two guys there, one sitting by an ordinary data display.

"Jesus! Who are you?"

"Dixie Mae Leigh." *As you must certainly know.*

The one sitting by the terminal gave her a broad grin, "Rob, I thought we were isolated?"

"That's what Gerry said." This one—Rob Lusk?—looked to be in his late twenties. He was tall and thin and had kind of a desperate look to him. "Okay, Miss Leigh. What are you here for?"

"That's what you're going to tell me, Rob." Dixie Mae pulled the email from her pocket and waved the tattered scrap of paper in his face. "I want some explanations!"

Rob's expression clouded over, a no-one-tells-me-what-to-do look.

Dixie Mae glared back at him. Rob Lusk was a mite too big to punch out, but she was heating up to it.

The twins chose that moment to make their entrance. "Hi there," one of them said cheerily.

Lusk's eyes flickered from one to the other and then to the NSA ID badge. "Hello. I've seen you around the department. You're Ellen, um, Gomez?"

"Garcia," corrected NSA Ellen. "Yup. That's me." She patted grader Ellen on the shoulder. "This is my sister, Sonya." She glanced at Dixie Mae. *Play along,* her eyes seemed to say. "Gerry sent us."

"He did?" The fellow by the computer display was grinning even more. "See, I told you, Rob. Gerry can be brutal, but he'd never leave us without assistants for a whole year. Welcome, girls!"

"Shut up, Danny." Rob looked at them hopefully, but unlike Danny-boy, he seemed quite serious. "Gerry told you this will be a year-long project?"

The three of them nodded.

"We've got plenty of bunk rooms, and separate . . . um, facilities." He sounded . . . Lord, he sounded embarrassed. "What are your specialties?"

The token holder said, "Sonya and I are second-year grads, working on cognitive patterning."

Some of the hope drained from Rob's expression. "I know that's Gerry's big thing, but we're mostly doing hardware here." He looked at Dixie Mae.

"I'm into"—*go for it*—"Bose condensates." Well, she knew how to pronounce the words.

There were worried looks from the Ellens. But one of them piped up with, "She's on Satya's team at Georgia Tech."

It was wonderful what the smile did to Rob's face. His angry expression of a minute before was transformed into the look of a happy little boy on his way to Disneyland. "Really? I can't tell you what this means to us! I knew it had to be someone like Satya behind the new formulations. Were you in on that?"

"Oh, yeah. Some of it, anyway." Dixie Mae figured that she couldn't say more than twenty words without blowing it. But what the heck—how many more minutes did the masquerade have to last, anyway? Little Victor and his self-terminating thread . . .

"That's great. We don't have budget for real equipment here, just simulators—"

Out of the corner of her eye, she saw the Ellens exchange a *fer sure* look.

"—so anyone who can explain the theory to me will be *so* welcome. I can't imagine how Satya managed to do so much, so fast, and without us knowing."

"Well, I'd be happy to explain everything I know about it."

Rob waved Danny-boy away from the data display. "Sit down, sit down. I've got so many questions!"

Dixie Mae sauntered over to the desk and plunked herself down. For maybe thirty seconds, this guy would think she was brilliant.

The Ellens circled in to save her. "Actually, I'd like to know more about who we're working with," one of them said.

Rob looked up, distracted, but Danny was more than happy to do some intros. "It's just the two of us. You already know Rob Lusk. I'm Dan Eastland." He reached around, genially shaking hands. "I'm not from UCLA. I work for LotsaTech, in quantum chemistry. But you know Gerry Reich. He's got pull everywhere—and I don't mind being shanghaied for a year. I need to, um, stay out of sight for a while."

"Oh!" Dixie Mae had read about this guy in *Newsweek*. And it had nothing to do with chemistry. "But you're—" *Dead*. Not a good sign at all, at all.

Danny didn't notice her distraction. "Rob's the guy with the real problem. Ever since I can remember, Gerry has used Rob as his personal hardware research department. Hey, I'm sorry, Rob. You know it's true."

Lusk waved him away. "Yes! So tell them how you're an even bigger fool!" He really wanted to get back to grilling Dixie Mae.

Danny shrugged. "But now, Rob is just one year short of hitting his seven-year limit. Do you have that at Georgia Tech, Dixie Mae? If you haven't completed the doctorate in seven years, you get kicked out?"

"No, can't say as I've heard of that."

"Give thanks then, because since 2006, it's been an unbendable rule at UCLA. So when Gerry told Rob about this secret hardware contract he's got with LotsaTech—and promised that Ph.D. in return for some new results—Rob jumped right in."

"Yeah, Danny. But he never told me how far Satya had gone. If I can't figure this stuff out, I'm screwed. Now let me talk to Dixie Mae!" He bent over the keyboard and brought up the most beautiful screen saver. Then Dixie Mae noticed little numbers in the colored contours and realized that maybe this was what she was supposed to be an expert on. Rob said, "I have plenty of documentation, Dixie

Mae—too much. If you can just give me an idea how you scaled up the coherence." He waved at the picture. "That's almost a thousand liters of condensate, a trillion effective qubits. Even more fantastic, your group can keep it coherent for almost fifty seconds at a time."

NSA Ellen gave a whistle of pretended surprise. "Wow. What use could you have for all that power?"

Danny pointed at Ellen's badge. "You're the NSA wonk, Ellen, what do you think? Crypto, the final frontier of supercomputing! With even the weakest form of the Schor-Gershenfeld algorithm, Gerry can crack a ten-kilobyte key in less than a millisecond. And I'll bet that's why he can't spare us any time on the real equipment. Night and day he's breaking keys and sucking in government money."

Grader Ellen—Sonya, that is—puckered up a naive expression. "What more does Gerry want?"

Danny spread his hands. "Some of it we don't even understand yet. Some of it is about what you'd expect: He wants a thousand thousand times more of everything. He wants to scale the operation by qulink so he can run arrays of thousand-liter bottles."

"And we've got just a year to improve on your results, Dixie Mae. But your solution is years ahead of the state of the art." Rob was pleading.

Danny's glib impress-the-girls manner faltered. For an instant, he looked a little sad and embarrassed. "We'll get something, Rob. Don't worry."

"So, how long have you been here, Rob?" said Dixie Mae.

He looked up, maybe surprised by the tone of her voice.

"We just started. This is our first day."

Ah yes, that famous first day. In her twenty-four years, Dixie Mae had occasionally wondered whether there could be rage more intense than the red haze she saw when she started breaking things. Until today, she had never known. But yes, beyond the berserker-breaker there was something else. She did not sweep the display off the table, or bury her fist in anyone's face. She just sat there for a moment, feeling empty. She looked across at the twins. "I wanted some villains, but these guys are just victims. Worse, they're totally clueless! We're back where we started this morning." *Where we'll be again real soon now.*

"Hmmm. Maybe not." Speaking together, the twins sounded like some kind of perfect chorus. They looked around the room, eyeing the decor. Then their gazes snapped back to Rob. "You'd think LotsaTech would do better than this for you, Rob."

Lusk was staring at Dixie Mae. He gave an angry shrug. "This is the old Homeland Security lab under Norman Hall. Don't worry— we're isolated, but we have good lab and computer services."

"I'll bet. And what is your starting work date?"

"I just told you: today."

"No, I mean the calendar date."

Danny looked back and forth between them. "Geeze, are all you kids so literal minded? It's Monday, September 12, 2011."

Nine months. Nine real months. And maybe there was a *good* reason why this was the first day. Dixie Mae reached out to touch Rob's sleeve. "The Georgia Tech people didn't invent the new hardware," she said softly.

"Then just who did make the breakthrough?"

She raised her hand . . . and tapped Rob deliberately on the chest.

Rob just looked more angry, but Danny's eyes widened. Danny got the point. She remembered that *Newsweek* article about him. Danny Eastland had been an all-around talented guy. He had blown the whistle on the biggest business espionage case of the decade. But he was dumb as dirt in some ways. If he hadn't been so eager to get laid, he wouldn't have snuck away from his Witness Protection body-guards and gotten himself murdered.

"You guys are too much into hardware," said NSA Ellen. "For-get about crypto applications. Think about personality uploads. Given what you know about Gerry's current hardware, how many Reich Method uploads do you think the condensate could sup-port?"

"How should I know? The 'Reich Method' was baloney. If he hadn't messed with the reviewers, those papers would never have been published." But the question stopped him. He thought for a moment. "Okay, if his bogus method really worked, then a trillion-qubit simu-lation could support about ten thousand uploads."

The Ellens gave him a slow smile. A slow, identical smile. For once they made no effort to separate their identities. Their words came out simultaneously, the same pacing, the same pitch, a weird humming chorus: "Oh, a good deal less than ten thousand—if you have to sup-port a decent enclosing reality." Each reached out her left hand with inhumanly synchronized precision, the precision of digital duplicates, to wave at the room and the hallway beyond. "Of course, some re-sources can be saved by using the same base pattern to drive separate threads—" and each pointed at herself.

Both men just stared at them for a second. Then Rob stumbled back into the other chair. "Oh . . . my . . . God."

Danny stared at the two for another few seconds. "All these years, we thought Gerry's theories were just a brilliant scam."

The Ellens stood with their eyes closed for a second. Then they seemed to startle awake. They looked at each other and Dixie Mae could tell the perfect synch had been broken. NSA Ellen took the dollar coin out of her pocket and gave it to the other. The token holder smiled at Rob. "Oh, it was, only more brilliant and more of a scam than you ever dreamed."

"I wonder if Danny and I ever figure it out."

"*Some*body figured it out," said Dixie Mae, and waved what was left of her email.

The token holder was more specific: "Gerry is running us all like stateless servers. Some are on very short cycles. We think you're on a one-year cycle, probably running longer than anyone. You're making the discoveries that let Gerry create bigger and bigger systems."

"Okay," said Lusk, "suppose one of us victims guesses the secret? What can we do? We'll just get rebooted at the end of our run."

Danny Eastland was quicker. "There is something we could do. There has to be information passed between runs, at least if Gerry is using you and me to build on our earlier solutions. If in that data we could hide what we've secretly learned—"

The twins smiled. "Right! Cookies. If you could recover them reliably, then on each rev, you could plan more and more elaborate countermeasures."

Rob Lusk still looked dazed. "We'd want to tip off the next generation early in their run."

"Yes, like the very first day!" Danny was looking at the three women and nodding to himself. "Only I still don't see how we managed that."

Rob pointed at Dixie Mae's email. "May I take a look at that?" He laid it on the table, and he and Danny examined the message.

The token holder said, "That email has turned out to have more clues than a bad detective story. Every time we're in a jam, we find the next hidden solution."

"That figures," said Eastland. "I'll bet it's been refined over many revs. . . ."

"But we may have a special problem this time—" And Dixie Mae told them about Victor.

"Damn," said Danny.

Rob just shrugged. "Nothing we can do about that till we figure this out." He and Danny studied the headers. The token holder explained the parts that had already seen use. Finally, Rob leaned back in his chair. "The second-longest header looks like the tags on one of the raw data files that Gerry gave us."

"Yes," sang the twins. "What's really your own research from the last time around."

"Most of the files have to be what Gerry thinks, or else he'd catch onto us. But that one raw data file . . . assume it's really a cookie. Then this email header might be a crypto key."

Danny shook his head. "That's not credible, Rob. Gerry could do the same analysis."

The token holder laughed. "Only if he knew what to analyze. Maybe that's why you guys winkled it out to us. The message goes to Dixie Mae—an unrelated person in an unrelated part of the simulation."

"But how did we do it the *first* time?"

Rob didn't seem to be paying attention. He was typing in the header string from Dixie Mae's email. "Let's try it on the data file. . . ." He paused, checked his keyboard entry, and pressed return.

They stared at the screen. Seconds passed. The Ellens chatted back and forth. They seemed to be worried about executing any sort of text program; like Victor's notepad, it might be readable to the outside world. "That's a real risk unless earlier Robs knew the cacheing strategy."

Dixie Mae was only half-listening. If this worked at all, it was pretty good proof that earlier Robs and Dannys had done things right. *If this works at all.* Even after all that had happened, even after seeing Victor disappear into thin air, Dixie Mae still felt like a little girl waiting for magic she didn't quite believe in.

Danny gave a nervous laugh. "How big *is* this cookie?"

Rob leaned his elbows onto the table. "Yeah. How many times have I been through a desperate seventh year?" There was an edge to his voice. You could imagine him pulling one of those deathcube stunts that the Ellens had described.

And then the screen brightened. Golden letters marched across a black-and-crimson fractal pattern: "Hello, fellow suckers! Welcome to the 1,237th run of your life."

At first, Danny refused to believe they had spent 1,236 years on Gerry's treadmill. Rob gave a shrug. "I *do* believe it. I always told Gerry that real progress took longer than theory-making. So the bastard gave me . . . all the time in the world."

The cookie was almost a million megabytes long. Much of that was detailed descriptions of trapdoors, back-doors, and softsecrets undermining the design that Rob and Danny had created for Gerry Reich. But there were also thousands of megabytes of history and tactics, crafted and hyperlinked across more than a thousand simulated years. Most of it was the work of Danny and Rob, but there were the words of Ellen and Ellen and Dixie Mae, captured in those fleeting hours they spent with Rob and Danny. It was wisdom accumulated increment by precious increment, across cycles of near sameness. As such, it was their past and also their near future.

It even contained speculations about the times before Rob and Danny got the cookie system working: Those earliest runs must have been in the summer of 2011, a single upload of Rob Lusk. Back then, the best hardware in the world couldn't have supported more than Rob all alone, in the equivalent of a one-room apartment, with a keyboard and data display. Maybe he had guessed the truth; even so, what could he have done about it? Cookies would have been much harder to pass in those times. But Rob's hardware improved from rev to rev, as Gerry Reich built on Rob's earlier genius. Danny came on board. Their first successful attempt at a cookie must have been one of many wild stabs in the dark, drunken theorizing on the last night of still another year where Rob had failed to make his deadlines and thought that he was forever Ph.D.-less. The two had put an obscene message on the intrasystem email used for their "monthly" communications with Reich. The address they had used for this random flail was . . . help@lotsatech.com.

In the real world, that must have been around June 15, 2012. Why? Well, at the beginning of their next run, guess who showed up?

Dixie Mae Leigh. Mad as hell.

The message had ended up on Dixie Mae's work queue, and she had been sufficiently insulted to go raging off across the campus. Dixie Mae had spent the whole day bouncing from building to building, mostly making enemies. Not even Ellen or Ellen had been persuaded to come along. On the other hand, back in the early revs, the land-scape reality had been simpler. Dixie Mae had been able to come into Rob's lair directly from the asphalt walkway.

Danny glanced at Dixie Mae. "And we can only guess how many times you never saw the email, or decided the random obscenities were not meant for you, or just walked in the wrong direction. Dumb luck eventually carried the day."

"Maybe. But I don't take to being insulted, and I go for the top."

Rob waved them both silent, never looking up from the cookie file: After their first success, Rob and Danny had fine-tuned the email, had learned more from each new Dixie Mae about who was in the other buildings on the hill and how—like the Ellens—they might be used.

"Victor!" Rob and the twins saw the reference at the same time. Rob stopped the autoscroll and they studied the paragraph. "Yes. We've seen Victor before. And five revs ago, he actually made it as far as this time. He killed his thread then, too." Rob followed a link marked *taking care of Victor.* "Oh. Okay. Danny, we'll have to tweak the log files—"

They stayed almost three hours more. Too long maybe, but Rob and Danny wanted to hear everything the Ellens and Dixie Mae could tell them about the simulation, and who else they had seen. The cookie history showed that things were always changing, getting more elab-orate, involving more money-making uses of people Gerry had up-loaded.

And they all wanted to keep talking. Except for poor Danny, the cookie said nothing about whether they still existed *outside.* In a way, knowing each other now was what kept them real.

Dixie Mae could tell that Danny felt that way, even when he complained: "It's just not safe having to contact unrelated people, de-pending on them to get the word to up here."

"So, Danny, you want the three of us to just run and run and never know the truth?"

"No, Dixie Mae, but this is dangerous for you, too. As a matter of fact, in most of your runs, you stay clueless." He waved at the history. "We only see you once per each of our 'year-long' runs. I-I guess that's the best evidence that visiting us is risky."

The Ellens leaned forward, "Okay, then let's see how things would work without us." The four of them looked over the oldest history entries and argued jargon that meant nothing to Dixie Mae. It all added up to the fact that any local clues left in Rob's data would be easy for Gerry Reich to detect. On the other hand, messing with unused storage in the intranet mail system was possible, and it was much easier to cloak because the clues could be spread across several other projects.

The Ellens grinned. "So you really do need us, or at least you need Dixie Mae. But don't worry; we need *you,* and you have lots to do in your next year. During that time, you've got to make some credible progress with what Gerry wants. You saw what that is. Maybe you hardware types don't realize it, but"—she clicked on a link to the bulleted list of "minimum goals" that Reich had set for Rob and Danny—"Prof. Reich is asking you for system improvements that would make it easier to partition the projects. And see this stuff about selective decoherence: Ever hear of cognitive haze? I bet with this improvement, Reich could actually do limited meddling with uploaded brain state. That would eliminate date and memory inconsistencies. We might not even recognize cookie clues then!"

Danny looked at the list. "Controlled decoherence?" He followed the link through to an extended discussion. "I wondered what that was. We need to talk about this."

"Yes—wait! Two of us get rebooted in—my God, in thirty minutes." The Ellens looked at each other and then at Dixie Mae.

Danny looked stricken, all his strategic analysis forgotten. "But one of you Ellens is on a three-month cycle. She could stay here."

"Damn it, Danny! We just saw that there are checkpoints every sim day. If the NSA team were short a member for longer than that, we'd have a real problem."

Dixie Mae said, "Maybe we should all leave now, even us . . . short-lifers. If we can get back to our buildings before reboot, it might look better."

"Yeah, you're right. I'm sorry," said Rob.

She got up and started toward the door. Getting back to Customer Support was the one last thing she could do to help.

Rob stopped her. "Dixie Mae, it would help if you'd leave us with a message to send to you next time."

She pulled the tattered printout from her pocket. The bottom was torn and smeared. "You must have the whole thing in the cookie."

"Still, it would be good to know what you think would work best

to get . . . your attention. The history says that background details are
gradually changing."

He stood up and gave her a little bow.

"Well, okay." Dixie Mae sat down and thought for a second.
Yeah, even if she hadn't had the message memorized, she knew the
sort of insults that would send her ballistic. This wasn't exactly time
travel, but now she was certain who had known all the terrible secrets,
who had known how to be absolutely insulting. "My daddy always
said that I'm my own worst enemy."

Rob and Danny walked with them back to the vault door. This was
all new to the two guys. Danny scrambled out of the pit, and stared
bug-eyed at the hills around them. "Rob, we could just *walk* to the
other buildings!" He hesitated, came back to them. "And yeah, I
know. If it were that easy, we'd have done it before. We gotta study
that cookie, Rob."

Rob just nodded. He looked kind of sad—then noticed that
Dixie Mae was looking at him—and gave her a quick smile. They
stood for a moment under the late afternoon haze and listened to the
wind. The air had cooled and the whole pit was in shadow now.

Time to go.

Dixie Mae gave Rob a smile and her hand. "Hey, Rob. Don't
worry. I've spent years trying to become a nicer, wiser, less stubborn
person. It never happened. Maybe it never will. I guess that's what we
need now."

Rob took her hand. "It is, but I swear . . . it won't be an endless
treadmill. We will study that cookie, and we'll design something better than what we have now."

"Yeah." *Be as stubborn as I am, pal.*

Rob and Dan shook hands all around, wishing them well.
"Okay," said Danny, "best be off with you. Rob, we should shut the
door and get back. I saw some references in the cookie. If they get rebooted before they reach their places, there are some things we can
do."

"Yeah," said Rob. But the two didn't move immediately from the
entrance. Dixie Mae and the twins scrambled out of the pit and
walked toward the asphalt. When Dixie Mae looked back, the two
guys were still standing there. She gave a little wave, and then they
were hidden by the edge of the excavation.

The three trudged along, the Ellens a lot less bubbly than usual. "Don't worry," NSA Ellen said to her twin, "there's still two months on the B0994 timeline. I'll remember for both of us. Maybe I can do some good on that team."

"Yeah," said the other, also sounding down. Then abruptly they both gave one of those identical laughs and they were smiling. "Hey, I just thought of something. True re-merge may always be impossible, but what we have here is almost a kind of merge load. Maybe, maybe—" But their last chance on this turn of the wheel was gone. They looked at Dixie Mae and all three were sad again. "Wish we had more time to think how we wanted this to turn out. This won't be like the SF stories where every rev you wake up filled with forebodings and subconscious knowledge. We'll start out all fresh."

Dixie Mae nodded. Starting out fresh. For dozens of runs to come, where there would be nothing after that first week at Customer Support, and putting up with boorish Victor, and never knowing. And then she smiled. "But every time we get through to Dan and Rob, we leave a little more. Every time they see us, they have a year to think. And it's all happening a thousand times faster than Ol' Gerry can think. We really are the cookie monsters. And someday—" *Someday we'll be coming for you, Gerry. And it will be sooner than you can dream.*

IN MEMORIAM

This page honors our colleagues who have recently died.

ANDRE NORTON
FRANK KELLY FREAS
F. M. BUSBY
JACK CHALKER
HUGH B. CAVE
SONYA DORMAN
PAT YORK
ROGER D. ALCOCK
ALFRED COPPEL
TETSU YANO
ROBERT MERLE
JOHAN SPRINGBORG
DILIP M. SALWI
ROXANNE HUTTON
KATHERINE LAWRENCE
ROBYN HERRINGTON
REX MILLER
BRIAN McNAUGHTON
PAULA DANZIGER
MICHAEL ELDER

Throughout every calendar year, the members of the Science Fiction and Fantasy Writers of America read and recommend novels and stories for the annual Nebula Awards. The editor of the "Nebula Awards Report" collects the recommendations and publishes them in the SFFWA *Forum*. Near the end of the year, the NAR editor tallies the endorsements, draws up the preliminary ballot, and sends it to all active SFFWA members. Under the current rules, each novel and story enjoys a one-year eligibility period from its date of publication. If the work fails to make the preliminary ballot during that interval, it is dropped from further Nebula consideration.

The NAR editor processes the results of the preliminary ballot and then compiles a final ballot listing the five most popular novels, novellas, novelettes, and short stories. For purposes of the Nebula Award, a novel is 40,000 words or more; a novella is 17,500 to 39,999 words; a novelette is 7,500 to 17,499 words; and a short story is 7,499 words or fewer. At the present time, SFFWA impanels both a novel jury and a short-fiction jury to oversee the voting process and, in cases where a presumably worthy title was neglected by the membership at large, to supplement the five nominees with a sixth choice. Thus, the appearance of extra finalists in any category bespeaks two distinct processes: jury discretion and ties.

Founded in 1965 by Damon Knight, the Science Fiction Writers of America began with a charter membership of seventy-eight authors. Today it boats over a thousand members and an augmented name. Early in his tenure, Lloyd Biggle, Jr., SFWA's first secretary-treasurer, proposed that the organization periodically select and publish the year's best stories. This notion quickly evolved into the elaborate balloting process, an annual awards banquet, and a series of Nebula anthologies. Judith Ann Lawrence designed the trophy from a sketch by Kate Wilhelm. It is a block of Lucite containing a rock crystal and a spiral nebula made of metallic glitter. The prize is hand-made, and no two are exactly alike.

The Damon Knight Grand Master Nebula Award goes to a living author for a lifetime of achievement in science fiction and/or fantasy. In accordance with SFFWA's bylaws, the president nominates a candidate, normally after consulting with previous presidents and the board of directors. This nomination then goes before the officers; if a majority approves, the candidate becomes a Grand Master. Past recipients include Robert A. Heinlein (1974), Jack Williamson (1975), Clifford D. Simak (1976), L. Sprague de Camp (1978), Fritz Leiber (1980), Andre Norton (1983), Arthur C. Clarke (1985), Isaac Asimov (1986), Alfred Bester (1987), Ray Bradbury (1988), Lester del Rey (1990), Frederik Pohl (1992), Damon Knight (1994), A. E. van Vogt (1995), Jack Vance (1996), Poul Anderson (1997), Hal Clement (Harry Stubbs) (1998), Brian W. Aldiss (1999), Philip José Farmer (2000), Ursula K. Le Guin (2002), Robert Silverberg (2003), and Anne McCaffrey (2004).

1965

Best Novel: *Dune* by Frank Herbert
Best Novella (tie): "The Saliva Tree" by Brian W. Aldiss
                    "He Who Shapes" by Roger Zelazny
Best Novelette: "The Doors of His Face, the Lamps of His Mouth"
   by Roger Zelazny
Best Short Story: " 'Repent, Harlequin!' Said the Ticktockman," by
   Harlan Ellison

1966

Best Novel (tie): *Flowers for Algernon* by Daniel Keyes
                 Babel-17 by Samuel R. Delany
Best Novella: "The Last Castle" by Jack Vance
Best Novelette: "Call Him Lord" by Gordon R. Dickson
Best Short Story: "The Secret Place" by Richard McKenna
Best Novel: *The Einstein Intersection* by Samuel R. Delany
Best Novella: "Behold the Man" by Michael Moorcock
Best Novelette: "Gonna Roll the Bones" by Fritz Leiber
Best Short Story: "Aye, and Gomorrah" by Samuel R. Delany

1968

Best Novel: *Rite of Passage* by Alexei Panshin
Best Novella: "Dragonrider" by Anne McCaffrey
Best Novelette: "Mother to the World" by Richard Wilson
Best Short Story: "The Planners" by Kate Wilhelm

1969

Best Novel: *The Left Hand of Darkness* by Ursula K. Le Guin

Best Novella: "A Boy and His Dog" by Harlan Ellison

Best Novelette: "Time Considered as a Helix of Semi-Precious Stones" by Samuel R. Delany

Best Short Story: "Passengers" by Robert Silverberg

1970

Best Novel: *Ringworld* by Larry Niven

Best Novella: "Ill Met in Lankhmar" by Fritz Leiber

Best Novelette: "Slow Sculpture" by Theodore Sturgeon

Best Short Story: No Award

1971

Best Novel: *A Time of Changes* by Robert Silverberg

Best Novella: "The Missing Man" by Katherine MacLean

Best Novelette: "The Queen of Air and Darkness" by Poul Anderson

Best Short Story: "Good News from the Vatican" by Robert Silverberg

1972

Best Novel: *The Gods Themselves* by Isaac Asimov

Best Novella: "A Meeting with Medusa" by Arthur C. Clarke

Best Novelette: "Goat Song" by Poul Anderson

Best Short Story: "When it Changed" by Joanna Russ

1973

Best Novel: *Rendezvous with Rama* by Arthur C. Clarke

Best Novella: "The Death of Doctor Island" by Gene Wolfe

Best Novelette: "Of Mist, and Grass, and Sand" by Vonda N. McIntyre

Best Short Story: "Love Is the Plan, the Plan Is Death" by James Tiptree, Jr.

Best Dramatic Presentation: *Soylent Green*

Stanley R. Greenberg for Screenplay (based on the novel *Make Room! Make Room!*), Harry Harrison for *Make Room! Make Room!*

1974

Best Novel: *The Dispossessed* by Ursula K. Le Guin

Best Novella: "Born with the Dead" by Robert Silverberg

Best Novelette: "If the Stars Are Gods" by Gordon Eklund and Gregory Benford

Best Short Story: "The Day Before the Revolution" by Ursula K. Le Guin

Best Dramatic Presentation: *Sleeper* by Woody Allen

Other Awards & Honors: Grand Master: Robert A. Heinlein

1975

Best Novel: *The Forever War* by Joe Haldeman

Best Novella: "Home Is the Hangman" by Roger Zelazny

Best Novelette: "San Diego Lightfoot Sue" by Tom Reamy

Best Short Story: "Catch that Zeppelin!" by Fritz Leiber

Best Dramatic Writing: Mel Brooks and Gene Wilder for *Young Frankenstein*

Other Awards & Honors: Grand Master: Jack Williamson

1976

Best Novel: *Man Plus* by Frederik Pohl

Best Novella: "Houston, Houston, Do You Read?" by James Tiptree, Jr.

Best Novelette: "The Bicentennial Man" by Isaac Asimov

Best Short Story: "A Crowd of Shadows" by Charles L. Grant

Other Awards & Honors: Grand Master: Clifford D. Simak

1977

Best Novel: *Gateway* by Frederik Pohl

Best Novella: "Stardance" by Spider and Jeanne Robinson

Best Novelette: "The Screwfly Solution" by Raccoona Sheldon

Best Short Story: "Jeffty Is Five" by Harlan Ellison

Other Awards & Honors: Special Award: *Star Wars*

1978

Best Novel: *Dreamsnake* by Vonda N. McIntyre

Best Novella: "The Persistence of Vision" by John Varley

Best Novelette: "A Glow of Candles, a Unicorn's Eye" by Charles L. Grant

Best Short Story: "Stone" by Edward Bryant

Other Awards & Honors: Grand Master: L. Sprague de Camp

1979

Best Novel: *The Fountains of Paradise* by Arthur C. Clarke
Best Novella: "Enemy Mine" by Barry Longyear
Best Novelette: "Sandkings" by George R. R. Martin
Best Short Story: "giANTS" by Edward Bryant

1980

Best Novel: *Timescape* by Gregory Benford
Best Novella: "The Unicorn Tapestry" by Suzy McKee Charnas
Best Novelette: "The Ugly Chickens" by Howard Waldrop
Best Short Story: "Grotto of the Dancing Deer" by Clifford D. Simak
Other Awards & Honors: Grand Master: Fritz Leiber

1981

Best Novel: *The Claw of the Conciliator* by Gene Wolfe
Best Novella: "The Saturn Game" by Poul Anderson
Best Novelette: "The Quickening" by Michael Bishop
Best Short Story: "The Bone Flute" by Lisa Tuttle
(This Nebula Award was declined by the author.)

1982

Best Novel: *No Enemy but Time* by Michael Bishop
Best Novella: "Another Orphan" by John Kessel
Best Novelette: "Fire Watch" by Connie Willis
Best Short Story: "A Letter from the Clearys" by Connie Willis

1983

Best Novel: *Startide Rising* by David Brin
Best Novella: "Hardfought" by Greg Bear
Best Novelette: "Blood Music" by Greg Bear
Best Short Story: "The Peacemaker" by Gardner Dozois
Other Awards & Honors: Grand Master: Andre Norton

1984

Best Novel: *Neuromancer* by William Gibson
Best Novella: "PRESS ENTER□" by John Varley
Best Novelette: "Bloodchild" by Octavia E. Butler
Best Short Story: "Morning Child" by Gardner Dozois

1985

Best Novel: *Ender's Game* by Orson Scott Card
Best Novella: "Sailing to Byzantium" by Robert Silverberg
Best Novelette: "Portraits of His Children" by George R. R. Martin
Best Short Story: "Out of All Them Bright Stars" by Nancy Kress
Other Awards & Honors: Grand Master: Arthur C. Clarke

1986

Best Novel: *Speaker for the Dead* by Orson Scott Card
Best Novella: "R & R" by Lucius Shepard
Best Novelette: "The Girl Who Fell into the Sky" by Kate Wilhelm
Best Short Story: "Tangents" by Greg Bear
Other Awards & Honors: Grand Master: Isaac Asimov

1987

Best Novel: *The Falling Woman* by Pat Murphy
Best Novella: "The Blind Geometer" by Kim Stanley Robinson
Best Novelette: "Rachel in Love" by Pat Murphy
Best Short Story: "Forever Yours, Anna" by Kate Wilhelm
Other Awards & Honors: Grand Master: Alfred Bester

1988

Best Novel: *Falling Free* by Lois McMaster Bujold
Best Novella: "The Last of the Winnebagos" by Connie Willis
Best Novelette: "Schrodinger's Kitten" by George Alec Effinger
Best Short Story: "Bible Stories for Adults, No. 17: The Deluge" by
    James Morrow
Other Awards & Honors: Grand Master: Ray Bradbury

1989

Best Novel: *The Healer's War* by Elizabeth Ann Scarborough
Best Novella: "The Mountains of Mourning" by Lois McMaster Bu-
    jold
Best Novelette: "At the Rialto" by Connie Willis
Best Short Story: "Ripples in the Dirac Sea" by Geoffrey A. Landis

1990

Best Novel: *Tehanu: The Last Book of Earthsea* by Ursula K. Le Guin
Best Novella: "The Hemingway Hoax" by Joe Haldeman
Best Novelette: "Tower of Babylon" by Ted Chiang

Best Short Story: "Bears Discover Fire" by Terry Bisson
Other Awards & Honors: Grand Master: Lester del Rey

1991

Best Novel: *Stations of the Tide* by Michael Swanwick
Best Novella: "Beggars in Spain" by Nancy Kress
Best Novelette: "Guide Dog" by Mike Conner
Best Short Story: "Ma Qui" by Alan Brennert

1992

Best Novel: *Doomsday Book* by Connie Willis
Best Novella: "City of Truth" by James Morrow
Best Novelette: "Danny Goes to Mars" by Pamela Sargent
Best Short Story: "Even the Queen" by Connie Willis
Other Awards & Honors: Grand Master: Frederik Pohl

1993

Best Novel: *Red Mars* by Kim Stanley Robinson
Best Novella: "The Night We Buried Road Dog" by Jack Cady
Best Novelette: "Georgia on My Mind" by Charles Sheffield
Best Short Story: "Graves" by Joe Haldeman

1994

Best Novel: *Moving Mars* by Greg Bear
Best Novella: "Seven Views of Olduvai Gorge" by Mike Resnick
Best Novelette: "The Martian Child" by David Gerrold
Best Short Story: "A Defense of the Social Contracts" by Martha
   Soukup
Other Awards & Honors: Grand Master: Damon Knight
Author Emeritus: Emil Petaja

1995

Best Novel: *The Terminal Experiment* by Robert J. Sawyer
Best Novella: "Last Summer at Mars Hill" by Elizabeth Hand
Best Novelette: "Solitude" by Ursula K. Le Guin
Best Short Story: "Death and the Librarian" by Esther Friesner
Other Awards & Honors: Grand Master: A. E. van Vogt
Author Emeritus: Wilson "Bob" Tucker

1996

Best Novel: *Slow River* by Nicola Griffith

Best Novella: "Da Vinci Rising" by Jack Dann

Best Novelette: "Lifeboat on a Burning Sea" by Bruce Holland Rogers

Best Short Story: "A Birthday" by Esther M. Friesner

Other Awards & Honors: Grand Master: Jack Vance

Author Emeritus: Judith Merril

1997

Best Novel: *The Moon and the Sun* by Vonda N. McIntyre

Best Novella: "Abandon in Place" by Jerry Oltion

Best Novelette: "The Flowers of Aulit Prison" by Nancy Kress

Best Short Story: "Sister Emily's Lightship" by Jane Yolen

Other Awards & Honors: Grand Master: Poul Anderson

Author Emeritus: Nelson Slade Bond

1998

Best Novel: *Forever Peace* by Joe Haldeman

Best Novella: "Reading the Bones" by Sheila Finch

Best Novelette: "Lost Girls" by Jane Yolen

Best Short Story: "Thirteen Ways to Water" by Bruce Holland Rogers

Other Awards & Honors: Grand Master: Hal Clement (Harry Stubbs)

Bradbury Award: J. Michael Straczynski

Author Emeritus: William Tenn (Philip Klass)

1999

Best Novel: *Parable of the Talents* by Octavia E. Butler

Best Novella: "Story of Your Life" by Ted Chiang

Best Novelette: "Mars is No Place for Children" by Mary A. Turzillo

Best Short Story: "The Cost of Doing Business" by Leslie What

Best Script: *The Sixth Sense* by M. Night Shayamalan

Other Awards & Honors: Grand Master: Brian W. Aldiss

Author Emeritus: Daniel Keyes

2000

Best Novel: *Darwin's Radio* by Greg Bear

Best Novella: "Goddesses" by Linda Nagata

Best Novelette: "Daddy's World" by Walter Jon Williams

Best Short Story: "macs" by Terry Bisson
Best Script: *Galaxy Quest* by Robert Gordon and David Howard
Other Awards & Honors: Grand Master: Philip José Farmer
Bradbury Award: Yuri Rasovsky and Harlan Ellison
Author Emeritus: Robert Sheckley

2001

Best Novel: *The Quantum Rose* by Catherine Asaro,
Best Novella: "The Ultimate Earth" by Jack Williamson
Best Novelette: "Louise's Ghost" by Kelly Link
Best Short Story: "The Cure for Everything" by Severna Park
Best Script: *Crouching Tiger, Hidden Dragon* by James Schamus, Kuo
    Jung Tsai, and Hui-Ling Wang; from the book by Du Lu Wang
Other Awards & Honors: President's Award: Betty Ballantine

2002

Best Novel: *American Gods* by Neil Gaiman
Best Novella: "Bronte's Egg" by Richard Chwedyk
Best Novelette: "Hell is the Absence of God" by Ted Chiang
Best Short Story: "Creature" by Carol Emshwiller
Best Script: *The Lord of the Rings: The Fellowship of the Ring* by Fran
    Walsh and Philippa Boyens and Peter Jackson; based on *The Lord of*
    the Rings by J.R.R. Tolkien
Other Awards & Honors: Grand Master: Ursula K. Le Guin
Author Emeritus: Katherine MacLean

2003

Best Novel: *The Speed of Dark* by Elizabeth Moon
Best Novella: "Coraline" by Neil Gaiman
Best Novelette: "The Empire of Ice Cream" by Jeffrey Ford
Best Short Story: "What I Didn't See" by Karen Joy Fowler
Best Script: *The Lord of the Rings: The Two Towers* by Fran Walsh and
    Philippa Boyens and Stephen Sinclair and Peter Jackson; based on
    The Lord of the Rings by J.R.R. Tolkien
Other Awards & Honors: Grand Master: Robert Silverberg
Author Emeritus: Charles L. Harness

The Science Fiction and Fantasy Writers of America, Incorporated, includes among its members most of the active writers of science fiction and fantasy. According to the bylaws of the organization, its purpose "shall be to promote the furtherance of the writing of science fiction, fantasy, and related genres as a profession." SFFWA informs writers on professional matters, protects their interests, and helps them in dealings with agents, editors, anthologists, and producers of nonprint media. It also strives to encourage public interest in and appreciation of science fiction and fantasy.

Anyone may become an active member of SFFWA after the acceptance of and payment for one professionally published novel, one professionally produced dramatic script, or three professionally published pieces of short fiction. Only science fiction, fantasy, and other prose fiction of a related genre, in English, shall be considered as qualifying for active membership. Beginning writers who do not yet qualify for active membership may join as associate members; other classes of membership include illustrator members (artists), affiliate members (editors, agents, reviewers, and anthologists), estate members (representatives of the estates of active members who have died), and institutional members (high schools, colleges, universities, libraries, broadcasters, film producers, futurist groups, and individuals associated with such an institution).

Anyone who is not a member of SFFWA may subscribe to *The Bulletin of the Science Fiction and Fantasy Writers of America*. The magazine is published quarterly, and contains articles by well-known writers on all aspects of their profession. Subscriptions are eighteen dollars a year or thirty-one dollars for two years. For information on how to subscribe to the *Bulletin,* or for more information about SF-FWA, write to:

SFFWA, Inc.
P.O. Box 877
Chestertown, MD 21620
USA

Readers are also invited to visit the SFFWA site on the World Wide Web at the following address:

http://www.sfwa.org

COPYRIGHT NOTICES